I0452361

FALLEN GODS

Act One:
The Resurrection Box
Susannah
The Moonsnatcher
Mister Foxwood's Holiday

RUSSELL PROCTOR

Illustration © 2018

Sophia Fredriksson

Cover design by

www.beyondbookcovers.com

ISBN: 978-0-6451490-1-2

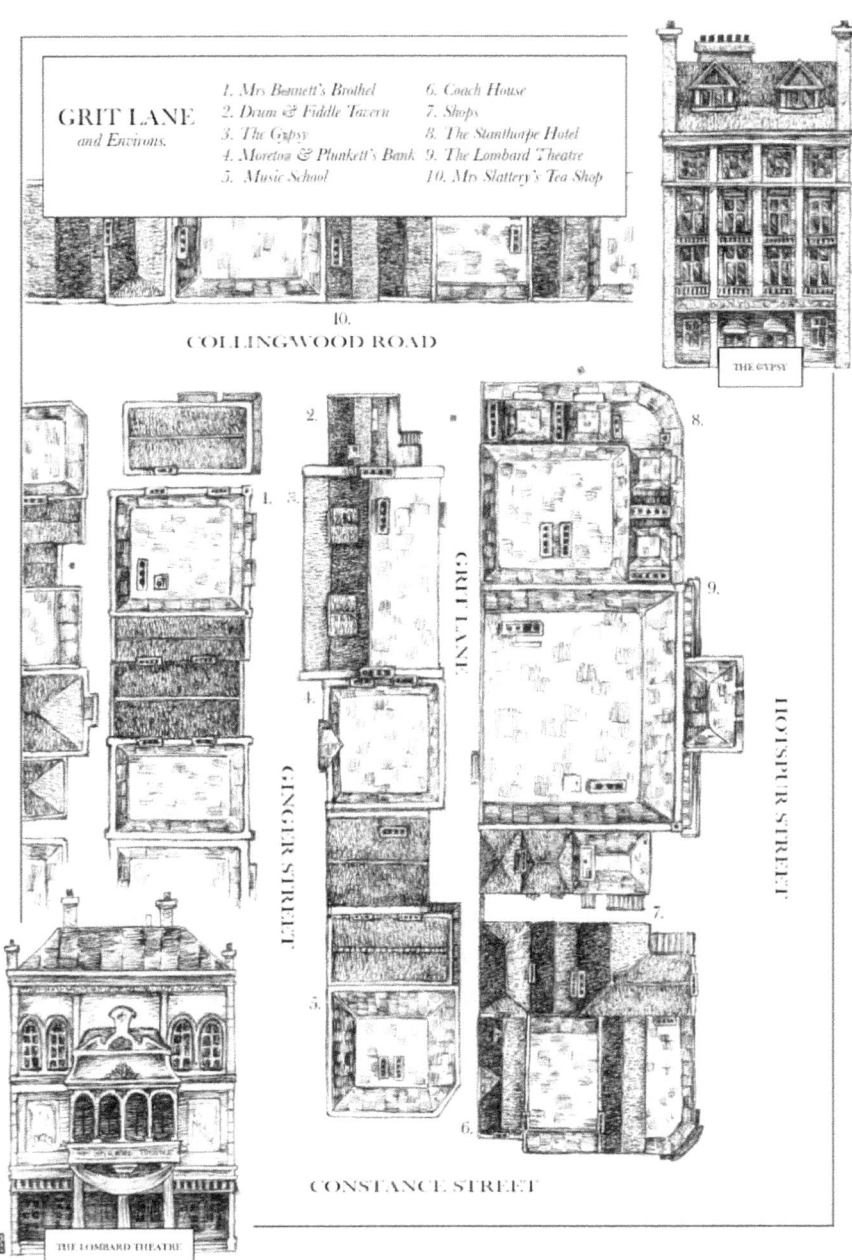

GRIT LANE
and Environs.

1. Mrs Bennett's Brothel
2. Drum & Fiddle Tavern
3. The Gypsy
4. Moreton & Plunkett's Bank
5. Music School
6. Coach House
7. Shops
8. The Stanthorpe Hotel
9. The Lombard Theatre
10. Mrs Slattery's Tea Shop

COLLINGWOOD ROAD

THE GYPSY

GRIT LANE

GINGER STREET

HOTSPUR STREET

CONSTANCE STREET

THE LOMBARD THEATRE

AUTHOR'S NOTE

In these stories, the character Leah uses a 19th Century form of sign language to communicate. The transcription of her words into English is simply for ease of reading and clarity of understanding and is not intended as a literal word-for-word translation.

FALLEN GODS

CONTENTS

SCENE ONE

August 1851

THE RESURRECTION BOX

I am the priest in a hidden house, guide to inner worlds. I am the idea of myself in my mother's belly, a bright trembling star in the memory of morning, a grain of sand blown east.

—The Egyptian Book of the Dead.

I

Porteous Merriman hadn't expected the gargoyle.

It crouched on a ledge above the stage door: a grotesque, leather-winged body, a long tongue protruding from the mouth, the eyes mere slits, long horns curved above a high skull. A trail of slime hung from the end of the tongue, beaded at the end with a drop of water.

Merriman was certain he had the right door. Theatre posters decorated the brick walls on either side and a rusted sign beside it read, *The Gypsy. Staff and Performers only.* He took a firm hold of the door-knocker and gave three hard raps.

The wind swirled dust from Grit Lane against his cheek while he waited a full minute. Just as he reached to knock on the door again it opened and a young woman peered into the afternoon gloom. A round face; high cheekbones; a long straggle of black hair leaking from under a cloth cap such as a workman might wear; brown eyes that needed sleep. On a good day she might have looked twenty-five years old.

"Yes?" she barked.

He removed his hat with a professional flourish. A card appeared in his hand as if out of thin air. "Porteous Merriman, conjuror and illusionist. Mr Foxwood is expecting me."

The woman didn't react to the production of the card. She stared hard at his face, sniffed and drew back so he could enter.

He indicated the wooden chest at his feet. "Find a man to bring that in, would you?"

The woman grasped the chest's handles and hoisted it without apparent effort. Merriman gawked; he always struggled with the weight of the thing. "Are you all right with that?" he asked, remembering his manners too late.

She merely inclined her head towards the stage door. As Merriman stepped under the gargoyle a drop of water fell from its mouth and rapped hard on his hat brim.

"Don't do that!" growled the woman.

"Excuse me?"

"What?"

"You said…never mind. Is Mr Foxwood in?"

"Wait here."

She put the chest down and went backstage.

The lobby consisted of a short corridor, flanked on one side by a small office behind a glass partition. On the rear wall of the office hung a gaudy tapestry, decorated with male and female figures standing atop a mountain, a thundering sky behind. In a plain wooden chair in front of the tapestry sat a short man, presumably the doorman, reading a book. Why hadn't he answered the knock instead of the girl?

The lobby wall facing the office had been almost totally plastered over with pictures and playbills. Half-clad dancing girls, acrobats, one woman in a feathered costume sitting on an ottoman, musicians, other magic acts. Merriman didn't recognise any of the magicians, but that was no surprise. He had only performed outside London until now.

"Quite a history," he muttered aloud.

The man behind the glass partition looked up and grunted. "Shut the door."

Merriman frowned at the impertinence of the request. The man regarded him with black eyes, the short stub of a pipe protruding from his mouth. He might have been sixty. His feet rested on a wooden box because they were too short to reach the floor.

"I beg your pardon?"

The man pointed at the open stage door with the stem of his pipe. A gold ring glittered on his right index finger. "Shut the door, you daft bugger. The dust's coming in."

"Aren't you the doorman?"

The pipe went back in and he mouthed around it. "Some people reckon so."

Merriman almost said something else, but chose to shut the door instead. No use arguing with staff this early in his engagement.

He turned his attention back to the pictures. One in particular caught his eye: a magician, posing with a female assistant. The man wore white tie and tails, a red-lined cloak thrown across his shoulders. He held a top hat in one hand while drawing a rabbit out of it with the other. Merriman thrust out his lower lip—his own act contained better and more mysterious illusions than that old classic. The assistant paraded her assets in a garment allowable only on a music hall stage, but that wasn't what had caught Merriman's attention. There was something familiar about the assistant, something he couldn't quite place.

The inner door opened and the woman reappeared.

The assistant looked a lot like her. Except the playbill was dated fifteen years ago, and the girl in the poster was about the same age. It couldn't be her. A close relative, then.

"This way, please."

He glanced down at the chest.

"Leave it," the old man muttered. "I'll make sure no one pinches it. Probably."

"Shut up, Gimble," said the woman. "Mr Merriman's a new act."

Merriman followed her through the other door and into the backstage world of the Gypsy.

He breathed in as the numerous smells of a theatre came heavy into his lungs. Turpentine, always turpentine. Dust and lime. The clay-smell of make-up. Oil. Sweat. The must of old clothing. A dim world, lit only by a single gas jet over the stage-manager's desk. Objects loomed as shadowy forms, not real, not definite. Even the form of the woman in front became no more than a silhouette as they approached the stage.

No performances tonight, being Sunday, so the house remained dark and the curtain up. As they crossed the raked boards of the stage Merriman glanced into the auditorium. Rows of empty seats and tables, the orchestra pit fitted with chairs and music stands, an old piano to one side, the conductor's podium hard against the first row of tables and chairs. Including the gallery at the back, which had seats without tables, the theatre could fit perhaps four hundred when packed. On either side of the pit were two closed-off boxes near the stage. Both had been boarded up as if unused.

They left the stage and passed through the left-hand wings. Heavy black curtains sealed out all light and sound from the backstage area. Beyond, a corridor led to dressing rooms.

"Mr Foxwood is up there," she said, indicating a flight of stairs with a flick of her head. "Knock once only, mind."

"Why?"

"Try knocking twice and see."

He bristled at her surly demeanour. Did no one answer polite questions here without an attitude? "May I ask your name?"

"You call me Mags." She retreated into the darkness. Neatly, soundlessly, almost like one of his own vanishing tricks. Potential there for a good illusionist's assistant, although audiences preferred svelte ladies with long legs and other attractive features. He thought again of the magician's assistant in the playbill.

The stairs ended at a green door. After a second's pause, he knocked once.

"Come in, Mr Merriman."

More smells: ink, paper, leather, all odours anyone might expect in a man's office. But another scent overlaid these, a cheap floral cologne that tickled his nose. The most prominent feature in the room was not Mr Foxwood but a large oaken desk on which perched an animal skull, perhaps that of a dog. An open bottle of red wine stood beside it, along with a glass bearing traces of recent use. Behind the desk, book-filled shelves surrounded a portrait of Queen Victoria. The room had a window, but the curtains were closed. A fire helped the two flaring gas jets illuminate the space.

Joshua Foxwood himself was barely visible. Merriman remembered him from his previous interview, which had not been held here but at the shady pub next door, the Drum and Fiddle, with shady customers to match. On that occasion he'd noted Mr Foxwood's extraordinary thinness. Seen here, behind the massive desk next to the towering wall of books, the manager of the Gypsy seemed overwhelmed by his surroundings. Tall, certainly, but with a cadaverous slenderness which revealed some bones normally hidden on a human frame. The narrow skull held two large, liquid eyes and a thin mouth. Only a few wisps of hair on the high crown. And the arms: long, spindly, the wrists jutting from the sleeves of his black coat like two white sticks, almost no flesh on them at all. Both blue-veined hands were clasped in front of him.

"Good afternoon," he said in a voice as thin as the rest of him. "It is afternoon, I take it? Please be seated. I'm glad to see you again." Just like at the previous day's interview, the man didn't stand up or offer a handshake.

Merriman sat in the only other chair available, facing his host. "Hello, Mr Foxwood."

"Welcome to the Gypsy. May I call you Porteous?"

"If you don't mind, sir, Merriman is my preferred choice, unless I'm in character, then it's The Miraculous Osiris."

Foxwood stared back, smiling. "I trust everything is in order,

Porteous?"

A tight ship here at the Gypsy. All right, he could knuckle under.

"Yes. There is one chest downstairs. I have another cabinet and other equipment, tables and so on that I use in the act. I can arrange for them to be delivered tomorrow morning. The chest has my costume and make-up. Perhaps I could have a dressing room to leave my paraphernalia in, or…"

"Or?"

On a performance night, there would literally be scores of people backstage. His equipment contained secrets, his magical illusions. And, of course, the Box. During his previous engagement, at the Solitaire in Birmingham, he'd been assigned a locked strong-room where his equipment could be left during the day away from prying eyes.

"Perhaps, for security purposes…"

"Don't worry, Porteous, your secrets are safe here. We are most professional. The acts here would no more dream of interfering with your trade secrets than you would theirs. You'll have a dressing room which you must share with—" His gaunt fingers lifted a sheet of paper, which he squinted at. "—Sebastian Riggs and Michael Hankey. Pleasant enough men, by all accounts. But you will have the privacy to prepare your act, of course."

"All the same, sir, as a professional man yourself, you must understand—"

"What I understand, Porteous, is that you will be paid for a three week engagement, following which your contract will be reviewed."

Mr Foxwood rose and seemed even thinner as he stalked over to a set of wooden filing cabinets, pulled open a drawer and put a sheet of paper onto the desk in front of Merriman.

"Please peruse, and, if satisfied, sign on the line."

A typical engagement contract: the artist agreed to perform twice a night Monday to Friday, and three times on Saturday including the matinee. Billing to be initially at the bottom of the poster, subsequently elevated closer to the top depending on the popularity of his act. Expectations included remaining sober while on the premises, following the directions of the stage manager and other senior staff listed (he noticed this included the name "Mags"—no surname), signing in at least one hour before his scheduled performance time and keeping his dressing room clean. Salary was also typical for the industry, two guineas a week, to be reviewed should engagement proceed beyond the initial three weeks.

He signed and added the date. 10th August 1851.

Foxwood took the sheet away and placed another in front of him, identical to the first. "Sign this one too, please. One for you, one for me."

It felt good to thrust the signed second copy into his pocket. Another three weeks' work at least. Birmingham had run dry of venues. Here in London there were more establishments, more call for his art, more chance to make a decent living. Magicians were passé unless they had something different, an "edge" they called it, to the act. He had one. Perhaps here in London it would prove more rewarding.

"Thank you," said Foxwood. "I wish you a decent run."

"What are audience numbers like?" Merriman asked, recalling but not mentioning the boarded-up boxes in the auditorium.

"Only fair for the moment. The Great Exhibition is still attracting many people. Have you seen it?"

"No. I arrived from Birmingham just last week."

"A most impressive affair. A little too magnetic when it comes to taking audiences away from us, perhaps. Another couple of months to run, of course, but I'll be glad when it's done and people start spending money with us again." Mr Foxwood sat down behind his desk once more. "That will be all then, Porteous. Mags will show you your dressing room."

Merriman was half up before he stopped. "My chest. It's a long way back to my accommodation. Perhaps it could be locked up somewhere safe? I mean, I don't wish to persist, but…"

Foxwood stared at him. For a long moment the two men remained still, and Merriman thought the faintest shadow of a frown crossed Mr Foxwood's face. Then the thin cadaver smiled.

"Of course. Remiss of me. Mags!"

She appeared so quickly Merriman suspected her of listening outside the door. The lock of hair still hung from under the cap on her head.

"Yes?"

Not "Yes, Mr Foxwood?" Perhaps the two were related, father and daughter or uncle and niece.

"Mister Merriman is now engaged here. Show him to number two dressing room."

Merriman hung back for a moment. The skull on the desk caught his gaze. Had there been a gleam from the empty eye sockets? Nonsense, of course. Such things were not possible, and yet...Or maybe the shadows in the room had changed. The fire burned a little lower. Yes, that was it: the shadows. A simple optical illusion. Nothing more. How remiss of him not to see the explanation immediately.

"Is there something else?" asked Foxwood.

"Er—no. Thank you. I'll see you tomorrow."

"No, you probably won't. I shall be far too busy. Mags will tell you anything you need to know."

Foxwood poured himself a glass of wine, turned his attention to the papers on his desk and didn't bother looking at Merriman anymore.

"This way," said Mags.

From the room behind, Merriman thought he heard a low, long chuckle.

At the bottom of the stairs the woman went past the stage entrance and turned left down a brick-walled corridor.

"Dressing room number two. We pay for the gas for two hours before and one hour after performance. The rest of the time it's your cost. Tuppence an hour."

The room felt cold and more than a little damp, but Merriman didn't mind. In his profession he had yet to find a dressing room that wasn't cold and damp to some degree. A wooden make-up table, three wooden chairs, a wardrobe for clothing; in one corner a ceramic sink served by two bronze taps. The room would do, although it lacked any privacy to set up his act.

"Mr Foxwood mentioned something about a space for my chest and equipment," he said.

Mags moved the lock of hair off her face. It immediately fell back to its original position. She didn't try to shift it again.

"There's a storeroom. Who are you again?"

He almost hauled his card out. "The Miraculous Osiris. An illusionist."

An unimpressed grunt came as the only reply.

He followed her further along the line of dressing rooms— another corridor, damper and darker this time, to the far end of the building. Mags unlocked a heavy oak door to reveal a gloomy brick-lined room fitted with shelves bent under the miscellaneous dross and cast-offs of a theatre: props, canvas flats, pipes and rubber tubing for gas and lime-lights, piles of old paper, wooden crates, metal tools. But enough space remained for Merriman to store his equipment and prepare his act. "It will do," he said.

Dust stuck to a hand Mags rubbed along a shelf. Merriman noticed a gold ring on her right index finger, similar to the one worn by the doorman.

"May I have a key?" he asked.

"You could ask the stage manager for one. Mr Simm."

"Is he here?"

A short bark from Mags and, for the first time since he'd met her, a brief smile that came and went like a sunny morning in winter: warm enough, but doomed from the beginning. "It's Sunday. He'll be drunk and losing at cards somewhere."

Not a good sign. Every other stage manager Merriman had ever met so far would have taken Sunday as a good chance to catch up on the myriad tasks involved in running a busy metropolitan music hall. He wondered if this Mr Simm might be trusted, and resolved to arrive promptly tomorrow and meet the stage manager to make his requirements known.

Mags led the way back to the stage door. Gimble still sat behind the glass partition. He barely seemed to have breathed in their absence. The chest blocked the path to the door.

"I need that locked up until tomorrow," said Merriman. "I'd hoped to get a private dressing room, you see."

The old man removed the pipe and leaned against the glass to peer down at the chest as if seeing it for the first time. "It'll be safe enough in your dressing room. Unless you think I'm going to steal it."

The alternative was to hire a cab and lug it all the way back to his hotel, and in reality it would be no safer there. Theatre people surely would understand his wishes.

"Can we put it in the store room at least?"

Mags shrugged and bent down to heft the chest up again. This time Merriman went to grab one handle to help.

"It's all right," she said, and clumped away with the heavy load. Merriman scampered after her, making sure the chest didn't get knocked against anything. In the storeroom she shoved it into a dark place between two shelves carrying rolls of cloth.

"Good enough?"

"Yes. Thank you. You didn't have to…it was heavy."

A shrug came in reply.

They went back to the stage door. Merriman shivered a little as the woman opened it, but not from the outside temperature He would have to walk under the gargoyle in order to exit to Grit Lane, and some inner sense chilled him at the idea. Another drop of water hung poised from the gargoyle's tongue.

"Well, I'll be back tomorrow then," said Merriman, pulling gloves from his overcoat pocket and donning them. "Eight o'clock. Will the stage manager be here by then?"

"Perhaps," said Mags.

The doorman chuckled. "Daft bastard."

Merriman stepped out into the lane. A single drop of water fell from the gargoyle's tongue onto the brim of his hat.

"I said don't do it," hissed Mags.

II

Leah sat in the pit in the Lombard Theatre with a pile of sewing and watched the dress rehearsal of *Hamlet*. A few other stage hands lolled around, hoping the set didn't fall down—or perhaps secretly hoping it did so they would have to work into the night and receive more pay.

On stage, the actor-manager Mr Julius Kent, as Hamlet, led the cast through the rehearsal. He never actually left the stage, even in the scenes without Hamlet. During those he stood to one side or other and kept shouting directions at the other actors, mid-speech. When it was his scene, he occupied centre stage and all the others, as required, moved aside to allow him full reign. It would have been annoying if the man wasn't so talented.

The rehearsal proceeded through to Act Three without too much interruption from Kent. Then came Hamlet's famous soliloquy, and Leah loved it so much she paused once more in her sewing to give it full attention, despite the flamboyant, pompous style Kent adopted in which to deliver it. Kent moved to the centre of the stage, placed one hand to his forehead, an expression of tragic grief on his face.

"To be, or not to be—"

Fierce hammering erupted in the wings, so sudden Leah almost pricked herself with the sewing needle. Kent broke character and glared into the wings. The hammering ceased. He exchanged his scowl for feigned tragic grief once more.

"To be or—"

The hammering recommenced.

"Who is making that obscene racket?"

The hammering continued for another few seconds, paused, began again.

The Lombard Theatre's manager entered from stage left. Sir John Fergus Rowley stood over six feet tall. A mop of dark hair fell to his shoulders, framing a long face highlighted by a pair of brass-rimmed spectacles. His nose protruded above a moustache that drooped around either side of his mouth to join massive side-whiskers. If roused to disapproval—anger didn't seem to enter Sir John's emotional vocabulary—he could be a stern task-master. Grizzled stage hands and bullying stage managers acquiesced to his commands without complaint, but Leah knew the persona was all bluff. She put down her sewing again to watch the imminent confrontation of Sir John's usual, calm, soft-spoken manner and the dynamic presence of Mr Kent. It might prove a better show than the play.

"Is there a problem, Mr Kent?" Sir John asked.

The actor rubbed his hands through his hair—actually a wig that made him look startlingly effeminate for the role of the Danish prince. But his hands were powerful enough, long-nailed, backed with blue veins.

"Sir John, I must protest!" His voice had no problem reaching the back row.

The hammering began again.

"There you are! I cannot act with that uproar going on! Fire that man!"

Actors and stage hands appeared from the wings, peering out. Leah noticed several were grinning, although at least one, the girl playing Ophelia, looked scared rather than amused. This was her first engagement with Kent's acting company, and she had the right to be anxious at the bad moods of her boss.

"That uproar is a necessary one." Sir John's voice also reached the back row, but without the thunder that accompanied Kent's. Leah knew the voice well, one that simply went without fuss and with perfect clarity where it needed to go. Years ago Sir John had been an actor himself, although a different quality to Mr Kent. "We must finish the set before the opening, and the castle walls are taking a deal of effort."

"Your workers do not need to—" The hammering recommenced. "Stop that immediately!"

The hammering ceased and a few seconds later the offender emerged onto the stage, hammer in hand. Charlie Stafford, one of the carpenters. He nodded to his boss.

"I'm sorry, Sir John, did you say something?"

"No, Charlie. Mr Kent did. Please return to your work."

"Very well, Sir John."

"And perhaps forgo the hammering for a while. Is there some quieter work that can be done on the set in the meantime?"

Charlie stared at the floor and thought. "Well, we could paint the buttresses."

"Excellent. Please paint quietly. There you are, Mr Kent," he said as Charlie retreated, "I trust this hasn't interrupted your performance too much."

Kent straightened a little, remembered his dignity, and stepped closer to the other man. Although a head shorter, he made up for it in sheer blistering presence.

"My performance has been ruined totally. Totally!" A stamp of his foot on the boards. "Why are your men working during a dress rehearsal?"

"Because they have no time else. Your…requirements for the set are taking a while to implement."

In her seat at the back, Leah smiled. Sir John had almost said "demands" instead of "requirements".

"The castle walls will take a long time to complete," continued Sir John. "They are particularly large and heavy."

"Those walls express the ponderous state of the Danish throne at the time of the play."

"It's a pity, then, that you didn't provide your own."

As a commercial company, Kent's troupe would normally have brought their sets with them, and all that would be needed was their erection in the new venue, a matter of hours rather than days. The necessity of building new walls meant considerable time and financial investment. Yesterday Charlie and the other carpenters had lugged in the timber. Somewhere a forest must be missing.

Sir John's comment seemed to quell Mr Kent. At any rate, he hummed for a bit and then said, "The fire was not my fault."

Leah remembered the story from the newspapers, and the backstage gossip. The fire had consumed the Empire down in Portsmouth where Kent's company last presented *Hamlet*. Sir John hadn't been amused to learn new battlements needed to be built at the last minute, even though it was Kent's duty to cover the cost. A delay in opening meant fewer tickets sold, hence the need to expedite the work.

Sir John clapped his hands together and smiled. "I presume that takes care of things?" He spun on one heel and exited before the actor could reply.

Kent stared after him for a moment, then did his own turn on the stage, sweeping his arms to include the rest of the cast. "Let us try to pick it up again!" He placed himself centre-stage, planted both feet firmly on the boards and once again placed his hand on his forehead. His black costume seemed to swallow the light, but that illuminated his face even more.

"To be or not to be," Kent intoned in a sonorous bass voice, so different from his everyday one. "That is the question. Whether 'tis nobler…"

He didn't move, but his face changed. The fierce scowl which was his standard Hamlet expression, no matter what scene, vanished. Instead, his features expressed pain. His eyebrows, great tufts of black hair, drew together. The sides of his mouth dropped.

Had he forgotten his lines? Impossible. He'd played Hamlet hundreds of times; it was his signature role.

Lurking in the wings, the actress playing Ophelia whispered hoarsely: "Whether 'tis nobler in the mind to suffer…"

He didn't seem to hear. Leah leaned forward, Rosencrantz's costume clutched in both hands, and watched his performance.

"To…suffer…" Kent croaked. "To suffer…"

The great actor-manager fell backwards, arms wide, until his skull crunched against the boards. He lay motionless, eyes open. The fingers of his right hand twitched a little. After three seconds, they too stilled.

Leah watched as the actor's soul rose from his body and hung above him. However individual people were in life, their souls were all the same after death, blue and sparkling with white lights like stars. She had seen many in her long life, but the unexpected appearance of this one made her stare.

Ophelia screamed. Charlie and several cast members ran to surround the actor. Sir John returned, but stood to one side rather than approach the man. Charlie slapped the actor on the cheek a few times in an effort to revive him. An actor leaned in and listened to the man's chest.

"No good, mate. He's dead."

The actress playing Queen Gertrude appeared from the wings and stood with one hand on her mouth, the other reaching out to Ophelia to comfort her, or perhaps obtain comfort for herself.

"Dead, you say?" Sir John gazed down from his lofty height. "Are you certain?"

"I think so."

"Send for a doctor." One of the stagehands scampered away. "All of you get back!" called Sir John, and Charlie tried to shove the onlookers aside. "Give the man some air."

"Won't be needing none of that," said another of the cast members, a minor player who didn't seem too upset about his boss's demise.

Charlie and the actor managed to force the mob back a little, but they hung round, joined by even more people at the edges. It began to look like a tableau at the end of a melodrama, chorus gathered around the dead hero in the centre.

Above the crowd, now hovering up near the light-battens, the soul of Julius Kent still gleamed. Dead souls would normally hang around for a few minutes, as if coming to terms with their fate, then slowly vanish like water on a hot rock to whatever final destination awaited them. With the right magical incantations it was possible to delay their disappearance and make them serve or prophesy, but Leah hadn't done any witchcraft like that for a long time.

Something else joined it in the air above the stage.

It looked a bit like smoke, a twist of grey vapour. Another spirit. It materialized near the soul, which seemed to back off a little from it, as if afraid. The curl of black smoke swirled, reached towards the soul, which ascended into the fly tower above the stage where the flats and drapes hung.

The dark spirit faded.

Ghosts and phantoms, souls that for some reason stayed on, could linger for centuries and appear to those who were sensitive to their form. But this was no ghost, no phantom. Something else. Leah headed backstage through the side door so as not to interfere with the onstage drama. Mags over at the Gypsy had better be told about this. Leah put her sewing in the costume room, collected her wrap, and left the Lombard through the stage door.

Grit Lane, running between the Lombard and the Gypsy, lived up to its name most days, as eddies and currents of London air stirred the dirt and dust along its length. But today, in the late afternoon, the passage lay still and silent. Leah made her way along the lane to the Gypsy stage door. The gargoyle leered down, smile wide and malevolent. Leah sneered at it, and the drop of water on the end of its tongue receded a little. She gave a few hard raps with the door-knocker.

Mags opened the door, glanced over her shoulder at Tom Gimble in his office, and stepped outside.

"What is it?"

Leah indicated the stage door of the Lombard.

"Has something happened?" asked Mags.

Leah exhaled silently and tried to take hold of her sister's hand. The woman could never learn the need for haste.

Mags wrenched her hand away and crossed her arms. The lock of hair from under her boy's cap fell across her left eye. "Look, I've got a lot of work to do. There's a new act and I have to—"

Leah put her hands together, pleading.

"No," said Mags. "Just tell me what you want. As I said, there's a new act and he's being a right troublement. I have to fix it all up."

Leah started to sign, her hands forming shapes that symbolized words. "*There's been a death.*" At the end of the sentence she tapped her right index finger on Mags's forehead to reinforce the message's urgency.

"Don't do that!" Mags snapped. "A death? All right. Give me a minute."

Mags went back inside and muttered something to Gimble. A cloud of tobacco smoke emerged from the dwarf's mouth as he gave a reply.

"We'll have to be quick," Mags said.

They walked along the lane, Leah in her cotton dress and wrap, Mags in a man's short tweed jacket flung over her scruffy muslin dress. The Lombard's doorman peered out.

"Oh, it's just you," he said as they approached. "Sir John's sent for the doctor and a policeman. Thought you might be them."

The two women pushed past silently.

Leah decided to avoid the backstage and passed instead along the right-hand side corridor out to the front of house. Passing the ticket booth with Mags in tow, Leah showed her a billboard erected there and pointed a finger at the top billing.

"*Hamlet,*" said Mags. "That'll be a good show. I remember—"

But Leah shuffled her into the theatre. No time for nostalgia. People crowded the stage, some who had a legitimate reason for being there and many who didn't. The corpse of Julius Kent, still in his Hamlet costume, remained centre stage, but with his collar removed and lying beside him. Sir John remained standing, arguing something with Queen Gertrude.

No sign of Kent's soul, or the other intrusive spirit.

Mags looked at the scene. "So he just collapsed on stage?"

Leah nodded.

"Who is he? Julius Kent? Was it an accident? How did he die?"

"I don't know." Trust Mags to ask more than one question at a time, faster than Leah could sign the answers.

"What then? What's it to do…You think it's not a natural death?"

"Not the death. What came after."

"What do you mean?"

"F."

"Foxwood? We should ask him? I don't know—it doesn't seem peculiar to me. An actor drops dead on stage. So what? Or did you see something else?"

"His soul. And something else."

"What?"

Leah used the fingers of both hands and waggled them over her head. It took a moment for Mags to catch on.

"Two souls?"

"One soul. And a spirit."

"A ghost?"

"No."

Souls, whether in or out of a person's body, seldom interacted with anyone or anything, especially not another soul. Most of the newly dead were preoccupied with the fact they were dead, especially someone like Kent who had died suddenly.

A policeman arrived and thrust himself among the commotion on stage with all due authority. The people parted slightly to let him through, but on nearing the corpse the officer merely looked down at it. Practically the whole population of the theatre had arrived by now.

"What do you want me to do?" asked Mags.

"Tell F."

"You think he's knows something about this?"

Really, Mags could be so dense sometimes. Leah pointed to the simple gold ring on Mags's right forefinger, and then to her own identical one.

Mags knew what that meant, at least. "The ladies? You think we're in danger? All right. I'll tell him. Any idea who the spirit is?"

Leah shook her head. Not another soul. Something nastier.

III

"The Miraculous Osiris, eh?"

The smaller half of Riggs and Hankey—Michael Hankey, if Merriman remembered correctly—blew smoke from his cigar and leaned back in his chair so that it balanced on two legs. He wore a cheap woollen suit that smelled of whisky.

"Yes," said Merriman. "I'm an illusionist."

"Well you would be with a name like that." Hankey didn't take his cigar from his mouth when he talked, so it rolled around wetly in one corner. "How long have you been at it?"

"That depends I've been doing illusions most of my life. I started as a boy at school amusing my friends—"

Hankey rolled his eyes. "I didn't want your life history, man. How long have you been in the business?"

"Ten years."

Ten long years. The last five...it always made him shiver a little when he thought about them.

Smoke from the cigar curled up to the ceiling in the still air of the dressing room. "Twenty-three years me and Riggs have been together. Twenty-three years and he still gets top billing. Riggs and Hankey. Always in that order. It's a brand, see? Like The Miraculous Osiris."

Riggs and Hankey were a comic duo presenting an act in which Hankey persistently tried to sing a love ballad to his absent girlfriend while Riggs kept interrupting with witty and (supposedly) hilarious comments, mostly at the expense of the girlfriend. A classic vaudeville double act. Merriman wasn't looking forward to seeing it.

"What's that mean then? Osiris?"

"He was the ancient Egyptian god of the afterlife, the dead, resurrection. That sort of thing."

"Sounds a bit morbid."

"It's my act. I resurrect things."

Another puff of smoke. "I see."

What was Hankey doing here anyway? Monday morning. The show didn't start until seven o-clock that night, so it was inconvenient he was here getting in the way when Merriman wanted to unpack his equipment.

He'd fetched the chest from the strong room and it lay open on the floor next to his dressing table. The trick cabinet and other equipment stood against the wall, waiting to be transferred to the strong room. Merriman refused to let any of his equipment out of his sight until that happened, so he took his own time sorting out the rest of his things. That Mags girl had been singularly unhelpful, and if his contract hadn't required him to follow her instructions he would have stopped asking for help altogether. Foxwood had a strange way of running a theatre, to include a woman among those in charge.

He smoothed down his thinning black hair and regarded the coat that formed part of his costume. It had seen a few years, like himself. Perhaps it was time for a new one—except that would cost a fair bit of money, given all the secret pockets and drawstrings that had to be sewn into it. Besides, nothing could be bought until payday. He hung the coat on a clothes rack. Looking at himself in the mirror gave him another pang of discontent: too much coarse cooking, too little exercise; but there was no time for exercise and no money for a better diet. Hence this turn at the Gypsy.

"Good bit of equipment you have there," observed Hankey.

"Yes. Please don't touch it."

Hankey put both hands up in the air as if under arrest. "Perish the thought. Riggs is the nosey one." He tapped his own nose significantly. "If you know what I mean."

"Not exactly."

"You'll see."

The other man gasped when Merriman drew the cloak out of the chest. The gold metallic cloth caught the gaslight in the room and sent a thousand reflections onto the walls.

"Neat," said Hankey.

Next came the headdress, similar to the double crown of ancient Egypt, tall, white, with a gilt serpent rearing on the front. Red and blue costume gems lined the front and back. He examined the crown carefully. One of the paste gems felt a bit loose; he'd have to chase up the stage manager later and see if they had any glue in the repair shop.

"All I wear is this bloody suit!" laughed Hankey. "Not like your get-up."

Without letting Hankey see, Merriman reached in and checked

that the secret compartment at the top of the crown still opened and closed easily. In transportation, that was usually the most likely part of the headgear to be damaged. Nothing to worry about. He hung the cloak on the clothes rack, placed the crown back in its box and set it on his dressing table.

"So what do you think of that Mags?" asked Hankey suddenly, after puffing silently on the cigar for a few minutes. "Bit of a saucebox, eh?"

"I'm still wondering about her. The doorman's a bit surly."

"That's Gimble. Ignore him."

When he'd arrived that morning Gimble still didn't answer his knock. It had been a small boy with red hair who had let him in. The old man hadn't stirred from behind his glass-fronted booth.

"You'll get used to him," continued Hankey. "I've never seen him do a scrap of work, but Foxwood keeps him around for some reason. We've been here six months now, me and Riggs. Gimble hasn't said a nice word to either of us."

"What are the houses like?"

"Good most nights. Second house crowds get a bit rowdy, but you'd be used to that I suppose."

Second house started at about ten o'clock after most of the patrons had fuelled up at the pubs and were more than ready to heckle and jeer lousy music hall acts. On the other hand, it also made them more appreciative of good ones. Merriman had received his fair share of judgements both ways.

"What do you think of Mister Foxwood?" He might as well ask someone who had been there a while.

For the first time Hankey removed the cigar from his mouth. "Strange cove, that old man," he said, with his voice dropped a third. "I sometimes think he's daft as a two-bob watch, other times he seems to know more than he lets on."

"What did he do before music halls?"

"Not wise to ask too many questions here. You might get answers you don't like." Hankey plugged his cigar back in.

All right, so this man played games too. Merriman preferred to make his own judgements about his work colleagues anyway.

Clothes arranged, make-up—mostly used to highlight his eyes to give them a vaguely Egyptian look—set out on the dressing-table. He again wished Hankey wasn't there to see the next thing taken out of the chest, but Merriman was anxious to check it for any damage: a carved wooden box, which he set on the dressing table under the gas light.

A cube, exactly twelve inches on a side, made of ebony and picked out in mother-of-pearl with designs of pyramids, Egyptian gods, crocodiles and a hawk in flight. All the figures stood in or soared over a desert in front of high mountains capped with clouds.

As usual, when he touched it, a soft whisper spoke in the back of his mind for a few seconds. The words were in some unknown tongue, but sometimes he knew what they meant. The voice instructed him to leave the box closed but unlocked, and each time he obeyed. He could no more resist the voice than shift a mountain.

Hickey whistled. "What's that?"

"Part of my act. I call it the Resurrection Box."

"What does it do?"

"Ah, that's a trade secret. I had it made in China."

"What's inside?"

Merriman didn't bother to reply to such an unprofessional question. He checked the outside of the box, noted that all was well, no chips or scratches. After a quick buffing of the upper surface with a piece of velvet he felt along the upper edge to the secret catch, but didn't activate it.

"Is it one of them Chinese puzzle boxes? You know, there's a trick to opening them?"

"Something like that. Watch my act and you'll see what it does."

Mags appeared at the door. Same cap, same dress, same lock of unruly hair as yesterday.

"I found the storeroom key," she said, with the same disinterested look as before. "Do you want some help with your equipment?"

"Oh. Thank you." Merriman stood over the box and looked at his gear in the back of the room. "The chest can stay here. The cabinet can remain backstage wherever the stage manager wants to put it. It goes on at the beginning of my act. The other stuff, and particularly this box, I'd like locked away until this afternoon. I can prepare things then."

The room became full as Mags's dumpy body entered. "Better let me take the heavy things."

She hefted a couple of suitcases and didn't seem to feel their weight at all. Hankey winked at Merriman. "Don't make 'em like that where I come from!" he mouthed around the cigar. "Hey, Mags, you ever going to have that drink with me?"

"I don't think your wife would like that."

Hankey laughed.

"And put that cigar out before Mr Simm smells it."

Merriman carried the Resurrection Box as they walked along the corridor to the room Mags had shown him the night before. With the two suitcases in hand, the woman's form blocked any view forward so he almost walked into her when she stopped abruptly in front of the open door. She put the suitcases down and pointed to the far wall. "Shelves at the back. You can have the first two but leave the top one empty, the stage manager says."

"Is he here? I need him to buy some props for my act."

She shoved a hand down the front of her dress and handed him a key on a chain. The metal was warm after its sojourn in her bosom. "Here's the key. Mr Simm'll turn up later. What props?"

"I'd rather talk to Mr Simm about them."

The bland look Mags sent was unreadable. She seemed neither miffed about his going over her head, nor relieved she didn't have to bother helping him further. He stepped to the shelves she had indicated and placed the box on one.

"What's that?" Mags asked.

"Just a piece of equipment. I call it the Resurrection Box. Part of my act."

"It's pretty." One hand came too close.

"Be careful. It's very expensive."

Her reaction came wild and hot. "What do you take me for? An idiot?" Mags whipped her hand back so hard the slap of it against her thigh reverberated in the small room. "You think I'd break it? I'm not some clumsy ox, you know. I wasn't going to touch it." The woman's scowl had come from deep inside; it twisted her face into something wild, untamed. Primal.

He swallowed. "Um…of course not. I'm sorry."

Once, a few years ago, someone in another theatre had become too curious and opened the box when Merriman hadn't been vigilant enough. The man's funeral several days later was well-attended; Merriman didn't go, in case anyone suspected him. Sometimes, in more sombre moments, he thought about the man and wondered if something like that would happen to him one day.

"If you want to get on here, mister," continued Mags, "you'd better treat us backstage people properly. Just because you're a high and mighty performer doesn't mean you're better."

"You're right." He struggled for words to calm the storm of her anger. "Without you people we'd be nothing at all. I've always thought that. It's just…well, the box was especially made for my act and sometimes people aren't as careful as you."

The flattery worked. At least, the woman stopped frowning and pointed at the two suitcases still on the floor. "You can handle them yourself I guess." The wild thing inside her had retreated.

After she left, Merriman grimaced. Not a good start.

"It's full of power," said Mags. "I felt it."

Joshua Foxwood swirled the glass of deep red wine and did not reply.

All things considered, he should have been a veritable oenophile, able to identify different wine varieties merely by smell and taste, able to propound the qualities and failings of any number of vineyards and vintages; but Mags knew from experience that the finer nuances of the art were lost on him, since his only use for wine was apparently to drink as much of it as possible. The swash and swirl of the ruby liquid around the delicate crystal glass made a pretty display.

"Ebony, you say?"

Mags nodded. "Yes, and covered in mother-of-pearl designs of gods and goddesses and things. Egyptian, they looked. And he called it a Resurrection Box. Is that significant?"

His eyes met hers for the first time since she'd entered his office. The red light reflected from the wine lit his eye sockets in intermittent flickers, so they seemed to flash by themselves. The thin mouth below them curled into a flat, sideways S-shape. For a moment his face resembled the fox skull on the desk.

"Well, I don't know," he admitted. "But it's a weird enough thing to call it, don't you think?"

After all her years at the Gypsy, Mags had seen many illusionists, some better than others. They had a habit of calling themselves by ostentatious stage names, and labelling their acts with spooky and mysterious terms. But something felt more than peculiar about the Resurrection Box. In ancient times Pandora's Box had given no clue as to what it concealed until opened. Then it all came out, except hope. This box was different: it gave enigmatic hints while staying firmly shut.

"So you're not interested in finding out more about it?"

Foxwood put the glass to his lips, held it there and then tipped it further and further as the contents disappeared down his throat. Mags watched his Adam's apple: it didn't bob once. His one and only swallow was right at the end as he put the glass back on his desk. She stepped forward with the wine bottle and proceeded to refill the glass. That lot disappeared in the same manner. When she attempted to fill the glass a third time he shook his head. "Business to do tonight. I need a clear head." He chuckled. " There's a first time for everything."

"So do you want me to do anything about Merriman's box?"

He frowned. "Eh? What box?"

She tapped her fingernails against the side of the wine bottle. *Wait for it…*

"Oh, that box. No, I wouldn't worry about it."

There were few occasions Mags had ever doubted her master's judgement. Usually—no, almost always—he was right. But something about this new act worried her. Ever since Merriman had turned up at the stage door, and had been spat on by the gargoyle. It only did that to people it didn't like. Or those it feared.

"I was thinking…"

Her master put his wine glass down and laced his fingers together. His long nose turned in her direction. "You were thinking, perhaps, that the box might have something to do with Leah."

So the old man did have concerns of his own.

"Yes." After three seconds of silence: "Does it?"

"I have no idea. What makes you concerned about her all of a sudden?"

"May I speak freely?"

He pointed to the chair and she sank into it, clutching the wine bottle. Foxwood held up one hand and a glass appeared as if from thin air. He placed it before her and she poured. "I never knew Leah back in the old days," she said, after taking a long sip. "You know, before she *was* Leah. I never met…"

"Yes. Two hundred years ago her name was Ingrid." Foxwood's voice was flat, unemotional. He never liked discussing the lives of his followers.

She ploughed on regardless. "All I know is she used to be a witch, then some god or other gave her a child, and later abducted him. He cursed Leah to silence and she hasn't spoken since."

He grunted, and the sound turned into a soft belch under the influence of the wine. "Used to be a witch? She still is, and don't ever forget that. But she needs my protection. That's why I keep her close: the vengeance of some gods can last for centuries."

"What did she do to make him so angry, to steal their son for himself?"

He took another swallow of wine and sighed. "You must ask her that."

"I have. She's never told me."

"Well then." His eyes gleamed. He knew, but the crafty old fox kept his secrets close.

"I was thinking," she continued, "could her child's father have come back for some reason? For more revenge, as you said. Maybe he made this box and had Merriman bring it to us."

"Don't worry about Leah," said Foxwood. "I don't think—*think*, mind you—the Box is anything to do with her. If it proves to be a problem we can deal with it. What about Tom Gimble? Have you asked him?"

"No."

"Well perhaps you could pay him the respect of a visit. Is there anything else?" He pulled a sheet of paper towards him with one hand, flipped open the inkwell with the other. "As you can see, I'm rather busy."

Mags pushed the cork back into the wine bottle and looked at the floor for a moment, silently cursing her master's casual dismissal of her fears.

"Well," she said. "There's been a death at the Lombard."

"Oh? How inconvenient. Not Sir John I hope?" He dipped his quill into the inkwell. "I quite like him. A little fussy, but an astute manager."

"No, some actor. Leah took me to the Lombard to see."

The quill remained vertical in the inkwell with Mr Foxwood's long fingers curled around it. "A death is always distressing, and often expensive. But why are you concerned? Did you see anything suspicious?"

"Just the dead man on stage. But Leah saw something with that second sight of hers. She thought there might be some danger, that you might know something about it."

He extracted the quill and held it poised over the paper. "Do you think I know something about it?"

Mags clutched the wine bottle tightly by the neck but said nothing.

"Sir John is perfectly capable of handling a death among his actors," Foxwood continued.

He seemed remarkably calm. He did own the Lombard, after all, along with the Gypsy, and a death was never good for business. But to persist further might invite scorn. Years of experience with his nettlesome moods had given Mags a healthy respect for the old man; along with it, however, went the knowledge that old Foxwood kept many dark secrets, Leah being one of them.

The quill scratched across the paper. "The fact you are still here in my office, Mags, leads me to believe there's something about the death you haven't told me."

"Yes. When the man died Leah she saw his soul, but there was another thing, too. Not just his soul, you understand. She called it a spirit."

For a single fraction of a second, the quill skipped on the page. He sneered and reached for some blotting paper. "What sort of spirit?"

"She didn't know. She normally only sees the souls of the dead, not other things. No more than the rest of us, that is."

"I see." He resumed writing, more slowly this time. "Ghosts might hang about a theatre, you know."

"She was afraid, sir."

"'Sir?' I don't get that often."

He appeared relaxed enough. If anyone should know about stray spirits hanging about the theatres, spirits that appeared at someone's death, it would be Joshua Foxwood.

"Do you think we should be worried? Does it have anything to do with Merriman's box?"

"Why would you think that?"

"I don't know." She stood and paced to the window. Outside, Ginger Street had begun to fill with evening crowds. Directly below her, a boy sold newspapers; on the other side of the street, outside

Mrs Bennett's establishment, two men talked, glancing occasionally at the house as if daring themselves to enter: the ordinary world, not concerned with ghosts or mysterious boxes. Mags sometimes missed such a mundane existence.

"Things have been quiet here for a long time," she said. "Then suddenly, a spirit and that stupid box." She sighed and turned back to face him. "I just feel something's wrong. Maybe it's nothing."

Foxwood paused in his writing and lines emerged on his brow. "It's all right, Mags. I've always taken my ladies seriously. See what you can find out. But be careful. If that spirit is—let's say an unauthorised visitor—steps may have to be taken."

She glanced at the ring on her finger. "I had a letter from Lucretia the other day." How long had it been since they'd seen each other? Ten years, maybe fifteen. Their sisterhood gatherings were rare, but Lucretia's letters were always full of titbits about life at her theatre in Edinburgh. "She suggested the possibility of a revel sometime."

"Indeed? 'For auld lang syne' as she would no doubt say. Touching. Well, that's for you ladies and Gimble to decide. Let me know."

"It is a valid point: we should gather together again."

"I've little time for such things now, Mags. You know that." He threw her a grim smile. "The rheumatics."

Mags stared at Foxwood's silhouette against the room's gaslight. Like a dead branch fallen from a tree, a twisted, thin, brittle cast-off, a discarded exoskeleton of a spider or scorpion. Nothing inside, and not much outside.

Her master had existed for a long time.

"All right. Good night, sir."

Scratch, scratch, scratch went the quill. For the first time, Mags noticed the rasping had the same dry sound as Foxwood's voice.

"Good night, Mags. And don't worry."

"Yes, sir. I mean, no, sir."

As soon as the door closed behind her, the sound of the quill ceased.

IV

It usually took Merriman an hour to set up his act, prepare the props, secrete the various objects on his person that would seem to materialise out of thin air and make sure the hidden drawers and catches worked smoothly and noiselessly. Donning his costume took a while too, especially the crown of Osiris that had to be checked to see the clockwork mechanism that operated the serpent on the front was wound tightly enough but not too tight—he didn't want another disaster such as had occurred in Birmingham the year before.

The preparation for his opening night at the Gypsy went well. No last minute repair jobs, no panic looking for a lost a piece of equipment. Locked in the storeroom he prepared everything and finally wheeled the table, piled with various pieces of equipment, backstage. Mr Simm directed him where to put the things until his entrance.

Despite his initial misgivings, Merriman had been impressed by Simm, who seemed the most pleasant person at the Gypsy so far. Mr Foxwood was too thinly cadaverous; Mags too surly; Hankey too dull. No chance yet to meet the other stagehands—indeed the other acts—under circumstances where a proper impression could be formed. Variety people tended to keep to themselves anyway. All in good time.

He waited, kitted out in his Osiris costume, under a dull blue light next to his table. The stage placard announcing his act, The Miraculous Osiris, had been painted that morning. He ran his eye over it critically. At his last venue some idiot had misspelled Osiris and a hasty correction had ruined the otherwise impeccable calligraphy. But this placard had a passable picture of himself next to the lettering. He wondered who had painted it.

The act before him was Riggs and Hankey, who were as ghastly as Merriman had feared. Although both wore the same style of cheap black suit and bowler hat, Riggs stood at least a foot taller than Hankey. He was indeed the nosey one—his proboscis stood proudly from his face and gave his speech an adenoidal twang. Every time Hankey began to croon a love ballad to his absent girlfriend (whose name was Primrose Plod) Riggs, who fastidiously peeled an orange the whole time, would interrupt with some wry observation or impertinent question about Hankey's relationship with the girl. The audience seemed to find this hilarious. Whether Hankey had a good singing voice or not was hard to tell, as he never finished more than a couple of lines of the song before Riggs came in with another broadside. It came to an end with Hankey chasing Riggs off the stage and pelting him with orange peel. Merriman stood ready and nodded to the two stage hands who would wheel on the table once the curtain closed.

The acts were announced by someone named Fred Bastable, dressed like a circus ringmaster, who sat in a box just beside the orchestra pit. Merriman hadn't met him yet, but the man had a clear voice which he could boom out readily enough over the noise of the crowd.

And it was indeed a noisy crowd. In his experience Monday nights were usually subdued. But tonight almost every seat held a patron, and the crowd happily cheered and jeered the acts. Merriman hoped the numbers were up because they wanted to see his act.

The curtain came down as Riggs and Hankey exited, and Merriman nodded again to the stage hands, who wheeled the table onto the pre-set chalk marks as another stage hand replaced Riggs and Hankey's placard with his own. Merriman went to the rear of the stage where a black curtain hung. It was split down the middle. Out front, Bastable announced him as the crowd still clapped and roared from the previous act.

"And now!" Bastable could really inflect enthusiasm into every word. "From the mysterious East! From the land of the Pharaoh! From the depths of time and the haunted mysteries of the ancient—"

"Get on with it!" some wit called from the back row.

"—sands, the Gypsy brings you wonders and delights that will astonish and amaze!"

Merriman readied a thunderflash in his hand as Bastable wound up.

"The Marvellous Osiris!"

Miraculous Osiris, you idiot!

He raised the thunderflash. As the curtain rose, he threw the firework to the floor.

A blinding light, the crack of gunpowder, and a billow of smoke. Under cover of the smoke Merriman stepped from behind his black curtain and appeared on stage, arms out wide so the golden cloak fell open, the crown of united Egypt on his head.

Applause at his sudden apparition out of thin air.

Worked every time.

The front rows of the audience stood out clearly in the spill of light from the stage. Working class mostly, the odd top hat among them, seated at tables piled with lemonade bottles, oranges and packets of nuts. The five musicians that passed for an orchestra waited poised and ready; the conductor raised his violin and led the band into a quick musical fanfare as Merriman turned to his table.

The first part of his act involved making objects appear and disappear, which he achieved using the various traps and secret compartments of his table and the hidden pockets in his coat. He kept up a steady patter, throwing in the odd magical phrase before each trick, hinting that the source of his powers came from a visit to the Great Pyramid twenty years before. This included a night he spent alone inside the pyramid, during which he received a visit from Osiris himself. The patter informed the audience that Osiris was the god of resurrection, among other things, and the audience would witness this marvellous power as the climax to the act.

The response to his act from the house was mostly positive. A few hecklers up the back said they'd seen it before, give us something new, and so on but they quietened down enough as his act proceeded. After each trick the orchestra would give a few dramatic chords and the audience would clap. A good enough reception for his debut.

The climax came soon enough.

"And now I can feel the power of Osiris!" he intoned, holding his hands out one more time to show nothing hidden up his sleeves—well, nothing now the act had almost concluded.

"Yeah, and I can feel this lady!" said a wag in the pit, his arm around a woman. She laughed, as did others in the audience.

"Good for you, sir!" Merriman quipped back. "I wish I could join you." More general laughter. "As I mentioned, Osiris is the god of resurrection. He himself came back from the dead with the power to raise that which has passed on." Merriman lifted the Resurrection Box from its place on the table and held it aloft. The mother-of-pearl decorations gleamed brightly under the stage lights. "This is his Box of Resurrection, which I received from the hands of Osiris himself.

Anything placed in this box will return to the living form it once had! Observe!"

He placed the box on the table and drew a bouquet of dead violets from his pocket, holding it out so the audience could see the wilted things, brown and dry. Actually, they weren't real violets at all, just a clever mock-up made from brown paper, but they looked genuine enough.

"Poor withered violets. I wish I could present a lovely lady with a living bouquet, but all is not lost. I place them in the box, so!"

He lifted the lid of the box using the secret release catch and placed the fake flowers inside, then closed the lid and gestured extravagantly while intoning his catchphrase, "By the power of Osiris!" Once more the box was opened, and Merriman extracted a fresh, living bunch of violets. He sniffed them deeply and tossed the bunch to a woman in the front row. "For you, my dear!" Then before the audience had a chance to applaud he continued: "I know what you're thinking! I had another bunch of flowers in the box! Such an easy trick. But may I have a volunteer from the audience to help me with the next resurrection?"

A pause. A few nervous chuckles, which is exactly what he expected. "Never fear, ladies and gentlemen, I'm not going to ask the volunteer to die!"

Laughter then. And a hand shot up: the young man who had made the joke about feeling his girl.

"Come on up, sir!"

Bastable showed the man how to make his way to the stage via the steps on the right.

"And what is your name, sir?"

"George."

"Well, George, people thought my last trick too simple, so how about you and I make it a proper resurrection this time?"

The man said nothing, just grinned foolishly and waved to his girl.

As Merriman turned back to his table a movement off-stage caught his eye. Mags stood there in the wings, staring at him. He could see others backstage: Mr Simm at his stage manager's desk, a few idle hands lounging about, a female singer who would be the next act slugging down a sip of something from a bottle. But Mags glared at him, arms folded across her chest, cap on her head as always.

Oh well, she had the right to observe a new act.

He removed a dead chicken from a canvas bag. "And what do you make of this, George?" He thrust the carcass into the man's face.

"Phew!"

The audience hooted. This was more their style, simple and direct stuff they didn't have to think about.

The chicken, obtained by Mr Simm at Merriman's request that afternoon, had been dead a while. It was genuine enough, and it wasn't part of his character to wonder how the animal had died or when.

"Can you assure the audience that this chicken is in fact dead?"

The man backed away, holding his nose, to the continued guffaws of the audience.

"Come on, examine it closely!"

More laughter. A voice in the back row made itself heard. "Garn, George, give it a proper sniff!"

The man leaned in and pretended to give a sniff at the corpse. "Yeah," he said. "It's dead orright."

"Now look inside the box, George, and make sure there is nothing hidden there."

He opened the front panel of the box so both George and the audience could look inside.

The voice came, whispering in his mind...words he could never catch...a deep voice, like gravel rubbed against the cheek, harsh, insistent...

"Put your hand in, George. Make sure there's nothing concealed inside."

George did so and nodded. Merriman turned the box to and fro on the table to make sure the audience could see no trickery lurked within. Then he shut the side of the box and opened the top panel.

"Now I place the dead chicken in the Resurrection Box." The smell of the thing lingered, but it could no longer be seen. He gestured histrionically. "And now I call upon the power of Osiris, the Great Ausir himself, to resurrect this chicken and make it as new again!"

A discreet thunderflash hurled to the stage, not a large one, just enough to provide some light and smoke, as if Osiris himself had done something marvellous. Merriman opened the box and pulled out a live chicken. The bird clucked loudly, proving itself very much animated, and fluttered its wings.

The audience applauded.

He put the chicken on the table where it strutted around briefly.

In the wings, Mags had uncrossed her arms but continued to look at him.

"Do another one!" came a call from the pit.

"Yeah, do it with something else."

"Do George!"

More laughter, but the healthy laughter of an audience enjoying itself, not the derisive howls that greeted an inferior act. Merriman was a hit.

"So, you want more? Very well!"

He lifted a cloth on the table and picked up a leg of lamb, also obtained by Mr Simm. "Now, George, once again I must ask you to assess the quality of this leg of lamb. Is it real?"

At least this one didn't stink, although the gas lights had raised its temperature enough for the lump of flesh to feel quite warm.

George summoned enough courage to poke a finger at the meat, and nodded.

"Once again, I show you the box contains nothing at all." He went through the routine of opening the false panel, revealing the emptiness of the box, and closing it. Then he opened the top lid.

"Now, I ask George here to place the leg of lamb in the box."

George did so. Merriman closed the lid, stepped back and turned once more to the audience.

"Great as the mighty Osiris is, it will take all my skill to call upon him for such a resurrection as this! I ask you, members of the audience, to repeat after me the intonation to restore this poor animal to life!" Merriman raised his arms. "Repeat after me: Oh great Osiris!"

In his head, the voice became louder.

"Oh great Osiris!" At least some of them tried to put some feeling into it.

"Restore to life this humble offering to your majesty and power!"

The audience repeated his words.

Another thunderflash. Three used so far—he would need to call upon a reliable fireworks manufacturer here in London to replenish his supply.

He turned to the box, opened it, and pulled out a living lamb.

The audience loved it. Although young, the lamb was patently too large to fit in the box. And the cloth on the table only reached to the edges. Plainly, no cage sat below the table from which the lamb might have been pulled.

Even Merriman didn't know how the trick was done.

Only the voice knew.

Great applause. He bowed and indicated George standing to one side so he could also receive his share of the ovation. The man grinned foolishly and scuttled back to his seat.

Merriman bowed again as the curtain fell.

The stagehands came to carry his table off—he amused himself observing the expressions on their faces. They took surreptitious glances under the table for any hidden mechanisms. But of course there were none.

"Hurry it!" whispered Mr Simm and the stagehands exited with the table, the living chicken roosting on top. Merriman, still with the lamb in his arms, made a quick check to see nothing had been left behind and followed them as the woman singer prepared to go on. More stagehands hurried to set up a bower of fake flowers under which she would present her medley of sentimental love ballads.

He stepped over to Mr Simm, no more than a shadow in the blue darkness of backstage.

"I hope the chicken for the second house is fresher than that one," he whispered. "It almost knocked me out. And I'll need two more each day, lamb legs and chickens."

Mr Simm shrugged. "It's the heat from the lights, Mr Merriman." As if in evidence he wiped his own beaded brow and pointed to the gas jets above their heads. "New props each night'll cost a bit. What happened to the ones you just had? Can't you reuse them?"

"Of course not."

He walked away before Simm could pry any more. He'd asked a good question, though, one Merriman couldn't answer.

Mags appeared at his elbow as the curtain rose once more and the band struck up with the next act's first song.

"An interesting performance," she said.

"Thank you."

"Can I speak to you please? In private."

He almost told her to remember her place. Stage crew simply did not fraternise with the acts in his experience of the theatre world. But the fierce expression on her face hinted he might have broken some unknown rule of the Gypsy.

"All right. Give me five minutes."

The voices of Riggs and Hankey could be heard from inside the dressing room.

"So he taps me on the shoulder and I ask him what he wants," said Riggs. "'I don't want nothing', he says."

"This was before you bought Maisie the pint of bitter?" put in Hankey.

"No, after. I said that before. Blimey, it's a funny story if you just shut up and listen."

They paused as Merriman entered with the lamb in his arms. It bleated once.

"My gawd," said Hankey. "Is that supper?"

Merriman deposited the lamb at the back of the room. It stood there, bleating softly. A stage hand appeared with the chicken, which Merriman shut in a cage beside the lamb.

"And lo, shall the lamb lie down with the chicken," said Riggs.

Mags arrived. Riggs and Hankey had started their conversation again and didn't take any notice.

"In private, I said."

Merriman nodded. "Perhaps we should step outside."

The night air of Grit Lane poked itself under his Osiris cloak. His head, relieved of the crown, felt lighter but also caught the cool breeze that stirred the dust.

"Now, Mags, what did you want to see me about? I have to reset my props for the second house."

She remained on the doorstep so her head was on a level with his.

"That box. The Resurrection Box."

"Yes. If you're about to ask me how it works, you should know I can't tell you. Trade secrets."

"Where did you get it?"

"I bought it. In China."

"From who?"

"From whom, Mags. Please, I can't tell you that either. He's a very talented wood carver who designed the box as well as made it. Now, if that's all you want to know…"

He made to enter the Gypsy, but Mags placed her hands on either side of the doorway so Merriman couldn't squeeze past.

"Mr Foxwood will want to know," she said.

"Well Mr Foxwood can ask me himself. But I won't be telling him either. Now, will you please let me through?"

"It's a dangerous thing, a box like that."

He took one step back.

Exactly what the Chinaman had told him. The box hadn't really been made in China, but it added to its mystery to say it had. He'd actually acquired it in Birmingham, from a Chinese man. Well, oriental at least. It had cost him quite a packet, too. But it had been worth every pound to make his act something special.

It's a dangerous thing, the man had said as Merriman handed over the cash.

"Never mind that," Merriman said. "It's a prop for my magic act. Now please, let me in or I shall complain to Mr Foxwood."

She stared at him, hands pressed against the sides of the entrance so tight the effort appeared on her face.

"Won't do you any good to complain to him. He'll just ask the same questions I did."

Then she removed hands and stood to one side to let him storm past.

"Stupid girl," he muttered loud enough for her to hear.

A drop of water fell from the gargoyle's tongue as Merriman entered the theatre. Gimble the doorman uttered a single grunt of laughter.

V

Charlie always slurped his tea when he drank, but Leah didn't mind. When she made a pot for the Rowleys at four o'clock each afternoon there was always enough extra for any of the stagehands who might be about.

He stood in the Lombard's tiny kitchen with his vest unbuttoned and the sleeves of his striped shirt rolled back to the elbows. One hand gripped the saucer, the other raised the cup to his lips. The smell of sawdust hung about him. When their eyes met Charlie smiled.

"Rum do about that actor chap dropping dead like that, I mean, I ain't never seen nothing like that before, don't know what they're going to do now with the play."

Charlie always ran his sentences together when speaking to Leah, probably to fill in for her lack of replies. Once, he made an effort to learn her sign language, but complained she signed too fast for him to keep up.

He took a considered sip. "Got any cake?"

She shook her head. Mr Kent's company had cleaned the kitchen out of food and hadn't bothered to replace it. Charlie took another, less contented, sip and winked at her.

"You're looking good today. I like you in that dress. Suits your eyes." He turned bright red and almost dropped his cup. "By that, I mean…don't get me wrong…I didn't mean to…"

She smiled and pointed at the teapot to ask if he wanted a refill. English coyness with flirting amused her. Not that she had any designs on poor Charlie, but their continued friendship sometimes encouraged him to make a rash remark.

"No thanks," he said. "I…er…I've got to get back to work." He put the cup on the narrow table and wiped his mouth. "I didn't mean to embarrass you just then. I'm sorry…"

She rose and reached out to adjust his neck-cloth which didn't really need adjusting but served as an excuse. After twitching the scarf into place she waggled her finger in front of his lips.

"Yes, all right," he said. "I can take a hint. Well, that set won't build itself. Not that there's much point in finishing it now."

She released him and Charlie touched his cap to her as he departed.

Leah set the tea things out on a tray and carried it upstairs to the Rowleys' office. With her hands full she had to kick at the door to signal her presence.

"Come in!"

Another kick. Sir John opened the door with a muttered apology.

They were both there, Sir John Rowley and his wife Esther, mutual managers of the Lombard Theatre. The layout of the room amused Leah, as it reflected her interpretation of their relationship. Each sat on one side of a partners desk set up in the middle of the room. It had two flat surfaces with a low divide down the middle. Sir John's side, closest to the fire, remained perpetually covered in letters, stationery, magazines and drafts of theatre programmes and handbills. Lady Rowley kept her side free of anything at all except a large ledger containing details of the theatre's finances. The rest of the room continued the divide: Sir John's side seemed to double as a storeroom, cluttered with various props, a pile of scripts and, for some inexplicable reason, a spinning wheel. Lady Rowley's half contained little more than a dressing mirror and an ottoman piled with cushions where she could rest after a hard day counting box office takings. The walls of Sir John's half, warmed by the fire, glowed a soft orange; the paint on Lady Rowley's side remained business-like grey. Leah preferred Sir John's side of the room.

She set the tea tray down on a side table and, falling into the role of servant to her employers, started to pour without being asked.

Sir John returned to his side of the desk and sighed. "Well, they've decided to press on with the production, although how it'll go down is beyond me."

"As long as it works, we'll bring in some money," said Lady Rowley. "But really, *Hamlet* without Hamlet? How do they intend to manage that?"

"Well, apparently the chap playing Laertes is going to step in. He's done the role before with a different company. So Laertes will be played by…" He consulted a sheet of paper. "…Horatio, who'll have a few lines to learn in the next week."

"Who's playing Horatio?"

He looked at his list again and shrugged. "They say they have it all worked out. Mrs Gower promised me they'd press on regardless."

"They don't seem to have mourned much for Julius Kent."

Leah put Lady Rowley's tea cup before her. The woman glanced at it. "No cake?"

"Leah, buy some more cake will you?" said Sir John as she handed him his cup. "No, it seems Kent wasn't the most liked person. I mean, a wonderful actor, but not amiable in real life as it were. Twice married, once widowed." He added after a slight pause, "No doubt there were one or two mistresses."

"Well the publicity might do some good. People will at least want to turn up to see what his replacement is like. Thank goodness it's *Hamlet* and not some obscure bit of modern rubbish."

Leah moved slightly to put Lady Rowley's back between her and Sir John and jabbed a finger at his wife. Just as the woman turned towards her, she dropped her hands to her sides again.

"That will be all thank you," said Lady Rowley.

"Actually, Esther," said Sir John, "I was wondering if you might go and have an urgent word with the stage manager. He has some purchases to make and needs to discuss the supplies account."

"Now?" She stared at her husband. "Couldn't it wait?" She indicated her cup of tea.

"Take it with you."

Lady Rowley rose and dusted down her dress. "All right. But we really need to discuss the publicity account for *Hamlet* before too much longer. And there's the next show to consider."

He smiled and held the door for his wife. Leah picked up the tea tray and stood to one side as Esther left, as if to follow her out. After the door closed she put the tea tray back and sat down in the vacated chair without being asked.

Rather than sit, Sir John stood by the fire, spreading his coat tails to catch the warmth. His facial expression had a lot less heat in it.

"You have something to discuss?"

A nod.

"Then out with it. We don't have much time before Lady Rowley finds out I've sent her on a false errand. Is it about the play?"

She signed quickly. *"Kent's death did not seem natural."*

"What, you think there's been foul play?"

"I don't know."

He took out his fob watch, fidgeted with it for a bit, then shoved it back in his pocket.

"All right. Thank you. I can understand your disquiet. Keep an eye open. See what you can find out. But I don't think Mr Foxwood would be so stupid as to allow a murder in his own theatre."

"*He knows much.*"

He laughed at that. A bitter laugh, without any humour. "Yes, if everything you say about him is true. He may be my boss, but it seems hard to believe he has quite the authority you grant him. But are you accusing him of murder?"

She shook her head, feeling her employer's questioning eyes, and met his stare. So much Sir John didn't know; so much he never could.

"No, of course not murder," he continued. "But after all, you and Mr Foxwood—and Mags for that matter—well, it's hard to accept." He looked at her sharply, as if trying to penetrate the secrets kept in her head. Not for the first time.

"*You can understand my signs.*"

He nodded. "Yes. There's that, I suppose. I woke up one morning and could read those hand moves of yours as if born to them. And you say Mr Foxwood granted me that ability?" A pause and a glance at her fingers, as if expecting a reply. "Oh, all right. What are you going to do? Ask Mr Foxwood about the death? If you do, I'd appreciate it if you'd let me know what he thinks."

A nod.

He paused for a moment. "Why are you telling me this? Is it something I should be worried about? Something that affects the Lombard?"

A shrug.

"The police seem satisfied there's nothing suspicious. A stroke, they said."

She put her hands together. A little plea. Not subservient, but definitely sincere.

"If you think the Lombard is in trouble you have a duty to me. But I guess you have a sense for such things. All right. Keep me informed."

The tea things rattled as she picked up the tray. Sir John held the door open for her. Just as she passed through, he touched her lightly on the arm.

"Be careful."

VI

Mags lived in a room in the fly tower above the Gypsy's stage, among the wooden beams and ropes used to haul the scenery up and down. Once the room had stored ropes, winches and tools, but she'd put in a single bed, a table and two chairs, and a few other pieces of furniture. The inner wall was dominated by a set of chimneys rising from below; on the Grit Lane side a window let in light during the day. The room was constructed across two massive wooden beams left over from before the building was converted into a music hall. Gaining access meant climbing a ladder into the flies then negotiating a narrow wooden staircase up to the very underneath of the roof itself. A water closet, fed by a cistern that gathered rainwater from the roof, had been installed ages ago for the use of the fly-men who spent hours up there during shows.

Over the years she'd done the place up in her own style. Posters of theatre personalities decorated one wall. Porcelain figurines of dryads and fawns lay scattered haphazardly about. A hat-rack stood beside the window, hung with scarves and her one piece of female headwear, decorated with artificial cherries, which Leah considered tasteless. A wardrobe for her few items of clothing and a dressing table with a mirror completed the furnishings.

A place to call home.

The second house didn't finish until eleven. After that it took an hour for the talent to depart, and another half an hour before Mr Simm dismissed the crew. Shortly before one in the morning, therefore, Mags made her way up to her room and struck a match to light the gas. Washing in one of the facilities attached to the dressing rooms could be left until the morning.

That night, the one following Merriman's debut at the Gypsy, she felt no more tired than usual. Sleep would come if looked for, but instead she took a deck of cards and played solitaire for a while.

Foxwood could think what he liked. The Resurrection Box intrigued her and not, as Merriman imagined, through any desire on her part to work out how the trick was done. The man's story that he'd had the box made in China hadn't convinced her. Osiris; resurrection; Foxwood played his cards close. He was probably just as curious about it as Mags but refused to admit that in front of her. Typical. Sometimes he infuriated her beyond belief.

She waited until the house became totally quiet, until the stage door far below shut for the last time. Rats emerged from their hiding places and scurried about on the wooden beams of the flies, making their way downstairs to hunt for crumbs and scraps left by the audience.

Still in her working clothes, but without the boy's cap, Mags joined them. The theatre was almost pitch black, but she needed no light, so familiar were the stairs and ladders to her. Besides, her eyes were like those of the rats, good at seeing in the dark. They'd become that way after years of being backstage, watching from the wings, keeping out of the bright stage lights.

The final ladder let her into the stage right wings, where Mr Simm had his desk. He'd left it littered with rubbish, but the drawer containing his bunch of keys opened easily enough. Mags extracted a key and headed towards the stage door.

The squeaks, chirps and scuttling feet of rats filled the space around her, but it was an auditory illusion caused by the almost total silence of everything else. No roar of burning gas, no thump of feet on stairs or quiet creak of the fly-ropes as the stage hands hauled scenery up around Mags's room. No murmur of the crowd, no whispered backstage words. Silence.

Mags relished it.

Gimble stood outside his office, puffing on his pipe. The bowl glowed red in the darkness. "This had better be worth my time."

"Thank you for waiting."

"I'm tired and want to get to my digs."

She led the way to number two dressing room, the one used by Merriman. The occupants had left it neat enough. Riggs and Hankey's suits hung on a rack, with the magician's costume beside them, the crown of Egypt sitting in a hat-box on the floor. Make-up pots stood lined up tidily on the dressing-table. No sign of the Resurrection Box.

No sign of the chickens or the lambs either.

"Well?" she said.

"What?" The dwarf puffed up a cloud of smoke and shrugged.

"Anything magical?"

"No."

"But the animals disappear. After each show, what happens to the animals?"

"Buggered if I know. He doesn't take them with him when he leaves."

They moved to the storeroom. A sudden uneasiness made Mags halt at the door. Things that lurked in shadows and rode the night winds hid away in daylight, like the rats in the ceiling. Perhaps dawn would be a better time to search.

Or perhaps not. That was the whole reason for this search, to find out if her suspicions had any grounds; if so, Mr Foxwood would have to pay attention.

As long as something didn't attack them, or cast a spell, or…Mags didn't know what.

Darkness inside the room. No windows to let in even a thin stream of moonlight or gaslight, no sound of rats, no trickle of unseen water, until Gimble kicked against something unseen and swore, foul and loud.

"Shh!" she hissed.

"Shh yourself. Nearly broke my bloody toe."

Better not light the gas; Mr Simm read the meters every morning and evening and would know it didn't come from her room. She took out a box of matches and struck one on the wall. The flame sputtered, illuminating the nearby shelves. Mags fumbled her way towards those assigned to Merriman.

Why did had she given him the ones at the back?

A moment of disorientation as her hands met the shelves far sooner than she'd expected and the match fell from her fingers and extinguished on the floor. She ducked to avoid a copper gas pipe that loomed in front of her, didn't duck far enough and bounced her head against it, not hard but enough to bring an oath from her lips.

"You see?" said Gimble. "Hurts, don't it?"

A squeak near her head: a rat balancing on the pipe, disturbed by her encounter with it.

"Watch it! Or I'll tear you apart," she hissed.

Feet scuttled away along the pipe.

Mags struck another match and groped further along until her fingers encountered a cloth. Part of Merriman's gear, no doubt. Yes, there was the edge of the table; the Box had to be nearby. Just as its hard, cubic form came into view the match burnt out.

"That's it," she said. "What do you think?"

Gimble felt the Box with the fingers of both hands and closed his eyes. He turned the Box one way, then the other. He inhaled deeply.

The Box opened. Light shone from within, driving away all the darkness. Mags's loose black hair flicked around her face, stirred by a movement of air. A voice, far distant yet also inside her head, came from ages long past, gasping with weariness, lost words in an unknown tongue. Inside the box a grey form swirled like smoke, coming nearer as the voice filled the room.

Mags slammed the lid shut. The light and voice both died.

"Was that magic?" she asked.

Gimble sniffed. "No. Not earthly magic anyway. Beyond my knowledge."

The dark room seemed smaller now, the chirrup of rats more threatening. A sudden need to leave came over her. The room felt like a trap. Her eyes were blinded from the sudden light, but there was no time to strike a match. She let go of the box and staggered back, instinctive memory of the room guiding her towards the door. She rushed through, Gimble following, and locked it. For a moment they leaned against the door, hoping it would hold firm if the owner of voice escaped the box and sought to follow. Even Gimble shivered.

Mags pushed an ear against the door but heard no more from the other side. But something was in there, something that should have been left alone. No wonder Merriman's trick looked so marvellous.

It wasn't a trick at all.

Back in Gimble's office, they conferred by the light of a single candle. Gimble sat in his chair and surveyed the tapestry on the back wall in silence for a few minutes.

"So, what do you think?" she asked.

"Give me a minute!"

The pipe went in for another few puffs. Mags could never detect anything in the figures in the tapestry, but Gimble seemed to see and notice all sorts of things. At last he said, "Nothing."

The tapestry moved a little, as if a draft had come under the door. Except Mags felt no draft herself.

"Are you sure? You touched the Box."

He turned and looked at it for a while, blowing smoke against the weave. The figures on the mountain top, dressed in a bizarre combination of clothing styles, didn't seem to notice.

"I'm sure. The Box itself isn't magical. What's in the Box, that light, the voice…well, I've never seen or heard anything like that before."

"And Merriman isn't a warlock?"

"Him? No way." He pointed at the tapestry. "He walks right past this booth—and this tapestry—each day. I would have smelt him if he was. No, he's just your usual stage conjuror. Sleight of hand and distracting patter."

If there had been any earthly magic involved, Gimble would have detected it. Because he couldn't, that meant a nastier possibility.

"Is Foxy here?" she asked.

"No. Gone somewhere as usual. Who knows?"

"Leah saw something when Kent died. A spirit. The Box had already arrived here."

He grunted. "That woman sees a lot of things. Some of them I swear aren't there." He took a few puffs and swore when Mags remained in his booth. "All right. Yes, it's possible. Anything's bloody possible. You leaving me alone is possible. But you seldom bloody do it. There's something going on, all right? But no magic to do with the Box or Merriman."

"And yet that light we saw when the Box opened," persisted Mags. "That came from somewhere. If you can't detect it, then that means it's not mortal magic. Which means the Box has a divine origin. Or it was made under the direction of someone divine."

"Why would a god give Merriman a thing like this?" Gimble asked.

Mags wondered sometimes why gods did anything.

"Thanks, Gimble."

He put on his overcoat. On his short frame the hem almost reached the ground. A chill wind blew in from Grit Lane when he opened the stage door and stepped out. He glanced up, as he always did, and managed to avoid the drop of spit from the end of the gargoyle's tongue.

Mags headed for her loft room.

VII

With a mouthful of pins, Leah knelt at Mrs Gower's feet. The actor now playing Hamlet, Jacme Palomer, was three inches taller than Mr Kent had been, so Queen Gertrude had changed her shoes and, consequently, the hem of her Act One gown needed lowering. While Leah inserted pins, Mrs Gower fed lines to Palomer, who sat in a chair at the make-up table, clad in Hamlet's costume above the waist, street clothes below.

"This doublet doesn't fit," he said, tugging at his collar. "I'm choking in it." No matter if in character or not, Palomer always spoke in his native Provençal accent. The audience would have to listen closely to understand his dialogue.

"Concentrate!" Mrs Gower roared. "Your cue is, 'Ah me, what act, that roars so loud and thunders in the index?', and you say—"

"'Look here upon this picture and on this…' I *do* know the lines, Eileen!"

"Then *say* them. We want you word perfect."

"I am word perfect. I've done the part before."

"When?"

"In '45. With Mr Higgins' company."

"You must have been a pup. Now: 'Ah me, what act, that roars so loud and thunders in the index?'"

Jacme had a long speech here. He carried it well enough, even slumped in the chair and despite his accent. Leah listened to the lilt and power of Shakespeare's words. How she longed to say such things aloud, to stand on stage and declare words that soared like eagles, ran like hungry lions hunting, lifted mere mortals to the stars.

Even just once.

It didn't have to be Shakespeare. To say any words at all, even to curse, to laugh, to sing. But in two hundred years, not a single sound had passed her lips, not a sigh, not a sob. Not since that day in the forest of black trees, when a horse bore away two people, the one she hated and the one she loved. Sometimes the memory made her cry, yet not even those tears could make any sound issue from her throat. No curses, either; they existed in her mind, thundered there wanting release, screamed at the taker of her voice—and, like all else, fell short of actual utterance.

Enough of that. The hem needed finishing.

"'Oh Hamlet, speak no more'," intoned Mrs Gower on cue.

Leah rose and stepped back. Mrs Gower continued her speech, not heeding Leah's indication that the pinning had been completed.

"'O, speak to me no more; These words like daggers fill mine ears...'."

Leah tried to catch her eye, but Mrs Gower leaned over to put her hands on Jacme's shoulders and continue her speech.

Although she'd never performed the play herself, even back in the days when she still had a voice, Leah knew *Hamlet* well. They were rehearsing the famous closet scene, as it was known, and any minute the ghost of Hamlet's father would make an appearance. Only Hamlet would see him, but he'd report the vision to his mother and the scene would end with Hamlet dragging out the corpse of Polonius. All good stuff and guaranteed, with some special effects like sulphur lights, to thrill the audience.

As Jacme built up to the moment, Leah found herself mouthing his words: *That from a shelf the precious diadem stole...*

Movement at the far end of the dressing room, where a small window let in some late afternoon grime from Grit Lane. A porcelain vanity basin stood there, serviced by a single brass tap. And yet Leah saw—thought she saw—something else, something not quite there, the merest shifting of shadows.

"'A king of shreds and patches...'"

For a moment Leah's eyesight blurred. A dead soul—blue lights, flashes of white—emerged through the far wall. In her mind came a recognition, as some external consciousness touched her and awakened her sensitivity to souls. She remembered this insubstantial pattern of light and shadow.

The soul of Julius Kent.

Jacme rose and pointed, but not at the ghost of Kent, rather at the opposite wall, where in his actor's mind he pretended to see Hamlet's father's spirit. "'Save me, and hover o'er me with your wings...'" Eileen turned around in role to see what he pointed at, spinning her gown so far out the pins almost caught Leah's own dress.

Both actors continued the scene, unaware of the form that floated towards Leah.

A soul could do no harm, or indeed interact with the real world in any way; a ghost, such as Kent had become, was capable of more. Ghosts sought something, or were held back by some means divine or magical—she had captured a number in her time as a witch. Ghosts could cause harm by spiritual means, and were notoriously unpredictable. For some reason Julius Kent's soul refused to leave the mortal world. Was he seeking Leah now for some evil reason? At least there was no sign of the other spirit, the dark shadow that had appeared at the moment of Kent's death.

The form floated over to her and hovered at eye level. She remained still with an effort. A warding spell came to mind, but without a voice she could not utter it.

Behind her, the actors rehearsed the scene in which the imagined ghost of Hamlet's father at last vanished and Hamlet and his mother argued over the body of Polonius. The real ghost continued to hover before her. No face, no actual form of a man, but Kent nonetheless; trust a dead actor to make an entrance right on cue. Perhaps his ghost would be sensitive to her thoughts.

What do you want? Why do you linger here? In the play, Hamlet was visited by his father's ghost to revenge his murder. Perhaps that was why Kent now appeared. *Were you murdered? Are you seeking or fleeing that other spirit, the dark one?*

No reply. The ghost backed off towards the wall. As effortlessly as it had appeared, it sighed away. Leah moved to the window and gazed out through the grimy glass, but could only see the dreary prospect of Grit Lane and the rear wall of the Gypsy.

Mrs Gower's voice brought her attention back to the dressing room. "Yes, that didn't go too badly. I think we can say that that scene at least will go over well."

Jacme collapsed back in his chair. "I told you I knew the words." He tugged again at his collar and glared at Leah. "What are you still doing here?"

She turned and indicated the costume Mrs Gower wore.

"Oh, yes," said the actress. "The hemming. I'm sorry, dear, I forgot."

Mrs Gower moved behind her dressing screen. Leah waited for the dress to be passed over the top.

In his chair at the mirror, Jacme continued to fret over his own costume. "Hey, girl, do you think you could do something with this doublet? Kent's neck must have been as small as his generosity, and it's also too tight under the arms."

The dress came over. Leah smoothed it out and folded it over one arm.

"Don't call her 'girl'," called Mrs Gower from the other side of the screen. "Her name is Leah."

Jacme grunted. "All right. Leah. Can you fix my doublet?"

She nodded and held out her free arm. Jacme proceeded to slip off the garment. "I need it by tomorrow's dress rehearsal."

Again, the nod.

"Say please," said Mrs Gower.

He scowled as he muttered the word, then added, "You don't say much, do you?"

"Oh don't be totally ignorant!" Mrs Gower emerged wearing a flannel dressing-gown. "Now, do you think we should run through another scene?"

A shadow passed across the window. Leah swung round—but it was just someone moving in the lane outside.

"Are you all right?" Mrs Gower inspected her hair in the mirror.

Leah nodded and retired to her sewing room.

Nothing had come back from the police about the cause of Kent's death, or whether foul play had a part in it. Perhaps the autopsy hadn't been conducted yet. The news had certainly made the morning papers. Many people who had already purchased tickets for the play had anxiously contacted the theatre. Kent's ghost couldn't be hanging around merely out of concern for the play's future.

Many supernatural things had crossed Leah's path. Mags would have laughed if she'd been there, or made some derisive comment to the apparition. Even Hélène, the youngest of the sisterhood at a mere ninety-six years old, would scarcely have raised an eyebrow. What troubled Leah was the other spirit, the dark thing that had appeared when Kent died. It was no remnant of a dead person's soul, but something else. Mister Foxwood should have warned her. Unless…the crafty old devil might think he protected her by not letting on. Why, after all this time, did Foxwood still think her incapable of looking after herself?

She thrust the angry thought back and focused on the costume. No use letting the rage overtake her now. Her sewing machine whirred away under the power of the foot treadle. Keeping the heavy Gertrude costume straight took her attention for a while. Then she started on Hamlet's doublet.

Kent's company planned a two month season with the play. Perhaps his ghost would lurk around for that time, perhaps it would move on once the show had opened. But whatever the outcome, something should be done to find out just why it lingered in the real world.

VIII

The beggar had no legs. A soldier, perhaps, wounded in the service of his country. Merriman automatically dug into his pocket and put a penny in the tin mug the old wreck held in one hand.

"Thanks, mate," muttered the old man. The stench of sour gin came with the words.

Merriman hadn't seen the man at the entrance to Grit Lane before now. Perhaps beggars took turns setting up in different places. That would suggest some form of organisation, some central authority of beggars and tramps. Or perhaps the agreements were less formal, arranged as necessary between particular mendicants.

As an artist performing at the Gypsy, Merriman should have told the beggar to move on instead of giving him a penny, or tried to attract the notice of a policeman. Theatre crowds, even those drawn to the coarse antics at the music hall, would prefer not to see such unfortunates when they sought a good night's entertainment. No good could come of encouraging vagabonds. He recalled the women standing at the back of the Gypsy each night, soliciting clients, the grunts that came from the lane through the dressing-room windows as one or another woman distracted a paying gentleman. Perhaps those ladies did second houses too.

He proceeded down Grit Lane, scarf over his mouth and nose to keep out the dust. At the stage door the gargoyle leered at him as usual. In the clear morning light the figure looked less ominous, less threatening. The dark patches that made it seem malevolent were revealed as no more than dirt and cobwebs, and the ridiculous ears, the grinning mouth with the tongue sticking out, were comical rather than startling. He smirked at the thing as he lifted the doorknocker.

The gargoyle's evil countenance returned as quickly as an actor could replace a mask. The image of the skull on Mr Foxwood's desk came to Merriman's mind. He fancied it had looked at him, just for a moment, after he'd signed his engagement contract. Now the gargoyle did the same thing, the eyes slightly turned down, regarding him with a quite unreadable expression. A trick of light and shadow, surely.

He rapped the doorknocker.

Not Mags this time, and not the doorkeeper either. A stage hand with a broom. Merriman thanked him and passed inside. Gimble the doorman sat in his booth, smoking his omnipresent foul briar.

"Good morning," said Merriman.

"Is it?" said the old man, exhaling a heavy cloud into his already smoggy interior.

"May I ask..." Merriman had had a late morning. The exertion of performing two shows for his opening night, and two the next night, the need to stay behind and check his equipment, to store it away in the locked room, the long, cold walk back to his lodgings and then a few drinks before bed meant he had awoken with a headache and a rather bellicose feeling towards his fellow man. "May I ask, do you ever answer the door?"

"I try not to."

Nothing followed this reply, and given its forthright and immediate nature, Merriman couldn't think of anything to counter it. He turned his gaze from the old man's face to the tapestry behind him. It seemed different too, in the daytime: less colourful, with fewer figures poised on their mountain top, the storm behind them not so tempestuous.

A thin chuckle came from the old dwarf. "Like it?"

Merriman ignored him and went to his dressing room. No one there, and no animals either. He wondered about the lambs and chickens that appeared twice a night out of the Resurrection Box— always by morning they had disappeared again. They were not the same each evening: different colours and breeds depending on the dead materials supplied by Mr Simm. He should feel frightened about their disappearances each night. Not thinking about them, and the drinks he imbibed each night, were the best ways to deal with his disquiet. Whatever power brought the dead remnants of animals back to life might be capable of anything. So far nothing bad had happened...well, apart from the man in Birmingham. Merriman closed the dressing room door on his guilt and headed for the storeroom.

Fresh rat droppings on the shelves and on the floor. Other than that, everything was in its place. No intruders, no curious handling of the equipment. No rough handling, either—some stage managers were known to be less than respectful to actor's gear if they needed storage space. At one venue in Glasgow a number of his items were damaged when some bumbling fools had dumped heavy sandbags on top of them.

The Resurrection Box sat on the lowest shelf. Merriman ran his fingers over it, felt the mother-of-pearl decoration. Such a curious thing. Mags had been understandably inquisitive about its origins, but he was miffed that the woman tried to probe its secrets. Only the box's creator knew how it worked, and whatever the devilish thing was inside that made the bewitching voice.

Wait…something felt wrong. The mother-of-pearl decorations on the side that faced him showed a depiction of the god Anubis crouched on a pedestal, glaring at the souls of several unfortunate people brought before him. That was not the way the box had been left on the shelf. He gave it a quarter-turn so another side faced outwards: the Eater of the Dead, a giant crocodile that consumed the souls of sinners. That side always faced out because it was the furthest away from the hidden release button, so if anyone did touch the box it was less likely they would trigger the catch.

But someone had touched it.

He examined the shelf around the box: more rat droppings, more than anywhere else on the shelves. Curious. More droppings on the floor, and burnt matchsticks.

That blasted Mags!

He stepped away, regarding the box with new fear awakening in him. Had the woman opened it? That would just like the impertinent minx, asking questions about it, trying to discover his secrets. Merriman had every right to complain to Mr Foxwood and insist on the woman's dismissal.

Instead, he ran back to the stage door, where the dwarf looked up from a journal and regarded him with a jaundiced eye, feet up on a footstool, the air thick with tobacco smoke. "What is it now?" asked the doorman.

"Is Mags here?"

"She's always here. Except when she isn't." That witticism produced a coughing fit that lasted a good while and plenty of movement as the old man rocked back and forth on his chair.

"Where is she now, do you know?"

The doorman slowly turned a page of his journal, which had a headline in Greek script. "Just yell for her," he yawned. "Everyone else does."

Merriman wasn't in the habit of yelling for anyone. Besides, his headache advised avoiding any loud activities for a while. But the old man said no more, so Merriman returned to the darkened stage.

"Mags!"

How utterly foolish. The woman could be anywhere.

"Mags?"

"What?"

He looked up into the darkness of the fly tower.

"Is that you, Mags?"

"Yes. What do you want?"

"Can I speak to you, please?"

"You already are."

He ignored the impertinence. "It's something urgent."

A curse came down that would have raised eyebrows even in a working-class beer hall. Merriman gasped to hear it come so loud and easily from the lips of a woman.

"I'd be most obliged," he managed to say.

A moment's pause, then, "Stay there."

The clatter of feet on stairs, then the metallic ring of ladder rungs as Mags descended from the gloom. The same incongruous mix of female dress, man's tweed jacket and cap. The same lock of loose hair. Every time, the same lock.

"Actually," she said, before he had a chance to speak, "there's something I wanted to ask you. I went to check on the animals after you left last night. They weren't there."

He swallowed, but people at other theatres had asked the question before and he gave the standard reply. "That's right. I took them home."

Her eyes rolled. "Ah, I see. I'm a country girl originally, that's all. Animals are kind of special to me. Just wanted to see they were looked after."

"I assure you they are dear to me, too." Perhaps he'd better secure a lamb and chicken and bring them with him each night if this woman was going to take a special interest in them. That would mean cages in the dressing room, and somewhere to put them during his act, so it looked as if they were on stage with him. And how to explain the different breeds of animals? Damn the woman's curiosity.

"My Resurrection Box," he said before she could open her mouth again.

Her dark eyebrows attempted to meet each other. "What about it?" Her hand went to the lock of hair and flicked it back. It fell forward to its usual position.

For God's sake, girl, he thought, *use a hairpin.*

"Has anyone been in the storeroom?"

"Not to my knowledge. Why?"

"Something…" How to explain it? Perhaps he should go directly to Mr Foxwood. But no, this girl had immediate responsibility for his equipment being in that room. "Follow me."

"I'm sort of…"

"Please."

He stalked off and a second later heard her follow. In the storeroom, their feet crunched the rat droppings underfoot. "You should keep a cat," he said.

"We did. The rats ate him."

He pointed to the Resurrection Box.

"See that?"

She held onto one of the shelves and peered at the thing. "It looks fine."

"It's not. Someone has touched it."

Mags didn't even blink as he said the words. A cool customer indeed.

"How do you know?"

"The side—not this one, another one—was wrong. I always leave one particular side facing out, and it's moved. And look: matchsticks on the floor. And there's the matchbox."

Three seconds of silence. Merriman started when the girl made some kind of noise in her throat.

"You don't give up, do you?" she growled.

He straightened, which gave him several inches over her. "What do you mean?"

"Monday night you accused me of trying to pry into your secrets. And now, you think I've gone and touched your precious box."

She shoved her fists into her pockets, but they continued to move so her jacket squirmed on her shoulders.

"If you didn't touch it then I'm sorry," he said. "I genuinely am. But I thought it most peculiar."

A snarl issued from her mouth, with a flick of her tongue like a lizard. In her eyes a light that reminded him once again of the skull. A sudden movement of her fists as they plunged deeper into her pockets with a rasp of tearing cloth. Her words came like knives.

"I've been here at the Gypsy for a long time, Mr Merriman. A long time. Longer than you'd think. And I've never had anyone accuse me of such a thing. I'm a professional, I am, and maybe I'm not so talented as you, but I certainly wouldn't do anything like that."

He held up one hand to stop the rush of words. "I agree." The flush in his face grew hotter. "I do apologise Miss…Mags. I spoke hastily. However—"

The fists emerged. So did some of the lining of her pockets. She put her hands behind her back, arms stiff, as if trying to stop herself hitting him. A few deep breaths exhaled so the lock of hair moved. Hard swallows. Rocking back and forth from one foot to the other. Eyes that opened and shut a few times, irises wide. Then, "All right. I'm fine now."

"Very well," he said. The woman appeared normal again, but her plump cheeks were red, her breathing heavy as if she'd just emerged from a fight. A fit of hysterics, perhaps, such as women were prone to. It would be best not to pester her further, but go directly to Mr Foxwood. "That's really all I had to say. Um…Are you all right?"

The hands came from behind her back to fall at her sides. The tension vanished, the eyes focused on him once more.

"Yes." Her voice returned to normal. "Look, I wouldn't worry about the box. You must have been mistaken. I've seen a few things in this room myself. The dim light and the creepy props can make you imagine all sort of things." She cast about for a moment "See that clown face there?" On a shelf to his right the head of a clown statue laughed at him. "Fair gave me a fright just a few nights back. Thought it was going to eat me alive!" A short barked laugh.

"Yes. Perhaps you have a point."

"Being eaten alive isn't right. The thing has to die first."

Did she say these things to startle him deliberately?

"Well, I have to check things for my performances tonight. If you'll excuse me."

But Mags didn't leave straight away. Instead she wandered through the shelves, shifting some of the items, sneering at the dust in the corners. Merriman couldn't start to work while she hung around, so after a couple of minutes he cleared his throat noisily.

"Are you looking for something?"

The woman took off her cap and scratched her head. Under the cap her long black hair had been tied up with a green ribbon. The cap went back on and she straightened her shoulders under the tweed jacket.

"Not in particular," she said. "I'll see you tonight."

The lock clicked behind her.

Her interest in the box was more than idle curiosity about his illusions. The woman had tried to discuss it before, and seemed angry at his implied accusation that she tampered with it. And then that peculiar fit a few minutes ago. Did Mags know something he didn't?

Merriman worked quickly, partly because the air in the room became stuffy after a short time, and partly because he wanted to visit an apothecary and obtain something for his headache.

He set up the Box last. Actually, it needed little preparation. The bunch of violets would be loaded at the last minute so as to remain fresh. All he really had to do was ensure the internal compartments and mirrors that gave the illusion the Box was empty worked smoothly and noiselessly.

The Box felt warm to his touch. He pressed the catch and opened the top. Nothing there. He snapped the upper lid closed and opened the side, the one that faced the audience and showed a false interior, so that the violets would be hidden from view.

Again, nothing.

But still, that warmth, like holding something living. Stepping back a pace he collided with the table.

He tried to remember the man who sold him the Box, Guang Jin. They met through a mutual friend, a fellow conjurer. Merriman had been looking for new tricks, something special to smarten up his act, and had become entranced with the Resurrection Box. It also fitted in well with his Osiris persona. Guang Jin claimed to have invented the device himself but offered no proof of that. However that may be, the Box had worked flawlessly every time and he'd made his money back many times over.

But Guang Jin had said nothing about the Box being warm. Certainly, it had never displayed such a tendency before.

He touched it again. The surface decorations were hot, and under his palms he fancied the sides moved in and out a little, as if the Box were breathing. He pressed the button that released the lid and flipped it open.

A pale glow, slightly golden, deep within. Merriman stared as the sides of the Box continued to swell and contract under his hands.

What he saw inside made him slam the Box shut and bolt from the room.

IX

Unlike Mags, Leah did not live where she worked, but at a hotel called the Stanthorpe attached to the Lombard on its northern side. Relations between the two businesses were such that a walkway had been established through the mutual wall, so that guests at the hotel could make their way to the theatre without the necessity of going out into the street. In inclement weather this proved most popular.

Leah had a room on the first floor of the Stanthorpe at the back, overlooking Grit Lane. There was no entrance to the hotel from the lane except one used for deliveries that led to the kitchens and storerooms. Living above the hotel kitchens meant that the smell of cooking permeated every corner of her single-bed room. Sometimes, Leah fancied herself reeking of whatever the guests at the Stanthorpe ate that night. Charlie would sometimes inhale deeply and make a guess; she didn't mind him leaning in close and sniffing her as long as they were alone.

Her room differed in other ways from Mags's austere but practical loft among the rafters of the Gypsy. Scrounging from second-hand dealers and pawnshops, Leah had obtained a number of bookcases, and these had been filled with many volumes. History, mythology, medicine and law featured, but most of the volumes were works on magic and supernatural arcana, both well-known and obscure. In one corner she kept a sewing table where she sometimes worked when the costume requirements of a play became too much for a standard work-shift. In another corner, just beside the window that overlooked the lane, were a music stand, a pile of sheet music, and a flute. It had been a long time since she'd played for other people.

Her bed, covered with a floral quilt, occupied the opposite wall to the bookcases, and beside it stood a small occasional table. On the wall above the bed, a landscape painting of a wild area of woodland, with the sea glimpsed a long way off. An armchair and a wardrobe completed the furnishings. The bathroom consisted of little more than a tub, wash-stand and water closet in a room only slightly larger than the space needed to contain them. The first floor accommodations at the Stanthorpe, particularly those overlooking Grit Lane, did not cost much.

Excusing herself from the evening's dress rehearsal, Leah had come to her room to think. A few books she'd consulted lay on the floor, open to pages that didn't tell her much. She sat in the armchair, a penny-dreadful open on her knees. On one page, a grisly drawing of a young girl being menaced by a ghost in a haunted house—on the other, the opening chapter of the story that went with the picture. The ghost looked absolutely nothing like the sparkle of lights that had been Julius Kent.

A rap at the window and a hissed voice: "Leah! I can see your light on, and you aren't one to waste gas!"

Leah went to the window and hauled it open. From the lane beyond the round face of Mags peered up. Her sister had flung a crocheted shawl over her male jacket as a further insulation against the fog that started to fill the lane. Her right hand held another pebble ready to throw at the window.

"Good, you're awake. I need you to come to the Gypsy."

Noises came in from the lane: the scratch and scrape of the Gypsy's tiny band warming up, stage hands outside the Lombard struggling with a large steamer trunk. From the Drum and Fiddle down the road came harsh shouts. A man and woman walked past, arm in arm, singing drunkenly.

Leah shook her head and showed Mags her book.

"No time to read now! This is important! Something to do with Kent's death, I think."

"*This is important too,*" Leah signed.

"Please, there's an act at the Gypsy I want you to see. It's business, not pleasure."

That kind of business, then, not theatre business but the sisterhood. Reluctantly, she nodded. Long brown hair, released from its usual tight pile on her head, fell about her face.

"I'll meet you at the front door of the Gypsy," said Mags. "It's too crowded to cut through backstage at the moment. Wear something warm, it's getting cool out here."

Leah hurried downstairs to the kitchens, in which the chef and his assistant were preparing the menu for the guests. They ignored her as she passed through. Grit Lane ended a short distance to the right. Collingwood Road, a fairly busy thoroughfare during the day, now swarmed with people heading for the various theatres and dining places around the area. She turned left again at the pub on the corner and down Ginger Street to the front of the Gypsy.

The contrast between the two streets always struck her as remarkable. After just a few yards everything changed. The half-decent respectability of Collingwood Road gave way to the grime of Ginger Street. Men lounged and smoked outside the Drum and Fiddle; boys chased each other; other people headed for the doors of the Gypsy. Across the road, men sought the more sordid attractions of Mrs Bennett's establishment, where the girls entertained gentlemen of chance acquaintance by the hour—or for as long as it took to finish business.

A few men whistled at her as she walked up to the flat black entrance of the Gypsy. Posters to either side announced the evening's acts. A man smoking a cigar stood in the doorway, arms folded, eyeing the patrons as they made their way in to the ticket booth.

"Come to see the show, young lady?" he asked, and tipped his head to indicate the ticket booth. "A shilling for the pit, sixpence for the circle. Or are you going to stand at the back?" Doubtless he assumed an unaccompanied woman could only be from Mrs Bennett's. Her girls were admitted without charge, since they attracted men into the theatre.

"It's all right, Jack, let her in."

Mags appeared in the entrance, and Jack stood aside.

"Friend of yours, Mags? Sorry, love, I didn't know."

"More than a friend. Leah; Jack."

The doorman touched his hand to his forehead like a sailor saluting an officer. "Pleased to meet you, Miss Leah."

"Jack's new here," explained Mags. "Still learning the ropes. Leah comes and goes as she pleases, Jack. No charge, no questions."

"I understand."

Leah passed in and Mags immediately pulled her into a curtained alcove next to the ticket booth. But not before Leah caught the unmistakable whiff of the Gypsy's front of house: cigar smoke, beer, and sweat.

"All right, I have to stay backstage, but I'll put you in the back row. Don't worry, gentlemen won't proposition you there. Mrs Bennett's girls go up to the gallery, so no one will accost you."

Leah almost resented the comment. Not that she wanted gentlemen to proposition her, but Mags's presumption that she could not personally deal with any over-amorous approaches riled her. Leah had at least a hundred years on her sister, and had chased off worse things than a drunken lecher in the back of a music hall.

"The act I want you to watch is on after Hankey and Riggs. A magician called The Miraculous Osiris. There's a trick he does with a box at the end."

Leah signed that she didn't understand.

"I don't want to tell you, it might influence your opinion."

"*F.*" The single letter bluntly reinforced Leah's impatience.

"Foxy knows about it but he's refused to do anything."

Whatever Mags had asked her to see would be revealed soon enough. Nevertheless, Leah wished she didn't have to sit through the rest of the acts.

They made their way through the pit door and along the back row of seats when the five-piece band picked up and most of the audience had gone in. The audience here consisted mostly of middle-class patrons and more well-behaved working class who could afford the extra cost and preferred to actually watch the show rather than partake in the antics of the gallery crowd. Mags led her to an empty seat at a table in the middle of the back row.

"Now stay here nice and quiet and I'll meet you in front of house at the end of the first half. I have to go backstage now."

Leah sat in the dark, clutching her shawl.

This certainly wasn't the Lombard. The pit crowd moved around, lounged in their seats and chatted. The Lombard presented plays by Shakespeare and Sheridan, and of course more contemporary works, especially melodramas and comic operas. Leah's preference for legitimate theatre was one reason Foxwood had sent her to the Lombard.

"Keep an eye on things there," he said years ago when he first bought the building. "You never know what might happen." She liked to think the real reason for sending her across the lane was that he found both her and Mags at the Gypsy too much to handle.

The show began. As she feared, most of the comedy acts were predictable or farcical. The singers weren't too bad. The ventriloquist had the audience roaring with laughter, and even raised a smile on Leah's face with one joke. Then came the act called Riggs and Hankey that Mags had mentioned. They were all right, except Leah wished Riggs would allow Hankey to sing more of his song before interrupting him. Hankey had a strong voice, wasted here perhaps in vaudeville. He should be in legitimate theatre, even opera.

That act ended and the master of ceremonies announced The Miraculous Osiris. With the burst of a thunderflash, the magician appeared on stage, clad in a gold cloak and tall pointed crown.

Leah almost rose in her seat.

A dark cloud hung over the magician. Man-like: no swirl and sparkle of lights as Kent's soul had been. It hovered like a hawk seeking prey, like a cloak of darkness spread over the stage. The magician didn't notice. Neither did anyone else.

It wasn't a soul at all. It was the spirit that had appeared at Kent's death—the same one, but clearer, more defined. A representation of the weird crown the magician wore surmounted the head of the shadowy thing beside him.

The conjurer went through a number of tricks of the usual kind, but after a few Leah turned her attention to the box on the table behind him. The spirit stayed near it; if the man crossed the stage for a moment, the spirit hovered around the box.

Now the magician drew the box closer and opened it. His patter rattled on about how Osiris could resurrect things, and proceeded to do so with a bunch of violets, which he tossed to a woman in the front row. Then he called for a volunteer from the audience and a portly gentleman stepped up. Osiris proceeded to resurrect a dead chicken and then a lamb from the box. These tricks drew appreciation from the audience. The portly man clapped hard too.

Whenever the magician "resurrected" something the spirit beside the box seemed to flash gold for a few moments, like the glint of sunlight through evening clouds. Leah was reminded of the way sun beams formed a triangular shape as they pierced clouds. Some said the ancient Egyptians had been inspired to build the pyramids from such a shape.

Realisation hit her as The Miraculous Osiris took his bows. Beside him, the shadowy spirit drifted, and when the man left the stage so did the apparition. No spirit at all; something far more dangerous.

Leah stood up and headed to the front of house to where Jack still stood in the doorway, watching the crowd pass by, and the lights going on and off at Mrs Bennett's.

"Hello!" he said. "I thought you were with young Mags. Didn't you like the show?"

And here came Mags, who pulled her out into the street.

"Watch it!" said a passer-by who almost collided with them.

"Well?" urged Mags.

Leah pointed back at the theatre and signed a few sentences to relate what she'd seen: the spirit, the way it stayed near the box.

"What do you think it is?"

"*A god*," Leah signed.

"Really? Which one?"

"*I don't know. My books.*"

"Did you see Kent's soul?"

A shake of her head.

Leah had not met many actual gods. The followers of gods, yes, the creatures they spawned in the world, surely. But not so many deities themselves. Most of those that still existed weren't even supposed to be in the human world anymore.

"Something's wrong," continued Mags. "Look, I have to get back to the show. I'll meet you for breakfast. Eight o'clock. Your room."

Leah nodded and Mags headed back into the theatre.

"Hope to see you next time, sweetheart!" called Jack as Leah stared at the front of the Gypsy.

She turned and headed back to her room to consult her library.

X

Mags hardly ever cooked for herself. Apart from possessing no talent for it, the small kitchen next to the green room at the Gypsy lacked the facilities to make little more than a pot of tea. Most of the time she ate at one of the dining houses dotted around the theatre district. Mrs Slattery's tea shop in Collingwood Road was a favourite, with its cheap but generous servings.

So, sneaking a breakfast with Leah had its advantages. The meals at the Stanthorpe Hotel would be better fare than Mags had had for a while, and the Lombard paid the bill.

The desk clerk was a new man. His gaze lingered on Mags, taking in the boy's cap, the man's tweed jacket, the muslin dress and the practical boots. She'd tied a pretty yellow ribbon around the errant lock of hair and the hem of her dress bore girlish frills.

"Are you supposed to be a man or a woman?" he asked.

"Don't be impudent."

He grunted. "Guess you're one of them."

"Probably. Precisely which one of them am I?"

"One of them theatre folk from next door." He didn't sound pleased at the idea. "Can I help you, madam?"

"Don't 'madam' me! I'm Miss! Miss Mags! I'm here to see Miss Leah," she said, putting on an accent she hoped sounded like it came out of Mayfair. Her acting abilities were not as good as her sister Lucretia's, but she could hold her own in a performance.

"Miss Leah who?" The clerk squinted at the guest register for a moment. "Oh, Miss Leah. Yes. They told me about her. Room 1." The man's gaze returned to the man's jacket she wore. "Just down that corridor."

Mags knew the way. She couldn't resist a parting shot.

"I'm her sister. Well, not blood sister, you understand. More like…well no, not like that, either. I'm not sure what it is, really."

"Room 1, miss."

With a swirl of her shawl, Mags followed the direction of the clerk's finger and knocked on the door to Room 1.

"Nice place," said Mags as she entered. When had she been here last? Two years?

Leah had ordered breakfast: eggs and mushrooms, toast and jam, and a pot of coffee on a bain-marie, laid out on the small table under the window. Cutlery, crockery and two delicate china coffee cups sat on one side. She'd pushed the armchair up to the table on one side and the bentwood chair on the other. Trust Leah to have far more effortless gentility than Mags could muster.

The business of eating proceeded silently. Mags loved the food, and ate most of it. Leah's muteness didn't encourage small talk. Not that Mags had ever felt comfortable about small talk.

On the second cup of coffee, when there were no eggs left and just a single surviving mushroom, Mags looked out of the window at the rear wall of the Gypsy just visible across Grit Lane.

"So. Last night. A god, you say?"

A nod.

"Have you worked out who yet?"

"*Osiris.*"

"What? Osiris? As in the one Merriman pretends to call on?"

"*Yes. I found him in a book.*" She pointed to an open volume lying on her bed.

There were a few forgotten gods left in the world. With only a few believers, powerful no longer, most had passed on to wherever gods went when no longer wanted. Like old actors, who thought themselves more important than they actually were, some old gods hung around, giving advice to people who didn't want it. In the end, actors and gods alike died anyway and remained only as memories, fondly remembered but not missed. Even old Foxwood would suffer that fate one day. While it was not unreasonable that an Egyptian god might come to the Gypsy, why he'd choose to do turns with a world-weary illusionist was anyone's guess. Gods were most peculiar beings, and the more you associated with them, the worse they became.

"Maybe the spirit you saw is just a follower of Osiris. A follower's not so important."

"*We are followers,*" Leah signed, tapping her own chest to emphasise the comment.

"Yes. And are we important?"

Not a movement in reply, not even a twitch of a finger.

"I thought not."

Leah clutched her hands over her heart and slumped in her chair with eyes closed.

"That actor chap who died in your theatre? You think he had something to do with this?"

"*I saw him.*"

"Yes, you saw him die."

A shake of the head. Pointing to her eyes again.

"What? You saw his soul? He's still around?"

"*Yes.*"

"It's the box I'm interested in. A box for resurrecting things." Such a device might be left behind in the world, an artefact of a vanished god. The way the chickens and lambs disappeared after each performance, how each night they were patently different chickens and lambs, hadn't escaped her notice. She'd have to work on Merriman again.

"So what do we do?"

"*F.*"

"I told you. Foxwood's not interested, although he might be if we could get some proof. Why would he care if some old god decided to drop in? He hasn't actually spoken to any of them in ages as far as I know."

"*Gimble?*"

Mags related her visit with him to the strong room.

Again, the dead actor mime.

"Foxwood cares even less about some actor dropping dead on stage. Died in harness, that sort of thing. Just the sort of drama he loves." Secretly, Mags could see the ironic side of it too. "I think we need to look at that box," she announced, picking up the final, cold mushroom and popping it into her mouth.

Leah nodded.

"And—we need to show it to Kent, or at least his ghost."

Leah mouthed, *Why?*

Common sense told them meddling with a god might be dangerous. There might be no connection at all between Kent's death and the Box, but Leah was right to be scared. They should show the Box to Foxwood, they should tell him what Leah had seen in both the Lombard and the Gypsy, a god or a follower manifesting himself—itself—where it had no right to be.

"Because if, as you suspect, Kent's death had something to do with whatever it is you saw, then we need to find that out. And the best way to do that is see if Kent recognises anything."

A look of fear on her sister's face.

"Well of course it could be dangerous. There's danger in everything, dear. Foxwood's dangerous. I'm dangerous. So are you. Even our sister Tahirah over in Cairo, who normally wouldn't hurt a fly, is dangerous when the frenzy takes her. We're Foxwood's girls after all. Now I don't know anything about Osiris, but if he's like most forgotten gods he's wanting to be taken seriously, not out to do anything really bad. He wants followers, not enemies. Besides, it might not even be him. A follower, as I said." She paused, then spoke with a rush. "Besides, you don't think it could be…well, something to do with you?"

That hit home. Leah's mouth twisted into a snarl and her right hand curled into a fist.

"I'm sorry!" Mags blurted. "But you've told me in the past that the father of your child might come looking for you. I didn't mean to…"

The fist uncurled and, after a few long breaths, Leah signed, "*It's all right. Yes. Forget it.*"

"Very well. I'll be at the Lombard stage door at one, with the box. Merriman should be eating lunch by then. Is anyone likely to be in the dressing room?"

A nod. She indicated her dress and spread her arms wide.

"What? A dress rehearsal? That makes it awkward." There would be a lot of people in the theatre, and the dressing rooms crowded. "All right, we'll have to wait until it's over and everyone's gone home. That means another night meeting. After the second house."

That would also mean another two appearances of Osiris or whoever it was. But since no one in the audience could see the apparition, perhaps no harm would come of it.

But she'd watch Merriman like a hawk.

"*What about Gimble?*" Leah signed. "*Should he join us?*"

Mags didn't hesitate in her reply. "No. Not him." She ignored Leah's raised eyebrows. "He'll just moan and complain." While doubtless Gimble would be an extra set of eyes and ears, Mags didn't feel like having to handle him and an unpredictable spirit at the same time.

She poured herself some more coffee and drank it without milk or sugar, a habit she'd developed through being unable to afford such things. Outside, Grit Lane lay like a stray dog, dirty and careless. Behind it, the Gypsy rose in black walls to the merest glimpse of grey

London sky. Her home. And before that, other theatres, including one on the south bank of the Thames, the Globe. And before that playhouses, tavern yards and miracle plays, stretching back to the thirteenth century.

She was so old.

At least in those previous theatres there'd been no Mr Foxwood actually in residence and therefore more freedom. Her boss wasn't looking over her shoulder constantly. When would the old fox go away and let her and Leah just get on with things? His other ladies were scattered around the world; he could spend more time with Annabelle, or Daphne, or any of the others. Of course, the old fellow did go away to visit them every so often, or to do something or other—he never said what. But never long enough for Mags to run the Gypsy her way. Foxwood could at least give her a chance.

Don't know why I bother with him sometimes, she thought.

But no. She did know. A glance at Leah told her that. Her mute sister sat looking at her, head tilted a little, a questioning look on her face. Mags glanced at the woman's flute resting on the music stand behind her.

That was why. Art. Performance. The theatre.

Mags knew no other passion as deep as the theatre: the thrill; the excitement; the laughter and tears; the pumping of the blood as one stepped onto the stage; the palpable energy coming from the audience; the soaring of the spirit as they were transported to another time and place through a few words, a simple gesture, a painted backdrop, a lilt of music.

That's why they hung around.

They couldn't help it. They had made their oath to Mr Foxwood and couldn't break it and live with themselves.

"Leah…" she began.

Raised eyebrows.

"Nothing. I'd better get going. The Gypsy's not the same without me."

XI

The final dress rehearsal of *Hamlet* started late, of course, as was the nature of dress rehearsals: last minute blocking changes; something wrong with the hydrogen flow for the lime-lights; an eleventh hour costume disaster that needed immediate repairs.

Stage hands scurried about while actors stood idle in the wings. Sir John and Lady Rowley sat in the front row, calm and expectant, but Leah noticed the frown on Lady Rowley's face and the gentle but persistent way Sir John tapped the head of his cane. Entitled to a cut of the show's proceeds, no doubt the loss of Julius Kent had them as worried as everyone else.

As Leah sat in the wings, having just delivered a hastily repaired set of tights to the actor playing Polonius, she wondered if Mrs Gower would like a cup of tea. The woman paced to and fro in the corridor behind the stage left wings. By contrast, Jacme Palomer waited calm and ready for his entrance. The characters Bernardo and Francesco, who opened the play, stood conversing in whispers together. Leah had just finished adding decoration to their sword scabbards before Polonius complained about his tights. It had called for quick pedalling on the sewing machine's treadmill.

Just before tempers were set to fray, Mr Cottard, the stage manager, roared through a bullhorn: "Places, please, for beginners!"

Leah consulted the watch pinned to her collar. The play ran for three hours, even with cuts. The dress rehearsal would finish late, and if the company insisted on another one, another three or four hours would pass. Even the second house at the Gypsy might be well over before they wrapped up here.

Leah recalled her failure to communicate with the ghost of Julius Kent. Whether or not she could make contact with whatever resided in the Resurrection Box remained to be seen. She had felt the fear and loathing coming from it. Even if not the actual Egyptian god, the spirit might make a mischief wandering at will through the real world.

And the other thing Mags had hinted at: that the spirit might have something to do with the father of her son, Torben. It seemed unlikely the spirit would be mixed up with that tragedy, but it might know something, or have been sent by her former husband. If that were the case, it would be her responsibility to face it, not Foxwood's.

The play started. Hamlet entered in scene two and pulled it off fairly well, enough for the rest of the company to relax and settle into the run-through. Perhaps there would be no need for a second. Polonius's tights held up—literally—during his opening scene and Gertrude looked suitably royal in her Act One dress, despite her previous misgivings. Leah started to enjoy the play, and shifted back a little to allow the actors waiting off-stage more room. She knew the fuss some actors could make if mere crew hindered their entrances and exits.

Charlie appeared beside her. He'd spent most of the previous night giving the battlements another coat of paint and wanted to make sure they looked right under the lights. Leah gave him a smile and he must have smiled back; it was hard to tell in the dim backstage lighting.

"He's doing all right," Charlie whispered during one of Hamlet's longer speeches.

When the ghost of Hamlet's father appeared Leah half-expected Kent's own spirit to materialise, like it had in the dressing room. The actor strode onto the battlements in full armour—well, cardboard painted to look like armour. Leah had had nothing to do with that bit of costume, thank goodness. The battlements didn't buckle under the strain of the rather overweight actor.

A light behind her— someone lighting a cigar or pipe? Totally against the rules. The offender would receive Mr Cottard's anger if it wasn't extinguished quickly enough. The glow continued, flickering slightly. Leah looked over her shoulder.

Julius Kent floated between her and the wall. A pattern of wavering blue light, visible to no one but herself. Perhaps he wanted to see the play? No, impossible: ghosts probably didn't sense the real world like that. Kent was dead, his body somewhere in a hospital morgue awaiting autopsy. These lights were just a memory, a hunger for the real world, a mote of desire adrift on the winds of eternity.

She slipped away from Charlie's side and went to Mrs Gower's dressing-room. The flickering spirit-lights followed her, and hovered near the wall as they had on the previous occasion.

How did one communicate with a soul? Of all those Leah had seen, none had ever spoken to her, or left any impression on her senses except sight.

We need your help, she thought.

Nothing at all in reply.

At any moment Mrs Gower might come in, or someone else with business backstage. They would not see Kent, but Leah would look odd standing there staring at the wall.

Communicating with thoughts had never worked—useless to try now. Leah remembered the ways she communicated with those around her: signing, body language and writing. No good: the ghost had no eyes with which to see the corporeal world. Emotions, perhaps.

Two hundred years ago the ability to articulate any noise at all had been ripped from her like tearing off a bandage. Then she'd known true fear, in the dark forest, bereft of sound and child. In her memory the vision of the horse racing away loomed large, defiant and invincible. Kent's ghost was similarly isolated, similarly scared. She closed her eyes and remembered the fear, the press of cold moss on her cheek, the tears that poured from her eyes. The scream imprisoned in her heart was the most painful thing of all.

From Kent's ghost came the softest, most subtle response, something that joined her own fear and sorrow. Wherever the soul had to go, it longed to do so, but something held it in the real world, waiting.

No words formed in her mind, just the image of the dark spirit.

The faintest echo from the soul.

He fears it.

Without thinking, she put out her hands to touch the dance of lights before her, and as her fingers passed into the cascade of colour came a shock as of static electricity.

Fear. Longing.

She put an image in her mind of the empty theatre, of the soul hanging above the stage, with herself and Mags standing below with the Resurrection Box. Would the soul understand? Would it come at all?

Music from the stage. A scene had finished. The dressing room door opened.

"Leah?" Mrs Gower held her arms towards her as if about to embrace. "Help me out of this dress, will you?"

When Leah looked again, the soul had gone.

XII

Porteous Merriman pulled a hip flask from his overcoat pocket and took a swig. The brandy burned his throat. Rough stuff purchased from the Drum and Fiddle tavern, but just the thing for the raw after-midnight chill.

He waited at the end of Grit Lane, watching the stage door of the Gypsy. The second house had finished an hour ago and, contrary to his usual practice, he'd left immediately after stowing his equipment and changing into street clothes. The audience had departed and one by one so did the staff. The other acts usually didn't wait around after their second run of the night so most of those had already gone by the time he had finished. He'd made sure that Mags and the doorman saw him leave.

By two o'clock the lane and surrounding streets were deserted. The pub had long closed and even Mrs Bennett's establishment had turned out the lights, although in her case that didn't necessarily mean business had finished.

He took another sip and pulled his overcoat collar up. Perhaps he'd been wrong. Perhaps Mags had gone to bed like any other sane person. He should do the same.

The stage door opened. For a brief moment the gargoyle appeared as a silhouette against the flaring gas light from inside, then someone turned the gas off and it sank back into the darkness.

Merriman pulled himself further into the shadows and watched as a figure moved across the lane towards the back of the Lombard. He followed quietly, not too closely.

Mags sure enough. As she neared the Lombard's stage door it opened and gas light spilled out. And in her hands, clearly, the Resurrection Box.

Time to make his move.

"Hey!" Merriman began to run as Mags looked over her shoulder and saw him. "Stop there!"

He reached the doorstep just as Mags cleared the threshold and he put out both hands to prevent the stage door being closed behind her. Shoving hard, he managed to enter before another woman ran up from the lane. Mags didn't halt, moving through to the dressing-room corridors. "Get him, will you?" she called.

The other woman grabbed Merriman by is collar and hauled him backwards. Nothing like Mags at all: the same age, perhaps, but with longer, lighter hair, narrow face, and wild eyes. She held a wooden staff, carved with a spiral pattern of what appeared to be vine leaves, surmounted with—of all absurd things—a pine-cone.

"What the devil…" Merriman put his hands up. "That's my box! That girl stole it! It's mine!"

The staff didn't waver. Neither did the woman holding it. Her eyes: power behind them, something almost frantic.

He took a step forward and everything went black.

Leah looked down at the man's body and gulped, sorry for hitting him. The old madness could still surface if allowed. Her thyrsus—the carved staff topped with a pine-cone—was normally used as a dancing prop, but it turned out to be hard enough when applied to a human skull.

He wasn't dead; his chest still moved up and down. He would recover soon enough. She shut the stage door, dragged him into the stage manager's office and laid him out on the floor. Just before leaving she took a cushion off a chair and placed it under his head.

Sorry about that, sir.

In the corridor, Mags stood with the Resurrection Box in her hands.

"Yes, this is it," said Mags. "Where's…Did you hit him?"

A nod.

"Oh dear. Not too hard, I hope?"

Leah pointed to the door leading to the stage. The building was deserted, the curtain closed. No second run had been necessary and the crew, including Charlie, had elected to go home rather than work any longer. They would be back in the early morning to put the finishing touches on the battlements.

They walked through to the stage and Mags set the box down in the centre, theatrically the place where the most important scenes took place.

"Where's Kent?" she asked. "Is he here?"

Leah pointed to the dance of lights above their heads, although of course Mags couldn't see them.

"Can you communicate with him?"

"*No,*" she signed.

"All right. Well, let's see what happens."

Without warning, the lid of the Box tilted upwards, and a golden-yellow light poured out. The Box kept on opening. More panels slid aside, until it resembled a hollow cube, sections turning, unlocking, revealing further panels within. Other parts slid aside, extended outwards. It kept opening, growing in size as each new section unfolded, to reveal even more panels that extruded other surfaces. Impossibly, the Box assumed the size and shape of a sarcophagus, standing upright on the stage of the Lombard. Sections of the outer panels emerged to create a relief design of a hawk. On top of the sarcophagus was emblazoned the double crown of Egypt; on the front, two crossed human arms, one holding a flail and the other a shepherd's crook.

The Great Osiris.

Leah gripped her staff, staring at the thing. What had Mags done, to bring this thing into her theatre?

"It's all right, sister," said Mags. "At least, I think..."

Osiris dwelt in the box, and now he had come.

Mags was an idiot.

Above them, the soul of Julius Kent hung in the loft, far up among the hanging flats and set pieces of Hamlet, as if shying away.

The sarcophagus opened, and from inside emerged the grey form Leah had seen the previous night in the Gypsy. It hovered a few inches above the stage, its head turning from one side to the other. No face, no eyes, nothing but a blank visage. No hands, no feet, just limbs that ended in stumps.

Mags backed off a little—she could see it too. No second sight needed now.

A stench of rotting flesh came from the form. A dying god. No place for him in the modern world. Slowly fading, like all the gods, but still able to influence things if given the chance.

Leah raised her thyrsus and the head turned towards her,

"No!" Mags, on the other side of the spirit, held up her hand. "Now listen here, Osiris! That's who you are, isn't it? Osiris the Great, first son of Geb and Nut, beloved of the Ennead. Yes, Leah showed me you in a book. And I've lived with gods long enough to recognise one when I see him."

Osiris turned to Mags and floated a little closer.

Meaning blossomed in Leah's head, an ancient language, coming as an overall impression, emotional connotation rather than individual words.

You speak well. I am Osiris, come to gather the dead.

"Well, I don't know how long you've been in that box," said Mags, "but things aren't the same anymore. There are new gods. The old ones have had their day."

Leah admired Mags's courage. Osiris was god of the dead, and dead they might both be if things went badly. She gripped her thyrsus tighter, looking for a chance to help.

Osiris looked upwards. High above, Julius Kent's ghost hung like St Elmo's fire around the rafters.

I can give him life, came the meaning from the mind of Osiris.

"I'm sure you can," said Mags. "But there are rules, see? At least, I think there are. You can't go around just resurrecting people. The new gods wouldn't like it."

But Osiris raised one arm and the ghost of Julius Kent drifted down and entered the sarcophagus, which shut by itself.

Soon you both will join him. Osiris raised one stump of an arm and pointed at Leah. *And all the world shall follow.*

"What the devil?"

Leah turned. The magician from the Gypsy stood stage right, holding his head where she'd belted him. He stared at the shadowy form of the god, at the giant sarcophagus centre stage.

"What's going on?"

Leah held out her hand to keep him back, but he took two unsteady paces forwards.

The god gestured in the air. *Come, my servants.*

Three large black jackals appeared on stage, one downstage centre, one near Merriman, and the third beside Mags. Snarling, growling

Leah gripped her thyrsus, glancing at Mags, who probably wished right now she'd thought to bring her own.

A jackal leaped towards her.

For ten seconds, all was confusion. Leah brought the thyrsus down on the jackal's head, the heavy shaft swooshing through the air. The blow hit it fairly, but the dog didn't stop. Leah dodged at the last instant, reversed the thyrsus and slammed the butt end down on the dog's body as it raced past.

Oh, the song of madness, the roar of blood in her veins!

The jackal skidded on stage, landed on its rump, and recovered itself. This time Leah had enough room to point the thyrsus at it, slamming the carved pine-cone end into the animal's mouth as it charged at her. The pine-cone went down its throat. The jackal stopped abruptly, hit the stage and rolled on its back. Leah tugged the bloodied end of the staff out of its mouth.

Mags had dealt with her animal, holding it by its throat in the air. Her face grew red as she squeezed. After a moment she dropped the carcass.

Stage right, Merriman lay pinned under his dog, which had its front paws on his chest, teeth bared inches from his face. Merriman tried to push the thing off, but its rear claws tore at his clothing.

Leah crossed the stage and raised her thyrsus to strike the dog. But all three jackals, alive and dead, simply vanished back into the thin air from which they came.

Not real at all. Phantoms.

Merriman groaned and Leah put out a hand to help him up. The voice of Osiris came again in her head.

So you are indeed with power. But it is too late. The resurrection is complete.

The sarcophagus opened again, and out stepped the nude, pale form of Julius Kent. He stared about him, shaking his head, then noticed the grey form beside him.

"My lord Osiris!" he said, and fell to his knees, arms above his head in worship. "Let me be the first of your new followers."

"Look, this has gone on far enough!" Mags sounded really angry now. Leah feared she might lose control, allow the sacred madness to take over, just like it had taken her in her battle with the jackal: the feeling of power and the glorious scent of blood!

Now I have a new follower, Osiris communicated. *There will be more.*

The shadow of Osiris was no longer faceless. Eyes had appeared, two dark dots in the centre, and a protrusion below that might be the beginning of a nose. A pale line below. He had feet and hands now, and stood proudly on the stage boards. He gestured again, and more jackals appeared, larger, fiercer, five of them this time, at all corners of the stage.

Leah raised her thyrsus, ready to defend Merriman. The jackals tensed, snarling.

The curtain parted slightly and Mr Foxwood walked in from the auditorium.

"No more of that now," he said, in that calm, measured tone of his. He pointed a long, manicured finger at Osiris, who turned to view the old man. Foxwood nodded at the two women, his bald head shiny under the gas lights.

"Are you all right, ladies?"

I don't know you, conveyed the fragment of Osiris that still clung to the world.

Foxwood nodded. "Not in this form, but we have met before. We're part of the same club. I'm a god, too."

Which one?

"Well, not a very important one, if you listen to some people. But I still have followers." Foxwood smiled. "My ladies have been rather naughty, opening boxes that don't concern them, poking their noses into the affairs of the gods."

Even Mags looked at the floor.

The jackals started across the floor towards Foxwood, who shook his head.

"Your minions can't harm me."

Your servants then.

"No! They are mine to deal with!"

You have not yet named yourself, god.

Leah caught Mags's eye. She nodded. The same thought. The forgotten gods had little omniscience left. In his day, Osiris had ruled the universe, or at least that part of it which had been his immediate responsibility. But in the long twilight of his decline, he'd lost much knowledge.

Mr Foxwood straightened himself up. "You're in a theatre. I am the god of the theatre. Also the god of wine and ritual madness. I like that last one particularly. Many years ago in far-away lands men called me Dionysus."

Leah heard Merriman give a startled grunt.

"And these charming ladies are two of my maenads." He stared at the grey form. "My retinue. I still have followers, Osiris, although sometimes I don't think they worship me all that much."

"You have your good days," admitted Mags.

Foxwood smiled. "Mags is a humourist. That's why I keep her near me."

I have come for your servants, not you. Osiris raised both arms. The jackals growled. Leah felt her palms damp around her thyrsus.

"You won't have them! Return to your box!" cried Dionysus.

The god of resurrection gestured one hand towards Dionysus, who promptly catapulted backwards, end over end, and slammed onto the wooden stage boards.

And the jackals leaped.

This time the battle raged fiercer. Leah pushed Merriman to one side as a white jackal rushed for him, bringing her thyrsus down on the beast's head. It buckled under the blow, but was up again in an instant. It turned on her, paws scraping across the boards, leaving gouges in the timber. Red eyes met hers, the mouth opening to reveal a double row of shark-like teeth.

You are not real, she thought.

The fur on the back of the dog rose.

You are an illusion. No more than the dream of a fallen god.

A scream from the other side of the stage. Leah didn't look, but at the sound the jackal sprang at her.

Her thyrsus had not been designed for battle, but it still weighed enough to slam down hard with all the strength of her belief in Dionysus. The thyrsus smashed into the jackal's skull and stunned it momentarily. The dog hit the stage with a single quiet whimper.

Leah felt the hot flush of madness rise once more inside her mind: the unfettered power of the frenzied god who was her master. It burned inside, filled her mind with the thoughts of blood, of total surrender to chaos and desire. Like a whirlwind, the hysteria carried her away. The fire of Dionysus consumed her. She dropped her thyrsus, picked up the stunned jackal and slammed it hard back onto the stage. Its spine snapped like a twig. A flash of white to her left. Another jackal, jaws agape, fangs seeking her flesh. Leah punched her fist into its head and felt the cracking of its skull.

A quick look around the stage: Merriman had gripped one of the leg curtains hanging down on stage left and hauled himself up, his right foot perilously close to a jackal snapping at him from below;

Mags held her own, a jackal lifted in her arms, using it as a club to keep off yet another dog from biting her; Dionysus and Osiris locked in a battle of wills, staring at each other, bodies rigid, eyes burning with all the power left to them.

Leah picked up her thyrsus and smashed it over the head of the jackal seeking to pull Merriman down from the curtain. It whimpered, fell to its belly and lay still. She reached up to help Merriman descend. He clutched at the curtain, only to trip on the bottom seam and fall into the wings.

Mags clubbed the jackal rushing at her. "Hey, sister!" she called. "How does it feel to stand to battle once more?" In her eyes was the same wild light that burned within Leah. The glory and wonder of the divine power of the god of madness.

Then Dionysus fell to his knees.

Osiris loomed over him, growing more real with each second. He flung his arms outwards and white flames enveloped the other god.

Leah launched herself towards the Egyptian god and struck him with her thyrsus. The stick snapped and the two pieces caught fire. The flames leaped towards Leah, who felt herself hurled back.

Neither maenad had the power to defeat a god; only Dionysus could do that, and he lay on the stage, white flames slowly consuming him.

Mags kicked at the jackal in front of her, sending it spinning into the flames. It howled and vanished.

"What do we do?"

Osiris roared as white fire whirled around their lord and master.

Then a new sound. A whirring noise that Leah could not identify. Movement behind Osiris. The sarcophagus unfolded again. New parts of it extended, a panel slid open and the whole Box tilted forwards slightly.

The flames wavered. Osiris turned to view the Box, roaring as if in pain.

From inside the Box, black tendrils of darkness reached out and wrapped themselves around the god, pulling him towards the opening. Osiris planted his feet, reached out to grab the sides of the Box to stop himself from being pulled in. But the tendrils encased him further and inexorably dragged him inside.

The panel slid shut so that Osiris was trapped. Then the sarcophagus started closing up. It shrank, folded into itself, collapsed back into the small Resurrection Box.

The flames vanished, as did the corpses of the jackals.

Silence.

Leah gasped for air as the madness died within her. Mags sat on the floor and brushed her hair with her fingers. Beside her, Dionysus lay with his eyes open, staring upwards. The old man blinked a few times, put his hands out to feel his body. Julius Kent was dead again. Leah saw his soul flash out of his corpse and fade into nothingness.

And beside the box, puffing hard, sat Porteous Merriman.

"Just a matter of knowing which button to press," he said.

XIII

Mags sipped at the wine in her glass. Not bad. When Foxy condescended to share wine with them, it was usually his cheaper stuff, but the old man hadn't stinted this time.

The upstairs room at the Drum and Fiddle tavern was one of the few places Foxwood frequented outside the Gypsy. Mags never understood his fondness for the dark and musty room. She had never seen the fire lit, and wind from the lane found its way under the door. The only furniture consisted of a long wooden table and a few hard chairs. She shifted uncomfortably as she took the glass from her god.

"You were bloody useless," she said.

Foxwood stopped pouring another glass for a second, then resumed. He handed the glass to Leah, who sat beside Mags, and poured a third glass for Merriman, who perched on a small chair beside the cold fireplace, staring at the others. Finally, Foxwood poured himself a glass and set the bottle on the table.

"Useless? Yes, I suppose I was." He eased himself into his chair. "Not what I used to be. Rheumatism. Old age. I need to feast on ambrosia again."

"Of course," Mags continued, "if you *had* been useful other than as a punching bag it would have been the worst ending ever. Deus ex machina. A good thing Merriman stepped in to help."

"Then I am happy to admit incompetence if you are happy to share the description. As I see events, it was you two who caused the trouble in the first place. Porteous saved the day." Foxwood drained his glass. "Imagine that."

Merriman looked bemused. "I knew there was another button in the side of the box," he said. "It never seemed to do anything, so I ignored it. But when I saw that…thing…attacking you, I took a chance and pressed it. Really, that's all I did."

"A button that only works when Osiris is out of the Box. A useful piece of knowledge, should he escape again."

"So all this is true?" Merriman said. "I thought I might be dreaming. You…" He used the small finger on his hand holding his wineglass to point at Foxwood. "You are the god Dionysus, and these ladies are your—maenads, did you say?"

"Precisely. As an illusionist, Porteous, you're used to seeing the supposedly miraculous. We truly are."

"I've lived with that Resurrection Box for years now. I bought it from a foreigner named Guang Jin. Certainly not an Egyptian. I knew the animals I revived with it had to come from somewhere, but I had no idea."

"Osiris had you under his spell. You knew there had to be something wrong, but he made you accept it without question. You worked under the persona of The Miraculous Osiris, who wanted to re-establish himself as a deity. The animal remains you fed him sustained him in the Box, but the resurrected animals hardly constituted sentient worshippers, so no doubt they were disposed of. A god of death and resurrection can unmake the living as humans can make flesh in the womb. But Osiris wanted more souls. Human souls. Believers. You were his first for a while. Kent was the second, and would, if allowed, have become a follower of the god. As Osiris himself threatened, there would have been more, perhaps the whole world. Your action imprisoning him back in the Box saved mankind. Not bad for a human."

Leah tapped her glass to call attention and pointed to herself and Mags.

"Yes," agreed Mags. "*We're* human."

"Now, Mags." Foxwood leaned forward on the table, hands clasped in front of him, eyebrows coming together over his nose. "What were you doing letting Osiris out without me there, eh? Not clever. And you, Leah, going along with her absurd plan. Have you no sense?"

The women looked at each other. Leah kept her signing hand in her lap.

"We thought..." began Mags, and then glanced sideways at Leah. "That is, *I* thought, we could reason with Osiris. Talk to him."

"No chance of that. The Egyptian pantheon always struck me as single-minded. Nothing mattered really, except coming back from the dead, growing crops and flooding everything once a year."

"Your sister Demeter is a crop-growing goddess."

A frown passed over the god's face. Foxwood never liked his family mentioned.

"Did Osiris kill Kent?" Mags changed the subject.

"No, I don't think so. He was there at the Lombard when Kent died, but I think that death had a natural cause, a heart attack or something. Kent's death, in medias res, as it were, gave Osiris the opportunity to begin his return performance."

"I sometimes had a queer compulsion to leave the Box unlocked," said Merriman. "Like a voice in my head. I didn't bring the box to the theatre storeroom with my other equipment, the afternoon poor Mr Kent passed, but left it at my lodgings. Just before going to the Gypsy to meet you, Mr Foxwood, I again felt that compulsion to leave it unlocked. Do you think it was Osiris himself?"

"No doubt," said Foxwood. "And he took the opportunity to pay a visit to the Lombard, just in time to see Kent die."

Merriman gulped and stared hard at his glass of wine. "I never knew that in doing so I was releasing Osiris. He might have killed many."

"Don't distress yourself about that," replied Foxwood. "I'm more interested in the Box itself. A divine sarcophagus is a natural enough home for a god of the afterlife, just like the theatre is for me. But how did he get hold of it? You say Gimble couldn't detect any human magic associated with it?"

"No," said Mags.

"*Osiris is a god. He could make it,*" signed Leah.

"He might," said Foxwood. "But I'm not so sure. Something doesn't feel right." He picked up Leah's broken, scorched thyrsus that lay on his table. "I will provide you with another staff, since this one gave its wholeness. You see how dangerous your encounter was? You should have told me."

"We did," said Mags. "You weren't interested."

Silence. Foxwood took a long sip of wine and swallowed. "I was doing my own investigations if you must know. The moment you mentioned the Box I wondered about its origins and its import. Something is afoot, some grave intent maybe by certain gods who wish to re-enter the world as more than mere—what's the word?—curiosities like myself."

"*We could have helped.*"

In the few seconds it took Leah to sign the sentence, Foxwood had refilled his glass. "Not this time. Not when the gods are concerned. They're too dangerous. New powers are at work. Osiris, or something else not human, made that Box. But there's more to it than that. I'd like to know who else might be involved and why." He smirked. "Things could be busy for a while."

"Do you mean to say," said Merriman, "that there are more, er, gods like you and Osiris? From all the pantheons?"

"Old gods never die," said Mags, "they just make nuisances of themselves."

"Now *that*," said Foxwood, glaring at Mags, "is one reason I didn't tell you."

"I was raised a Christian man, sir." Merriman drew himself up a little. "I find such remarks unacceptable."

"As you like. But if Osiris does not really exist, what's in your Box, eh?"

Mags yawned. There had been no sleep following their adventure. Cleaning the mess in the Lombard had taken a long time.

Foxwood leaned back in his chair. "First of all I need to know more about this man, Guang Jin, from whom Porteous bought the Resurrection Box."

"What will happen to me?" asked Merriman.

"What? Oh. Do you want to stay on at the Gypsy and complete your contract? You can't use the resurrection trick anymore. We don't want Osiris out of that box. While you managed to manipulate its controls once to trap him, he will be wary of that a second time. In fact the Box should never be opened again."

"I think, if it's all the same to you," said Merriman, "I'll move on. I have to find a new climax to my act. And a change of stage name is probably in order, too."

"Where's the Resurrection Box now?" asked Mags.

"I put it in the storeroom," said Foxwood.

Mags almost choked on her wine. "You're *keeping* it?"

"It'll be safe enough there on one of the dusty old shelves at the back. Don't worry: Osiris is still inside, but he can't get out as long as the Box is kept closed. No more souls to gather. Someone has to teach the gods their place."

"Yes," said Mags, glancing across at Leah, who smiled into her glass.

SCENE TWO

October 1851

SUSANNAH

Prepare for death, if here at night you roam,
And sign your will before you sup from home.

—Samuel Johnson,
London–An Imitation of the Third Satire of
Juvenal.

I

The night Mags met Susannah, she also saved the girl's life.

During most performances at the Gypsy, girls from Mrs Bennett's establishment across the road came to ply their trade among the customers. The girls felt safer off the streets, away from the reaches of the law. If a patrolling bobby did shove his nose inside, which didn't happen often, the girls could say they were watching the show. Mr Foxwood didn't mind—he liked to maintain a good relationship with Mrs Bennett and the idea appealed to him anyway. Any rebellion against society's norms tickled his fancy.

Things didn't always go smoothly, however. Mags had witnessed a few uncomfortable encounters, such as when men pushed their desires on a lady who had already declined them. Usually the lady ended up leaving or one of the Gypsy's security staff moved in to escort the man off the premises. Bad Ben did his job well.

The night Mags saw Susannah propositioned by an undesirable customer Bad Ben had taken the night off. His "lads", a couple of louts he'd recruited from the streets, had also decided to spend the night at the Drum and Fiddle. It was a Tuesday, not normally a full night anyway, and they reasoned if Bad Ben could shirk his duties, they could too. So Mags hung around the back of the gallery, lounging at the top of the stairs leading down to the front of house, keeping an eye on things.

During the second house a few of Mrs Bennett's girls wandered in. Jack, the spruiker out the front responsible for encouraging people to enter, let them in without paying. All part of Mr Foxwood's "live and let live" approach. Normally the girls would pass through the gallery crowd, letting the gentlemen at the back see them. Most would have a customer within minutes and wouldn't come back for a while.

Only a few hopefuls that night: slim pickings on a Tuesday. Most were regulars who waved hello to Mags, but there was a new girl among them: blonde hair visible under her bonnet, a small face with large, liquid eyes. Eighteen, maybe. She came in with the others and stood at the back, looking about carefully.

The other girls didn't stay long. Mags watched them leave with customers, until only the new girl remained. If she was new to Mrs Bennett's, or even new to the trade, it was a bit unfair of the other girls to leave her to fend for herself. Mags moved closer just as a man approached the new girl. He said something to her and the girl pressed herself up against the rear wall. Mags couldn't catch the man's words: the noise in the gallery almost matched the noise on stage. The hecklers liked to sit at the front of the gallery so their voices carried across the entire auditorium. Why heckle from close up to the stage where no one could hear you?

The man said something more. The girl glanced at him and pressed herself a little harder against the wall. A quick shake of her head. Then he ran his finger down her cheek. The girl flinched. Although she might eventually permit the man to touch her in all sorts of places, no money had yet changed hands. He leaned closer, muttering to her. She turned her face away, either because of his breath or his words.

Mags placed herself next to the girl so she could overhear while pretending to watch the show.

"What's the matter?" the man asked in a voice slurred by alcohol. "You wouldn't be standin' here if you weren't open for business." He reached for her left breast but she twisted her body away in time.

"I'm waiting for someone else," the girl replied in a heavy cockney accent. She must have been born right under Bow Bells, never mind within earshot of them.

"That ain't true!"

"I don't want you."

"Now see here, bitch!"

Mags gripped his hand just before it connected with the girl's arm. "None of that, mate." He tried to pull away, but Mags tightened her hold. "If I want to, I could break your wrist. No problem at all." She squeezed and gave a slight twist to show it was no idle threat.

"Let go!" His eyes grew large.

"Apologise to the lady first."

"Go to hell!"

Mags kept her grip on his wrist, almost disappointed he didn't give her an excuse to snap his arm. The madness of Dionysus lay waiting so close beneath the surface. The rage, the frenzy—one small twist would cause that heady sound of shattering bone...

Mags exhaled heavily and released him. "Say you're sorry to the lady and move on."

The man glared at both of them as he wrung his hand. "Pair of bitches!"

"I guess that's the closest you'll get to an apology." Mags pointed to the exit. "I've got a theatre full of people who just want to enjoy the show. If you're after a girl, Mrs Bennett's is right across the road."

He muttered something and staggered downstairs. Mags followed to make sure he left.

Jack at the front doors came over. "Trouble?"

"Not any more. Don't let him back in."

The man went into the street, shouting abuse at Mags.

Up in the gallery the girl sat on the floor, back against the wall, her shawl pulled across her face.

Mags leaned down and touched her shoulders. "Are you all right? Did he hurt you?"

Her face appeared from under the shawl. Pretty, but with the premature care lines of the working class, the pallor of the under-nourished. The blonde hair that escaped from beneath her bonnet needed brushing; the make-up emphasising her eyes and rosy cheeks had started to smear a little under tears. A long day at work.

"Stand up." Mags held out a hand. The girl hesitated for a moment, then allowed herself to be helped upright. They walked downstairs to front of house.

The girl sniffed and wiped her nose with her sleeve. "Where's that man?"

"You're safe from him."

"Please don't give me to the peelers!"

"What do you take me for?"

"Where are you taking me, then?"

"Backstage." Mags pushed open the door marked *No entry*. "Now keep quiet, there's a show on."

Finding a private spot backstage would not be easy with the show in progress, performers milling around and the crew lounging or working depending on their duties. Dressing room number five hadn't been allocated to anyone. It would do.

People glanced at the two women as they passed through the corridor. One of the flymen said, "Who's your friend?", but Mags just sneered in reply. The dressing room itself was quiet enough.

Mags locked the door, put a match to the gas lamp, and as it spluttered into life pulled out a chair. "Sit down."

The girl drew her shawl closed against the coldness of the room. Mags sat in another chair and shoved her hands into her pockets.

"Cold as a witch's tit, isn't it? Sorry there's no fire. My name's Mags. I work here. What's your name?"

"Susannah." She took a handkerchief from her sleeve and proceeded to dab at her face.

"That bully—don't worry about him. Jack won't let him back in, and he'll think twice about approaching you again."

Another sniff. "I didn't…"

A burst of applause came from the auditorium as the current act finished. Mags ought to go back to patrolling the gallery, or at least help out backstage. This girl wasn't her concern. She'd seen enough wretched people in her centuries on Earth, but something about Susannah made her stay.

The girl hiccoughed and put her hand over her mouth. The tears, and her dabbing, had smeared her make-up even more.

"Your hair's come undone," said Mags. "Turn to face the mirror there and I'll get it right for you."

The girl did so. The flaring gaslight threw her face into sharp detail. Mags regarded it as she removed Susannah's bonnet and started pulling out hair pins. "I haven't seen you around before."

A pause, then: "No. I've only worked at Mrs Bennett's for a week. The other girls suggested I come across tonight."

"Mrs B's girls can be a bit rough on the new ones." Mags hesitated a moment before asking the next question, gathering some of Susannah's hair in her fist and holding it in place while she secured it with a hair pin. "Why didn't you go with that man?"

Their eyes met in the mirror. The girl seemed to resent the question for a second. "I just didn't like the look of him."

"Me neither. And he was obviously drunk."

"Oh, the drunk ones usually aren't that bad. Most of 'em fall asleep before you get too far into business, or they can't make things happen in the first place, if you know what I mean." She held one finger pointing down and waggled it feebly. "I just didn't like him."

Most of Mrs Bennett's girls weren't so fussy. Mags stabbed another pin into her hair.

"I've worked at the house this last week, but I wanted to see the theatre. That's really why I came. I love the theatre."

Mags grinned. "I know what you mean."

"Maybe that's why I didn't want to go with the man. I wanted to see the show."

"You still can if you like. What's left of it, anyway."

"No. Thank you. I'm going to be in trouble. I'll have to bring in some money tonight. Mrs Bennett gets half, see?"

Rental on the room, no doubt.

"I'll have to find a customer. The old witch'll really get mad if I don't."

Mags made the final adjustments to Susannah's hair, placed her bonnet back on and let the girl tie the ribbons under her chin. "That looks a lot better. There's a basin in the corner if you want to wash your face. I can heat up some water and fetch a bit of make-up for you to refresh if you like. Not that you need to—you're pretty enough."

"Thanks. But I'd better go."

Nothing could be plainer than that the girl was in no condition to pick up a customer that night. Ordinarily Mags didn't care much for Mrs Bennett's girls. Nothing to do with their profession (there but for the grace of Dionysus might have gone Mags herself), but they just didn't seem terribly interesting as people. But Susannah liked the theatre, and anyone who was that way inclined deserved her attention.

"Wait here, if you can stand the chill a bit longer," she said. "I'll be back."

Mags cut along to the wings and climbed the ladder into the flies. Harry Banks, one of the pull-men, saw her and waved.

The noise from the stage was muffled up here. The stage had, of course, been designed to project the sound out into the auditorium. Only a fraction of it drifted into the fly tower, which was a good thing at the moment, since the current act was old Becky Slocum, who belonged to that school of singers who believed being slightly off-pitch could be compensated by sheer volume.

Mags pulled out a metal box from under her bed, extracted two coins from a leather purse inside, and then began the long descent down to the wings again. Harry frowned as she reappeared.

"Forgot something?"

Mags ignored him and returned to the dressing room, where

Susannah still sat in the chair, staring at her reflection.

"Hold out your hand."

The girl did so. Mags deposited the coins in her palm. "Two sixpences. One for Mrs Bennett, one for you. Sorry I can't spare more."

Susannah rose. "No! I can't take your money. You've already done enough for me!"

"You go to Mrs Bennett, give her one sixpence, say you got it from a mark in exchange for an upright one in Grit Lane, and then get home. You have a home?"

"I usually sleep in the doss down the road with my brother Bobby."

Many of the girls who worked the streets slept in the boarding houses. A bed for a night if they could pay. The girls worked for their bed money and a meal—and also to get drunk in order to forget how they earned the money.

"I see. Does he work?"

"He used to, at a cotton mill. He's twelve. But he had an accident."

"No parents?"

"Mamma died when Bobby was born. Papa was killed last year. He…"

The start of tears again. Mags pulled her own handkerchief out and handed it to Susannah, who used it while telling Mags her story, as old as time itself. The government provided no support for orphans, they just had to make the best of the crappy life handed to them. Once a worker in a mill had an accident, and became useless for their allotted task, they would be shown the door. And no other company would hire a disabled worker. Unable to pay the rent when their father died, Susannah and Bobby had taken refuge on the streets. A tough life. One that Mags had managed to avoid.

"You could get work somewhere else. A lady's maid, perhaps, or a shop assistant."

"I tried. But you need references, and I got none. You need to know someone who knows someone. I started doing…this…when Papa was still around, trying to earn a bit more, pay my own way. He didn't like it, and drank most of what I earned. It's all I can do, now. And with Bobby to look after all by myself, well, it's too late, innit?"

Never too late to change your life, thought Mags. *But no good telling that to someone who's already deep in it.*

She found herself holding Susannah's hand, but couldn't remember taking it. "Tell you what. There's some food left over in the kitchen. The acts bring in their dinners, and sometimes there's a bit left over. Most of them don't want it because it's all gone cold, so I usually end up eating it. That's how I got my superb physique, see?" She indicated her stumpy form with her free hand. Susannah raised a smile. "So let's go to the kitchen, have a feed of what's there, and you go home. Tomorrow you come back here."

"Why?"

"You said you loved the theatre, didn't you?"

"Yes, but—"

"No buts. Tomorrow you get yourself here and I'll show you all around."

The look on the girl's face brightened for a moment. Then sank again. "I can't. I love watching theatre, but don't know anything about it. And there's Mrs Bennett—I have to work tomorrow night."

"We'll be long finished by then."

The gas hissed for a few moments. Mags could see in its light a play of emotions across Susannah's face.

"All right," she said at last. "I'll do it. What time?"

"I'm always here. Just knock on the stage door—I'll show you where that is. Come whenever you can."

They feasted on buttered buns and cold roast potatoes and half a beef pie in the kitchen while the show continued. Some of the acts who'd finished their turn noticed them but knew Mags's habit of late night demolition of the food, so said nothing. The last slice of pie was wrapped in a scrap of newspaper for Bobby. As the final act began, Mags said she'd walk Susannah down to the doss house.

"Oh, no!" the girl protested with enough vehemence for Mags to briefly wonder if in fact she'd been telling the truth about that. "I couldn't let you do more than you have already!"

But Mags insisted with the determination developed from decades of having to deal with Mr Foxwood. In the end they ducked out of the front door just as the second house closed. Ginger Street started to fill up with people now the theatres had finished.

"You pop over to Mrs Bennett and hand her that sixpence and I'll wait for you here."

Ten minutes later the girl returned, slightly flushed. "Mrs Bennett wanted me to go out again, but I told her I had a headache."

"So it's all good?"

"Yes, but I have to earn more tomorrow. Sixpence ain't enough."

A determined business woman, that Mrs Bennett.

They proceeded along the street, jostling through the late night crowd. Mags didn't go out much, but when she did it often startled her to see people—real people, not the pretend characters of the vaudeville. The world of grease-paint and costumes and pasteboard props had been left behind. Here reality reigned, which was sometimes lovely when the better-dressed people passed by: two lovers arm in arm, or a man helping his wife into a carriage; sometimes sordid: rough, drunk men scouring for trouble, or a woman and man emerging from an alleyway hand in hand, both looking slightly out of breath.

All the world's a stage, thought Mags. *And all the men and women merely players.* She'd loved that line ever since she'd first heard it at the Globe Theatre. William Shakespeare had been standing right beside her, waiting backstage for his cue to go on in his own play. Shakespeare knew she was a maenad—indeed, Mags had haunted the Globe just like the Gypsy—and he had thought of writing one as a character into a play, but he never did.

The doss house where Susannah and her brother usually stayed was a few streets along, just outside the district of theatres and pubs. The crowd diminished and the buildings became even older and more disreputable. Occasional shop windows were boarded up or lacked glass. The street-filth became deeper, catching the hem of their gowns, and the pong of unwashed bodies, unwashed clothes, and general grime infiltrated their nostrils. So quickly the mystery and polish of the theatre district wore off to reveal the vast, grubby city that lay beneath.

"Left here and along," said Susannah, turning down a laneway.

Their footsteps weren't the only ones that turned. Mags halted, pulling on Susannah's arm.

"Shh!" she hissed when the girl gave her an enquiring look.

Behind them, the other footsteps halted.

"Someone's following us," whispered Mags. "Just keep walking as normal."

No more than three steps along, and a voice called harshly: "You should have taken my money!"

Mags urged Susannah on. If they could reach the boarding house, there would be people gathered round, trying to secure beds at the last minute. A crowd meant safety.

A shadow stepped out in front of them, the man from the theatre. They halted once more and turned. Behind them, another man, with a knife in his hand, blocked their retreat.

"You've been a naughty girl," the man from the theatre said. "Both of you."

Mags pressed Susannah against the wall of a house and stared back at the speaker. He must have been waiting outside the Gypsy and followed them, madder, humiliated, and now armed. Some men never gave up.

"We don't want any trouble," she said.

"Too late for that, missy. I thought you might be heading for this doss house; it's the only around here."

So that was how he managed to have an accomplice in place to box them in. No simple street thug, then, but someone with brains. That made him even more dangerous.

"Now, I was going to play nice with your friend earlier and pay her. But you showed me up back there. So I won't be paying for it, see, but I'll still be having it. And my friend here can have you."

A whimper from Susannah. Mags squeezed her hand.

"She doesn't want you," said Mags, and couldn't help adding, "I can't say I blame her."

The man lashed out with a hand to strike. Mags caught his wrist. "Stupid," she said. "We've been in this position before. You know I can snap your wrist like a twig."

"Tom!" cried the man and his accomplice stabbed in with his knife, too fast for Mags to do more than parry his arm with hers. The knife slashed the sleeve of her jacket and the flesh beneath. But her hand caught Tom's arm. Despite the pain, she thrust him hard against the wall. Tom dropped the knife and fled into the shadows.

"Let me go!" the other man yelled. "Let me go!"

"Not until you make a promise. You leave this young lady alone. You got that?"

Tears of pain traced down the man's cheek. Mags could keep twisting, even tear his arm off. The desire to do so rose swiftly as the mad fire kindled inside her soul.

Let me set it free... Give me an excuse... Do it!

He nodded. With an effort, forcing the insane desire down, she let go. The man loped off down the alley.

Susannah peeped out from behind her. "Dear God!"

"No, there aren't any dear gods. Just used ones."

"What?"

"Never mind. Let's get to your boarding house."

"Wait! Your arm!"

Mags had forgotten about her wound. Blood dripped from the cut, which stung like fire. "It's…not too bad." Well, maybe a little bad.

Susannah took off her shawl and wrapped it around the wound. "Let's get you to the boarding house. They'll have something to bind you up."

Boarding houses did a brisk trade late at night. People who were too drunk or too frightened to go home, or who had no home, crowded in their doors as midnight approached. As long as they had the money, and there were enough beds, they were welcome. Once the place filled the doors were closed, and those left outside had to fend for themselves. Susannah explained she and her brother had a system whereby Bobby turned up in time with the money for two beds and secured them. She never knew quite what time she'd be in, depending on her success with customers, so her brother arrived first. He stood now just inside the doorway, as proof of having entered the premises, and waved as Susannah approached. Twelve years old, with the small frame of the starving, and an unruly mop of black hair. Mags immediately noticed he lacked a left hand. Quite some accident at the cotton mill.

His grin faded when the boy saw the wounded Mags.

"Bobby, this is Mags," said Susannah. "She's been cut."

The owner of the house stood on guard to prevent anyone without money from entering. He knew Susannah from previous nights, but wouldn't let Mags past.

"Look at her arm," persisted Susannah. "She needs attention."

But the owner stood firm. "No one gets in unless they spend the night, and we just run out of beds."

"It's all right," said Mags. "I can't spend the night away from the Gypsy anyway. I'll fix myself up when I get back home. You go in. You're safe now."

"But—"

"Rules are rules. That's what Mr Foxwood would say. I'll be fine." In fact the pain of the wound had already diminished from a howl to a grumble. "I'll see you tomorrow. Pleased to meet you, Bobby."

A few more protests from Susannah, but Mags merely laughed and stepped off into the night.

She made it back to the Gypsy without being accosted again. The night had shifted to early morning as she took out the small medicine chest kept in the green room. She unwrapped Susannah's shawl and looked at the cut. Not too bad, but it would leave a scar. It still bled as she bound the wound tightly with a linen bandage. A couple of glasses of brandy took the edge off the pain.

The climb up to her room in the loft took longer than usual and, despite the brandy, sleep took even longer to come.

II

Mags woke when the morning was well advanced. The light that entered through the only window in her loft room touched everything inside with a soft radiance.

The events of the previous night came back to her as she clambered out of bed and shuffled in her nightgown to the water closet: Susannah, the man in the theatre, the feast in the kitchen, and the sordid skirmish in the alley. The girl would be coming here today for a visit. Mags had better move to finish her chores before then.

While brushing her hair (just a few strokes—Mags didn't believe in making a fuss over something that would be buried under a cap most of the day) her bandaged left arm gave her no pain. By the look of the bandage even the bleeding had stopped.

She sat on the bed and unwound the dressing, then moved into the shaft of light from the window to take a closer look. Most peculiar: the only sign of the wound was a completely healed scar, a mere white line across her forearm.

Had the injury actually happened? Of course it had. Mags's mind may have lost some memories over the years: her childhood, her place and year of birth. Even those milestones had to make room for other memories in a life as long as hers. But there was no problem recalling events from a few hours ago. That thug had slashed with a knife. Not easy to forget.

Yet now there was no wound, just a scar.

Perhaps Mr Foxwood had done something, although healing people was not usually in his power. *Causing* wounds, perhaps. But not the opposite. Not his style at all.

As it turned out, Mags had no time to ask him about it, as he went out almost straight after breakfast. When he did leave the building it was usually either to the Lombard or the Drum and Fiddle. But this time he had gone further afield.

At ten o'clock Susannah arrived at the stage door, and her brother Bobby was with her. Both wore the same clothes from the night before.

"I hope you don't mind," Susannah said. "He wanted to come."

Mags stepped aside to let them in. "Of course not; he's welcome."

"Thank you for this, miss," the boy said.

"Call me Mags."

In his booth, Gimble glanced up from his game of solitaire and grunted. "Who's this then?"

"Behave yourself. They're guests, not an act."

Bobby stared at the dwarf in the office. "You look funny!" But Susannah chuffed him and said, "Don't be rude!"

Gimble pulled the pipe from his mouth and blew out a scented cloud. "That's not rude. You want rude? You can both get fu—"

"Shut up!" Mags pushed her guests through to the back stage. "Don't mind Gimble. Mr Foxwood, the manager, keeps him as a curiosity, I think. Just to see how far he'll go."

The man's hoarse laughter followed them backstage.

"How's your arm?" Susannah asked the question while staring around her at the inner world of the Gypsy. The house was dark, the curtain down, isolating them in a pocket of quiet and warmth.

"A bit better, thanks."

"Show me." The girl leaned closer, reaching for the arm. Mags stepped away.

"What? Why?" If the girl saw Mags's healed arm, questions would be asked. Unanswerable ones.

"Please."

"It's bandaged."

"Don't look like it," chimed in Bobby.

"Shh!" His sister glared at him. "All right, you don't have to show. I just thought it might be better."

"It is a bit." Mags had to stop herself rubbing the arm, and pretended to wince while moving it.

"I prayed for you last night," said Susannah, not making eye contact. "I thought maybe there'd be an improvement."

"You did what?" The word *pray* always made Mags uncomfortable. She didn't pray often, and when she did Mr Foxwood didn't always grant her request. She'd stopped asking after a couple of centuries. No use flogging a dead horse, or in Foxwood's case a live horse that was simply too self-absorbed to react to the flogging.

"I prayed that your wound would heal quickly."

Something a little too earnest about the girl's tone made Mags cautious. "Who did you pray to?" she asked.

"Who?" Susannah glanced at Bobby and put his arm around his

shoulders. "Who do you think?"

Mags let that one go. For the next hour they toured the theatre. The backstage, the dressing-rooms, the green room, the auditorium, the front of house. Susannah took in everything, a radiant smile on her face, head turning back and forth, asking a myriad questions. The girl had seen a number of shows in her time, the money scraped together somehow (or worked for on her back) but had never penetrated into the backstage world. Bobby seemed entranced too, but his questions were more curious than practical.

"Is this place haunted?" he asked after gazing up into the loft, where the floor of Mags's room could be dimly seen.

"Not in the normal sense."

"In what sense then?" The boy had penetrating eyes that caught Mags's own and held them.

"A lot of performers have died here. But I've never seen a ghost." It was intended as a joke: an actor "died" when their act went over badly. Actors who died on stage too often at the Gypsy had their contracts terminated. Mr Foxwood had standards.

Susannah caught the joke. Bobby just frowned.

They finished back in the green room, sitting at the rough deal table with a pot of tea.

"It's all so splendid," said Susannah. "I wish I could be an actress."

"There's no reason why you couldn't. My sister Lucretia is one. You just go to the theatres and try out for the companies."

"Are you an actress?" Bobby asked.

Mags had died on stage herself a few times over the years, but her preferred world was the dark one behind the scenes. "Not anymore," she said. "I used to help out a magician with his act, and played the patsy in a few comedy sketches. But I haven't got the figure for anything else, and I can't play a musical instrument. I can sing and dance a little."

When the frenzy takes me, she thought.

"I used to sing to Bobby and Papa quite a bit," said Susannah. "When he wasn't drunk, that is."

Bobby said nothing but kicked at the table leg.

The events of last night put an idea in Mags's mind. Susannah needed some other form of income—best to keep her where Mags could see her. "Would you like to sing here at the Gypsy?" she said over the rim of her teacup.

The girl glanced at Mags, then at Bobby, then back at Mags. "I don't know. I'd be nervous. Singing to Bobby's one thing, but…"

"You have a beautiful voice," her brother chimed in, nudging her arm.

"And it might get you out of Mrs Bennett's." Mags hoped her voice sounded as casual as she intended.

Susannah lifted her teacup but didn't drink. "I don't know…Do you think?"

"Sing *There's a Nightingale at my Window*," urged Bobby. The song was popular. One of the previous night's acts had included it.

The girl hesitated for a moment, then began the song, quietly at first, but putting in more volume as confidence set in. Even without music to accompany her, she hit the notes fair and square. Good enough for the Gypsy at any rate. They might hesitate to give her the lead in an opera at Covent Garden, but the Gypsy crowds would be looking at her more than listening to the song, especially if her hair was let down.

As Susannah finished the song Harry Banks put his head in the door. "Better keep it down," he said. "Mr Simm is back."

The stage manager liked his theatre quiet when dark.

The two visitors left a few minutes later. Mags rubbed her arm where it had been cut and thought a lot.

Harry Banks scratched his chin while contemplating the tangle of rope in front of him. The rasp of whiskers carried across the stage.

"The problem, Mr Foxwood, is the ropes are gettin' old. There's a lot of stretch in 'em now and they don't grip as much as they used to. We need new lines all round is my opinion."

Mags stared at the mess of rope and agreed with Harry, but it wasn't her place to comment until asked. Mr Foxwood prodded the ropes with the toe of one highly-polished shoe and sighed.

"I'll think about it."

Harry started to coil the rope preparatory to re-reeving it through the pulley.

"Can we talk?" Mags leaned towards her boss so that Harry didn't hear. She didn't hold out much hope. Her master was apparently not in a generous mood, but she wanted to help Susannah as soon as possible.

"I'm inspecting things at the moment," he said, watching Harry with the line. "Is it something important?"

"I think so."

He stepped into the orchestra pit where the band leader and Fred Bastable were discussing something about the coming night's acts. Bastable had been the host at the Gypsy for about ten years now. The males in the audience loved his coarse humour and the women thought him quite handsome. The problem was, Bastable had the same opinion about himself. He winked at Mags as she joined them in the pit.

"Something in your eye?" she asked.

Foxwood spoke with Bastable and the band leader for a few moments, then turned away and gave a little start when he saw her still there.

"Yes, Mags?"

"Can we talk?"

"I'm all attention."

"I mean..." She pointed upstairs towards his office. "Talk."

"Ah. I see. It's not really a good time. I'm going out again shortly. Important meetings."

"All right, come over here then." They went to the far side of the pit. "Look at this." She rolled her sleeve up and showed him the white scar line. "Did you have anything to do with this?"

He looked at her arm. "No. What is it?"

"I fought off an attack last night. Just a footpad who got between me and a friend. Nothing I couldn't handle. But he cut me with a knife. Did anyone..." She cleared her throat. "...*pray* to you last night?"

"Pray?" The word seemed as disturbing to him as it did to Mags. "If only that were true."

There were a number of ways to tell if old Dionysus was being less than totally candid. His fingers had a habit of lacing together; he tapped one heel on the ground; and, most telling of all, he stared at the ceiling. Mags watched closely for any of these signs, but saw none.

"No private prayers to you last night?" she asked.

"Not in about two thousand years, except for you maenads and satyrs. Speaking of which, some of you have been a little remiss—"

"So you had nothing to do with healing me?"

He shrugged. "It's not really something I do. You know that."

No private prayers from Susannah, then. So who had healed her?

"All right. Thank you." She rolled her sleeve down. "On another note, I'd like to audition a new act. A singer. I've heard her and she's good."

A bell went off in Foxwood's stomach. He pulled out his pocket-watch and glared at it. "I have to go. All right, yes, whatever you like. Audition her. I trust your judgement—you're the Gypsy's maenad after all. And that old goose Mrs Slocum is coming to end of her contract anyway. We need a new voice for the second half."

III

Edward Paynter slammed the empty glass down and pushed his chair back. It struck a man leaning against the bar, who cursed and muttered, "Watch it!"

Paynter slurred an apology. Sweat trickled down his face—too much alcohol always made him sweat, never mind the oppressive atmosphere of the Red Admiral tavern. No more money meant no more drinking for the time being; his brain still worked enough to appreciate that. Another burglary would be needed to replenish his funds, and burglaries were risky here, with the teeming masses and the peelers. It would be necessary to find a new target house outside of the City, and that would take time. Holborn might suit, or Clerkenwell. He needed to speak to Tom about it, but his accomplice was lying low for a while, cowed by that homely girl from the Gypsy who had beaten off his attack a few nights ago. What a fool, to be scared of a woman! All the same, Paynter rubbed his arm where she had gripped him and remembered her strength.

He pushed his way through the crush of men, women and children, earning more reprimands. At the door he paused for a moment to light his one remaining cigar and stepped out into the night. Too drunk now for anything but bed. A curse on the woman who had humiliated him and the blonde whore with her! Women were all the same. A desire to thrash one, to beat and tear at a woman's flesh, thrilled through him. He would have done that to the whore had that bitch not stopped him. Who cared about a beaten harlot? Just another useless rag in the world.

Who cared about anything?

"Edward Paynter."

A small, dark-haired girl stood in his path: maybe ten years old. She wore a red print skirt, white blouse, and a dark jacket. Two black ribbons in her hair hung down like plaits on her skinny shoulders. She held a thick leather leash; on the other end loomed a large black dog, almost as tall as herself.

"Out of my way," Paynter muttered, but the dog stepped in his path, baring its teeth.

"I want a word with you," said the girl. Her voice sounded right for her age, but the tone held command, assurance.

"How do you know my name?"

"The dispossessed are known to me."

That made no sense. He had no time for a brat's games. He squinted at her, a tiny girl he could thrust effortlessly into the gutter. But the dog looked able to rip him open if it chose. If he turned and walked off in the other direction she might follow or set the dog on him. He felt chilly, and not from the wind that bustled along the street.

"It's late, girl. Run along home to your mam now."

"You do not command me," the lass intoned.

None of the passing pedestrians seemed to acknowledge the girl, or even notice the great slavering dog. A waif might be nondescript in a London street, but the dog not so. Almost as big as a wolf. And yet people walked by and didn't even turn to look.

"Who are you?" His hand edged towards his jacket pocket where he kept a small but sharp knife.

"Your guide."

He smirked. "Don't be daft."

"You have nothing else left. No family, nothing."

He remembered the cigar lodged in the corner of his mouth and puffed at it for a moment, squinting at the girl through the smoke. How did she know of his misfortune? Not just the loss of his money and his house and his family. Everything. All in the last year. A lesser man might seek release from life in the dark waters of the Thames, or take a pistol and blow out his brains. A lesser man.

"Aye," he found himself saying. "Nothing left."

A man walking past heard his words and glared at him.

"What you staring at?" roared Paynter, and the man hurried on.

"Only you can see us," said the girl. She tugged on the dog's leash and started to walk along the street. After a few paces her voice came back, as clear as if she still faced him. "Come with us." Paynter hesitated until the dog looked back and snarled. He stumbled after them, hand on the knife and breathing deep draughts of night air to clear his booze-addled brain.

No street lanterns here, just the damp darkness, but the girl's form was easily visible as it moved ahead of him, her shoes barely seeming to touch the cobblestones, as if she weighed hardly anything at all. A dream? A delusion brought on by his drunkenness? Yet he followed, and his heart felt as cold as the air that nipped at his fingers.

At the end of the street she turned the corner abruptly into an empty lane. High in one wall a single light burned in a window, enough to outline the entrance to a stable on the other side. A water pump stood forlorn in the middle of the road. But no girl, no dog.

"Where are you?"

"In here."

The girl and dog appeared like ghosts in the doorway of the stable. Paynter shuddered in the closeness of the alley. Pitch darkness behind them, and the smell of hay and dung.

"Good," said the girl. "You seek me. That's as it should be."

His mind was cleared of the drink now. He could focus on asserting himself. "What's all this? What do you want from me?"

"Service."

Burglary did not constitute his only income. He sometimes performed chores for people with the right money, desperate people who needed discretion as much as a solution to their problems. But he'd never considered doing such things for a mere child. He decided to act dumb. "What do you mean?"

She reached a skinny hand to stroke the head of the dog. It growled a little, a bass note that could almost be felt. The moon emerged from behind a cloud, casting its silver light into the alley. For the first time he saw the girl's eyes clearly: all dark, no whites, and placed closer together than normal. For some reason Paynter couldn't take his gaze away from the face.

"You have a need," she said. "So do I."

Those eyes, staring, liquid, penetrating, bored ever deeper into his brain. The bitch knew his thoughts.

"You have nothing left," the girl said, stroking the dog's back. It emitted a soft growl. "Except a desire for revenge. I can help you."

"Can you indeed?" His words sounded hesitant even to him, but her gaze continued to needle into his brain.

"I can give you power," she said.

What did that mean? The question rose in his mind, but his lips could not form the words.

"I can help you move with the night, to remain hidden, to seek those on whom you would exact revenge."

"I don't..." He trailed off before adding the words, "need your help", but the dog growled as if it understood their talk, and more.

"You can do much service for me and others."

He pulled the cigar from his mouth and dropped it on the wet floor. The faint hiss filled the space. "Others? What others?"

And the girl's eyes became all of Paynter's world, as they seemed to grow and engulf him. The stable vanished; he floated in a place of dark, towering forms, of fire on the horizon, of bestial screams that came from afar. Other figures were there, forms both human and different, monsters from nightmare that swung by and mocked him, or grinned with mouths full of sharp teeth, or reached out to pluck at his clothes. Lost souls, drifting.

"Work for us," came the girl's voice. "Be one of our servants."

Paynter found himself nodding even as he tried to shy back from the passing forms. The stable reformed around him. His hands clenched into tight fists as he stared at the girl, who hadn't moved.

"Put out your hand," she commanded.

Almost of its own accord, his right hand reached out. Dirty nails, black hairs on the wrist. Such things it had done, yet it no longer seemed a part of him.

With a growl the dog snapped its jaws around the hand, bit hard, then let go and sat quietly as if it hadn't moved at all. Too stunned by the speed of the attack, Paynter gripped the wounded hand with his other. No pain, but blood trickled between his fingers.

"I give you a gift," said the girl who was not a girl at all. "You will be my hunter in the night, unseen, silent."

"Who are you?"

"The maiden of destruction. The first of the first. The stealer of children."

"What's that mean?"

"You shall know me better soon. For now, you serve me. And the tribe."

"What tribe?"

But the girl continued in the same low, thrilling voice that sounded like the dog growling. "Fetch us souls. Many of them."

At last something he understood. "I will bring you twenty. My gift to you."

"Yes. Twenty. And after that, we will be stronger and we will harvest twenty million."

Silently, Paynter left the stable and returned to the streets of London that had now become the darkest place in the world.

IV

Mags and Susannah halted at the kerb of Collingwood Road and waited for a carriage to pass. An old man with a broom began sweeping the road, clearing a path through the mess of manure left by passing horses so the women could cross without soiling their gowns.

"Oi! None of that!" barked Mags. Normally Mags just ploughed across the roads and didn't bother that her gown became soiled. All the Gypsy's laundry was sent out, so cleaning it wasn't her concern anyway. Originally a country girl, she had no city-bred qualms about a bit of healthy animal dung. She stepped out into the road but stopped when Susannah remained on the kerb. "Come on," she said.

Susannah picked an apple out of her basket and inspected it. Small, but without any bruises. She turned it round to check all sides, then sniffed at it. "Have you ever heard of Sir Isaac Newton?"

Frowning, Mags scratched her armpit. "Yes. Why?"

"He got hit on the head by an apple, they say, and discovered gravity."

"Really? If someone crowned me with an apple I'd bloody well hit 'em back."

"No, nobody *threw* an apple at him. He was sleeping under a tree, and the apple *fell* on him."

"Well it's a bit daft to lie under an apple tree when it's in season. I thought Newton was supposed to be smart."

Mags grabbed Susannah's arm and pulled her into the road before the old man could sweep any more. As they passed he held out a hand, palm upwards.

"We didn't want you to sweep it," said Mags, walking on, but felt Susannah pull out of her grip. The girl dug into her purse and handed the man a halfpenny.

"There you are, father," she said. The old man showed a toothless smile.

On the far side of Collingwood Road Susannah stopped again to rearrange the cloth cover over the fruit. Mags glanced back at old man, now waiting for another customer.

"That was a nice thing you did," she admitted.

The other glanced up from the basket. "Excuse me?"

"Nothing." Mags looked over at the squat, black-bricked edifice that was Mrs Bennett's house of unrestrained entertainment. No sign announced its purpose, but a few men lounged around the steps leading to the front door, waiting for girls to emerge, or, more likely, summoning up the courage to enter. They were all the advertising Mrs Bennett needed. The peelers kept an eye on the place, of course, and occasionally conducted raids. They would arrest the girls and the customers—never Mrs Bennett herself—and she would close its doors for a few days, only to re-open with just as much audacity as before. Such a laissez-faire attitude by the authorities proved more useful than shutting the establishment down for good. The police found the girls a handy source of information and had more than once caught known criminals while being entertained. It was hard for a wanted man to flee when literally caught with his pants down.

"Are you sure you want to go in?" asked Mags. "I mean, you've got the Gypsy now."

Susannah had easily passed her audition. They had started rehearsals a week ago and she would open next Friday night, once she'd signed the contract with Mr Foxwood.

"I need the money," Susannah replied. "Until the Gypsy pays me…"

True enough. Foxwood wasn't going to give any money in advance, especially not to a debut act. He'd need to see an appreciative crowd before he granted any favours.

"I'll lend you something until pay-day." But it was a wrench saying that. The purse in the box under her bed had become lighter lately.

"Oh, Mags, don't be silly. Now come on, I want you to meet the girls."

So that was why Susannah wanted to walk home with her. Mags eyed the loitering men and felt queasy at the prospect of walking past them. "What? I'm going in with you?"

"It'll be fun. Don't worry, we don't use the front entrance." She started up the narrow lane beside the building. "Come on, it's all right."

The side of the building had a narrow door on which Susannah knocked. A grate slid open, a man's face appeared, the grate slid back and the door opened. They entered a hallway, plastered and whitewashed. The man, cigar in hand, regarded them as they passed in. He ran a hand over his unshaven cheek and looked Mags up and down apparently about to say something.

"Shut it!" growled Mags.

The look on his face might have made Mags feel better had she been in the mood.

"Through here." Susannah ushered her into a sort of boudoir. Heavy red drapes covered three walls, in front of which were several plush sofas. They, too, seemed draped with cloth, until Mags realised the fabrics were in fact the clothes of several ladies who reclined or sat on the sofas. Mirrors set at intervals around the walls reflected the light from the functional gas jets mounted on the fourth wall. Under them was a purple curtain across a door to the front of the building. The air of the room was thick with perfume, some of which must have issued from the necks and wrists of the reclining ladies; the rest apparently came from a brazier burning in the centre of the room.

One of the reclining ladies looked up from perusing a dog-eared journal and declared, "Hello Audrey! I didn't think you were coming in today."

Mags stifled a laugh. "Audrey?"

"My professional name."

"I prefer Susannah."

"So do I. But it's house rules." She put the basket of fruit down and stripped off her shawl and gloves, holding her hands near the brazier to warm them. "Nippy out this morning. How's business?"

The girl who had spoken before turned a page of her journal and slapped the paper into place. "Slow."

"It should pick up this evening," Susannah said, turning to Mags. "After the men finish work and before the theatres open."

Mags wanted to repeat her earlier statement that Susannah didn't have to work there anymore, but held her tongue. Not her place to dictate how another person should live their life. Besides, her own history was hardly innocent—everyone had regrets, and being almost six hundred years old meant she had more to repent than other people.

"Well, I'll leave you to it," she said, wrinkling her nose in the heavy air. "Now remember, you have a rehearsal tomorrow. You have to be there for that."

"Oh, don't go just yet. I want you to meet the girls." Susannah clapped her hands. "All right everyone, this is Mags, a friend of mine. May I introduce Miriam, Cynthia and Claire."

Mags found herself making the rounds as if at a tea party or ball. Each girl deigned to look up and extend a hand, which she took awkwardly, not sure quite what to do. Cynthia, the one who had spoken earlier, said, "Are you a new girl?" and gave Mags a long, heavy look, like a butcher assessing the saleability of a slab of meat.

"No!" said Mags. "I'm not...that is, I don't..."

Shut up before you say something stupid.

"No, silly!" put in Susannah. "She's a friend from the Gypsy."

"Oh yes," said Claire. "I've seen you there before, when I've popped in on business. Didn't know you worked there. Better stay with that game, love, not this one."

Titters from the others, although Claire could have lost a few pounds herself.

"Mags saved me from a footpad last week," Susannah dropped into the brief pause.

That made an impression. Claire fetched a newspaper from a corner and flipped through the pages loudly. "There was something I saw this morning....There!" She held up the paper so the others could see. Mags leaned in and read a small headline: *Murder in Holborn.* "A man was killed last night. A charwoman found his body this morning, just laying in some garbage."

"Happens all the time," said Miriam. "Why up my way—"

"But this was so gruesome," said Cynthia, dragging the final word out far longer than necessary. "He was stabbed twenty times. *Twenty times!* You'd think once you'd killed someone that'd be enough."

"May I?" Mags reached for the paper and read the article. The victim was a toff, a respectable lawyer who had apparently been out late the night before (for what reason was presently unknown) and had come across foul play. No possessions were taken, but his body had been pierced twenty times in the back with a knife, probably the type used by butchers, and the corpse unceremoniously dumped in an ash pile beside a horse-trader's.

Miriam was right. Murder happened all the time somewhere in London, but twenty stab wounds seemed unduly savage.

"All the more reason," Mags said to Susannah, pointing with her thumb in the direction of the Gypsy. "You know what I mean."

Susannah bent down to her basket of fruit and set it on a table. "I brought you all a present!"

There were apples, peaches and oranges. The girls crowded round the basket, the murder forgotten. "I haven't tasted a peach for a year!" said Cynthia, holding one to her nose and inhaling the aroma. "How did you afford all this?"

The inner curtain swished aside and a woman swept into the room. Immediately the girls became silent. Mags pursed her lips to stifle a laugh.

She was a tall woman, with an enormous wig of black hair piled high. For a moment nothing else could be discerned, since her garments flowed out and obscured the body beneath. It was only when the woman came to a stop that the clothing settled. The costume resembled something from the Arabian nights, with wide pants, a tiny vest that failed to fully contain her white bosom, and a veil that covered her face from the eyes down.

The girls hastily put their fruit back into the basket, all except Susannah, who kept hold of an orange.

"Good afternoon girls!" said the woman, although her voice lacked the warmth that usually accompanied such a greeting.

"Good afternoon, Mrs Bennett," they chimed as if in school.

"Who is this?"

Susannah stepped back a pace to stand beside Mags. "A friend of mine, Mrs Bennett. She's just leaving."

The woman peered short-sightedly at Mags and nodded. Any other expression remained masked by the veil. "You're from the Gypsy, aren't you? Joshua Foxwood's girl."

Mags found herself doing a small curtsy, stopped at the bottom of it and stared at the apparition. "Yes, Mrs Bennett."

The veil came away at the touch of the woman's hand. Bright red lips, rouged cheeks, and a large nose to match the rest of her. "That's all right, then. Joshua is most kind to my girls. But it's time for business. Audrey, there's a gentleman waiting." She nodded at the door.

"But I was just about to share this fruit—"

"None of that. It's your turn. Go and show yourself to the gentleman and see if he wants you. Hurry!"

Without another word, Susannah left. Mags waited until the curtain fell back into place, then turned to leave.

"Wait!" Mrs Bennett didn't touch Mags, but the voice felt like an iron clamp had gripped her. "What's this I've heard about a job for Audrey?"

Mags narrowed her eyes. "How did you know?"

"I know everything about my girls. And what I don't know I find out. Now tell me."

"She's rehearsing an act for the Gypsy."

"What sort of act?" The woman took a step closer, the diaphanous garment sending out trails of silk. Up close, Mags could see through the thin cloth covering her midriff. The woman obviously ate well; a roll of fat flopped over her waistline. The urge to laugh rose again.

"Well?"

"She's a singer."

"Ha!"

Cynthia said, "I've heard her, she's good."

"Shut it, you! Audrey ain't been here long, but it's plain the trade itself isn't new to her. If that girl goes then I lose business, you see? There's no way the Gypsy'll get her."

Mags clenched her fists tightly to shove down the rising rage. "Then I suggest you take the matter up with Mr Foxwood." Her voice wavered a little, but not from fear. "You'd do better to worry about your girls prowling the streets with that killer out there."

Again, Cynthia piped in, this time pointing at the paper. "She's right, Mrs B. I'm scared to go out there. Did you read what happened?"

A bell rang somewhere. Mrs Bennett pushed her nose into the air as if sniffing, and declared. "A customer. Go and see, Cynthia."

"It's Miriam's turn."

"No arguments! She filled in for you yesterday."

The girl cast a wistful look at the fruit basket and headed for the curtain, muttering.

"Sell yourself, girl!" cried Mrs Bennett. "Chest out! And sashay— you walk like a flat-footed washerwoman!"

The silence after Cynthia's exit remained almost palpable. Mags stood her ground, while the other girls wandered back to their sofas. Claire noisily flapped open the newspaper and peered at it.

"I'll speak to Mr Foxwood," said Mrs Bennett, refixing her veil. "And it would please me if you didn't frequent this place again."

A deep breath and Mags settled herself. "I'm sure he would be most interested to discuss things with you. Goodbye, Mrs Bennett."

Outside, Ginger Street had settled into the long afternoon. Mags strode across to the Gypsy's entrance, and paused to look back at Mrs Bennett's establishment. The lounging men had moved on—or in—and the doorstep lay waiting for fresh prospects to occupy it. A vision of Susannah in there with her customer, naked and letting him do all sorts of things, brought a heated flush to her cheeks. Much better the girl came to the Gypsy as soon as possible, away from that sordidness. The murder of the toff showed working girls took a big risk. And this killer was ruthless and violent.

The Gypsy was closed at that time of day, so Mags dug into her bosom for the key. A small girl stood looking at the front doors holding a black dog, almost as tall as the girl, on a leash. Two long black ribbons bound the girl's hair.

"Hello there, love," said Mags. "We aren't open yet."

The lass looked at her. Two coal-black eyes, no whites. Now that was odd.

"Are you all right?"

The dog growled, and shifted on its haunches as if preparing to leap. If it did, the child would be far too small and light to hold back its rush. Just then the door of the theatre opened from inside and Jack, the spruiker, appeared with a sandwich board to set up in the street announcing the opening times of the night's shows. He nodded to Mags and whistled as he placed the board on the street.

"Coming in?" he asked, about to close the door again.

Mags glanced at the girl and dog. "Yes."

Inside, Jack went into the ticket booth. Mags leaned on the counter. "A timely arrival. I thought that dog might attack me."

"What dog?"

"The big dog. With the girl."

"What girl?"

Mags tapped her fingers on the counter for a moment, then said, "Sorry. Talking to myself."

She opened the door a fraction and looked out. No girl, no dog.

V

"It's not safe on the streets nowadays." Sir John Rowley looked in the mirror leaning against the wall of Leah's sewing room in the Lombard Theatre, took off his top hat, replaced it at a slightly different angle, and stared at the change. "Not for anyone. The seventh murder in two weeks."

Leah waited for the clothes iron to heat in the fire, wishing Sir John would explain his presence. Not that he couldn't go anywhere he liked in his own theatre, but he had never been in her sewing room before, and any breach of routine for Sir John meant his mind was unquiet.

"You're lucky," he continued. "You can go next door to the Stanthorpe Hotel when you leave here, but the other employees have to brave the streets to go home at night."

She fetched the iron from the fire and began on the stack of shirts fresh from the laundry. Sir John liked his orchestra to look smart, but twelve separate shirts, and twelve starched sets of collars and cuffs to be attached to them, took a bit out of her afternoon.

"You never know who he'll get next."

The newspapers, hungry for sales, had delighted in the grisly tales of the murderer stalking London's streets. The atrocities had made for thick black headlines and even blacker borders to front pages each time another body turned up in the cold light of morning. Always in the morning. Seven so far, men and women, each stabbed twenty times as if the killer delighted in the act of plunging metal into a warm body over and over again. Leah herself knew that sensation—not the delight, but the actual feel of a blade entering flesh, the vibration that passed from the blade into the hands, and then through the whole body. Never a human, of course, but to cast a spell some incantations required animal sacrifices. Not that she had done much magic of that sort in the two centuries since losing her voice.

"The thing is," said Sir John, idly watching her pressing the shirts with practised care, "I'm worried for the safety of the staff."

She nodded while continuing to iron.

The man paced back to the mirror. "This top hat's too small.

Esther bought it yesterday and it doesn't fit!" He scowled at his image for a moment, then whipped the hat off. "Damn it, these murders are odd!"

Leah, halfway to the fire with the iron, almost dropped it.

"Almost as if…" Sir John continued in a lower voice. "Well, there was that affair a few months ago, with that magician at the Gypsy, what's-his-name, Merriman."

So Foxwood had told Sir John about that. Probably a necessity, given the damage that occurred to the stage of the Lombard from the fight with the minions of Osiris. She recalled that Sir John had asked her to keep him informed about the Resurrection Box, and she had failed to do so. If his intention was to reprimand her, no rebuke could be heard in his tone.

"What I mean is, that was something supernatural. Is this?"

She shrugged. The newspaper reports contained nothing to rouse that suspicion.

"Is that all your opinion? A shrug?" He stormed to the door and then stopped and turned back. "I'm sorry. I suppose I'm just anxious for my employees and the actors."

That was an understandable concern. They would be anxious for themselves as well. "*We appreciate that,*" she signed.

"I remember when that actor died—Julius Kent—that was part of that magician thing, too. As it turns out…well, I'm not sure exactly *how* it turned out."

"*This doesn't seem supernatural. Just a maniac.*"

"Very well, then." He sighed as if to move the matter to the back shelf. "Now, I understand you want to be excused attendance at tonight's performance. Something on at the Gypsy?"

Leah nodded. The light musical comedy being presented at the Lombard had drawn full houses most nights. Leah had watched the show enough times now to practically know every song by heart. Perhaps that's why she kept going, because it should be her singing on stage as the young female lead. It was a silly tale, but popular: a sailor who loved a girl was shipwrecked, but returned to marry her in the final act after being rescued by a mermaid. Tonight, however, Leah would miss the show and go over to the Gypsy during the second house. Mags had invited her over to see a singing act that had opened the week before, some girl Mags thought better than most of the warblers who passed across the music hall boards. Her sister certainly appeared to be in a better mood since taking on the protégée.

"Well, all right," said Sir John. "I ask only one thing: don't go the long way around. Duck across Grit Lane. Get the doorman to accompany you."

"*I promise*," she signed. "*Thank you*."

He had a point. The latest killing, just five nights ago, had been only two streets away—an old man found dead with twenty knife wounds in him. He'd been attacked, apparently, without anyone hearing. A sad way to go: in the dark, terrified, alone. The streets around Grit Lane were perfect for a killer to skulk waiting for a victim. There were plenty of hiding places where an intoxicated person might go looking for a dark place to urinate, or prostitutes and their clients would seek somewhere private to conduct business without the bother of going to Mrs Bennett's house. While Grit Lane itself was a suitable place for an ambush, it took only a few seconds to nip across from one stage door to the other, and there were usually performers from both houses chatting or smoking.

A newspaper lay open on the table, a sketch of the latest body's discovery prominent in the middle column. The crumpled form of the dead man had been depicted in lurid detail by the newspaper artist, who must have taken grisly delight in drawing the multiple stab wounds all over the victim's back. Seven victims so far, one every few nights. The police scoured the streets and still the killer struck. No clues, no apparent motive. Some madman with a delight in killing, targeting people simply by opportunity. No one was safe.

When Sir John had gone, taking his unsatisfactory topper with him, Leah ploughed on with the shirts. The ironing took longer than planned, but it had to be done to Sir John's standards. Lady Rowley kept tight control of the books, but even she agreed that stiff white collars needed plenty of starch.

She completed the shirts, took them to the orchestra's dressing room and folded and put away the ironing sheet. Nothing to do now unless a costume disaster befell someone in the cast. Not likely, since Leah took her job seriously, although just last week one of the chorus had spilled chicken pie all over his blouse just before the curtain rose. Leah read a book in her sewing room until the play was well into the second act. As the sailor began a duet with the mermaid she passed out the stage door without requesting the doorman to accompany her. At the stage door of the Gypsy she nodded to Gimble as she passed through. Mags appeared out of the shadows.

"I'm so glad you could come," she said, taking Leah's hand and leading her through the tunnel to the back of the auditorium.

Entering the pit of the Gypsy felt different each time. The audience at the Lombard behaved itself—once the show had started a sort of reverential silence came over the patrons, who watched the performance and clapped politely at the end. The noise from the Gypsy's crowd was far more abundant and loud, and people passed in and out of the curtained auditorium door all the time, heading out to get a drink at the pub next door, or turning up to watch a particular act and then leaving.

The Lombard was fantasy; the Gypsy was life.

On stage a ventriloquist approached the end of his act: a tall, thin man and a short, ugly one sitting on the same chair. The usual bad jokes and jibes at the audience. It took Leah a moment to realise the tall man was the puppet.

The act finished and the curtain closed briefly while Bastable did his spiel to introduce the next act, Susannah the Songstress.

"This is her." Mags nudged Leah's ribs.

To a slam of Bastable's gavel the curtain rose to reveal a blonde girl lying on a settee, draped in a voluminous blue gown and clutching a bouquet of obviously fake roses in her hands. A table set with tea things stood slightly downstage.

The audience settled down as the band struck up; no catcalls or whistles, which normally greeted attractive young ladies on the Gypsy stage. Instead, all eyes watched her in anticipation.

Susannah the Songstress launched into *You Left Me Standing at the Altar*, a song guaranteed to bring tears to the eyes of the women in the audience. Their companions liked it because it gave them an excuse to put an arm around their ladies by way of comfort. While Susannah lay on the settee and sang about how her fiancé had never turned up at the church, from the auditorium came nothing but a few sobs and sighs.

The number wound down but before the audience had a chance to applaud the band launched into an entirely different song, a raunchy ballad about what the singer would get up to with a new beau after she'd forgotten her previous intended husband. Ribald puns about climbing poles and plunging depths and finding safe harbour in her scented garden abounded.

The thing that really sold the tune, though, was when Susannah rose from the settee and left her blue dress behind.

At first Leah wondered if there had been some horrendous costuming accident. But no—the dress came away intentionally, revealing a second one underneath. No trace of the jilted bride remained: this girl had something far more basic in mind, and didn't mind saying so.

The audience picked up and the cheers and laughter started once more as some of the single men shouted coarse remarks and informed Susannah that if she wished, they could easily fulfil her desires. She acknowledged one or two of the more raucous ones with a smile and wave of her finger, chiding them while still keeping up with the song.

At the end of that tune the orchestra gave time for applause, which filled the place. Leah found herself clapping too.

"What do you think?" Mags looked at her with eyes shining brightly.

"*I like her*," Leah signed.

Two of Mrs Bennett's girls stood beside the exit. They weren't clapping. "Audrey's done well," said one. Her companion nodded. "Yes. Couldn't understand the words, though. She won't last."

Leah had clearly understood every word of the songs.

The music began again. Susannah acknowledged the applause and moved down to the tea table. Leah wasn't sure how the trick was done. A quick shrug of the shoulders, perhaps a flick of a hand to some unseen stay and her gown fell away to reveal yet another one underneath, a floral one in keeping with the tea setting. A parasol appeared in her hand as she sat, poured imaginary tea during the opening bars and came in right on cue with another popular song, a parody of the etiquette of the middle and upper classes, the sort of disrespectful fun the working-class audience loved.

At the end Susannah spilled tea down her dress—all part of the act, of course. She threw a mock-disgusted look at the audience, which burst out laughing.

As the curtain fell Leah clapped again, until Mags herded her out into the front of house.

"Well, what did you think?" Mags asked quickly.

Leah grabbed her sister's hand to squeeze it. The act was entirely suited to the Gypsy—nothing like it would ever appear at the Lombard. One or two suggestions came to mind about the costumes, but they could keep for later.

"*Your idea?*"

"Yes. The dresses took a lot of work. I would have asked your advice but we didn't have time. Our sewing girl here did a good job but I'd welcome your thoughts."

Leah mouthed singing and put her hands up to question.

"She did well at the audition—which Foxy didn't attend. The rehearsal pianist agreed with me about the girl's voice and together we dreamed up the act. It opened last week. Mrs Bennett didn't want her to go, even made her a large financial offer to stay. Well, large in Mrs B's eyes. But I insisted. Want to meet her?"

Leah gave an enthusiastic nod to end the rush of words.

They headed through the backstage door and along to the dressing rooms. The normally yellow brick walls that formed the corridor glowed a peculiar green in the gas light. In the dressing room Susannah sat pulling her costume off while a young boy fiddled with make-up sticks on the table. Both looked up as the women entered.

"Wonderful work, tonight, Susannah!" Mags called. They hugged and then Mags introduced Leah. A formal nod of the head from Susannah this time. Up close the girl looked even more beautiful than on stage, although her eyes were tired.

"Leah works at the Lombard," explained Mags. "She haunts it like I do this place."

"Haunts?" Bobby stared at Leah.

"I'm sorry," said Susannah, starting to don a plain muslin street gown. "Bobby's obsessed with ghosts and spirits. He don't mean no harm." Her cockney accent contrasted sharply with Mags's more cosmopolitan one.

"Are you a ghost?" Bobby asked Leah, who shook her head.

"Leah doesn't speak," said Mags.

"Doesn't, or can't?"

"Now, Bobby, that's enough!" Susannah chided. "Don't be rude."

Leah signed that no offence had been taken and Mags translated.

They waited while Susannah finished changing. Like most of the acts at the Gypsy, she headed home after her second house turn and didn't wait for the end of the show. Leah remembered the warning Sir John had given, the need for caution in the streets.

"Who's walking us home tonight?" Susannah asked while collecting her personal effects.

"I usually do that," Mags explained to Leah. "We can't be too careful with that madman out there. But I can't tonight. Bastable has some problem or other he wants me to deal with. I have to see him immediately the show finishes. And Bad Ben has to stay and make sure the crowd leaves."

"I'll take her."

"Are you sure? I thought you'd be busy with the show at the Lombard."

The light opera could look after itself for tonight. The only likely accident would be to the mermaid costume, and they had a spare if any irreparable disaster happened. Leah felt quite sure they could do without her. If Sir John complained, well, Leah could deal with Sir John.

"I'd love it if Leah could walk us home," said Susannah. "If she's all right with that."

"Don't you worry, Leah can handle anything I can."

Leah's ability as a maenad was to see the souls of the dead for the usually brief moment they existed in the real world. She didn't have Mags's belligerence or strength. Leah had seen her maenad sister throw burly sailors and labourers out of the Gypsy. Regular customers knew not to mess with her. Such aggression was not Leah's usual method of handling a crisis, even with her unleashed maenad rage. If an attacker did appear, a swift retreat might be the best tactic. But before they left Leah fetched a large carving knife from the Gypsy's kitchen.

Grit Lane had become colder, and the perennial dust drifted and swirled in a light breeze that channelled between the buildings. A couple of drunks from the Drum and Fiddle scrapped with each other at the end of the street but the three pushed past them. Only Bobby glanced back.

Paynter had many friends.

The night cloaked him so he could wait enshrouded in its shadow for the next recipient of his gift to come by.

His knife, the deliverer of his gift, was honed to a fine edge.

The fear in the minds of men and women, who kept to the bright places because they did not want his gift, was another companion. It unmanned them and he forced it on them in his generosity.

The girl who was his mistress had given him the power to move silently through the streets.

All these were his friends.

Paynter stalked the fog, unseen, silent, searching for his next victim. The fog opened before him, closed behind and left no trace of his passage. Under a cold gaslight he paused, sniffing the air.

"I am here."

As the girl who ruled his soul emerged from the gloom, her black dog striding beside her on its leash, Paynter wondered at the change.

He had already murdered seven people in her name, and the deaths had given her stature and years. A little girl no longer, now fourteen years or more, still dark-haired, still with the black ribbons in her hair, but graceful now, starting to show the curves of a woman.

"You have done well," she said. Beside her the dog growled. "Your gift makes us stronger."

He nodded. The gift of twenty souls. One thrust of his knife for each of those he had lost. One for his wife, two for his parents, four for his children. And the rest: three for his brothers and sister, the remaining ten for the brothers-in-arms who had died in war.

Twenty people gone from his life.

So he returned the favour. Twenty thrusts for each person, and soon twenty victims.

And each victim became an offering to the girl, who voraciously guzzled their power.

He raised the collar on his jacket and pulled his hat further down. His friend, the night, had brought the fog from the mouth of the Thames, but no moon penetrated the pall of cloud.

"I am seeking another for you," he said, but the vision of the girl faded.

Had she been there at all?

He stalked on, wondering at the nature of the being that ruled his life, who gave him the chance to find revenge on the streets.

Several people passed by, hurrying through the fog, but he left them alone. Each victim needed careful choice: older people for his parents, men for his lost soldier friends, a woman about twenty for his sister. Each time he avenged a different soul who had passed out of his life.

"This is awfully good of you," said Susannah. "Mags insists I have an escort, ever since that time we almost got stabbed." She related the incident as they walked. No boarding houses for Susannah and Bobby now. Thanks to her turn at the Gypsy they could afford a room at a proper establishment, a room to themselves without different bed-mates every night.

"I marvel at Mags's strength," Susannah continued. "She smashed that man against the wall so hard!"

"I wish I'd seen it!" piped in Bobby, walking a few steps ahead. He slapped the stump of his left wrist into the palm of his right. "Crunch!"

"Now, Bobby, that ain't nice!"

Fog drifted up from the Thames, the thick yellow murk only that river could produce with its proximity to the sea, laced with the gritty smoke-soup of London. The pedestrians thinned as they plunged through the miasma.

"It's not much farther," assured Susannah. "So you work at the Lombard? What do you...Sorry, I forgot you can't talk. That must be terrible. Not trying to cause offence, mind."

Fortunately the girl knew how to talk without the need for replies. She prattled on as they walked. It allowed Leah to focus on listening and watching.

"Working at Mrs Bennett's—and before that on the streets down in Bermondsey—well, this is much steadier work," continued Susannah. "And a lot more likeable. Mr Foxwood suggests that men would like to see me in my dressing room after, but I don't want to do that sort of thing anymore."

Leah would have laughed if she could. Mr Foxwood had all sorts of ideas.

"Oi! Bobby! Come back!"

The boy had gone too far forwards, anxious to be home perhaps, and had disappeared totally into the fog.

"Bobby!"

Leah put her arm on Susannah's to ask her to be quiet, but the girl wasn't familiar with her forms of communication and kept calling Bobby's name.

"It's all right!" The boy's voice came back after a few moments. "I'm here!"

"You come here this instant!"

A scuffle of steps and Bobby appeared from out of the haze.

"Don't go straying away again!" she ordered, shaking a finger at him. "He's a good boy, just doesn't use his brain too well sometimes. He can be real disobedient when he wants to. It's his missing hand's made him act addled, I'm guessing. He gets frustrated."

Leah knew all too well the hindrance of a physical disability.

"It's cold and I want to get home!" the boy whined.

"Home," said Susannah. "I never thought I'd have one again. Oh, I know it's not much, but it's better than living in the streets. And now I'm actually in the theatre, getting flowers from admirers—imagine that! I never got flowers before. Most of my previous customers just wanted to do the thing and then leave, not so much as a thank you most of the time. They just…" A pause. "Sorry, you probably don't want to hear about that."

In fact, Leah could have regaled the girl with things worse than being a prostitute. Seven centuries of her life lay behind her, a vast stretch of time filled with both joy and sorrow, love and hate, the elation of performing on stage and the despair of watching the black horse gallop away with her son and husband. And her lifetime held, too, the power of her witchcraft. Susannah had performed three songs tonight, but Leah knew many other songs, mighty spells that she hoped would one day take revenge on the god who stole her voice.

"Bobby!"

The boy had run off again.

"I'll murder that little…"

Leah stopped. Someone ahead, someone not Bobby. She held up one hand to Susannah to indicate she should remain, and ran ahead into the swirl of fog.

A tall, shadowy form, arm raised and lowered again and again.

A huddled form on the ground.

"Leah?" Susannah's voice came to her from behind.

Ahead, the stooping form straightened, lowered its arm. Leah saw his face clearly for a second, before he vanished into the fog.

She reached the huddled form on the ground.

Blood poured from a dozen wounds on Bobby's back.

Susannah appeared beside her. Leah stood and tried to turn her away, but the girl saw her brother's body, wrenched herself free and fell down beside him.

Bobby's soul rose from his body, pale blue, shot with lights like stars. It drifted away, above the reach of the street lights, and faded into nothingness.

Susannah put her hands on the boy's heart and muttered words that Leah didn't catch, but which sounded like a prayer, the same few words chanted over and over. She pressed harder, ejecting the words through gritted teeth.

But it was no good. Bobby was dead. His soul had gone.

Susannah kept chanting until the police came.

VI

"Please don't blame yourself, Leah."

Mr Foxwood stood with his back to the cold fireplace in his office, arms crossed in front, head down. The cuffs of his black suit jacket pulled away from his bony arms to expose the soft white flesh underneath. Mags thought he looked like some predatory bird, although his voice contained genuine concern.

"He's right," she said, taking one of her sister's hands in her own. "There's nothing you could have done."

As the god of wine, theatre and perilous ecstasy, Dionysus did not have the power to bring Bobby back. Gods could not work outside their sphere of responsibility. Also, the strength of a deity's powers was determined by his followers. With just a few maenads, one satyr and some other questionable believers scattered around the world, Foxwood simply lacked the power, even if revivification had been something available to him. Mags thought briefly of the Resurrection Box in the store room, but of course they couldn't use that without setting Osiris free once more.

"*My fault,*" Leah signed. "*If only I'd seen the man earlier.*"

Mags hugged her. "I would have failed, too, I'm sure." She tried to smile at her sister, saw the latter's hollow cheeks and the dark circles under her eyes. "No one's blaming you, dear. Whoever this killer is, he's a quiet one."

"An interesting point," said Foxwood. "That a maenad—Leah especially—should fail to hear or see his approach. It makes one think."

Mags pushed a lock of Leah's hair back into place. "Would you like a nice cup of tea, perhaps?"

"*No.*" Leah turned away to stare into the fireplace.

"I'll light a fire for you, then." Mags reached for the coal scuttle.

"*No!*" A flick of her left hand for emphasis.

Mags sighed and removed her hat, a real lady's hat from the Lombard's costume store, not her usual man's cap or the dreadful monstrosity that was her sole concession to lady's millinery, and placed it on the desk. The funeral had finished a bare hour ago, just themselves and Susannah and one or two of the acts from the Gypsy who had formed friendships with the girl. No one else.

Of course, Susannah had ceased her act, two shows a night six days a week. She'd declined to come back with them to the Gypsy after the funeral, insisting that she wanted to be alone, and the others had reluctantly conceded to her wishes. Mags would give her a few hours then go around to check on her.

"She'll be back singing again," said Foxwood, guessing her thoughts. "Give her time. A true artist will always go on eventually."

"Oh shut up!" snapped Mags. "She'll make up her own mind!"

The god didn't flinch, but his sparse eyebrows came towards each other as he stared at her.

"I'm sorry, sir," muttered Mags. "You saw her act, then?"

"Yes. Her opening night. A lovely piece. I enjoyed the sudden costume changes particularly. And her voice: an unexpected treasure there."

"We can't let her go anywhere else. She has to come back to the Gypsy."

"Leave it to me. I'll have a private word with her. I sense an extraordinary talent in her."

The Lord of Theatre might feel confident he understood the minds of performers. Mags, more practical, knew it would take a bit of coaxing to get Susannah back on the boards again.

She felt her arm through the sleeve of her gown. Even the white scar had healed now. "Leah said Susannah muttered something over Bobby's body. A prayer, it sounded like."

Dionysus looked up. "Indeed? Did you catch any words?"

Leah pulled herself back from dark thoughts and shook her head.

"Look at my arm," said Mags. "Completely healed now. Not even a scar. That was Susannah's doing, I'm sure of it."

"*A prayer to her god*," signed Leah.

"Possibly," said Foxwood. "But I think there's something else at work here."

"You suspect the power is her own?"

"Yes," said Foxwood. "After all, you ladies have certain talents." He cleared his throat. "Well, I think that's all we can do at this stage." He clapped his hands together. "We have to find a temporary replacement act for Susannah. The show must have a singer in the second act until she's back."

Mags glanced at Leah. She had had a lovely singing voice,

centuries ago. It wasn't fair. Mags wanted to punch whoever had stolen Leah's voice right in the face. Just one punch. Really hard. And then another one. Even harder. And keep on punching.

"What have you been up to, by the way?" she forced herself to ask Foxwood.

He glared at Mags as he sat behind his desk. "What do you mean?"

"You're hardly ever here. Where have you been?"

A scowl passed across his face as fleeting as if a bird had cast a shadow in its flight. He patted the fox skull on his desk.

"Never mind. You have a theatre to run."

No, he was supposed to run it. She was just the maenad. But Foxwood said nothing more.

"Come on," she growled to Leah. "I want that cup of tea."

VII

Paynter's last victim, two weeks ago, had not been a good kill. The boy had come running out of the fog almost straight onto his knife. But after only twelve stabs a woman had appeared. Paynter had panicked and run before he could complete the other eight thrusts. He had slunk back to his home and prayed to the dark-haired girl, had asked her advice, but no reply came.

Tonight he must do it right, wait for the perfect victim to come along. It had to be a woman this time. Tonight was for his sister. Like his son, she had been starving, but the man who raped and murdered her had not cared about that. If she hadn't been starving there would have been no need to sell herself, and no encounter with the man who took her life.

Someone would pay for that. And the girl, his new mistress, would flatter him once more.

Footsteps approached. He slipped his hand down to the haft of his knife. No need to hide, for the girl had given him the gift of darkness. None of his victims had ever seen him before he fell upon them from behind, for he was just a twist of fog to people's eyes. The footsteps drew closer.

Not the heavy tread of a man, but the click-clack of a woman's lighter boots on the cobbles. Perfect. If the right age, she would do for his sister. Her soul would be a present for his hellish ladyship.

He drew his knife and grasped it tightly. In four more steps the woman would be close enough. Three, two, one...

She emerged from the fog. Blonde hair, just like his sister. Bright-eyed, so still sober. A flower-patterned dress, a white shawl thrown over to keep off the night air, a hat with a narrow brim.

The women stopped and passed her gaze over him.

But how? The fog, his mistress's magic, rendered him invisible.

"You can see me." The words emerged from his mouth before he could prevent them, so great his surprise.

The woman kept her hands behind her back. "Of course I can."

"Who are you?" he demanded. He wondered if he had displeased his mistress and she had taken back the gift of coming unseen upon his victims.

He stepped forward; she didn't retreat, just gazed at him with large eyes. "How can you see me?"

"Because I've been looking for you," the blonde woman said, and thrust a pistol to his face. An ancient flintlock, the hammer drawn back, the wide barrel inches from his head.

The spark of the flint on the frizzen illuminated the street for a quarter-second. The girl's face stood out in sharp relief, a triumphant smile wide across it.

Then the powder in the barrel ignited and the ball slammed into his skull.

VIII

Mr Foxwood carefully replaced the duelling pistol back in the case with its companion.

"I do love the pattern on the butts of these," he said. "You don't see such painstaking work like that anymore."

He put the powder-holder and bag of bullets next to the guns, closed the case and slipped it back into the sideboard.

Mags sneered. "You've gone behind our back again."

Beside her, Leah nodded. Both sat at Mr Foxwood's desk. Standing to one side, near the door, Susannah looked at the floor, loose blonde hair covering most of her face.

He locked the sideboard and turned on Mags. "If I had told you, you might not have let her go."

"Not by herself. She should have had Leah and me with her."

"Better to take her own revenge. Neater, and it doesn't incriminate you."

"*He has a point,*" signed Leah. Mags pouted a little that her sister didn't support her.

"Mr Foxwood explained it all to me," came Susannah's soft voice. She raised her head, but kept her eyes averted from them all. "How I could avenge Bobby's death, and save London from the scourge of the killer."

Mags had to admit she would have done the same thing in her place. "He deserved it."

"Then it was my place to do it!" The words came from between tight lips. For a moment Susannah's face lost its sweetness and beauty. Mags recognised the growing anger in her, the uncontrolled rage that could overwhelm the followers of Dionysus.

"Not now!" barked Foxwood. "Come back, Susannah!"

The girl shook her head. Her face became young again and she took a long breath as if rising from deep water. "I'm sorry, sir," she whispered.

"That rage is something you must learn to control, my dear," said Foxwood. "There is a time and place."

Susannah had become a maenad. The girl had sworn allegiance, done worship to Dionysus, had performed the appropriate ceremonies. On her right forefinger, a gold ring, and leaning against the wall beside her a thyrsus staff, topped with a carved pine-cone. There hadn't been a new maenad in ages. Not, at least, one that Dionysus had told them about.

"You are a crafty old fox aren't you?" said Mags. "You should have informed us about making Susannah a follower. After all, we're her friends."

Foxwood ignored the metaphor. "From the moment I saw her I thought she would make a good maenad. Such people are rare, and have talents to attract the notice of a god. Just like you with your strength, or Leah's gift of seeing souls. Susannah can heal."

"They get us all in the end," explained Mags in reply to Susannah's frown. "Your ability to heal is innate, instinctive. It's not been granted by any god. Every so often a human is born with a special power, and they usually end up attracting the notice of one or other of the gods and becoming a follower."

"I see," Susannah said. "So all those miracles throughout history were…"

"Not really miracles at all," said Foxwood. "Well, some were, those actually performed by gods. The rest were done by special people like you."

"I always knew if I prayed hard enough that wounds would heal," said Susannah. "I did it to myself, to my family, to friends, but without them knowing it was me. But I never knew it *was* me, I thought…well, being a Christian I thought…" She blushed. "I thought it was…"

"Never mind, my dear," said Foxwood. "We all make mistakes."

"*Did you try to heal Bobby's missing hand?*" signed Leah.

When making her a maenad, Dionysus gave Susannah the ability to interpret Leah's signs. His gift to all his followers, so they might better protect her.

"I tried to, many times. I prayed hard, that is, because I didn't know it was actually me. But it never grew back. I guess I can't do everything."

"No one can," said Foxwood mournfully. "Not even gods."

"*Our talents only go so far,*" signed Leah. "*I can't always see souls.*"

"With your new status comes a new life," said Mags. "You must be dedicated to the theatre. And other things, too. You are aware of that?"

"She's fully aware," said Foxwood. "I do know what I'm doing, Marguerite."

"Don't call me Marguerite. I haven't been Marguerite for…well, longer than I care to remember."

Leah rose and hugged Susannah, a long embrace, and then pulled back to hold the girl at arm's length and look at her for a long time. Eventually, she nodded.

"All right, all right." Mags rose and did the same thing. "I really am happy for you," she whispered in Susannah's ear, and meant it. "So is there to be a revel to welcome our new sister?"

Foxwood shrugged. "That's up to you ladies."

"It is the custom. I've a vague memory of some sort of celebration when I became a follower." Most of the things that happened during a revel seemed to be forgotten once sanity returned. The moral part of the mind blanked it out. Probably a good thing. One clear image of a particular night remained, however, even after all this time. "You danced on a table."

"Well, there's always a lot of dancing at those things."

"You wore nothing but a fox skin. And that slipped. I didn't know where to look."

Foxwood cleared his throat. "As my follower, you were supposed to be looking at *me*. With all due adoration."

"I must have been too drunk to remember my commitments. You can't criticise me for being drunk, Lord of Wine."

He ran a hand through his thin locks. "So many girls have come and gone. You remember them all?"

"Not all. I wasn't there at the beginning." Mags felt a lump rise in her throat. Foxwood had struck home with that remark. There had been many satyrs and maenads, men and women in his service, over the centuries. She tried to think of some names from the past: Marianne, Erik, Anika, Christof, Edithna, Viola…who could forget sweet little Viola? Perhaps no more than a dozen maenads still existed, and only one satyr, the sour old Tom Gimble.

"So many," muttered Foxwood. "I feel old."

"You *are* old," said Susannah.

Leah smiled and pointed at her in agreement.

"Now don't teach her bad habits!" Foxwood's surprisingly serious glare denied any more hilarity.

"It's not an easy life," Mags said. "You're going to live a long time.

People around you will die, go away, move on, and you'll always be here."

"I have no family now." Susannah twisted the gold ring on her finger.

Sometimes, Mags spent a lot of time looking at the bare walls of her room in the loft and wondering if things might have been different. Six hundred years ago Dionysus had tapped her on the shoulder, and looked into her eyes and ensnared her, the same god who had supplied the newest maenad with the means to kill. No knowing what might have happened if he hadn't made Mags a follower, if she'd lived the life she'd been born to.

A rap on the desk from Leah interrupted her thoughts. "*Susannah needs a theatre to haunt.*"

"Ah, yes," said Foxwood. "Now she is one of the sisters."

"She could stay here," put in Mags immediately. But Foxwood frowned.

"You know my rules. Only one maenad per theatre. But it should be easy enough; there are many theatres without one."

Too true. Thousands of theatres and music halls all around the world. And precious few with a guiding spirit.

"I thought it might be good to send Susannah to Italy," he continued.

Mags frowned. "Italy? She's not—do you even *speak* Italian?"

"Si." A grin had come at last to Susannah's face. "Parlo molto bene Italiano. Mio padre era da Firenze."

"You see, Mags?" said Foxwood, his eyes gleaming. "I do know something about her. Firenze, eh? Florence, as Mags would call it. That would be good. There are any number of theatres there, and no maenads yet. Yes, I think Italy will be good. Besides, London is no place for her now."

"Why not?" asked Mags.

"She's a murderess. There's no proof the dead man was the same one who's been committing all those atrocities. Susannah will be arrested if it came out. Voluntary exile is the only safe option."

Susannah nodded. "It's all right, Mags. I'll go. And I promise to write."

Yes, perhaps the Continent was the safest place, although it was a wrench to lose a new friend. With Bobby gone, Susannah had no family at all. A good thing, really: now she was destined for a lifespan far beyond that of mortal women, having no kin was an advantage. With a theatre of her own, safe from arrest, perhaps she would thrive. Mags would miss her singing.

"What about the killer? What motivated him?"

The god of theatre patted the fox skull on his desk. "Yes. That worries me. Such evil mortals can commit, and yet his was beyond that of most criminals."

"If I may, lord..." said Susannah, and Mags detected a skein of fear in her voice—regret, perhaps, at her decision?

"You don't have to 'lord' me," said Foxwood. "The occasional 'sir' is sufficient. We seem to be on less formal terms these days." He pouted at Mags, who bristled at the hint of blame for the lapse in the etiquette of divine adoration.

"The man I killed. He seemed surprised that I could see him. He asked me a couple of times. Why wouldn't I be able to?"

Foxwood held out his hand and a glass appeared in it. Three more materialised on the desk. Mags took the cue and proceeded to uncork the bottle of red wine that had been warming on the mantelpiece.

"Yes, his question was a peculiar one for an ordinary person to ask," he said. "You said there was a good deal of fog about, but even so, face to face like that, it seems odd. So we must assume that he didn't expect to be seen, that he, for some reason, thought himself invisible to his victims. Something to do with the fog, perhaps, but I doubt it. He must have had supernatural help."

Mags sloshed wine into each glass and didn't wait for Dionysus before taking a long sip from her own.

"Then how could I see him?" persisted Susannah. "And how did I know *he* was the killer?"

"The same reason Leah could see him," said Mags. "You're a maenad. Your mind now resonates to some things ordinary people can't see. Some of us do it better than others. Leah here sees souls, and I can't. But you *could* see past a simple enchantment placed on an ordinary mortal to render him invisible."

"Well done, Mags," said Foxwood. "As for recognising him, that was my doing. Leah told me what he looked like, and I put the image unconsciously in your mind. But..." He took another large swig of wine. "We have another problem. If the murderer *was* under enchantment by some arcane power to hide his form, who cast the spell? I've made contact lately with one or two gods about recent events, those I can trust."

All three maenads leaned forwards to listen, the older two from habit, since Foxwood revealing information occurred so seldom, the new one because her sisters did so.

His hand ceased to caress the skull and paused in an overly dramatic way. "I found nothing."

Mags felt a strong temptation to take out the pistols and hold one to his head. Not that it would do any good to shoot an immortal being, but the theatricality of the act would not be lost on him.

"*Don't lie to us.*" Leah stamped her foot to add emphasis.

A glance to each face, and then he shrugged. "All right. The attempt by Osiris to gain followers last August worried me enough to start asking questions. As you know, gods manage to pop in and out of the world occasionally, although most don't make any fuss—they know their place. But something new has begun. Some enemy we should be worried about. No, not your enemy, Leah. Another one. That killer—he could have had links to them."

"*And now he's dead.*"

Foxwood smiled. "Well, *dead* is a relative term, I understand. Don't worry, he won't be disturbing this realm any longer. But he had links. Contact with something else. I need to look into it more."

"Which means you'll be away more?" Mags glanced at Leah. Perhaps now the Gypsy would be run more on her terms. Perhaps she would see more of Leah.

"Every so often. But I'll still be here to keep an eye on things." He straightened his skinny form and put his hands behind his back. "Ladies, I think we're in trouble."

The nervous laugh he threw at them didn't make Mags feel any better.

SCENE THREE

March 1852

THE MOONSNATCHER

There is no greater hell than to be a prisoner of fear.

—Ben Jonson

I

As the music ceased and the dancers ground to a halt, Leah took her gaze from the rehearsal on the Lombard Theatre's stage and looked over at the left hand audience box.

Someone's large, bare hand rested on the railing. A dark form loomed behind it, but no details were visible. Leah's pulse quickened: something about the form, something unnerving. No one should be there. Given that the box doors were locked between shows, theoretically no one *could* be there. How did they get in?

The voice of the choreographer, Leonard Daintree, who sat in the front row of stalls, brought her back to the rehearsal. "The performer's art is an ephemeral one," Daintree said, smoothing his long hair back with a slow sweep of one hand. "An artist paints a picture, a writer writes a book, and the results may be enjoyed forever. But not so for the dancer, the actor, the musician: even when you witness the actual execution of their art, nothing remains of their accomplishments but a few memories. And even they fade over time. So please, ladies, give the audience something worth remembering. Let's try it again."

The rehearsal pianist struck up and the dancers once again began the third act ballet for the Lombard's new play. Sir John Rowley, sitting next to Daintree, tapped the end of his cane and stroked his moustache. Leah could tell he was bored with the dance rehearsal already. These girls were chorus, not the première danseuses and coryphées who danced downstage in bright costumes. These were the back rows, the less proficient dancers and the new girls who might one day work their way downstage. Leah had not laboured on their costumes quite as much as the front ranks, given that these dancers would not be seen as clearly.

Leah stared again at the left hand box. The hand was gone from the railing, but someone still sat there, hunched back in the shadows, as if trying not be seen. A cleaner? But box cleaning took place just prior to the theatre opening for the night. A stage hand slouching off his duties? But no, even a stage hand would need a key to enter the box. The keys were normally kept by the box-keepers, but Sir John insisted that duplicate keys be hung on a rack near the stage manager's desk. The person would had to have used one of those.

Sitting up in the gallery with Charlie watching the rehearsal had seemed a good idea at the time. Charlie had brought up a couple of bottles of stout and a seed cake. They drank the stout and dropped crumbs and watched the dancers go through the ballet.

At the conclusion, Daintree rose to his feet again to address the lines of performers. "Might as well get a machine to do it, some arrangement of marionettes that the stagehands could manipulate. We'd save a bit of money in the long run."

"You're the choreographer," spoke up Sir John. "If you don't like it, change it."

"No time," said Daintree. "Maybe we could get the conductor to have this piece played double time and get it over with sooner." The girls pouted but said nothing. Leah felt sympathy for them. Like all performers, they had to work with tough bosses occasionally, but Daintree always came across as a man whose reputation counted more than mere dancers' ambitions.

"Nice bit of dancing, that," Charlie said. Leah disagreed; the men down in the pit were right: the dance had little promise in it. Charlie's view probably reflected that of the gallery public, but the true dance lovers near the stage would see every flaccid kick and emotionless twirl up close. Leah could do better than most of these girls at a revel. Even Mags could throw herself around when the occasion demanded it.

Daintree gave directions for a few minutes, told the girls to try again, with more verve this time. The pianist slapped his hands on the keyboard with more than usual vigour in an attempt to put some energy into the piece.

Leah looked once more at the dark form in the box. The hand was back on the railing, tapping time to the music. Something metallic gleamed. She touched Charlie on the shoulder and signed her need to leave. Charlie hauled out his watch and glared at the dial. "Lunch isn't over yet, is it?"

She shook her head and indicated for him to stay.

Leah checked the rack of box keys. All there. She took the key for the box and went up the stairs. Red velvet on the box doors, sumptuous carvings of sprites and nymphs on the woodwork. Some of England's loftiest lords and ladies had graced these seats, and expected value for their money. Could the person inside be the boxkeeper? But why would he be there—she'd never known any of the Lombard's keepers to take time out to watch a rehearsal.

She unlocked the door and pushed it open enough to peer through. Six plush-leather chairs lined along the front, another six behind them and three more at the rear, a place for a service table. A man sat in the first seat of the front row. Long hair spilled down the back of an over-frock coat, a wide-brimmed hat lay on the seat next to him. Light from the stage illuminated his face. Old, lined, pale yellow skin; white-hair; intense blue eyes; a long beard swept over his chest. But his body hinted at formidable strength, and he sat upright. His mouth bore no malice, a long line just visible under his bristling moustache.

"Good evening," he said. Plain enough English, but spoken hesitantly, as if not a language familiar to him. He rose, a tall figure with a bandaged right hand. His over-frock coat fell open to show plain working-man's clothes beneath, and, strapped around his waist, a large broadsword in a silver scabbard inscribed with Nordic runes. Black stones adorned the hilt.

"I presume you have the sight of a follower," he continued, "since only such a person can see the divine without consent."

Her pulse quickened as she curtsied, eyes on the sword. The desire to retreat into the corridor made her take a step backwards, but she resisted. A stupid idea, to run from a god!

"Do not be alarmed," he said. "I mean you no harm."

She nodded and glanced down into the auditorium. Charlie waved from the gallery but gave no indication he could see the god.

"Silent?" The god pulled his overcoat closed. "But you understand my words. If I have the right place, then you must be a follower of Dionysus. I assure you, I come in peace."

Another nod. She forced herself to take a step closer, so as to put one hand on the back of a chair. The last deity she had met apart from her own was Osiris, and the meeting had been less than cordial.

"I am Máni," he continued. "One of the Norse pantheon. I am the god of the Moon."

Of course! She should have recognised him. He was from the old pantheon of her own Viking people. But they had become Christian before she was born almost eight hundred years ago. Time enough to forget much about her people's history. Her change of faith to follow Dionysus had further clouded her knowledge of the old beliefs.

Máni, lord of the Moon, brother to the Sun. There had once been numerous moon deities: Arma and Mawu, Yarikh and Selene; others from many faiths. No divine monopoly existed over the Earth's satellite. What had happened to the others was unknown. Evidently this one at least remained worshipped by someone, somewhere. Just as Dionysus personified the spirit of theatre and wine, Máni in some way represented the essence of the moon.

The Man in the Moon. Had she been able to laugh, a giggle would have escaped her lips.

Light spilled from his hair, a silver glow that seemed to drive back the yellowish gaslight, like glare from one of the great, flaming lime-lights that could illuminate the whole theatre, but not so harsh or hot. His eyes shone like moonbeams on a dark night reflected off a pool of water, the golden-white light of the full Moon, seen through laced tree branches.

He'd said he came peacefully, and it didn't sound like a lie. This god was not like Osiris, burning with jealousy of the deities still worshipped. Not even like Dionysus, grumpy and drowning his sorrows in wine.

"It is plain you cannot speak," the god said. "Therefore I will ask no questions that cannot be answered with a shake or nod of the head. I must ask a favour. I came to seek the advice of your master, Dionysus, or even his protection if his benevolence reaches that far. But he is not at home, and I still need counsel. Is there somewhere we can be talk without these vassals overhearing?" He indicated the auditorium with a dismissive sweep of his good hand.

There might be some private place to talk with Máni here in the Lombard, although anywhere alone with this god might be dangerous. Máni had kept himself invisible to ordinary mortals—and presumably inaudible as well—and so no one would come to her aid if he threatened her.

Nothing for it. The smell of ancient rock and dust hung about Máni as they went backstage, and light spilled from his hair enough to cast her shadow on the wall. But they passed a stagehand in the corridor who didn't bat an eyelid. So little were the old gods acknowledged.

Dressing room two was empty, although the costume racks bore the street clothes of some of the rehearsal dancers. Máni opened the window over the sink and looked out at Grit Lane. In the late afternoon several people could be seen: workers at the back of the Drum and Fiddle, a cart unloading at the kitchen door of the Stanthorpe Hotel; further along, two men smoking and kicking at the dust.

"The Moon is not up yet," he said.

A few deep breaths managed to calm Leah. She stayed near the open dressing room door, resting her back against it, keeping as much distance as possible between her and the god.

"My fellow lunar gods and goddesses are still on the Moon," he said, "but I have fled the Moonsnatcher."

Given a few minutes with her library back at the Stanthorpe, Leah might be able to find out what that word meant. For the moment it might be better to pretend prior knowledge. After all, he'd sought her master out deliberately to ask a favour.

He held up his wounded hand. Blood soaked through the bandage, which appeared to have been torn from an old shirt. No, not blood, but ichor, the fluid that served the gods for blood. While it looked almost like its human equivalent, it was darker and more sinister in its implications. Only something equally divine could have harmed him. She shuddered a little, and not from cold.

"Do you have a better wrapping for this?" he asked. "I will be healed of it soon enough, but for the moment…I think the sensation is called pain. It is unpleasant."

She nodded and hurried to the stage manager's desk to fetch a small medical kit. Back in the dressing room she took out a roll of bandage and clean lint. Máni unwrapped the hand while Leah cut off a suitable length of bandage. The wound looked fierce, a deep tear across the palm and other, smaller rips around the wrist. "I've never felt pain before, in all the millennia I drove the Moon across the sky," he said, as Leah wrapped the wound. "Am I supposed to cry or laugh?"

She closed the medical kit and distanced herself from him once more, standing back near the open door.

"You continue to fear me," he said. "I'm sorry for that. Perhaps your experiences with gods has not been agreeable. There are few among us I would recommend." A grim smile appeared briefly. "When will your master return?"

A shrug. Foxwood never told her where he went. Even the news he had gone at all was usually conveyed by Mags.

"I would have sought out my own followers, but I know not where they are." He stared at the floor. "I am not a popular god."

Somewhere, someone must believe in him. An astrologer, perhaps, or even a Moon-worshipping witch. At the least, he was humble enough to admit his own shortcomings.

"I need your help," he said suddenly. "If Dionysus isn't here, then it must be you and the other maenads. Are there more of you?"

A reluctant nod.

"I must meet with them. There is little time. Even now, my enemy pursues me."

What enemy did the Moon have? Leah tried to recall the Norse legends. When the gods died at the time of Ragnarök a giant wolf would devour the Moon and the Sun. But it could not be that apocalypse yet, or the universe itself would already be crumbling around them.

Voices came from the corridor. The rehearsal must be over, and the dancers coming backstage to change into their street clothes.

"Hello, love!" one cried on entering, seeing Leah but not the tall god standing by the window. "Something you want?"

Leah fled the room, followed by the god. Back at the stage manager's desk she found a notebook and pencil, wrote a hasty note in Elder Futhark runes and gave it to Máni. No guarantee he could read, of course, having come into existence long before the development of writing, and having spent almost all of his existence in the sky or on the Moon.

He nodded as she showed him the paper.

"Tomorrow? Very well. And please, bring the other maenads."

II

Up in her loft, Mags pulled a wooden chest from under her dressing table and unlocked it. Her selfishness chest, as she called it, contained a few bundles of papers tied together with string. She took out the top one and pushed the box back into it hiding place. In the pale gaslight the words on paper seemed darker, more mysterious, the black ink sharp and clear against the white sheets.

Except they weren't all that dark and mysterious. In fact, they were supposed to be the exact opposite.

It shouldn't be that hard to write a play, surely?

For a year now she'd hacked away at the thing, rewritten whole scenes, introduced and expunged characters, rearranged the order of events. And still the thing eluded her. She knew how the play would end, had even sketched the final tableau on one page, but how things reached that point remained a mystery.

How did other playwrights manage to do it?

She tried to pick up from where the last page left off. It had been a month since writing the words, scrawled in frustration at the bottom of a page covered in crossings-out.

POLICE CONSTABLE: *Put the gun down, sir.*
HAROLD: *You'll never take me alive!*

Had she actually written that? The lines had seemed so perfect when first penned, so exactly right for the actors to boom out while the audience gasped in anticipation. Now they made her want to scrunch the paper up and throw it on the fire. Perhaps killing Harold off might not be a bad idea. At least he'd stop using terrible dialogue. She scratched the words out and sucked her quill pen while contemplating an alternative wording for Harold's defiance.

Nothing came, just the taste of feather.

Red light drifted through the only window, illuminating a patch of floorboards next to the threadbare rug laid across them. The red light looked almost like that produced in the theatre by hanging coloured scrim-silk in front of the lighting battens, except here the effect was stronger and more pronounced. It couldn't be moonlight. Perhaps a fire burned somewhere. Except the light didn't flicker, and in order to illuminate the floor, it had to come from above.

She peered out of the window over the London skyline. The Moon, a few days off full, shone down, surrounded by torn clouds.

A blood-red moon.

That's not right.

Maenads danced under the Moon at revels, shaking their thyrsi, stripping off clothes as the dance grew more heated and they entered the ritual madness. It represented the inconstant moods of the theatre god, the cycle of nature, rebellion against the stilted mores of society, that sort of thing. Usually Mags just felt naked and cold.

Tonight the Moon appeared bright scarlet, perhaps because of some dust in the atmosphere. Or maybe there was a lunar eclipse; the Moon turned a dirty red colour when it passed into Earth's shadow. But the eclipses she'd seen didn't look like this: too red, angry. More suited to Mars than the Moon. Perhaps Mars or Ares had dropped by the Gypsy for a visit. But why would the gods of war affect the Moon?

Something to check with Mr Foxwood when he returned from wherever he'd gone. Perhaps he expected a visitor. He might have warned her. "Oh, by the way, Mags, don't be concerned if the Moon turns red. Just one of my friends stopping by." Something like that.

Someday I'm going to sit him down where he can't get away and give him a bloody good talking to.

Mags yawned. The play-script held no attraction, and the mystery of the Moon could not be answered immediately. Despite her curiosity about the satellite's colour, it might be best to go to bed and worry about it later.

A rat scuttled across the floor, entering the pool of red light and for a moment its glossy fur picked up highlights of the colour. It looked at the woman for a moment, snuffling its nose and raising its front paws up to its mouth as if begging for food.

"No! Go to sleep!"

The rat scuttled away into the shadows of the far wall.

The crimson moonlight looked like a patch of blood after the gas had been turned off. Lying in bed, Mags watched it slowly move across the floor as the Moon followed its path through the sky, until after an hour it had shifted away from the window entirely to cast its lurid glow elsewhere.

Tom Gimble liked to read the *The Times*. He never seemed much interested in an intelligent conversation with anyone, but every morning he'd sit in his booth poring over a copy of the newspaper. Each day when he arrived at the Gypsy—always one of the first to do so—one of the callboys would run out to buy that day's edition as soon as it hit the streets and bring it to the satyr in his booth. After finishing his read, which was done over several pipes of tobacco, Gimble usually flung the sheets out into the lobby, where the cleaners would eventually dispose of them. Few staff desired to read the crumpled mess he left it in.

"What do you do with it?" Mags asked him, while sneering at the grubby, torn pages in the corner. "Eat off it?"

"No. I wipe my—"

"Never mind!" She searched the pages for the daily almanac. Moonrise that day would be at 4:01 pm, three hours before the start of the first house. She'd be too busy then to watch the Moon for any length of time, so would have to wait until after the theatre closed near midnight. The Moon would be high in the sky.

There was no mention of the blood-red Moon, no eclipses *The Times* could be relied on to report such things, so perhaps she had imagined it. The vision of the rat illuminated in the ghastly glow came back. No illusion.

"Did you look at the Moon last night?" she asked Gimble.

He took his pipe from between his teeth and pointed upwards with it, probably in a vague attempt to indicate the Moon, although it had long ago set for the day. "What's the point? It's always there."

"You should have. It was red."

He grunted. "That must happen once in a blue moon."

"Oh, shut up." She sneezed and started for the stage door.

"Why this sudden interest in the Moon?" Gimble asked as Mags paused under the gargoyle to pull out her cap and slap it on over her unkempt hair. "Stupid great lump."

"Me or it?"

"Don't tempt me to answer. Where are you going? There's a new act coming today, and the gas-reader."

"Breakfast."

The gargoyle spat on her cap as she crossed the threshold. Mags glared up at it as she swiped her thumb across the moist patch left by the drop. "Hey! What's the idea?"

The thing glowered down, as silent as ever.

"One of these days I'll fetch a sledgehammer to you."

On days she could afford to, Mags would breakfast at Mrs Slattery's tea shop on the other side of Collingwood Road. The shop served broiled fish, fried eggs, sausages and all that was holy in an English breakfast. Most of Mag's meagre funds went on food. Mrs Slattery maintained a generous table, and was also generous with the local gossip.

"Morning, Mags!" Mrs Slattery shouted as she opened the door to her first customer of the day. Chronically incapable of talking softly, the woman must have reckoned that being loud and voluble made people notice the speaker, which meant they were more inclined to enter her shop. "You're early today!"

Mags removed her cap as she entered and sat down at her usual table looking onto the street. Lace curtains and a row of potted petunias framed her view, which included the entrance to Grit Lane and the front of the Drum and Fiddle. The passing parade of humanity always made an interesting spectacle before the general exertions of another day at the Gypsy.

"What's it today?" asked Sylvie, Mrs Slattery's youngest serving girl, as she wiped a dust cloth over Mags's table and unnecessarily rearranged the already perfectly placed tableware.

"An omelette and beef sausages, please," said Mags. "And toast with lots of butter. And my usual Darjeeling."

No need to look at the bill of fare. Mags knew it by heart, and the day Mrs Slattery changed her menu would be a glacial day in the infernal regions.

Sylvie returned with a pot of tea before too many minutes had passed and Mags poured her first cup.

"May I ask a question?" she said before the girl could hurry away.

"I suppose." Mrs Slattery, while unreservedly outspoken herself, frowned upon her staff spending too much time in idle chatter.

"Did you see the sky last night? The Moon?"

The girl paused before replying. "The Moon?"

"Yes." She added milk and sugar to her tea and resisted the urge to say *That big round thing in the sky.* "Did you see it?"

"I was in bed."

"So you didn't see it?"

"Should I have?"

Mags smiled. "No. Thanks, Sylvie." The girl scurried off.

Why did no one look at the Moon? City people—Londoners particularly—had an appallingly low interest in celestial objects. Mags conveniently ignored the fact she hadn't looked at the Moon herself for some time before last night.

The Stanthorpe Hotel next to the Lombard could just be made out in the frame of her window. After breakfast she'd go and see Leah and ask her opinion. Not that Leah had a habit of looking at the Moon, but her sister would have no doubt been up late last night after the play finished at the Lombard and might have noticed something.

Just as the eggs and sausages arrived the shop bell tinkled and Leah walked in.

"Hello!" cried Mags. "I was coming to see you!"

She pulled out a chair for Leah to sit down. "How are you today, sister?"

Leah signed a greeting, but glanced over her shoulder like there was some kind of problem, or something not for Mags's eyes.

"What's wrong?"

Her sister maenad slid into the chair as Mags fetched a second cup and saucer from the counter and filled it with tea. "Well?"

Leah sipped at her tea and kept staring out at the Stanthorpe Hotel.

"Did you see the Moon last night?"

The question produced an odd reaction. Leah lowered her cup and pointed out at the street. Then she waggled one hand as if the answer could be either yes or no.

"What? Did you see the Moon or not?"

A nod.

"So what colour was it? Red?"

The hand waggle again.

"*Sign* it."

Why did most people in Mags's life annoy her so much? Leah couldn't help being mute, but sometimes communicating with her had its downside.

"*Yes. I saw the Moon. I mean, really saw him.*"

"What do you mean?"

Leah mimed writing.

"Hey, Mrs S! Do you have a pen and paper?"

Sylvie came over a minute later with a sheet of paper and a swan-quill fountain pen with red ink. After a few moments of sketching, Leah passed the paper across.

A picture of a chariot chased by a dog-like beast. Next to it a circle with the word *Moon* inside, and an arrow pointing to the charioteer. Under the beast Leah had written, *The Moonsnatcher.*

"Huh?"

Leah rolled her eyes and tapped the pen on the charioteer.

"Yes, I got that much. That's supposed to be the Moon. So the charioteer is some kind of Moon god? And this big dog is—I don't know, running after him or something. Moonsnatcher? What's that?"

"*I met the Moon god.*"

"Really?" Before becoming a maenad some centuries earlier, Mags would have found such a statement nonsensical. Now she merely sipped at her tea. "Well what did he say? I mean, did you talk to him?"

Leah tapped the picture again. "*This is how he is shown in one of my books.*"

"Very pretty."

"*He is meeting me tonight. You must come too.*"

Leah's rigid posture, the way she kept fiddling with the pen made Mags reach out one hand across the table. Her sister gripped it hard.

"Well, of course," Mags reassured her. "I mean, if you want me to. But what's going on?"

The last time they'd encountered a god other than their own, there had been trouble. Both of them had almost died.

"*I'm not sure. Come to my room tonight.*"

"All right. But I'll hold you to a full explanation. Now get some breakfast into you. Sylvie!"

III

Mags had a problem with fate.

To her mind, predestination had a nasty habit of making one resigned, complacent and generally dissatisfied. The concept of something being inevitable, unavoidable, already laid out and cast in stone, annoyed her. Many Christian people believed in the coming apocalypse, the return of Christ, the resurrection of the soul at the Day of Judgement. So they tried to do good in order to be one of the winners of the contest. Most only succeeded in becoming self-righteous about the whole thing. All her long life, Mags had fought against foregone conclusions. The one time that really changed things was the day she admitted that becoming a maenad was the most desirable thing in the world.

It had happened after the performance of a miracle play in York in 1256. Up until then, her life had been perfectly straightforward, living with her parents until they both died from the plague on her thirteenth birthday. Mags worked as a serving girl for a middle-class family, and that hadn't been too unusual either, although there had been comments about her remarkable strength. But on a day during Easter, the town guilds presented the annual mystery plays and she stood in the square to watch. There were the usual Bible stories presented by rough-cast actors trying their best, but it had been the story of Noah's Ark, enacted by the Guild of Carpenters on the back of a wagon, that completely overwhelmed her. The sheer beauty of the performance, the magnificent words rolling out of the actors' mouths, the costumes and the crude but ornately painted cloth backdrop depicting a seemingly endless parade of animals marching into the huge ark, had entranced her soul.

As the play finished, a tall, thin man tapped her on the shoulder. For some reason, Mags didn't run, but listened to him, intrigued both by his audacity and another quality she couldn't name, a sort of temptation that Mags had been brought up to consider sinful. It turned out the thin man was the god of the theatre, and the madness it could engender in the unwary. Almost without effort, but certainly with a will, Mags became a maenad. Dionysus didn't believe in fate either, he admitted to her once. It was an illusion, he said, a fabrication by mortals to make sense of a senseless world. Only in ritual madness, in the abandonment of order, did Truth emerge.

Now, sitting in Leah's hotel room with Máni, the Norse god of the Moon, Mags appreciated his fear of being eaten by a wolf, but thought his acceptance of its inevitability a bit disappointing.

One of Leah's books on mythology lay open in her lap. The Norse pantheon had never really been a study of hers, but she had a vague idea the legends involved lots of warriors and battles. Like all cultures, the Scandinavians had implanted their deities with their own beliefs.

Foxwood often said it: *We gods are dependent on you.*

She glanced at the frontispiece of the book: a picture of Ragnarök, with Odin battling the Fenris wolf.

"A time to come. Perhaps soon," Máni said when she showed it to him, his eyes wide, daring her to disagree.

Another picture, the inspiration for the one Leah had drawn in Mrs Slattery's: Máni and his sister Sol, the goddess of the Sun, riding through the sky in chariots pulled by horses made of light. Wild hair flowed from both, cloaks streaming behind them covered the sky, and mounted on each chariot was a lantern: one for the Sun, one for the Moon. Close behind, loping through the sky as if on a flat road, two huge wolves with jaws agape.

The god grimaced. "Yes. That is us. My sister and I, and the beasts that pursue us. The Moonsnatcher and the Sunhunter. Children of the Fenris wolf. Poor Sol. She will be next."

"Surely, you're not going to just let this happen?" Mags asked.

The old god—yes, that was the word, old—held up his wounded hand. "The wolf has already attacked me once. I barely escaped."

"But, you see, you escaped!" Mags looked at Leah for support, but her sister stood near the window with her arms crossed, looking rather desperate. "If you had just accepted your fate, you'd be dead now. Eaten by the Moonsnatcher. But you're alive. Well, not actually alive in the dictionary sense of the word—you're a god after all. But certainly not eaten."

She looked again at the book. In Norse religion, the Sun and the Moon, Sol and Máni, were both to be devoured at the end of time by the children of the great wolf Fenrir as part of Ragnarök, the final conflict that would supposedly be the death of the universe and the start of a new one. Many gods and monsters would die in that conflagration. The rest of the world's population too, for good measure. Typical of the gods, not to think of others at a time like that. Gods were a peculiar lot. On the one hand, they grumbled and griped that no one believed in them anymore; on the other, they continued to act as if they held the keys to the universe. Sometimes Mags wondered why she bothered.

"I fled the Moon when Hati—that is the Moonsnatcher's name— caught up with it," said Máni slowly. "But he chased me, hunted me with all his cunning. That's when this happened." He held up his bandaged hand. "A near thing. It's why the Moon is red, of course, from my spilled ichor. It will shine white again once I heal."

"*You and the other moon goods actually live on the Moon?*" Leah signed. Mags translated for the god's benefit.

"In a manner of speaking. It is our responsibility, so we congregate there. Much like Dionysus and the theatre."

That sort of made sense.

"We lunar gods and goddesses take our tasks seriously, even if others do not."

The first thing that came to Mags to say was that it sounded like the Moon was run by a board of directors, but that might not make sense to the god. Besides, if he became angry it might not go well for them. She tried to think of something else.

"It depends on what you want to do. I mean, if you stay here, won't Hati just catch up with you again? Where does that leave us?" She indicated Leah and herself.

"But he must not eat me! It would mean that Ragnarök has come! The end of the world!" The Moon god rose and seemed to fill the room for a moment, a little god-power leaking out at the edges of his chosen incarnation. "History would fall! All things come to an end."

"*Maybe not that bad,*" signed Leah.

The trouble with the fallen gods stemmed mainly from their total incapacity to understand their lack of importance. New gods had taken over. Naturally, Máni feared Ragnarök. So did all the Norse gods. But it was a personal matter between themselves. The other pantheons that had different end-time scenarios might not be worried about the consumption of Máni and his sister, Sol. The Moon and Sun would continue to exist, surely?

Leah stepped forward and picked up the book. She flipped through the pages briefly and showed Mags a picture. Gods and monsters battled together. A huge wolf with jaws agape featured prominently. A gigantic serpent lay coiled in the background. The Yggdrasil tree was falling. Total chaos. Beneath it the caption read *Ragnarök in full rage.*

"Are you saying it *won't* necessarily be Ragnarök if the wolf eats Máni?" asked Mags.

Leah shrugged.

"But don't you know? He's one of *your* gods. You were born in Norway, weren't you?"

"Trondheimsfjord. In 1056. But we were Christian by then."

"I came to Earth seeking gods who could help me," interrupted Máni. "But the only one I have found is Dionysus. Where are the mighty ones of old?"

"I think there are a few still around," said Mags. "We don't know where they are. Dionysus might, but I'm afraid he's not here."

"Where is he?"

"We don't know."

Dionysus the Fox had taken himself away somewhere. Long absences seemed to be his habit these days, more so since that business with Osiris and the Resurrection Box. It didn't affect the theatres much; Mags and Simm could run the Gypsy between them, and Sir John managed the Lombard with Leah's help.

"It's vital I speak to him. I must have protection from the Wolf. Never have the grandsons of Loki caught up with us. Always Sol and I have managed to ride our chariots ahead of them. But now, who can guess how the world changes?"

The sound of raucous singing came in from the lane, a drunkard from the Drum and Fiddle probably. From somewhere farther away a voice yelled at him to shut up.

"I don't see how Dionysus could save you from a wolf that's been chasing you for thousands of years," said Mags. "You want Ashur, perhaps, if he's still around. Or Mars..." She glanced at Leah. "Who's the Scandinavian god of war?"

"Tyr," Leah signed.

"Him. Does he have any followers?"

Máni's startled expression became a frown. "I am the Lord of the Moon, Master of the Night Sky, and you are just two human beings! You cannot tell a god what to do!"

"We're maenads. Dangerous women. We tell Dionysus what to do all the time."

"*Not that he listens.*"

"But it's the principal of the thing."

Leah's hands formed Futhark rune-shapes so Máni could read them directly. "*We are sorry.*" She mouthed the ancient Norse words to reinforce the meaning

The drunken singing outside abruptly stopped.

That, by itself, didn't make Mags look up. Many drunks passed along the lane, and some woke up the next morning, heads sore and clothes streaked with vomit. What did make both her and Leah turn to the window was the strangled choking that immediately followed the stoppage of words.

"Someone's in trouble," muttered Mags.

Leah nodded. Even Máni seemed concerned, sitting on the edge of his chair, eyes bright in the gaslight.

Like many London streets, Grit Lane had its share of deaths, although too many corpses in this vicinity was not good for business. But most of those who died there did so quietly: drunks who either expired from too much alcohol or were robbed and murdered as they lay helpless; beggars quietly submitting to starvation; once, a man was found with his throat cut, unable to cry out as his vocal cords were severed. Foxwood had disposed of the corpse quietly and not told Sir John.

But this strangled gurgle chilled Mags. A person emitting such a sound had not been strangled or knifed cleanly and unexpectedly. It held fear as well as pain. Wrenching up the window so hard the glass rattled, Mags leaned out into the dusty air of the lane.

To the right, the lane ended at Collingwood Road a short distance away. To the left, a dark shadow fled along the lane. Worth investigating. Mags took any trouble in Grit Lane personally.

"Wait here!" she called to the others and swung her legs over the sill. A stack of wooden crates beside the Stanthorpe's kitchen door provided a landing place, although the timbers creaked under her weight as she lowered herself down.

A tapping in the window above. Leah leaned out and tossed her thyrsus down for Mags to catch. Her sister had a point. Going unarmed into a possible dangerous situation might not end well.

"Stay there! Keep an eye on Máni!"

The maenad rage that made itself known in times of crisis asserted itself as a thrill deep within her soul. Better keep that under control. Letting her unbridled anger loose would not be helpful. She swallowed hard and breathed out heavily to calm herself.

The hotel's delivery door was open. Inside could be seen the pantry, where a couple of assistant-cooks worked. Behind them, the kitchen glowed red as the chefs prepared dinner for the hotel's guests. No one seemed to notice Mags's descent from the window.

She held the thyrsus in both hands and wished for a better weapon. If it came to defending herself against man or beast, the staff might not be heavy enough. She eased along the lane, listening. The Drum and Fiddle loud behind her, the slam and clatter of food preparation in the Stanthorpe's kitchens, dim sounds from the streets beyond. At the Gypsy's stage door, she glanced at the gargoyle. It remained impassive as always, but Mags fancied its stone eyes had shifted to look along the lane where the shadow had fled.

"Did you see anything?"

No reply. The thing never spoke, even if it occasionally gave the impression it wanted to. A thing of stone, nothing more.

The stage door of the Lombard was open, and several people could be seen inside, half in costume. The doorman nodded to Mags, who threw a quick grin.

"Did you see anyone along there?" she asked.

He glanced towards Constance Street. "No, but then I've been inside."

"Someone cried out a minute ago."

"Sorry, love."

She stalked behind the bank and the leather-goods seller. At the rear of Harcourt's Drapery Emporium a dark form lay huddled on the ground: an old man, bearded and portly but well-dressed—he could have been a patron of the Lombard. He lay in a pool of blood, and more was splashed over his waistcoat. On his chest was a gaping wound.

Mags placed the thyrsus on the ground and felt the man's pulse. Nothing. Broken ribs could be seen through his chest wound. Something had ripped him open. Grimly, she peered into the ragged hole. No sign of the man's heart. It had been torn out. Bile rose in her throat. She swallowed again and looked away from the grisly sight.

A change came in the light about her, a softening of the darkness.

The Moon had emerged from behind a cloud. The dim light brought the dying man's features into sharper relief. A thick moustache. Side whiskers. Maybe forty years old.

She found a wallet in his coat pocket. The fact that it and his watch were still on his person showed he was not the victim of a mere street thug. Besides, whoever had torn open the man's chest possessed strength beyond that of a human being. Beyond even her own. Perhaps it hadn't been such a good idea to come.

Standing, Mags looked about. No sign of anyone else Even Constance Street, just a few yards away, seemed deserted. But the lessening of the darkness made the shadows of Grit Lane smaller, and behind the bakery loomed a deeper darkness. Someone stood there, a vague shape, the head obscured by shadow, the moonlight illuminating one shoulder. Even in the dark, Mags sensed massiveness and strength in the figure.

Time to retreat. She bent down slowly as if to re-examine the corpse, and gripped Leah's thyrsus, her eyes keeping watch on the shadow. It moved slightly, the legs shifting as if preparing to leap.

Mags rose like a sprinter off the starting line and raced back along the lane. Behind her, heavy breathing and the thump of feet in the eternal dust. She ran, thyrsus in one hand, the other lifting her encumbering skirts, the lock of hair from under her cap whipping past her shoulder.

At the Lombard, a young man half-dressed in a Cavalier's costume stepped out. He paused in the act of lighting a cigar, glanced up at the shape pursuing Mags and ducked back inside.

Passing the Gypsy, she thought for one second of seeking refuge within, but knew that she would not be able to do so fast enough. Even if that did happen, the thought of leading her pursuer backstage at her theatre terrified her. Gimble could hardly stop whatever it was, and everyone else inside would be utterly helpless.

Ahead, Leah leaned out of her window above the kitchens, pale oval face staring wide-eyed at whatever pursued Mags. As she approached, her sister lowered a knotted sheet.

Mags tossed the thyrsus into the window, gripped the sheet and, with Leah's help, scrambled up. Below her, two clawed hands covered in fur grabbed the end of the sheet. Two glaring red eyes peered up.

She brought one booted foot down on the man-thing's hands. It just gripped harder. Beside her, Leah smashed the butt-end of the thyrsus down onto the eyes and there came a grunt out of the darkness. The hands let go.

The women whipped the sheet up and slammed the window shut. Something hit the wall outside. The scrabble of claws on masonry, and a face appeared in the window: a long snout, red glowing eyes and yellow teeth. The face of a wolf.

Máni backed away to the other side of the room, hard up against Leah's bed. He held his sword in his left hand, its scabbard in his bandaged right.

At the window, the wolf-man placed one hand on the glass and pushed. The glass held for one moment then smashed in.

Máni ran to the door. Leah stayed, pointing her thyrsus at the creature standing on the shattered glass, fully revealed in the room's light. Beside her, Mags halted as well, seeking inside for the maenad rage, feeling it ignite deep in her soul.

In form the wolf-man appeared human, but with a long beard, whiskers that jutted far out to either side of the head, and an elongated face. The hands were clawed and hairy. The eyes glared short-sightedly, darting back and forth in the light. Taller than a man and broader, dressed in a long overcoat, which fell open at the front to reveal a torn and dirty shirt. A bandana wrapped around the neck, working-man's corduroy trousers, booted feet. Its mouth opened and a thin white mist wafted out. The wolf raised a clawed hand and pointed at Máni, who wrenched open the door and fled.

The maenads trembled as the wolf came closer, even as the burning rage in their souls begged for release. Mags thrust it back reluctantly—too few of them, too strong an opponent.

"Run!" she yelled, shoving Leah after the Moon god. Mags followed, backing away from the beast, and slammed the door shut. The wolf clawed and thudded against the wood. The door wouldn't hold long. Along the corridor, Leah and Máni headed for the front desk.

"Go!" Mags screamed, "It's coming through!"

Another blow against the door. Timber cracked. Mags planted her feet and shoved against it. Another blow, and the creature's arm thrust through one of the door panels. Splinters struck Mags's face. She ran.

At the front desk, the concierge peered over his desk as the women emerged into the lobby.

"Hey!" he called. "What—"

The women streaked by and out the front door. Papers on the desk stirred in the rush of air as the unseen god and wolf ran past.

Mags noisily sucked in great gasps of air as she drew up to Leah, who leaned against a brick and plaster wall, one hand to her head, the other clutching her thyrsus. Above, the crescent Moon shone down as bright as a lime-light.

"Where…is he?" Mags managed to gasp, hand on her bosom, her cheeks flushed red. "Máni?"

Leah took her hands away from her head, looked at her fingers as if expecting to see blood. There was none.

"What happened to you?"

"*I hit this wall*," Leah signed.

"Here, let me look at you." Mags peered at her sister's scalp, but the darkness prevented a detailed examination. She touched Leah's head, and the woman pulled away, grimacing.

"Sorry. It looks all right, what I can see of it. Just a bit of skin missing."

Mags remembered running along the street past the entrance to the Lombard, holding her skirts up. People turned and stared. Máni showed a good turn of speed, fleeing in front of them. There was one horrible moment when they almost collided with a group of men standing on the corner. Leah upset a fruit cart, but they kept running.

Until now, halted by sheer exhaustion and Leah's wall.

They stood in a grimy street near a set of steps leading down to dark water. From the stink of raw sewage, it was undoubtedly the Thames. At the bottom of the steps, a rowing boat dipped and tilted on waves stirred up by a fresh wind. Somewhere near Westminster, perhaps. A good distance from the theatre district.

"Máni?" she called, looking about.

Nothing. Above them the Moon shone down radiantly; the Moon god himself had vanished.

"Maybe the Wolf got him." Mags dusted herself down and put a hand on Leah's arm. "Are you all right?"

A nod, but Leah's hand stayed on the place she hit her head.

The street was not one ladies should be in at night, fleeing a wolf or not. Several shady-looking individuals walked along the riverbank, clearly visible in the shocking light of the Moon. Something was wrong there—even when full, the Moon never blazed like that.

"I wonder what the time is?"

Leah took out a watch and showed it to Mags. Eight o'clock.

"What about the wolf?"

Although invisible to ordinary people, if Máni and the Wolf came to blows innocent people could be hurt. One man was already dead in Grit Lane, so presumably the police would be asking questions, not to mention the staff at the Stanthorpe, who took a dim view of broken windows and guests racing through the foyer.

"All right, so where are they?"

From somewhere in a nearby street, a dog growled.

Both women turned towards the sound. Mags felt her sister grab her arm.

"Please, just be a dog," pleaded Mags.

The growl again. No dog: too deep, too primal. Full of blood and hunger.

"What do we do?" Leah's signing had a frantic pace to it.

A vision passed through Mags's mind: her lying safe and content in bed while around her London was torn to bleeding shreds. Two maenads armed with a wooden stick could not halt the swathe of destruction. Even Dionysus would concede that the Wolf was beyond anything they could deal with—even he, for that matter, would baulk at taking on Loki's grandson. Two women and the god of intoxication—hardly a match for the primordial hunger of a monster that had chased the Moon for millennia.

Another growl and what might have been a man's shout came out of the darkness.

"Over there." Mags pointed towards the disturbance, and Leah shrugged in submission. Nothing for it. Even if they could do nothing to help him, they could not abandon Máni.

More shouts and crashes. The sounds led them away from the Thames and into a small stone courtyard fronting onto a boatshed. A half-built fishing dinghy lay upturned on wooden slats. Beside it, a carpenter's bench with sawdust and wood shavings ankle-deep beneath it. The only light came from the burning Moon overhead.

Leah tapped Mags on the shoulder and pointed upwards.

On top of a wall, framed against the night sky, was the Wolf. From the courtyard it seemed even more alien, more feral than it had been in Grit Lane, the human clothing highlighting the animal nature more than disguising it. It hadn't noticed the two women but looked down on the opposite side of the wall.

"We have to warn Máni," whispered Mags.

Before they could move, the Wolf leaped down the far side of the wall. A shout, heavy thuds and bangs, and then the lower part of the wall collapsed as something came through it. Brick dust showered the maenads as they retreated, dodging whole bricks that came their way.

The Wolf landed on its back amid the rubble and lay there, stunned. Máni emerged through the cloud of brick dust, sword in hand, ichor trickling from his mouth. A light shone around him. A god indeed, in all his glory, striding towards his enemy.

The women were nothing, mere atoms against the two immortals, and they stood there helplessly watching as Máni towered over the Wolf and prepared to strike the death blow.

But the creature lashed out with one leg and sent the Moon god backwards through the hole. The creature clambered to its feet and faced its enemy once more.

A hand on Mags's shoulder—Leah pulled her back away from the combat. This was no place for either of them.

The Wolf paused, then turned as if to leave the courtyard by the road. It came face to face with the two women.

"Run!" screeched Mags.

But Leah's grip on her shoulder held even her in place. Mags soon saw why. The Wolf walked past them as if they didn't exist, didn't even turn to look. It strode back along the way they had come, circling around to approach its foe from a different direction. As it passed within a yard of them, they smelt its sweat, heard the rasp of breath in its throat. But its eyes never even glanced at them. They were not its target.

Leah's grip pulled Mags towards the hole in the wall which was half-filled with fallen bricks. No Máni, just a scrapyard piled with rubbish. Much of it lay scattered as if violently disturbed.

"Where's he gone?"

They looked all around. Overhead, the Moon shone down on the dark world. Framed against its light Mags saw, or thought she saw, a shape moving. It was her turn to grip her sister's arm.

"Look!"

A shadow moved across the face of the Moon in the shape of a horse-drawn chariot, with a figure like flame standing, whip in hand, urging the beasts on. Behind, a dark shadow in the form of a wolf, jaws agape, tail streaming out in its wake.

Mags sat down on an old bentwood chair that stood forlorn in the scrapyard and dusted her clothes down. Leah remained staring at the retreating figure of the Moon god and his pursuer. Both were soon lost to sight as they passed into the night on the other side of the Moon.

"*Interesting,*" signed Leah.

Mags felt the rapid thudding of her heart as she leaned back in the chair, which creaked ominously. "That's all you have to say?"

"*I found it so.*"

"Oh, yes. Fascinating. The next time you want to stand there while a monstrous wolf comes towards us, let me decide for myself."

Leah threw her a withering look.

Outside a closed pub they found a cab stand, but no cabs. As they waited, a police constable strolled by on his beat and cast a professional eye over them. Doubtless he thought them up to no good—only one reason for women to be out and about at this hour, one that would involve paperwork on his part should his suspicions turn out correct.

"Evening, ladies. Can I help you?"

"We're just going home," said Mags, smiling.

"I hope so. You be good girls, now."

"Oh, we are, sir. We're waiting for a hansom."

"I see that. Mind if I wait with you, then, and see you safe? It's been a wild night, it has."

"Really?"

"Someone killed up near Constance Street. Nasty business."

"What happened?"

"Now that's nothing for young ladies to know." As he said the words, he eyed Mags's tomboyish appearance. "I expect it'll be in the newspapers tomorrow if you're still curious then."

A cab rattled around the corner; the policeman signalled it to stop. The cabbie climbed down to open the door and assist the women inside. As she climbed in Leah turned to the officer and pointed her thyrsus at the Moon. Its light lit the man's face like a lantern.

"Yes, miss?"

She kept pointing until he followed the direction.

"What?"

"She can't talk," said Mags. "She's asking you to look at the Moon. Does it seem…strange…to you?"

The man squinted. "No. Should it?"

"Probably not."

"Funny thing to ask, then. Has your friend had too much gin, perhaps?"

Leah scowled at the officer as Mags gave the cabbie directions for Grit Lane.

IV

"I've never liked intermission in the gallery," complained Lady Rowley.

The difference in the audience up here was obvious: the gallery seats were cheaper, so the audience there lacked some of the gentility and breeding that the more serious theatregoers in the pit displayed. Lady Rowley often expressed her wish that the audience consisted entirely of acceptable social classes—that is, hers or higher—but the fiscal side of things demanded a cheaper section. At least the Lombard had not yet lowered its standards and put in stalls like some theatres.

"Bums on seats," Sir John would sometimes declare, although not in his wife's presence. "The only way a theatre pays is with bums on seats."

Saturday matinees were typically rowdy times. The fifteen-minute interval meant that the ginger-beer sellers in the gallery were hard-pressed to serve all those requiring refreshment. Downstairs in the pit, the more refined audience could purchase cups of tea and coffee—hot liquids would not sell so readily in the heat of the gallery, where the gas lights raised the temperature beyond comfort. As Lady Rowley declared whenever anyone bothered to point out that fact, the audience got what it paid for. Or in this case, didn't.

Leah set down the case of ginger-beer she'd carried up from the cellar and wiped her brow. It *was* hot up here today. Even Lady Rowley, who kept an eagle-eye on the vendors to make sure they didn't slip any spare change into their pockets, made use of a large hand-fan.

"It's not the heat so much, my dear," said Lady Rowley. "It's the *smell.*"

To Leah's knowledge Lady Rowley had never been in the gallery at the Gypsy next door. The atmosphere of unwashed bodies in that establishment had to be experienced to be believed. The mild pong of sweat engendered by the heat here in the Lombard could hardly be noticed by comparison.

The curtain bell rang, the signal for the audience to return to their seats for the second act. A few last-minute sales and then the vendors started to close up shop. Leah hastily loaded her crate with empties before the show recommenced, so the rattle of glass didn't disturb the performance. Lady Rowley took a final look around, seemed satisfied, and headed back downstairs as the curtain rose. Heaven forfend she should carry any heavy crates of bottles.

A man leaned over the railing, bottle in hand, his own body obscuring a sign which read, *Please do not lean over the railing*. If the bottle slipped from his grasp, it might injure someone in the pit below. If Leah pointed out his error, he would no doubt tell her, a mere woman, to mind her own business. Fortunately, he sat down as the gas lights dimmed and the second act began.

Just as she bent to pick up the crate of empties a callboy tapped her on the shoulder. "Someone to see you, miss," he whispered. "At the stage door."

Leah frowned. The Lombard staff had learned to read her body language intelligently, even young callboys like this one. "I don't know who," he continued. "A right weird cove, but."

Grimes the doorman should know better: no visitors during a performance. She went into the dim but crowded backstage. Grimes sat there at his table frowning at the bearded man on the doorstep. He wore a plain dark suit and top hat, from under which hung long dark brown hair, and carried a walking stick of the current style.

"You have a visitor," Grimes said. "You know the rules. Take it outside."

Grit Lane was warm in the afternoon sun. Over at the Gypsy stage door a couple of stagehands lingered, smoking, even though the matinee had started. She led the visitor along to the back of the Stanthorpe, where men unloaded vegetables from a handcart under her room's window.

The visitor awkwardly doffed his top hat and then placed it back. "I think that's how it's done. I'm not used to your customs, or to such a peculiar headpiece."

She stared at him.

"I am Máni," he said.

The Moon god was not at all like he had first appeared. Shorter by several inches, no sign of the silver hair, or the ethereal light that had glimmered from him at their first meeting in the Lombard. Like Foxwood, he had taken full human form. Even her maenad eyes had been deceived.

"It is a burden to be visible to the mundane," he continued, his voice weary. "But perhaps such a mortal frame may fool the Wolf. I hope you and your sister prosper."

Leah crossed her arms. He'd get no information until he gave some.

He pointed upwards with his cane. "The Moon will set in a few hours. It follows its course without me. My horses pull an empty chariot."

A week had passed since their flight from Hati. There had been some trouble with the Stanthorpe and Leah's smashed window, a few lies had to be told to cover things up. As far as the hotel was concerned, a man had broken into Leah's room, and she had fled. The window had been replaced but it had taken Sir John's intervention to reassure the hotel owners that Leah had not been entertaining dangerous men—or any men at all—in her room.

She raised one eyebrow.

"I am well," he said, grinning a little foolishly. Two teeth were missing from his lower jaw. "If that is what you're asking". Other things besides the missing teeth betrayed past violence and unease: scratches on the back of his left hand, the wild eyes, the way he kept looking over his shoulder.

"Hati still pursues my chariot. He circles the world each day, but if I stay here disguised and in one place, at least it gives me respite."

Why had the Wolf killed that innocent man in Grit Lane? The newspapers had been quite graphic in describing the killing. The *London Standard* suggested a tiger had escaped the zoo, a suggestion the zoo emphatically denied.

The god raised trembling hands in the air. "The Moon falls towards the horizon. Hear it!"

Leah heard nothing but a burst of applause from the Gypsy. The two stagehands returned inside.

"Until tonight, I am safe. Your almanacs predict the Moon's movements with great accuracy, but I know in my heart when it will return. And when it does, so will he."

"*What then?*" Leah signed.

"I don't understand your signs. Perhaps your sister might be of assistance." He stood with hands on hips, as if waiting for someone to pay him the respect due to a god.

Yes, perhaps Mags might. Leah walked towards the Gypsy stage door and indicated for him to follow. Inside, Gimble sat in his glass-fronted booth, feet planted on his stool, apparently listening to the music drifting out the from the five-man band and the warbling, plaintive singing of a soubrette on stage.

He opened his eyes and glared as Leah and Máni entered. "What do you want?"

Leah pointed at Máni, then at Gimble. The god strode to the booth, filling the narrow corridor with his presence. "I am the Moon!" he declared.

Gimble grunted, a small smile cracking his face. "And I'm the bloody Sun, mate. Pleased to meet you."

"No!" The glass window cracked as Máni smacked his hand against it. "She is my sister."

Gimble looked at Leah, his smile twisting at one corner. "Who's your friend?"

"*The Moon,*" signed Leah.

The satyr gazed at the tall stranger, hand still pressed against the cracked glass. "You can pay for that damage, whoever you are."

"*He's the Moon god.*" Leah jabbed a finger at him to emphasise the point.

Gimble stared at Máni, brow furrowed, then leaped up as realisation hit and pressed himself against the tapestry on the back wall, arms out as if to protect it.

"Don't you come near me now!" he growled through clenched teeth.

"You tell a god what to do?"

Leah stepped between them, but Máni raised a long hand at the satyr as if about to destroy him with a blast of divine wrath. A long moment passed as they stared at each other, and then the god lowered his hand and used it to adjust his tie.

"*We need to see Mags,*" Leah signed to the satyr.

"Mags is busy!" said Gimble, still pressed against the tapestry. He side-stepped across his office and tugged on a bell-rope. A few seconds later one of the callboys appeared. The Gypsy's boys differed from those at the Lombard. These were real street urchins, ragged, dirty, doing the job for a few pennies handed out grudgingly by Mr Simm. This one had a mop of untidy red hair and a limp. The lad stared open-mouthed at Máni.

"Go get Mags!" roared Gimble. The boy scampered away.

Máni stared at the pictures on the opposite wall, the old acts that had performed at the Gypsy, but his face betrayed no thoughts about them.

Mags appeared.

"Mags!" Gimble called. "See what your sister's brought home!"

With a sigh, Mags took in the tall man idly gazing at pictures on the wall. Her puzzled look vanished as she inhaled noisily. "Is he...?"

Leah nodded.

The satyr returned to his chair and crossed his arms, staring at Leah. "You bloody daft woman, bringing him here. The master's away, in case you didn't know."

"Of course she knows!" cried Mags. "I do all the work around here while you skulk—"

A tap on the window glass. Leah pointed at Máni. The maenads each took an arm and pulled the god out onto the stage door steps. With a curse, Gimble followed them outside. The gargoyle leered down in a most disapproving manner.

Máni rose a few inches in stature, standing straight in his leather boots, but perhaps also adding a few inches to his height by some divine power. The look on his face suggested the latter. "The Moon has just set," he said. "And hours will pass before it rises again."

Leah tapped her sister on the shoulder so she looked at her, then signed, "*Ask him what he wants.*"

"Yes," said Mags. "What do you want from us anyway? We're not your minions. We serve Dionysus, not some god who can't keep ahead of a wolf."

The Moon god twitched his coat back into position and scratched his beard.

"I came to Earth seeking the help of a god, or at least sanctuary with one. But there are no gods to be found, only yours, and he is far away. So I must ask your help."

"Oh? Really? Did you need our help the other night? Last we saw you were riding away in your chariot, chased by Hati."

"That has been going on all my existence."

"*So continue to do it. It seems to work.*"

Mags translated Leah's signs. The god shook his head. "No longer. That's why we must decide the contest once and for all."

"Forgive us if we don't understand," said Mags.

"I don't understand either," grumbled Gimble. "Mister Foxwood isn't going to like another god traipsing around. What's he doing here, anyway?"

In a few sentences Mags filled the satyr in on the situation. He sneered when they mentioned the encounter with the Wolf. "Daft way to do things," he said. "And what's he expect Foxwood to do?"

Leah agreed. Why could gods never be straightforward, even with followers? In a minute Mags would storm back into the Gypsy, Gimble would say something insulting and that would be the end of it. Leah wanted to shake some sense into Máni, show him that on Earth things were different.

"The Moonsnatcher will return," the god said. "There will be more combat between us. If I die…"

He paused. The others stared at him, Mags with her arms crossed, Leah with hands by her side, long hair stirred a little by the stiff afternoon breeze along the lane. Gimble scuffed the dusty flagstones with his feet.

If Máni died, Leah wondered, what would happen? Surely the Moon would continue to orbit the Earth. Humans had imagined Máni and his sister Sol into existence; the Earth's satellite and its sun were older than their gods. If Máni ceased to be, nothing might change for humanity: tides would continue to rise and fall, lovers would look up at the moon and make declarations to each other and sailors at sea would still navigate. But something intangible would be lost: romance, perhaps, the essence of magic and mystery that surrounded the Earth's satellite. Science would continue, but human art would suffer.

"The Moon is not a cold, dead, world," said Máni, as if guessing her thoughts. "At least, not to me. It is my home, my being. Imagine if the theatres were to be removed from the world. How would you feel?"

"But Hati is not trying to remove the Moon," said Mags. "He's only trying to remove you. One less god to worry about."

The red-headed callboy pushed his head out of the stage door.

"Hey, Mags, Sal's nearly finished, time for the magic act."

The warbling singer had completed her turn, and Mags was needed inside to help with the change-over to the ventriloquist. She glared at the boy for a moment, then said, "Sam can help strike the bower. And make sure the magician's table is set further upstage than yesterday. It was half in shadow last night."

"But Sam's got—"

"Go away!" roared Máni. The boy scuttled out of sight.

"You asked why I must confront Hati when for all eternity I have fled him," continued Máni. "It isn't just a personal grudge on my part. The time is out of joint."

Mags wondered when the Moon had learned Shakespeare.

"The world spins through space," continued Máni. "Your savants and scientists can predict the position of every celestial body with their mathematics. Yet it seems they don't see the truth."

"Now you're making no sense at all." Gimble slapped his pockets looking for his pipe and cursed.

"The world is not just what is seen and experienced by mortals!" the god said. "You know this—you are part of the real world. At Ragnarök this world, this cosmos, will cease to be. But I refuse to let that happen. Hati is Hate. He does not stop. If someone encounters him, they are killed merely for practice. Hati consumes their hearts. He wishes to consume mine. But I will slay him first."

"So basically," said Gimble, emitting a short grunt, "your problem is *you*. You don't want to go with the fate destiny has in store."

For the first time, Leah saw real anger in the god's face. Deities became angry in different ways. Foxwood became quiet, deliberate in his movements, as if holding in check forces that would destroy the mortal who had angered him. Ahti, the god of oceans—the father of her child—made the sea rage with his fury. Leah trembled to remember when he had become angry at her and stole their child and cursed her to silence for eternity. For a moment she feared Máni might destroy Grit Lane—but he merely kicked at a wooden crate near the stage door. The staves broke and a dark liquid trickled out.

"Careful!" called Gimble. "That's needed for the kitchen!"

"So why did you flee from the Wolf the other night?" asked Mags.

"I did not flee!" Máni thrust a finger at her, but Mags just stood straighter instead of retreating. "I wanted to take the carnage away from you, to protect you! We fought among the stars."

"Then take your combat there now."

For a second it appeared that Máni would kick Mags as he had the crate. Instead, he stood and glared at all of them.

"You humans are so stupid! So naïve. I moved the fight away from you, to save your own lives."

Leah knew he was lying. He didn't give a fig for her or Mags. He hadn't cared about the man in Grit Lane the Wolf killed, and he didn't care now. He had another agenda. A drop of water plopped onto Máni's head. The gargoyle sneered down.

"Did you do that? I'll remove you," Máni said, shaking his fist at its motionless face. "I'll turn you into a statue."

"You're too late," said Mags.

Leah had to admire her sister's courage, but Máni ignored her remark. "I had a chance to slay the Moonsnatcher last week. Almost I succeeded. But he evaded me." Máni ran his hands through his beard. "I had a chance, and I will seek the next opportunity. I have fled too long. He can be slain."

A burst of music from the Lombard. The second act ballet. A few cast members of the show spilled out of the stage door but paid no attention to Máni. Peculiar people were not a rare sight at the back of a theatre.

"All I need is a chance to hide until the Moon sets. Then I can prepare to hunt Hati and kill him before he kills me."

"*What about other people?*" Leah signed.

The deaths of innocents would continue, the god had said, if Hati hunted here on Earth. In the sky, it didn't matter—only one goal there for the Wolf. But here, on Earth, among the bustle and crowds of London, Hati had much more prey.

"All the more urgency that I slay him first," said Máni, after Mags had translated Leah's signs. "But I must hide until he chases the Moon to the other side of the Earth."

"So?" Gimble had stepped back into the Gypsy but remained looking out. "You're a god. Hide."

"Perhaps I can hide here for a while." The god brushed past the satyr. The maenads followed. "What is this place?"

The sound of applause following the singer's exit came from the auditorium. Bastable was introducing the next act, the ventriloquist. "There are people here," the god said, peering into the corridor leading to the dressing rooms. "Lots of people. I'll put myself among them." He walked backstage.

"No!" Leah and Mags ran after him.

V

Although Mr Simm ruled the backstage world during performances, Mags sometimes felt irked by his authority. He didn't live in the Gypsy; she knew every cobweb in the place. While he issued orders to the staff about maintaining the lime-lights—a fiendishly delicate operation at the best of times, involving pure hydrogen—she had risked being burned by doing the job herself on a number of occasions. In many ways, the Gypsy was *her* theatre. Especially, like now, when Foxwood was away. She was the Gypsy's maenad, and therefore had a spiritual relationship with the place. So, the sight of Máni calmly walking backstage into her music hall sent her scurrying hard on his heels.

He passed down the corridor of dressing rooms, glancing into those that were open. Mags caught up with him halfway along and dared to pluck at his sleeve.

"You can't just walk in here," she declared. "There's a show on."

In one of the rooms a man stood half-dressed, affixing a false moustache to his upper lip prior to his turn on stage. "That's an odd practice," said Máni. "Do all humans attach their hair like that?"

"This is a theatre!" declared Mags, as Leah caught up with them. "If you want to stay here, I guess I can't stop you, but you have to sit in the audience."

The god ignored her and stalked to the end of the corridor. The green room and kitchen were on the left, ahead were the stairs leading to Mr Foxwood's office. Onstage, an illusionist was preparing to saw a woman in half. The maenads each took one of Máni's coattails and just stopped him from walking on in the middle of the act.

"Behave yourself!" whispered Mags, resisting the urge to give him a slap like she would a mischievous boy. Leah signed something but Mags didn't have time to look.

The illusionist introduced his assistant, a young girl clad in a suitably exotic costume. She climbed into the coffin-like crate while the illusionist gave his patter to the audience and demonstrated the sharpness of his saw. Máni continued to watch, fascinated.

"What do we do?" Mags said to Leah.

"*Can he stay here?*"

"Not backstage! We have to get him into the green room."

A stagehand walked by, glancing at the tall man being held by the two women.

"*He could become invisible.*"

"Máni!" Mags tugged at his coat. "Make yourself invisible. You're not supposed to be here."

But the god remained enthralled by the illusionist's act. All that could be seen of the girl was her head at one end of the box and her feet at the other. The illusionist flourished his saw and, to the delight of the audience, proceeded to saw the girl in half down the middle.

"How does he do that?" asked Máni. "I had no idea mortals had such power."

"It's not real," grunted Mags, who had been sawn in half herself when she worked as a magician's assistant. "Come away." She gave a hefty tug and the god's coat-buttons parted at the front. One of them flew onto the stage, but fortunately the audience was too focused on the act to notice.

As the illusionist completed his cut and turned the two halves of the box around so the audience could see the girl was apparently separated, yet still smiling at the audience, Máni applauded loudly along with the crowd.

"No!" cried Mags as the god took a step forward, sliding out of the coat still held by the maenads and walked boldly on stage.

All eyes turned to the tall man appearing suddenly from stage left. The applause died away, although Máni himself continued to clap. The illusionist stared in horror at the apparition. The girl, facing away, didn't see him and continued to smile at the patrons.

After a few seconds of silence, during which they anticipated Máni was part of the act and expected him to contribute to it in some way, the audience started laughing. The Gypsy's patrons were typically an enthusiastic lot, not holding back from expressing opinions about the acts, but not often did someone boldly try to interfere.

The illusionist, professional to the end, ignored the interruption and carried on with the act. He pushed the box back together and explained to the audience his intention to re-join the girl's halves. But they ignored him, too intent on what Máni might do. Sawing a woman in half was all very well, but a cheeky, and probably drunk, audience member promised to be far more entertaining.

"*Let's get him off,*" signed Leah. But just as they stepped forwards Bad Ben and one of his lads entered from the other side and escorted Máni off. The audience booed and made a few remarks. Máni threw his escorts off and raised a hand as if to strike.

"Stop that!" Mags hissed.

"Now look here—" started Ben, but automatically keeping his voice down as they were only just off-stage.

"Shut it!" Mags and Leah hauled Máni further back towards the green room. "Now listen, this is a theatre. You can't go onstage."

The Moon god glanced back at Ben and his assistant but said, "I merely wished to see the wizard perform."

"He's not a wizard," groaned Mags. "It's a *trick.* Come into the green room and stay there."

Once seated at the table, the god said, "Those men who grabbed me, are they followers of Dionysus?"

"No. Just ordinary men doing their job." Mags felt the beginnings of a headache. The day had been long enough. Being a Saturday, there were still two houses to go. Three shows in one day were enough trouble, never mind a silly god who couldn't tell reality from illusion.

"*I'll stay with him,*" signed Leah. "*For this house anyway.*" She would have other duties in the Lombard, which was busy with its own matinee performance.

"But I wish to see the wizard," persisted Máni.

Mags considered the options. Máni would no doubt make a nuisance of himself in the green room, with performers coming and going all the time, not to mention the stagehands and even Mr Simm himself. Simm had seen the intrusion onto stage and would certainly not permit any more interruptions. If he tried to argue with Máni he might end up on the wrong side of the god's wrath. She pictured Simm as a pile of moondust on the stage, and her having to sweep his sorry remains into a bucket. Explaining that to Foxwood would not be a pleasant task, either.

"You can watch the show from the audience," she announced. "But stay in your seat."

Leah frowned at the folly of the plan, but Mags had the final say. The Gypsy was her theatre.

They escorted Máni around to front of house and admitted him to the pit, placing him at a table up the back. Leah remained with him to ensure his good behaviour. Mags returned backstage and expected the worst.

Fortunately, he wasn't too bad, although hardly quiet. He roared with laughter at every joke, even those that weren't that funny, slammed his fist on the table to show appreciation and even cried at one point when a singer warbled a particularly sentimental ballad. The audience, recognising him as the former intruder on the stage, found him almost as much fun as the performers. But here were no more attempts to walk on stage. At the end of the show Mags joined them as the audience left. He continued to sit at the table and stare at the closed curtain as if expecting another act.

"He behaved himself?" Mags asked, feeling the tension in her muscles relax a little now the show had finished.

Leah nodded. "*I must return to the Lombard.*"

"Yes. I'll sit with him for the next show." She tried to keep the disappointment out of her voice.

But Máni arose as the last patrons were herded out by the staff. "I must prepare for the hunt." His form glimmered a little, as if shedding moonlight, and his hair began to gleam silver.

"Don't change here!" Mags glanced around, but only a few cleaners were in the auditorium and none were looking. The god's metamorphosis ceased, and he faded back to his mortal form.

"Then I shall depart and wait for the Moon to rise again. When it does, the hunt will be on." He stalked towards the exit.

The maenads stared after him. "*Do we follow him?*"

Mags was tempted to. Allowing the Moon loose on the streets of London might not have a happy ending. She was about to follow him, but just as he reached the exit he vanished. Not even her maenad eyes could detect him.

"Well, that's inconvenient," she said.

Leah signed, "*Heaven preserve us from gods.*"

VI

Leah lay awake in bed, listening to the night and thinking of her son, Torben. A small family group seen in the foyer of the Lombard had reminded her of him: a man and woman, and between them a small boy holding their hands. The woman smiled down at the lad and said something which made the boy laugh, and the man smiled to see the boy's happiness. The sight made Leah imagine herself in their place. After two hundred years, Torben's face remained clear, and his voice came to her in dreams. As the child of a god, he might still be alive somewhere, perhaps married, with children of his own. He might even now be making them laugh like the parents she had seen in the theatre.

Am I a grandmother?

Over two hundred years ago and a thousand miles away, her name had been Ingrid, a Scandinavian witch who had already been a maenad for centuries. The god Ahti, lord of magic and the sea, had found her as she walked on a beach of black pebbles. She knew the ancient legends about him, knew the joyless marriage to his gloomy wife. Leah worshipped Dionysus in those days but, foolishly in hindsight, allowed Ahti to win her heart. He in turn, like other gods before him, had been captivated by a mortal woman. The affair was, as usual in such circumstances, a brief but fruitful one. She gave birth to Torben, a black-haired boy with his father's dark eyes and the pale skin of his mother's race. Ahti had insisted Leah follow him instead of Dionysus, but she had refused to renounce her bonds to the theatre god. They argued long, but her pleas did not sway the sea god. Dionysus intervened on her behalf, but Ahti grew impatient. He took Torben.

The memory of her last view of the child remained vivid. In a dark forest, trees dripping rain, Torben's father wrenched him away from her arms, the gloat of triumph on the god's face. And Ingrid, helpless, pleading as they rode off on the huge black horse with hooves that scattered sparks in their wake, away under the branches, never to be seen again. Torben looked back at her, arms held out imploring, the anguish on his face tearing at her heart. The horse vanished between the twisted trunks too quickly for even a farewell.

It took a long time to free herself from the ropes binding her. She was still bound, fettered with the curse Ahti shouted even as he stole their son. From that day, that moment when her heart had shattered, she had not been able to utter a single sound, not even to weep. Torben's father had taken not just her son, but her voice, took it so completely that not even Dionysus could restore it. The coward god Ahti ran from her witch's magic as much as her wrath, knowing that without her voice she could not curse him.

Can you hear me Torben? she thought into the darkness. No reply came, as it never had the countless times before.

Dionysus insisted she took a new name and lived under his protection, although she declared her own intention to seek for her son. Nevertheless, she had agreed to bide her time until Dionysus deemed it right. For two centuries Ingrid waited as Leah, some years more patiently than others, bound by her promise, a promise that became no easier to keep as the years passed. And all that time she had dreamed of her revenge. When it came, as one day it must, then Ahti the god of magic and the thundering sea would know the true anger of a maenad.

Pain in her jaw brought her back to the present. She had been clenching her teeth. She rose from her bed without lighting the gas and opened the window. A slight breeze blew in from Grit Lane, redolent with the ubiquitous odours of unwashed bodies and refuse. The sensory impact further cleared her fevered mind. She took up her flute and stood in the window to play. Her anxiety further settled as the music drifted out into unhearing, uncaring Grit Lane. A slow tune, one she'd written many years ago, every note burned into her brain. Soft, low notes representing Torben's voice alternated with the high, shrill keen of her loss. The tune had never been written down, but was always reworked, new touches added, the register changed, the melody slightly modified. A tune that would never be finished.

A knock on the door. One single rap.

She broke off playing, startled, then sobbed as reality came back once more. No Torben, no comfort, just her lonely room at the Stanthorpe. It took a moment to compose herself and answer the knock.

Mags was almost unrecognisable in the light of the candle clutched in her hand. Her stray lock of hair had been tamed at last, pulled back under a man's top hat. She wore moleskin trousers, a cotton shirt and vest, over which was flung her tattered tweed jacket, topped with a woman's shawl. A cotton bandana covered her neck to her chin. Over her shoulder was a leather bag. In one hand she carried her thyrsus.

Leah frowned at her sister, her mind still partly on her music, partly on Torben.

"Time to look for him," said Mags, ignoring the frown.

"*Who?*"

"Máni of course. The Moon is up, and Hati the Wolf has no doubt returned."

"*Why us?*"

Mags deposited her bag on Leah's bed. "Because the other night we almost got killed, and I don't fancy Máni's chances. Foxwood will want to know what's going on when he gets back. We have to at least see what our two visitors get up to."

A good point, if not exactly a welcome one. Yes, the other night they had almost been killed, and there was no reason to suspect tonight would be safer. Leah nodded but took time putting her flute away.

"Do you have trousers?" asked Mags.

Leah sneered and indicated her wardrobe's lack of masculine garments. Mags took a pair of cotton trousers and a shirt and coat out of her bag. "Put these on. They're from the Gypsy's wardrobe department, but they're clean."

The pants and shirt fitted well enough, but the jacket bulked too large on her thin frame.

"And don't forget your thyrsus." Mags went to the window and looked up at the crescent moon just visible over the roof of the bakery down the lane. "Come and look at this."

Leah joined her and signed, "*That's not right.*"

"No, it's not. The Moon's supposed to be in last quarter, and low in the sky right now. But that thing…"

That thing was a thin crescent and high in the sky, and huge. Not the real Moon at all—or perhaps the Moon as the gods saw it, the divine Moon, not the dead satellite that orbited the Earth. The two women stared at it with open mouths.

"At least it should make our task easier," said Mags. "It probably means they're still in London."

Máni had stated a desire to find Hati in a place that would avoid contact with humans as much as possible. That meant meeting him away from the city, but in which direction? And how would they patrol the city fast enough to find him? And what, above all, could they do if they did find him?

"You're all right on a horse, aren't you?"

"*Yes. Are you?*"

"Not funny."

They climbed out of the window to avoid passing through the hotel foyer and eased themselves down into the lane. Only a few drunks behind the pub at this hour. Leah sensed the looming mass of night-time London around them, a place of lurking crime and dire intentions. Somewhere in all the chaos of the city Máni prepared to battle his hunter. Nothing to do with them, except that Mags was right: in the absence of Foxwood, they had a duty to keep an eye on the situation, whatever the danger.

At the end of Grit Lane, opposite the music school, Foxwood had a coach-house where he kept a brougham and two horses. The animals knew the maenads and waited patiently while the two women saddled and mounted them. Hooves clopped on the cobbles as they proceeded along to the corner of Constance and Ginger Streets.

The moonlight waxed even brighter. No one about. Even Mrs Bennett's house had all windows shuttered, no lights showing. A single gas lantern flickered at the intersection, but its glow added nothing to the overall brightness cast by the Moon.

The women pulled up their horses under the lantern, thyrsi balanced across their saddles. Where in all of London, or outside it, would they find Máni? Leah lifted her eyes to look past the glare of the lamp, trying with her maenad second sight to detect any disturbances in the air that a god might leave. Nothing. She shrugged her shoulders and shook her head at her sister.

The gas lamp gave off a great deal of heat, more than any such lantern Leah had ever known, almost like the warmth of daytime. Sweat broke out on her forehead and her clothing prickled against her skin. The heat came not from the gas lamp at all.

Leah remembered the first time she'd looked at the Moon through a telescope when she'd been working at a theatre in Paris. On a quiet night between performances, she had taken the telescope to the roof and pointed it at the Moon hanging low over the skyline. It had surprised her to see such detail on the surface: mountains, craters, dark seas, and bright highlands. It looked more like a place of life than barren desert.

It was the same this night, but without the need of a telescope. Most of the Moon was in shadow, but the bright nail-paring curve of the visible surface glowed, and the detail of mountains and valleys appeared close enough to touch. Almost, she reached out a hand towards it.

"I see it too," said Mags. "Like it hangs just over our heads."

Not only light came from the Moon: heat too, as if the orb burned. Mags removed her top hat and fanned her face with it.

The pull of the Moon felt like a tidal drag, inexorable, eternal, stirring their blood. Even the horses, with their animal instincts, seemed to react to the enormous curve in the sky. The maenads submitted to the Moon's influence. Leaving Constance Street, they headed east and a little north, past Finsbury Circus and Spitalfields Market, entering after a good hour into Hackney Road. The streets were deserted, only the occasional sight of a policeman who stared at the women as they clattered by.

Every minute or so Leah glanced up at the Moon, still burning hot, still summoning. Blood sang in her ears. Even her heart seemed drawn to the huge crescent in the sky as if held by a warm hand. Perhaps the other moon deities guided them, led them towards Máni. Or perhaps not; gods could be so selfish.

Mags, riding slightly ahead, pulled up abruptly. "What's that?"

A group of people ahead in the gloom—or rather it seemed more like the gloom slid away from them as the women approached, tendrils of darkness peeling reluctantly aside. A police officer—no, two officers, one holding onto a younger man in working clothes, a hat half off his head, as if the peelers had been shaking him. On the ground at their feet lay a dark form. The officer not holding the young man shone a lantern on the horses as they approached.

"Who's there?"

They stopped. The young man struggled a bit. The other police officer shook him to keep him still, and in so doing stepped away from the huddled shape on the ground. A dead man with a bloodied shirtfront. An upturned top hat and a walking stick lay beside him.

"We're no one important, officer," called Mags.

He held the lantern so the light played across their faces and clothes. "What are you two ladies doing out here this time of night?

And on a pair of nags, too?"

"Going home. We've put in a hard day at the theatre, and now want nothing more than supper and bed."

While Mags engaged the policeman, Leah tried to peer past him at the dead man. Hard to see much with the light on them rather than the corpse.

"What names, then?"

"Really, sir, do you need those?"

The policeman set his lantern down in the road and pulled out a notebook and pencil. "Just in case we need to know who you are, there's a good woman." His eyes flicked back at the corpse. "Bad business here, and on a dark night it's my job to ask questions. Now, names."

"I'm Marguerite and this is Leah. We work at the Gypsy and Lombard Theatres."

"What kind of names are those? Surnames too, and quick about it."

Leah's horse shifted back and forth a little, perhaps scenting something approaching and eager to be off; perhaps the pull of the Moon, the great tidal attraction, disturbed it. Her blood tingled, churning under the Moon's supernatural heat.

"I'm Marguerite…Foxwood. And this is Leah…as I said."

The policeman looked at Leah. "Name, miss?"

"She can't talk. Her name is Foxwood too."

"Is it? You don't look like sisters." But he scrawled the names down in his notebook. "What're those sticks you're carrying?"

The white staves shone in the moonlight.

"Just props from the theatre."

"Daft looking things."

"*Ask him if they saw or heard anything unusual,*" Leah signed.

After Mags asked the question, the first police officer picked up his lantern again and took a step forward. Leah's horse, still restless, bucked a little and it took her a moment to calm it down again.

"Now what are *you* asking questions for?" the policeman demanded. "Did *you* see anything? You come along here all sinister like, no lights, dressed in men's clothes like you don't want to be recognised, carrying what I might regard as weapons if I chose to. Suspicious, I call that. And there ain't no theatres around here. Did *you* see this chap doing anything?" He waved vaguely at the young man.

"I didn't do nothin'!" the youth yelled. "Just walkin' home I was, and came across this here stiff. Not my doin'!"

"No one said it was," said the officer holding him. "But you're not co-operating too well, are you, Jack?"

"Did you see anything?" Mags persisted. "Did you see the man killed?"

Jack stared at the women for a moment. "I saw..." He hesitated when the note-taking officer put his hand on his night-stick. "I saw somethin', yeah. Horrible it was." Then he spat on the ground.

"Now look here!" The officer drew his nightstick. "Any more of that and I'll—"

"Please, officer," said Mags in a strained voice that Leah knew well. She had to force down her own maenad rage. "The man saw something. Let him speak."

It apparently dawned on the policeman that that might be the logical course of action. At any rate, he nodded.

"Horrible. Huge, black. Bigger than a man," spluttered Jack.

"Did it remind you of a wolf?" Leah's hands moved urgently.

Mags translated.

"A wolf? No, nothing like that. Something else. And the smell— phew! Worse than cholera miasma it was. I know, I worked down the sewers a few years ago. Stank like that, only worse. And something about it was burning."

"Burning?"

"Like it was on fire. Made it harder to see any details." Jack's voice became louder as he gained confidence. "Like its head was on fire."

The policeman looked up from scribbling in his notebook. "Don't be daft. You give a proper report, now, or you'll get what's coming."

The maenads ignored him. "Its head was on fire?" Mags asked, glancing at Leah, who shrugged.

"Maybe it was holding a torch or something," continued Jack. "I don't know. It ran off that way before I got a proper look." He pointed in the direction the women had been headed. "I didn't get close enough. I couldn't abide the smell."

"How long ago?"

"Not thirty minutes."

"All right, that's enough, now," said the officer. "You better come with us to the station."

Something flicked across the Moon's face. Both women looked up, blood singing, but whatever it was had gone. Not a cloud: too fast, too small. The policeman holding Jack licked his lips and looked up. He had noticed it too.

"Bright moon tonight, isn't it?" he said.

The other officer grunted. "What did you say, Stan?"

"Er…nothing." But he continued to stare up at the Moon, holding Jack's collar almost nonchalantly now.

"Let's go," said Mags, chittering her horse forwards. They ignored the police officer's protests and continued along the street towards the beckoning Moon.

"Smelled like shit it did!" Jack called after them.

"*Remember that.*" Leah added a tight twist of her mouth to her hand signs.

"I wish we could have had a look at that dead man."

The hunt continued, until Leah was quite lost. But the pull of the Moon, the unmistakable call, guided them on. Fifteen minutes later Leah hauled on the reins and halted outside a fire station. A different part of the city entirely, and still no sign of life.

Mags stopped also. "Is something wrong?"

The Moon was bleeding. A slash across the top horn of the crescent dripped lines of scarlet across the rest of the surface.

"That must mean Máni's been injured again."

Injured or dead? Leah spurred her horse on, but Mags, slightly ahead, held her thyrsus out to stop her. "Listen!"

A cold keening on the air, the long howl of something not remotely human. Mags's eyes shone.

"Something's happened!"

Leah pointed ahead and they continued, but slower, more cautious, letting the horses have their own pace. Their hides rippled with fear or excitement; Leah felt her own breath catch in her throat. She had to force herself to take a few deep gasps of air.

The howling stopped. No movement anywhere, no sound at all to show they rode through the midst of a mighty city. The buildings on either side had become mere black shapes, the cobbled road a dull grey path between. Gas lights burned without their usual roar. After ten minutes, the women arrived at metal gates set in a stone wall. A sign hung on them announced their location. London Field.

Inside the gates were grass and trees, an area of pastureland in the bustle of the city. Working class people regarded the place as their domain, distinct from West End areas like Regent's Park and Kensington Gardens. Here, during spring and summer, flowers grew in abundance. In winter, frost killed even the grass, but the park remained a popular site for winter games.

Now, to the eyes of the two women, the ground gleamed like metal.

"Do we go in?" Mags eyed the gates dubiously.

Leah nodded, dismounting and tying her horse's reins to the gates. The animals shivered; their instincts shied away from anywhere a wolf might prowl. Their nostrils quivered as they snuffed the air. Leah shook the railings and the gate opened, creaking a little. The lock had been cut, not smashed or prised, but completely sliced in two, the bright metal halves gleaming on the pavement. Leah picked up the cut lock and showed it to Mags as she dismounted.

"I didn't say we'd have fun doing this," was the only comment.

They pushed the gates open and looked into the park. Trees obscured the immediate view, but beyond were open fields, even in those modern times still used for pasturing stock on the way to London markets. Far on the other side the city started again with crowded buildings and tenements, but here all was quiet, just a slight wind stirring the cropped grass.

"How do you feel?"

Leah peered into the park, but saw nothing. How did she feel? The Moon still heated her body, and the sight of the fields made her shiver a little. *"Too quiet."*

"Yes. Oh well, let's see if they're in here."

Leah stepped forward a few paces, thyrsus held out. From behind her, a movement of air and a crash of metal. She turned, and found the gates closed. And no sign of Mags.

VII

Heat and light.

And a smell of shit.

Where am I?

Mags blinked at the light. The Moon, even larger now, a good yard across to her maenad eyes, hung like a bow in the sky. Craters and mountains stood out in sharp relief, as clear as on a paper map. And across it, a splatter of blood, dark red against the white.

A cool wind whipped at her hair and dried the sweat on her face. She stood on the roof of a house. On the opposite side of the street below were the gates of London Field, shut tight. Tiles slid under her feet. When she thrust out her thyrsus to steady herself, the end of the staff pierced the rotten timbers of the roof. A loud clatter as tiles fell into the street; another step and the whole roof might give way.

If I weren't a lady, I'd say a few choice words right now...

No sign of Leah. Mags opened her mouth to call but stopped before any sound issued. From behind her came the rasp of heavy breathing and the smell of sewage, strong even for London's fetid streets. She pulled her thyrsus from the beam it had sunk into and gripped it in both hands. Without moving her feet, she turned slowly at the waist to look behind.

I might say those words anyway...

The thing perched on the roof of the house vaguely resembled a human being if a human had four arms and a head of burning hair. Two of the hands held curved swords, and the other two were clenched into fists. The monster wore dark trousers and a body-hugging shirt. Its dark brown skin looked like old leather, wrinkled and folded as if several sizes too big for it. The eyes, dark pools that reflected its burning hair, regarded Mags coldly.

Mags took a step backwards and swayed as one of the roof beams bent under her weight. A loose tile skidded away and smashed a moment later onto the road below. Her stomach tightened at the thought of the same thing happening to her. The rotten roof timbers creaked as she turned slightly to glance down the slope. Remaining there on the roof was not an attractive option.

She lifted her right foot, which sent another tile sliding down to smash in the street. The creature took a step down from the rooftop, the tiles cracking under its weight.

Maybe she could lure it down and it would fall through instead. Whatever it was, it seemed focussed on her, only moving when she did. She put her right foot down carefully, the toe of her boot catching on a tile, but finding safe purchase. The thing took another step down. A timber creaked beneath its clawed feet. It paused, looking at where it stood.

Come on, a few more steps…

She faced the thing squarely now and held her thyrsus in both hands. If it decided to use the swords it would kill her in an instant; the heavy metal blades looked capable of slicing right through the thyrsus, not to mention her, without slowing down.

The creature paused, glanced down with eyes that shone in the light of its burning hair, and took another step.

Just six feet away from Mags it halted again. The stench of it made her gag; if she hadn't lived in London for so long, with its sorry excuse for a sewerage system, she might have been overwhelmed. The burning hair never seemed to be consumed, and the crackle of it gave off a palpable heat even over the Moon's warmth.

"What are you?" Mags managed to croak, not really expecting an answer. She licked her lips, felt them hot under her tongue.

Another step forward on the tiles.

With a loud crack, the roof gave way. The monster flayed its arms and howled as it fell through the rotten timbers. At the same moment, the roof heaved as a beam lifted right under Mags's feet, toppling her backwards down the slope. She let go of her staff and slid down headfirst, desperately clawing at the tiles as her head reached the edge of the roof.

Her thyrsus slid down past her torso. Mags grabbed it with one hand before it fell over the edge and then lay there, not daring to move again.

A crash from below. Had the beast fallen all the way to the ground inside the house? She tried to lift her head up to look, but the motion caused her body to slip slightly downwards. Any more movement would send her tumbling to the street three stories below.

Another few seconds lying there trying to work out what to do. Sounds came from the house, crashes and thuds and once a long moan that might have meant anything. The thing might be injured or just tearing the place up. Any people in the house would be in danger.

If only she had something to hold onto, she could twist to one side and prevent herself falling off. But her fingers found nothing but loose tiles. Even breathing seemed to shift the timbers under her. Slowly, Mags started to slide off the roof. In another five seconds, it would be all over.

A hand gripped her left foot tightly and hauled her back onto the roof. Another hand reached down, grabbed the front of her jacket and pulled her upright. Another two hands flashed razor-sharp swords in front of her eyes.

The monster had just saved her life.

"You will not die that way," it growled.

Fangs gleamed and a tongue emerged, purple, covered in what looked like boils. Carrying her in its hands as if she weighed no more than a doll, the being walked up the cracking, creaking roof and deposited her on the tiles at the top. Mags gagged with relief and fear.

She decided to remain seated, held down not only by the threat of the two swords within inches of her head but also the need to regain her breath. The creature reared above her, silhouetted by the enormous curve of the Moon, which seemed even closer now, filling half the sky, scarlet with the blood that flowed in streams over its surface.

"The Moon god dies," said the thing.

She found breath at last. "Where's Leah? Where's my sister?"

"That does not concern you."

"I'll bloody well tell you what concerns me. *Where is she?*" All the force and power of a maenad's rage went into her words.

The creature frowned, and for a moment seemed almost uncertain. "With my mistress," it said slowly. "Your sister will die tonight along with the Moon and yourself."

Mags tried to stand. A plan formed in her mind to leap down the hole through which the beast had fallen—obviously it hadn't gone very far and had climbed back out soon enough. But a sword came down and landed flat along her cheek.

"Stay!"

She stayed, putting one hand to her cheek that smarted from the blow. The maenad rage boiled inside, ready to be released. But to do so would surely be her death, unarmed against those blades it wielded so expertly.

"Who are you?"

The creature's two free hands went to the hips—apparently it could also appreciate human gestures, while the swords remained ready to carve her like a Sunday joint of beef.

"You are not worthy of knowing my name." It clashed the swords together.

"All right. So I don't know *who* you are, but I think I know *what*." Even under threat of death, Mags's mind worked well enough. The creature was not a god—she knew that sort a mile off. It was more like something out of Leah's witchcraft books, a being that should not be on Earth, that usually only came when summoned. "You're some kind of demon," she said.

The creature nodded. "You are clever. I am one of the Rakshasa. Strong. Fearless." He grabbed his crotch and leered. "Potent."

"Oi! That won't scare me. You think I haven't seen one of those before?"

The flaming hair of the creature burst into new heat as it surveyed the park across the road. Darkness shrouded whatever happened in there. Not even the fierce Moon could illuminate its interior.

"The fight goes well. Soon the Moon will die, killed by the Wolf, and all will happen as it should."

Mags searched her mind for information about the rakshasas. She knew they were part of the Hindu pantheon, and could take the form of any living thing, especially human. But how to defeat such a monster, what its purpose here might be, she had no clue.

"How did I get up here? Did you bring me?"

"Yes." It grinned, showing yellow teeth.

"I don't remember that."

"That is no surprise. You humans are weak, easily overwhelmed."

She let the comment go. "What are we doing here?"

"You will be sacrificed when the Moon dies. And then I shall devour you. Listen to the combat!"

"I can't hear anything."

"Their fight is not for mortals to hear or see."

"I'm not strictly mortal."

The eyes glared at her again, and Mags wished they hadn't.

Leah peered through the gates. No sign of Mags. No sign of anyone. No sound but the faint stir of wind along the street and the rustle of leaves on the trees.

The horses shifted a little, but didn't seem unduly frightened, so there was nothing out there with them. She rattled the gates for a moment, but they remained closed; the cloven lock still lay in the street outside, so some supernatural force held the gates shut. She was trapped inside, and although it would not be impossible to climb the wall, or even scale the gate for that matter, it would be hard avoiding the spikes at the top. The barrier had been built to keep people out; equally, it kept her in.

Mags had gone—presumably whatever had locked the gate had removed her as well, which meant it intended to separate them.

She turned and entered the fields. Beyond the belt of birch trees the pasture opened out. No grazing animals, just grass and bushes under the Moon. There had been no attempt to make the fields attractive to people, like nearby Victoria Park. This was a commercial area, and although people did use it during the day it remained largely undeveloped.

A sound to her right. A low keen, similar to that heard earlier. She held her thyrsus in front of her, searching for the owner of the voice. Only darkness in that direction.

Sound now to her left, like heavy breathing, and the flash of something metallic.

Leah stopped amidst the smell of hay. To the right, the low cry continued, almost like a wounded beast. To her left, coarse breathing. All around her, stillness and silence. She placed the butt of her thyrsus on the ground and waited.

The sensible part of her mind told her to hide, that being exposed here tempted the same fate as the unfortunate victims who'd already died. But Máni and the Wolf hunted each other now, so perhaps they would leave her alone. In any event, the only shelter was under the same trees from which the breathing and the howling came.

"Maenad."

The voice was young and full of warmth, a female voice, one with blood behind it, but a coldness of tone that Leah felt in her soul.

"Servant of a rebel god," the voice continued.

Leah could see no one, just hear a voice in her head, taunting her. One that knew her identity, her allegiance to Dionysus.

Something loomed ahead in the darkness, a small, slight figure, walking towards her through the field of grass. Leah raised her thyrsus as the figure continued to advance.

"Put down your stick, witch," came the voice. "It serves no purpose here."

The figure halted a few yards from Leah. Its form was plain now: a woman, perhaps Leah's own apparent age, long hair tied with two black ribbons that hung low over her simple grey gown. A long face, with eyes sunk deep, mere black holes under the high forehead. Her two pale hands were held out palm upwards, as if to show she carried no weapon.

Who is she?

"One who understands your thoughts."

Leah gripped her thyrsus tighter and instinctively took a pace back. No one could read her thoughts, not Mags, not even Dionysus. The curse of silence by Ahti had been so complete even her mind was psychically barred from others.

Who are you?

"If you have true knowledge, you will recognise me."

Stay back or I'll call upon my god.

No laughter, no word, could have shown more contempt than the thin smile that appeared on the woman's face. "After the Moon dies, so will you."

As a witch, Leah had often made animal sacrifices to call upon the favours of gods and spirits. The killings had sickened her sometimes but had been necessary. No power came without cost. The heat and scent of blood came back to her, memories of flickering candlelight and her chanting voice as she sliced the throat of a helpless animal. What she had never contemplated before was being the sacrificial victim herself.

More growls came from the trees on the right. The Wolf was in there, hunting under the white-hot Moon.

You are a goddess known to my master.

"You are quick in your deductions. I am not just any goddess, but one you should worship instead of that lame lord of oblivion."

If Leah had her grimoires, and her cauldron, and time and the necessary materials, and above all her voice, she might have conjured something to ward herself against this deity. But she had none of those things.

Only my faith.

"Your faith is nothing," said the goddess. "Now, await the outcome. Here they are."

A bestial, primal grunt broke into her thoughts from the right. Leah raised her thyrsus as the sound ceased. Someone emerged from the trees to her left, silver hair shining in the moonlight. Máni, sword in hand, with a long trail of blood down his leg. His trousers were ripped to shreds. But there was strength and determination in him yet; the blade rose firm in his hand. He saw Leah and gestured to her, but she could not understand his meaning. Then he looked beyond to the trees on her right.

Over there, emerging also from the darkness, the long, lean shape of Hati Hróðvitnisson, son of the Fenris wolf. More lupine than before, nude, with black hair rising from chest, back and arms, his face elongated into a muzzle. The eyes remained man-like, and gleamed. He, too, appeared wounded, a dark stain of blood on his left arm. Spittle dripped from his mouth as he howled again at the sight of his quarry.

Wordless, the two combatants charged at each other, and the ground thundered under their feet.

At the last second Leah realised she stood directly in their path and dived aside as they met. Dirt scraped her face as she landed on her side, rolling away from the clash of man and wolf.

From the goddess, watching from the other side of the combat, came a shout of joy.

Máni fought with his sword, which rose and fell with hammer-hard force. Hati responded with teeth and claws and moved like lightning to avoid the slash of the weapon. He leaped and dodged and every so often almost closed with his quarry, only to fall back as the sword came in time after time. Over both, the hot Moon cast a ruby glow on the scene.

Leah rose, thyrsus in hand, and watched as the combat continued. No way to intervene on either side. To step into that conflict would mean a swift death. But neither did she flee, standing and watching as the wolf attacked, and the Moon defended, in anger and ferocity.

She felt a presence beside her. The goddess, pale hands still held out, watched the contest, a smile on her face as if anticipating the death of either combatant.

"When the Moon dies, so will you," said the goddess. Leah saw a flash of light and a knife appeared in the goddess's hand, a katar with a short steel blade, and black handle and cross-pieces.

If I run, she will pursue me.

Hati found an opening as his opponent stepped back for a moment. Coming in low, head down, back arched to provide the impetus for a spring, he hurled himself at the god and latched his jaws around his sword-arm. Máni screamed as the teeth ripped into his flesh. The wolf hung on, legs finding purchase on the slippery grass, and wrapped his arms around the god. For a moment Máni managed to stay upright, until the weight of the Wolf brought him crashing down. Leah took a step towards them but halted as the Wolf's eyes rolled towards her. Máni howled again as the beast bit into his arm. The sword dropped from his hand and fell beside him.

Another cry as Hati tore Máni's arm off below the elbow. It threw its head back and in one gulp swallowed the limb, bones and all. Leah stared in horror at the god's mangled stump. A second later Máni lashed out with his left arm, grabbing the monster by its throat, squeezing with all his might.

A battle of pure strength followed. Hati could not remove Máni's hand and tried instead to lean in and bite his throat. With his left hand, Máni choked the Wolf, fingers straining on the beast's neck, his own teeth bared.

For a long moment, the two figures remained still as they strained and pushed and squeezed, neither able to defeat the other. Leah glanced at the sword, which had fallen beside the struggling bodies and wondered if she dared try to take it. At any second one or other combatant might free himself, and then she would be crushed or torn apart in the melee.

Hati's jaws closed on the god's throat. No sound came from Máni as the jaws closed and tore his throat out. Again the flesh disappeared into the monster's mouth as even now it obeyed its divine destiny to devour the Moon. And still Máni squeezed the Wolf's throat, preventing it from swallowing. Flesh hung from the beast's mouth; ichor sprayed from the god's neck, the thick liquid of the gods, red like blood but darker, more primal. Some drops hit Leah on her cheek; the liquid smelled of perfume, not iron, and was cold like the blood of a serpent. She wiped the stuff away. Slippery like oil.

Overhead, the huge arc of the moon dripped with gore.

Nothing but my faith remains. My faith in Dionysus. In myself.

In one smooth movement, Leah dived forwards, as if plunging into the sea. She cleared both bodies, rolled as she came down the other side. Her hand scrabbled for the sword in the cold grass, and her fingers fixed around the hilt.

The goddess hissed but did not move to strike with the katar. "Leah!" she cried. "The sword of a god is not for mere followers to use!" More words followed, an incantation meant to bind and disarm.

You cannot conjure me. Leah is not my real name.

She plunged the sword into the Wolf's side, pushing hard. The unearthly steel drove deep into the beast. Leah kept pushing until half the blade had penetrated the torso.

The beast fought on. It grabbed Máni's hand and tried to force his fingers apart, and with the other hand clutched its side where the god's sword skewered it. The jaws continued to snap and seek Máni's heart. But slowly the struggles of the Wolf lessened. Its eyes rolled and the tongue protruded. Gobs of god-flesh dropped from its jaws.

The beast collapsed and lay still over the other's body. Hati Hróðvitnisson, grandson of Loki, was dead.

With both hands, Leah tugged the sword free and raised it over the corpse, ready for an attack by the goddess. Knife against sword.

You have no power over me. You don't know my name.

"I can read your thoughts. I can find it."

A presence entered Leah's head, a seeking eye that scanned her mind, a squirming worm that burrowed deep. It might indeed find her name.

You want names? Then here are those of my sisters.

The names of dead maenads filled her thoughts. Some she had known, some she had only heard of. Dionysus had known them all. Elisha. Siobhan. Viola. Prija. Marie-Jeanne. The names flowed from Leah's long memory, and the ghosts of her maenad sisters were all the goddess found. Calpurnia. Berenike. Niloufar. Riya. Renata. Yende.

"These are not your names."

The goddess had no power over the dead, but the dead protected Leah now, at least from the spells it might pronounce. Dropping her thyrsus, she raised the sword high over her head in both hands. The black stones on the hilt gleamed in the bright moonlight.

But the goddess gave way no further, her lips moving as she continued to mutter spells, seeking one that would have effect, the worm still searching for her name.

A shaft of yellow-white light hit the goddess. She howled, covering her face. Leah strode in and slashed down with the sword, but the deity retreated into the darkness; nothing but the night remained. The worm in Leah's head disappeared.

She turned to look at Máni, who had his hand raised with light streaming from it. Even as a thin smile broke out on his face, his hand fell. The light faded.

Leah knelt and gripped his ichor-stained hand. The Wolf's corpse still lay on top of him, but neither he nor Leah had the strength to move it.

Thank you.

She stayed beside him until he died.

Mags stared at the rakshasa as it sniffed the air.

"What is it?"

"Shut up, turd."

She rose, balancing on the top of the roof, and strained to see into the park. Still nothing. But something had happened—she could feel the taut night air, as if a note of music, above the range of hearing, hung over the world. Something was ready to give way.

"The god is dead." The demon smiled and the arms holding the swords swung high. Mags backed off, almost losing her footing again. But the swords did not come down on her. "The god is dead. His fate is sealed!"

His fate, not hers. Mags hoped that meant something positive. But no, this thing had said she would be sacrificed, and Leah.

Time to go.

The edge of the roof might be close enough to reach before he cut her open, but then came the three-story drop to the ground, and not even a maenad could survive that. But there was the hole made by the demon earlier. Mags had no idea of what lay below, but it was her only hope. The rakshasa hadn't fallen very far, so maybe neither would she.

Worth a try, anyway.

The hole was about three large paces away, maybe four for her. Gravity would assist in clearing the distance down the slope of the roof. Then a jump into the hole and pray she didn't kill herself.

Pray? All right, no harm in that for once.

You hear that, Dionysus, my lord? I'm praying to you for once. Guide me.

The demon faced her in that moment, and raised both swords over its head, muttering dark words in an unknown language. Any second now, the swords would come down on her head.

She flung herself down the roof.

One step, and the demon slashed the air with the swords where Mags had been standing.

Two, three. Her boots slammed into the tiles, breaking and dislodging them. On the final step, the awful feeling of a beam giving way under her as she pushed off with her right foot and leaped for the hole, crashing through, feet first, into a room. The floorboards mercifully didn't give way under her. Eight feet, maybe a little less, but enough to hurt. She landed among rubbish and wreck from the demon's fall, rolling to soften the impact.

Through the hole, the demon looked down, swords swinging back and forth.

"Filth!"

She ignored it and looked for a way out in the gloom of the house's interior. A door in the far wall. As she reached it the demon jumped down into the hole. The boards shook at the impact, even as Mags turned the doorknob. Mercifully, the door opened and she ran through. But the demon had already reached her and swung a sword down to slam into the wall. The weapon sliced through plaster, brick and wood as if they weren't there. Mags took the stairs three at a time.

How did one fight a rakshasa? Leah would have known what to do, with her knowledge and her books. All Mags could do was run.

A landing at the bottom of the stairs. The demon followed behind her as she started down the next flight. She stopped half-way and turned, thyrsus held up. A beam of bloody moonlight through a broken window illuminated her face.

"Stop there!"

To her surprise, the rakshasa halted ten feet away and glared down. "Are you prepared now to be sacrificed?" it roared.

She shook her thyrsus. "Do you know what this is?"

The demon laughed. "A stick."

True; a stick topped with a ridiculous carving of a pine-cone. The thyrsus wasn't magical, it held no powers, but maybe it could be used to bluff.

"It's a holy symbol. I serve a god."

"So do many."

She held it upright before her. "The thyrsus of a maenad is like a cross to a Christian. A symbol of faith and divinity. Anathema to one of your kind."

"You serve one of the lesser gods. It matters not."

I was afraid of that.

What was a Hindu holy symbol? Again, Leah would know; Mags hadn't a clue.

The demon advanced, swinging one sword, holding the other above its head. The blades had sliced through the wall of the old house; her flesh, her neck, her spine would be no obstacle for them at all. She backed down the stairs, still holding the thyrsus out towards the demon.

"The Moon God is dead," said the monster. "Now is the right time for you to die also."

It halted under a beam of moonlight. In its gory glow, the demon's face stood out in sharp relief, as sharp as the mountains of the Moon. It turned its gaze to the light.

"The crescent moon is a holy symbol too," said Mags, as she continued to back down the stairs to the final landing, "to a follower of Allah."

The demon seemed mesmerised by the light, gazing at it with wide eyes. For a moment the swinging sword halted, and the other arms reached out towards the window as if to grasp the Moon in their claws.

Mags thumped down the stairs to the ground floor hallway. Blinded by the moonlight, she bumped into several objects, furniture perhaps, trying to find the way out. An outline of red light guided her, and she found the door handle with trembling fingers. Then the demon appeared, its flaming hair illuminating the hallway. Mags glanced over her shoulder and continued to tug at the door. The demon roared, and that sound contained all the hate, all the fear and suffering of Hell. Mags sobbed as she tried desperately to open the door.

At last it gave way and the familiar sight of an ordinary London street came into view. Outside, the Moon gleamed down, reduced once more to its normal size, without heat. The sight stopped her. The universe had returned to its natural state. Had Máni killed the wolf, or was it true what the demon said, that the Moon god himself had died?

A monstrous hand descended on her shoulder before she could run out. The heat of the burning hair struck her like a wall. The hand forced her down to her knees. She dared not turn around, dared not look at the thing which held her down with two hands while the other two raised their weapons high to strike.

Dionysus, aid me now!

Mags lifted her thyrsus and jabbed upwards over her head into the monster's face. The demon grunted. A quick twist and her shawl came off her shoulders. She slid from the monster's grasp and ran across the road to the gates of London Field. The horses had broken free of their tethers and were nowhere to be seen. The gates were shut and did not yield to her furious attempt to force them open. A quick glance over her shoulder at the house, but no sign of the demon. People in night attire appeared, attracted from surrounding houses by the noise. Mags continued to pull and push at the gates.

Wait a minute, I'm doing this wrong.

"Leah!" she called. "Leah! It's Mags! Are you there!"

Mags had a good set of lungs on her, together with a powerful breath control developed over years of having to reach the audience in the back row and penetrate the cloth-ears of stagehands.

"Leah! Time to go!"

A cry from across the road: for a moment Mags thought the rakshasa had appeared and attacked a bystander, but the scream was from nothing human. The roar of the demon itself.

It emerged into the street, swords swinging, seemingly bigger than before, its hair blazing high enough to reach the timbers of the house. Passers-by screamed and ran, while others stood frozen in fear. The demon ignored them and stalked towards Mags, fangs bared, leathery flesh putrid and oozing slime.

"I see you!"

Mags rattled the gates; no escape this time. There might be time to run along the street, but the demon would chase her and its powerful legs would no doubt make it faster than her, despite its bulk. Pressed against the gate, Mags shivered, awaiting her fate.

Something struck the gate bars a huge blow from behind her, forcing Mags forwards. The demon reached the pavement a few feet from her, but then another figure stood beside Mags, someone tall and slender, carrying the sword of Máni the Moon god.

In her other hand Leah carried her own thyrsus, which she handed to Mags. Leah raised the sword, stepping towards the demon, putting herself between her sister and the monster.

It paused, its own two swords wavering a little in its grip. Leah seemed tiny in comparison, a frail woman standing up to the gargantuan strength and power of the rakshasa. Yet she stood firm, sword gripped in both hands, mouth set in a fierce line.

But she had no words. Mags stepped beside her and yelled at their enemy, raising both thyrsi high. "Be gone! You cannot face the sword of a god, even one held by a mortal! Be gone back to your infernal regions! Leave us!"

The demon laughed.

"I can face any sword, held by a god or not."

And it leaped high over their heads, landing on the wall surrounding the park.

Across the street a crowd had gathered. Women screamed, men stared and tried to push people back. A few braver souls found stones and hurled them. One landed close to Leah's feet.

The demon leaped again, crashing to earth between Mags and Leah. It swung both swords at the same time. Mags fell backwards. The sword aimed at her sliced open the edge of her jacket but missed her flesh. The one aimed at Leah met Máni's sword with a ring of metal.

The god's sword knocked aside that of the demon, and continued into the monster's flesh, carving a long gash across its stomach. The monster howled and brought its other sword around, and again the weapon was parried by Leah, who followed through, slicing another gash across its chest.

Screaming, the rakshasa leaped once more, but this time away from the women. For a second it hissed at them, fiery hair bursting into even greater heat and light, and then it turned and ran, leaving only a twist of foul-smelling smoke in the night air.

Mags looked up at Leah, who looked as shocked as she felt. "Are you all right, sister?"

The crowd remained on the other side of the road, still unwilling to approach the gates where the monster had been. Mags stood up and gripped her sister's hand. "Come on, let's get out of here."

VIII

The rat sat back on its haunches and waved its forefeet in the air, whiskers twitching. The end of its tail almost dipped into the inkwell on Mags's desk.

"Go away!"

The rat squeaked, paws still begging.

"I've nothing for you!"

She lifted the animal down and set it on the floor, whereupon it scuttled across the boards of her loft-room and out through a hole in the wall.

Mags turned back to the papers spread out on her desk. Her ideas for the play had changed, and Harold was no longer cornered by the police. That bit of banality at least had been expunged. She nibbled at her pen for a while, dipped it into the ink, and began to write.

(An open place. Storms clouds gather in the background. HAROLD stands at the top of a cliff, staring up at the sky. A flash of lightning.)

HAROLD: A gathering storm, I see. Something coming. The heavens work against me, and there are gatherings in the nether regions as well. All right, let them come! I shall stand firm against the onslaught! I fear neither the gods nor the infernal legions! I am Harold Montgomery Stewart and I defy all supernature!

She paused and sucked on the pen again. This was good stuff! Melodramatic, suspenseful, and really opening Harold up as a character. Besides, she'd just figured out his middle name—it came to her in the heat of composition after nagging her for months.

Though the gods themselves oppose me, I shall prevail, for I have the truth on my side. I dwell among gods but have the heart and soul of a human being. That is my secret weapon.

(He draws his sword. Note: he has to get a sword somewhere in Act Two, Scene Three.)

She looked up at the shaft of moonlight coming through the window in the roof: plain old moonlight again now, the colour it should be, and the orb itself back to the right size. Not that anyone besides those immediately involved had noticed anything about it. No mention of anyone dead in London Field itself, neither man nor beast. The bodies of Máni and Hati had both vanished. People had seen the rakshasa, of course, but police had suggested that some criminal had escaped while dressed in a fancy costume, or a lunatic from Bethlem Hospital perhaps. The two women seen outside London Field, one carrying a sword, might have been part of some nefarious but unknown plot by foreigners. There had also been a note about an unfortunate man killed in Hackney Road. A man had been arrested in relation to the killing, although he continued to deny involvement.

The world could be overrun by gods and demons, and humans would assume they were pranksters in fancy dress.

"People are dumb," she said out loud.

She had seen little of Leah since they'd had a long talk in at the Stanthorpe the day after their adventure in London Field. The arrival of the rakshasas was no doubt significant, but they would have to wait for the return of Dionysus before they could ask him what to do. That a demon stalked the world was not alarming in itself— strictly speaking, the idea of demons had always haunted the fears of mankind. Succubi, incubi, the galla of ancient Mesopotamia, the rakshasa tales of the Hindus, the myriad denizens of Hell from a thousand pantheons, had always been feared. But for an actual rakshasa to take an active interest in the vendetta of two deities from another pantheon, to prepare sacrifices, that gave cause for worry.

On the positive side, Leah thought they had avoided Ragnarök somehow. Both Máni and Hati had died in the conflict, and Leah had told of the mysterious goddess who witnessed the killing, and who had threatened Leah herself. Another enemy. The Moon god's presence had not been a chance encounter; the barriers between Earth and the divine realm had been breached.

Trust Foxwood to take a holiday just when things became dangerous. Mags dipped her pen again and made some notes under Harold's half-finished soliloquy.

Why are the rakshasas involved in whatever is going on? When did Leah learn how to use a sword so well? Possibly took lessons for a play once. But that's stage fighting, not the expertise she showed against a demon. Ask her, and threaten violence if doesn't tell? When will F. return? He's been away ages now.

She re-read the notes and then Harold Stewart's words above them. Ridiculous stuff. She drew two diagonal lines through the script, sighed, and corked the inkwell.

The rat poked its nose out of the hole in the wall and stared at her.

"You'd better run," said Mags. "There's a storm coming."

SCENE FOUR

June 1852 and August 1855

MISTER FOXWOOD'S HOLIDAY

How can the past and future be, when the past no longer is, and the future is not yet? As for the present, if it were always present and never moved on to become the past, it would not be time, but eternity.

— St. Augustine of Hippo,
Confessions.

I

"Mr Foxwood, I am so glad to make your acquaintance."

The hand that Guang Jin held out to grasp Foxwood's own was wrinkled, with long blackened nails, as if its owner were a raptor bird rather than a man. And yet the rest of him appeared ordinary enough: black hair, rather long but neatly styled, a thin black moustache over a wide mouth, broad shoulders that hinted at considerable strength, enough muscle on the body to be evident under his dark, tailored suit. He looked closer to sixty than fifty, and although he sported a walking stick, he didn't lean on it for support.

"It is rather my pleasure, sir," said Foxwood, taking the hand and feeling unexpected warmth in its grip.

The man, who against all expectations looked neither Oriental nor particularly clever, smiled and showed a set of magnificent white teeth. Even Foxwood, divine as he was, had to acknowledge they were almost perfect in their straightness and gleaming purity. Perhaps they were fake, fashioned of porcelain and rubber.

A man cried out, followed by the heavy thud of a body hitting canvas. Foxwood glanced at two men in a boxing ring, both stripped down to leggings. One stood over the other who lay on the floor of the ring. Both men were bleeding from the nose, and the one standing had his bloodied fists raised as he stared down at his fallen opponent, daring him to rise. The other man shook his head, sending red droplets to the canvas, and held up an open hand. The victor reached down and helped him to stand. A third man, looking on dourly from outside the ring, threw a towel to each of them.

"Interesting," said Foxwood. "Do you train them?"

Guang Jin looked indolently at the boxers. "I pay Nicolai to do that, the man with the towels. They are a handy source of income when they win, and a liability when they do not."

He snapped his fingers and both men looked at him, chests heaving as Guang Jin spoke in Romanian, railing at the defeated man and giving sharp criticism to the other. Foxwood pretended not to understand the language. After a minute the men sidled away to their buckets of water. Two small boys came to assist with their ablutions. Nicolai spoke to them in short, stabbing sentences.

"Moraru, the defeated man, will not be with me much longer if he cannot learn to block," said Guang Jin. "He has yet to win a fight. I cannot afford to keep him, and he will go back to being a sheep herder in the Moldavian hills where I found him."

Foxwood wondered if that was not what Moraru preferred, if his daily keep here meant being beaten to a pulp. But he merely nodded and snuffed the scent of blood that remained in the air.

"Come, walk with me," said Guang Jin. "I would offer you some refreshment, but I am a busy man and must keep my appointments. Had I known you were coming..."

"My fault entirely," said Foxwood.

Learning about Guang Jin had not been a problem, for his status among the less reputable classes of Bucharest made him a known figure. Finding him had been more difficult. Some leads had proven false, one almost had Foxwood arrested, and other contacts had refused to discuss him at all. But the final lead, paid for at considerable expense, had ended at this dilapidated old building on the edge of the city, where Guang Jin trained his fighters—just one of his many business enterprises.

They left the building, the street front of which showed considerable damage. Rubble lay piled in the gutters, and the metal gate they passed through hung off one hinge.

Guang Jin nodded at the mess ruefully. "There is still damage around the city from the recent revolutions," he explained. "Wallachia and Moldavia wish to be united as one country, Romania, but some...well, they have other ideas."

What nationality was Guang Jin? Wallachian, or Russian, perhaps, or even English. Nothing about him gave away his origins. Foxwood watched him carefully as he shut the gate—a pointless exercise given its broken state—and tried to read the man. Centuries among humans had given Foxwood some insight into their eccentricities and foibles. He himself had sometimes tried to imitate them, more for amusement that anything else. This man, who had sold the Resurrection Box to Porteous Merriman, remained a cipher, whether through innate personality or some deliberate deception.

Guang Jin re-joined him, slapping dust from his hands. "Real estate is cheap here, especially when the building itself is falling down. I buy such places, renovate them if they can be saved, or knock them down if they cannot and sell the scrap, and then resell the land."

"You seem to have many initiatives," said Foxwood.

"And I know which it is that you desire to see me about. Something theatrical, no doubt. Your reputation proceeds you."

Indeed? That could be either flattering or dangerous, depending on what this man knew of him.

"Come, let's walk," and Guang Jin went so far as to place a hand on Foxwood's shoulder and indicate the way along the street with his other. "As I said, I have another appointment that cannot wait, but I'm happy to discuss—what are they, business matters?—with such a renowned man as yourself."

Another prickle of suspicion went through Foxwood. In London he owned two theatres, and around the world several more, or had shares in them under various names. No one, not even the managers of various banks with which he did business, had any suspicion of his full assets. His reputation in London did not amount to much. Many other theatres there had far greater status, and attracted more numerous and discerning customers, than the Lombard and the Gypsy. How then did this man, here in the far-flung eastern extremes of Europe, know of him?

"I hardly think—" began Foxwood, but Guang Jin had already started a rapid walk along the footpath. Foxwood caught up to him and they passed along a broad, almost deserted, street. The neighbourhood seemed chiefly residential, but here and there a coffee house or bakery or sweet shop peeked out from behind lines hung with washing, or bright blue, yellow and red flags. Old men, smoking thick, scented tobacco, lounged in doorways and regarded them as they passed by, calling out occasionally, "Bună seara." Dogs snuffled for scraps in the gutters and eyed them with more suspicion than the old men.

"I am not an easy man to find," said Guang Jin as they started up a slope of cobbled road, "so your efforts must have had some strong impulse behind them."

Since he had no idea where they were going, or how long it would take them to get there, Foxwood decided to come to the point quickly. "Porteous Merrimar."

The other man never broke stride, never sent any sharp look at Foxwood, but perhaps there was the slightest intake of breath, before he replied. "I cannot recall anyone of that name."

"An English illusionist," Foxwood continued. "He performed in my music hall a while ago. People found his act remarkable."

"I imagine so. Only the greatest artists appear in your halls, sir."

Flattery usually worked well on gods, but not today. Foxwood struck his cane hard against the cobbles as he kept pace with Guang Jin up the slope of the street.

"You are too kind. His act was fairly mundane in my opinion; even an employee of mine knew many of his illusions from being a former conjuror's assistant herself. But he had one act of legerdemain that received ecstatic response from the audience, and which seemed to defy explanation. A resurrection trick."

They reached the top of the slope and Guang Jin halted to pull out a spotted silk handkerchief and mop his brow, although the wind up there was chill. Two streets led off to right and left, but Guang Jin was in no hurry now. He indicated a water pump and walked across to it to fill a metal cup attached by a chain to the pump handle. After offering the cup to Foxwood, who declined, he drank.

"I assume despite your denial that you do in fact recall Mr Merriman, or at least his illusion."

"A remarkably perspicacious observation, sir. But you are right. I do recall him now, and what I sold to him."

Their gazes met. Hostility there, but something more, another emotion under the sharp light that Foxwood caught in the man's eyes. Amusement? If only his maenad Lucretia, who knew when people lied, were here; or Daphne, who could follow the man silently and spy on him. As a god, Dionysus had lost so much power. Dependency on his followers irked him as much as it did them.

"Merriman had a device he called the Resurrection Box," he said, again keeping his statements honest while watching the other man's body language.

"Yes." Guang Jin's eyes glittered as he returned Foxwood's stare.

"He told my employee that you had designed and built the box."

The man refilled the water cup and drank again. It clanked against the fountain's masonry as he set it back down.

"Your worker flatters me beyond words."

"That's true, because you didn't make it. It's not a thing of this world, and you know that. And I suspect, you know I am more than merely a theatre owner."

Cards on the table there. If Guang Jin did know he was a god, then the stakes had been raised high; if not, his remark was vague enough to explain away.

"Yes, I know."

The man glanced around. The few people who braved the overcast sky and high wind stalked by with collars up and hands thrust into overcoat pockets. A horse clopped by with no human leading it. No one paid attention to them, but Guang Jin eyed the passers-by carefully. Such a man might have allies lurking nearby, ready to come to his aid.

Foxwood leaned in a little, lowering his voice. "How did you come across the Resurrection Box? Who gave it to you? Or did you find it?"

"I have an appointment, sir."

"So you keep saying."

Guang Jin pointed to the building next to the water pump. A two-storeyed edifice of grey stone, fronted with rococo decorations and tall pillars, but severely damaged. "It is the greatest coincidence, then, that this is the building where I am due. Please enter with me and we can talk further."

Without using a key or knocking, Guang Jin entered the building. They met no one on the stairs as they climbed to a large room on the first floor. Rubble littered the front half of the space. A trompe l'oeil fresco on the ceiling, showing a flight of angels among clouds, gave an illusion of height. Thin sunlight came through glassless windows. Across the street a man sat in a chair behind a pile of cabbages, with a wooden box at his feet. A carriage rattled past. Two police officers walked by, pistols on their belts, hands behind their backs. A woman shuffled along, bearing heavy bags. Neither officer stopped to help her.

"Now," said Guang Jin. "What is it you wish to say?"

"You are not Guang Jin."

A grunt of amusement. "You are not human."

"I take a form that is convenient," replied Foxwood.

A smile made itself known under the thin moustache. "I take whatever form I wish."

"As I feared." Foxwood drew himself up, planting the end of the fox-head cane firmly on the worn floorboards. "I have followers in London who encountered a rakshasa demon a few months ago—I was away at the time, but they informed me of the encounter upon my return. You are a rakshasa? A shape-shifter?"

The other laughed. "I salute your intuition. We rakshasas delight in assuming any form, particularly human. I copied the form of Guang Jin before he died."

"Did you obtain the Resurrection Box from him?"

"No. He was a remarkable practitioner of the magic arts, but, as you surmise, not skilled enough to construct such a thing as the Resurrection Box. I acquired it from its maker, but that was not Guang Jin."

"Who, then? Osiris?"

"Let us change the subject. You say your followers met one of my tribe. That would be my son, Prince Geneth."

"Prince? Then you are a queen of the rakshasas?"

Guang Jin's eyes rolled back in his head until only the whites showed, and his mouth pulled back in a gleaming smile. His face changed, melting away as if made of water, and reforming into a different visage: a demon with dark eyes and pale skin. Yellow fangs appeared at the corners of the mouth. The brow wrinkled and a third eye formed in the centre, red and glaring. The man's clothes altered, the upper half disappearing to show two breasts, the lower becoming a red skirt that fell to the creature's knees.

The sharp tang of sulphur. Foxwood sniffed it disgustedly and lifted his fox-headed cane like a sword between them. "I see you now, rakshasi."

"And I you, Dionysus," the creature hissed, the words slithering like snakes from her mouth. The demon's third eye, independent of the other two, rolled in its orb to stare at him. Wings that had been folded against her back spread out, bat-like, covered in skin. "I am Queen Malanu Negrashi of the Sevenat, soon to be Mistress of the World, First of All Creatures. Why have you sought me out?"

"I'm concerned with your plans for humanity. Osiris attempted to garner souls as followers. If you imprisoned him in the Resurrection Box, you must have designs beyond mere mischief. And my followers encountered another malevolent deity, a goddess who refused to name herself. You are linked with her, too?"

Queen Malanu cast a cold eye over Foxwood. "You're a god who takes an interest in mortals. How unusual."

"What are you doing in this world?"

"*Our* world!" Spit flew from Malanu's lips. "It is ours as you well know, Dionysus!"

That was true. Earth had been the home of the rakshasas until the gods, freshly born from human minds, expelled them to give their charges free reign. But that only made knowing the rakshasas' intentions more urgent.

"You lived here, but the planet was no more yours than anyone else's."

"We were here *first*: before life had the audacity to struggle from the oceans onto land, we had mighty realms. The Earth belonged to us." The rakshasi took a step towards Foxwood, one fist clenched.

"I'm not here to argue about precedence." Foxwood stood his ground. "Why did you use Osiris? Why the Resurrection Box? You stole it from the real Guang Jin and sold it to Porteous Merriman. Why?"

"You are right: Osiris made the Box. Guang Jin was his only follower. But I desired it and took it from him. Merriman seemed a convenient way to resurrect the dead so that Osiris might have power once more. He would release Osiris at performances and the god could convert who he wished."

"And Osiris agreed to such imprisonment? He let you slay his follower, Guang Jin?"

"The Box is his realm, all he has left when bereft of worshippers. And I never killed Guang Jin; he died as any mortal might. After that, only the Resurrection Box sustained Osiris until he could find more followers. He had no choice but to depend on our help."

"Why would you desire to help him?"

"Not all your kind are our enemies. Join us. There are fallen gods who would rejoice in returning to power."

"That other goddess, the one who helped the Wolf kill the Moon—she is another of your allies? Who is she?"

"Help us reclaim the world and find out. You remember the war between gods and demons. You were there."

"Yes. We won and your kind was exiled beyond the borders of the universe."

"My tribe, the Sevenat, will reclaim the Earth for our own. The humans have been such bad custodians. Look at them: the lords of the world who fight and starve and suffer because they can't help themselves. Human beings are on the verge of a golden age of industry and science, and they continue to squabble and bicker."

Wallachia had been involved in a civil war, and other wars were even then being fought around the world. Dionysus could not argue with that. "But they are beautiful, too," he said. "Full of hope and kindness. It's there if you look."

"My tribe disagrees. We will teach them the true meaning of science and industry. We have plans." Malanu regarded him with her gleaming red eye. "I see your potential, Lord of Wine. That's why I allowed you to find me as Guang Jin, why I show my true form to you now, why I tell you these things. If the legends speak rightly, your mother was mortal. You have much influence among the people with your theatres and your lordship of wine. You can help us."

He shook his head. "That's true. But I don't direct humanity. They direct me."

"You have followers like any god."

"Yes." He pointed with his cane. "And your son the prince tried to kill them."

"Yes. He took the opportunity to find a mortal to sacrifice. He is rash sometimes. Over-enthusiastic. I apologise for his misjudgement. In the end he received wounds that will make him more discerning next time. But set that aside and join us now."

Foxwood thrust the temptation aside with the contempt it deserved. "The Earth belongs to humanity," he growled.

"Ah, such a pity. Then I shall kill a few of these people," she said, indicating the street, "just to demonstrate your inability to prevent me, to show I am more powerful than you. And then I shall leave."

"No! Leave now, rakshasi, and I will spare your life."

Malanu did not actually laugh, but the right-hand corner of her mouth twisted slightly, to reveal the base of the tusk. "You think I am one of the lesser? That you can kill me so easily?"

She had a point: he knew little of the rakshasas. Nor was he a fighting god, like Ares or Anat, just a drunk old man. Malanu might well prove the stronger in any test of power, which flowed from her almost palpably.

"Do not kill anyone," he commanded. "Depart."

The demon took a small pistol from skirt and pointed it at the cabbage vendor. "It is you who should leave, unless you wish to revel in their deaths."

"No!" Foxwood lunged forward and brought his cane down on the rakshasi's arm. He may as well have struck a wall for all she felt it.

"Watch how easily it is to stop the life of a human." She fired—the cabbage vendor clutched his chest as he toppled from his chair.

"Murderer!" Foxwood dropped his cane and made a grab for the gun with both hands, but in that instant she spread her wings and flew to the ceiling among the painted angels.

"A god who cannot fly? Pathetic."

The murdered man lay in heap. Several people gathered to help him. One man massaged his chest, another ripped his shirt open to expose the wound.

As with Osiris, Foxwood prepared to battle Malanu with whatever power he had, a contest of wills to dissemble the creature. Better do it now, before she became more potent.

The rakshasi dropped down to the floor and again aimed her pistol. A second man fell while crouching over the first trying to help him.

Foxwood flung his hands up, divine wrath surging through him, a silent command to desist and bend to his command. Queen Malanu merely smiled and flew through the open window, into the brazen sky and away. Seeing the demon emerge, the crowd around the man panicked. Some ran, others crouched behind various objects.

Foxwood ran down the stairs and out into the street. He bent over both crumpled forms of what had mere seconds ago been living men.

I am a god, and yet I can't bring them back to life.

"Has the devil come?" asked a bearded man brave enough to show his head around the edge of a doorway.

"Yes," said Foxwood. He rose and gripped his cane. "Yes, she has."

II

"More coffee, Joshua?"

Mr Foxwood nodded without looking at the tall, olive-skinned goddess beside him. The sound of coffee being poured into his cup seemed over-loud. Outside, the rain fell in a steady sheet, making the landscape—what could be seen of it—a flat, dull grey. Beyond the thin stretch of visible beach, the waveless Mediterranean Sea blended with the sky on a white horizon. A single boat passed, rowed slowly by a man in a raincoat. The south of France failed to rouse any early summer warmth that day.

"You're deep in thought," observed the goddess.

"Hmm."

His fingers curled around the carved fox's head on the end of his cane. The symbol's significance had palled lately, like the fox skull on his desk back in the Gypsy. A relic like himself.

"I'm old," he said.

Tamar Snake-Rider of ancient Colchis, goddess of the seasons and the glowing sky, captor of the Morning Star, chuckled while pouring herself a fresh cup. No milk or sugar: the coffee came hot, black and bitter. "So am I. So are we all. That's no reason to be morbid."

As the rowing boat vanished into the haze of rain Foxwood turned to look at her, removed his hand from his cane and placed it near his coffee cup.

"That man, now. The one in the boat."

"I didn't see."

"He'll live his life out and never know of us, or our problems."

She sipped her coffee, holding the cup in both be-ringed hands. The tattoo of a snake's head showed on the back of her left hand. The body of the serpent continued under the sleeve of her dress, the tail just visible above the high neckline. The snake's eyes gleamed gold. Foxwood knew they could see him.

"The man is mortal," Tamar admitted. "Mortals know little, and what they don't know they make into myth. Our problems don't concern them. Besides, your man in the boat has his own priorities: finding food, shelter and love. That's enough for anyone. Even a god."

"They'll have other problems if Queen Malanu gets her way."

The rain kept people indoors except for a few hardy souls who ventured out perhaps because they'd paid good money to come to the French coast and were determined to enjoy it despite the weather. A parti-coloured tent set up on the shingle optimistically offered sticky confections and lemonade to whomever might venture by.

The world of humans kept on despite everything. But what if the rakshasas chose to change it? Defeated ages ago and exiled to the outer darkness, they had had plenty of time to plot revenge. And he could not stop them. Two thousand years ago he had far greater power than now, able to work miracles with a few well-chosen words.

"Why now? The rakshasas have had millennia to take the world from people if they chose. And why kill humans in front of me?"

The Snake-Rider reached out to select a pastry from a small plate. The woman had a decent appetite, no doubt about that.

"To defy you?" she suggested. "To defy all gods who would resist? For pleasure? Who can tell the motivations of their kind?"

He remembered the arrogance of Queen Malanu. She had mocked his weakness, and rightly so. The time of the ancient gods had passed. Others had stepped in to take the place of the old pantheons.

"You need cheering up," Tamar said. "A walk on the beach might do you good."

"It's raining."

She looked out as if noticing the weather for the first time. "So it is. Does that matter?"

"I suppose not. You're a sky goddess, so you can stop it."

"Would you pick grapes at the wrong time? Would you stop a play halfway through the first act on a whim? It's raining because it's the right time for rain. Besides, I rather like it."

Foxwood smiled and emitted a shallow sigh. Tamar had once been worshipped in ancient Colchis, that was now Georgia, on the Black Sea. A different pantheon, a different culture. No worshippers for a long time—fewer followers now than himself, perhaps. But as long as people prayed to her for rain or shine, as long as they had faith that spring would follow winter, then she could remain in the world.

The lot of the fallen gods.

"We had our days, didn't we?" he said, at last picking up his cup and taking a measured sip. He grunted and added sugar.

"Goodness me, is *that* what's bothering you? Nostalgia? Really, Joshua, you're quite the end. Stop being morose."

"Why shouldn't I be?"

A long silence, broken only by the rain hammering on the roof of the restaurant.

"Once you could alter the seasons," he continued. "Never mind something as paltry as stopping the rain. You controlled the winds and the storms, painted the rainbow, guided the stars in their courses. For my part, I could create madness, bring forth the vine from the ground, lord of the dance and all things anarchic. People worshipped me by becoming outrageously drunk and morally uninhibited. I had hundreds of maenads and satyrs—now, a dozen only, in all the world. Of course I miss the old days. Don't you?"

"Yes, but they're gone."

He listened to the drumming rain. "In the old days," he said, and ignored the slightest breath of a sigh exhaled from the sky goddess, "we would not be sitting here drinking coffee like two decrepit mortals." He straightened up and winked her. "Two thousand years ago, I would have seduced you."

"Would you now?" The merest flicker of a smile gleamed like the sun between clouds. "Indeed, Bacchus, you are a bold one. Don't you recall I am the eternal virgin?"

Bacchus—he hadn't been called that in a while. "I was bold once. But my Greece has gone, and your Colchis. And now we drink coffee and eat pastries in a barbaric land."

"It sounds to me," said Tamar, and her voice slowed as she chose her words carefully, "that you wish to replace the modern world with past glories."

"Oh, no, of course not. Mortals may be irascible and unpredictable, but it's quickly becoming their world, not ours. Gods like Osiris may make occasional attempts to return to power, the rakshasas might wish to dominate in their turn. But it's not right. The world belongs to human beings."

The snake tattoo caught his gaze once more—reproach in the serpent's eyes? He fancied the mouth opened and its forked tongue licked out.

"Let's go for a walk," Tamar said, rising.

They paid for the coffee and descended a flight of stone steps to the beach. Foxwood held out his arm and she linked hers into it. He felt the snake squirm a little under her sleeve before it settled down once more. The rain continued but no drop reached them, a mild conceit of Tamar's. As they passed the tent selling confectionery, Tamar adjusted her red-ribboned hat and ran fingers through her coal-black hair. "Once," she said, "I had a fierce beauty."

He chuckled. "Once I looked good in a fox-skin and nothing else. One of my women pointed out recently I'd lost that part of my appeal."

"Why does she worship you, then?"

"I think worship is the wrong word when it comes to Mags."

Marguerite's headstrong nature often grated on his godly sensibilities, although he would never have chastised her for it. Leah had another destiny. Secretly he sometimes feared what she could do when roused. The other maenads each had their own strengths and vulnerabilities, although he only saw them during his absences from London: Lucretia in Edinburgh, Susannah in Italy, Maria in Brazil, Natsuko in Japan with her puppet theatre, and the other ladies scattered around the world. He really needed to travel more. If only he had the energy.

More companionable silence. They came to a clutter of rocks lapped by the unenthusiastic Mediterranean. Tamar relinquished his arm and sat down on a boulder, her booted toes lapped by salt water. Foxwood remained standing, regarding her.

At the other end of this sea, three thousand years ago, existed the civilization that had brought him into being. He'd always regarded the body of water as a whole world, thundering, dynamic, a thing worthy of the legends told about it. Now it washed at a woman's boots. He dug his cane into the sand like a sword and let it stand by itself. Tamar shifted slightly on her rock.

"You've told me of your meanads' encounter with a rakshasa in London, one with a head of flame," she said. "Your adventure in Bucharest confirms the demons are up to something."

"There's more," said Foxwood. "When my maenads told me of the demon in London, they said they also encountered two deities. The Moon god Máni came seeking help, and I wasn't there to give it to him even if I could. And when he died, Leah was threatened by a goddess who could read her mind. My maenads were to be sacrificed to her by the rakshasas."

"Which goddess?"

He kicked sand into a little pile with the toe of his shoe. "I don't know, but I have my suspicions. It's clear she's helping the rakshasas. They've already sought to manipulate events through an alliance with Osiris. Malanu said her people had plans. She asked me to join them." He felt the need of a drink and contemplated creating a bottle of wine and two glasses, but the coffee still churned in his stomach. "There are gods who harbour resentment against mankind. I was lucky with Osiris. He's now a prisoner in one of my theatres."

"He must resent that."

"I don't care what he thinks. It's his own little world in there. He created it, a boxed kingdom. But my maenad Leah drew a picture of the goddess who witnessed Máni's death—the sketch reminded me of Lilitu. Someone like her would certainly be up to mischief."

"Lilitu? I don't know her."

"I never met her, but a nasty piece of work by all accounts. The goddess of demons."

"She sounds fully qualified for the alliance, then. If the rakshasas are making a bid for the world, then we should find allies among the gods to defeat them."

"But who? I trust you because we go back a long way. But who else?" Most of the old gods had pushed themselves beyond the limits of the world. Those, like he and Tamar, who clung pathetically to the world of men, had no fight left in them. "Demons have always dabbled in men's affairs behind the scenes. But now they interfere boldly."

"Perhaps we need to be more vigilant."

"What do the demons imagine, that they can rule the world?"

"Why not? They did once before." Her face became grave as she stood up. "You must come with me."

A wind from the sea bent the rain inshore. No water reached them, but the wind did, flapping the tails of his frock coat and wafting Tamar's hair.

"Where?"

"We should consult the Wyrd." On her arm, the snake head blinked its eyes. The tongue flicked out and back.

Tamar's simple words chilled Foxwood. The Wyrd had many names in many cultures: the Fates, the Norns, the Weird Sisters. The beings that wrote the story of the world. At least, augury had been their original function. Now, like the gods, their powers were held in check by other forces, but they still had meaning and significance in the minds of the forgotten lords of the universe. The Wyrd could prophesy the doom of the world, if they wished to, and in so doing might reveal the plans of the rakshasas and any gods who allied with them. But there were more than simple auguries: they could reveal or withhold knowledge at a whim, play on fears and hopes, manipulate even the gods if they desired.

The breeze felt cold on his skin as he said, "Why do you need me? You could consult them without my help."

Her hand reached out to touch his. A thrill of power, just a little passed between them, one to the other and back again. Tamar smiled. "You're afraid to meet them?"

"You aren't?"

"Our friendship goes back many years, Joshua, an acquaintance I've always treasured. And you mentioned if you'd been younger you would have seduced me. I like that thought, even though it's one doomed to fail. I have to trust someone, and you still have some credit among the mortals. Your maenads adore you. You still have earthly responsibilities: wine and the theatre. It gives me hope that you want mortals to continue."

She put her hand on the sand and the snake emerged slowly from her sleeve, green and gold, white underbelly, red eyes staring about as the triangular head turned each way.

"Ghame will take us," said Tamar the Snake-Rider.

Foxwood chuckled but stepped back as the serpent slithered towards him across the damp sand. "Can he bear us both? I may not have much flesh to my bones, but he is a little small."

"Of course." She picked the snake up and whispered to it. Foxwood had the odd feeling that it stared not at him, but at something over his left shoulder. He looked, but only the flat beach and the grey drizzle of the rain could be seen. The confectionery vendor had apparently decided the weather was too bad for business and worked at lowering the front part of his tent.

"Come. Take hold." Tamar held the snake in front of her.

The serpent hissed as Foxwood touched the scales of its back. They felt surprisingly soft and warm for the skin of a reptile.

The world faded, the shingle bleached away, the Mediterranean swirled into a bland mix of colour.

They stood in the shadow of stone walls that rose into the sky.

Foxwood let go of the snake and brushed down his frock coat. Not that it had any dirt on it, but instantaneous journeys always made him feel slightly uncomfortable, as if the space between locations was like Grit Lane, dusty and shabby.

Tamar held out her arm and Ghame slithered back up her sleeve, its head emerging after a moment and settling back into a tattoo.

No sign of rain, just worn stone walls that enclosed on all sides, one broken with an opening that might have been man-made but had partly collapsed and filled the gap with rubble. Grass and bushes grew on what had once been the floor of a room. The castle had not been occupied by men for an age. Over one of the walls he could just sight dark mountains. The air smelled of wildflowers.

"The Castle of Ortega," said Tamar. "In the Pyrenees. Spain is not far that way."

"The Wyrd is here? I thought they were in Germany somewhere."

"They move. It's not safe."

Sometimes Foxwood regretted his self-imposed exile. Much happened in the universe without his knowledge.

They passed through the gap in the wall and came to a bare slope that fell sharply down to a gully. Saxifrage and sandwort bushes dotted the mountainside, offering a pretty prospect but poor purchase to climbers.

"Watch your step," warned Tamar. "Down and to the left."

She led the way, balancing perfectly on the slope; Foxwood used his cane to help him on some of the more treacherous parts. They had cleared the castle walls and now walked on the bare rock of the mountain. At the bottom, where the gully flattened out a little, they found a hole behind a large boulder.

"In there."

He fitted fairly well due to his thinness; Tamar had slightly more trouble squeezing through the gap in her day dress. Inside a tunnel opened up a bit more and led down. Dirt covered the floor; the walls were hard granite. He touched the right-hand wall: cold, smooth lines of cut stone.

"Who built this?"

"It was part of the old foundations, a bolt-hole for the occupants if the castle was taken. There used to be another entrance from inside the keep, but it has long since collapsed. We came in what was originally the exit."

Mankind never ceased to fascinate Foxwood. Able to accomplish such things as the castle and a secret tunnel with labour, and yet unable to hold onto beliefs for more than a few centuries. Proud, vain, war-like, yet also capable of art and music. That was why he continued with his two London theatres—he could observe all the oddities of humanity without having to search for them.

At the bottom of the slope, they entered a room and an almost palpable darkness. He and Tamar could see well enough with their divine eyes, but there was hardly any need since the room contained almost nothing.

"There has been fire here," said Tamar.

Scorch marks on the walls and the tang of char and ashes.

"Torches for the Wyrd to see?" he suggested.

"Not in those positions. Besides, have you forgotten? They're blind."

Perhaps a battle had been fought here when the castle had been occupied, one of the myriad conflicts of human history. The room led into another passage. The first had been meant for defence, to confound attackers who located the secret exit. The passage here led straight into the mountain for a good while. They had to be directly under the castle now. They arrived in another room, and here Foxwood could feel a presence before seeing it. A form lay against the far wall, a bundle of clothing perhaps, but as he drew closer under the low ceiling he saw a hand and a face belonging to a person or creature, unmoving.

"They're here!" Tamar knelt beside the form. Foxwood held back, staring as the goddess removed part of the cloth covering it.

Some things could surprise even him. This was a sight perhaps for a circus freak show, or the field of battle after the war had finished, a shattered, monstrous travesty. He saw at first little more than a head, dull grey flesh pulled tight over the skull, eyes too large for the head, with huge pupils. A long nose ended in a single nostril, the closed mouth lined by black lips. As the head moved slightly to one side, another appeared, and another: three semi-human heads under the single set of clothing. A hand reached out to push the cloth down. A torso, grey and wrinkled, with two bare breasts like collapsed balloons. Two arms. On either side of it, two more shrivelled bodies, all in the same shapeless clothing.

The Wyrd.

"They are injured," said Tamar, and indicated a blotch of dark blood on the first one's stomach. Another wound on the second. The third lay unmoving, eyes closed, breath coming in shallow gasps. "Who would attack the Wyrd?"

"It makes no sense to try and kill them—they're outside of time," said Foxwood. Perhaps the attack had not been to kill at all. Revenge might still be sought on beings that knew the future but only revealed what they wished.

Tamar touched the cheek of the liveliest head, the one first seen. The second opened a blind eye but did not turn to face her. "Who did this?" Tamar asked.

All three then opened their mouths, showing black teeth. So old these things, these hags, these speakers of fate. Older than Foxwood himself, older than any god. A hiss of breath came from the three, nothing more.

"Who did it?" persisted Tamar. "The rakshasas? Please, we must know."

Blind eyes rolled in their sockets, turning completely around to show blank white, gazing inward to see the things that would be. The mouths spoke in unison, one voice, three mouths, the same tone, the same pitch, identical words.

"The price shall be paid."

Tamar looked at Foxwood, who shrugged.

"Who attacked you?" she asked.

A second while the creatures gazed into fate. "Those that would conquer."

Obvious, and not much help. Foxwood examined the injury to the Wyrd in the middle. The open wound pumped dark ichor onto the floor where a dark puddle already lay. He looked into the pool of ichor and saw movement. Something above him, reflected in the liquid? No, nothing there. He looked back into the spreading pool.

"There!"

A glimmer of movement, a face, the beat of heavy wings.

Tamar glanced at the ichor. "I see it."

Something large, anthropoid, a faint shadow within a roiling cloud.

"What is that?" Tamar peered into the pool.

The dark form grew larger as if approaching them. Black cloud swirled. A flash of lightning scored the background. For an instant the thing's face became visible, a twisted visage, tusks emerging from the mouth. Wild black hair. A third eye in the forehead. Then darkness again.

"Her again," said Foxwood. "Queen Malanu Negrashi." He chuckled sourly as lightning flashed again. "Suitably melodramatic theatrics, but more illumination needed downstage."

A moan from the Wyrd. They closed their eyes and the middle one placed both hands over her gaping wound. All three mouths opened again. "The time shall be done again."

"What are you talking about?" asked Tamar.

But Foxwood knew it would be useless to ask for clarification. "We'd better go," he said, rising to his feet. "The Wyrd never reveal more than they wish, and often less."

"We cannot leave yet," insisted Tamar. "I would now more, and the Wyrd are wounded."

But the Wyrd sat up slowly, all three together, the robes slipping further off to reveal their pale grey bellies. Long white hair fell from the hood that covered their heads. Their wounds had closed, the ichor had ceased to flow. Even more slowly they rose to their feet, still huddled together under the one set of clothing.

"Welcome back, sisters," said Foxwood.

The central face gazed at them, hands moving as if in time to music. The third face, the one with closed eyes, opened them and groaned, a sound that seemed to come from the depths of the Earth, so deep it was.

"The she-demon has gone," said the first face. "We live again." Something like a smile might have passed across all three faces, but the eyes remained sad—the sisters knew the ultimate doom of the cosmos. Whatever else happened between now and then could not alter that inevitable entropic nothingness.

"Tell us about the attack," said Foxwood. "Did you not foresee it?" The pronouncements of the Wyrd were not inevitable. Future events would only come to pass if nothing were done to prevent them. Means could alter ends. The Wyrd merely announced, it did not declare. If they foresaw their own fate, then they could have taken measures to prevent it happening.

"It came from beyond our sight," said the first face.

"One shall bring flame," said the second.

"Who?" Tamar took a step closer to the Wyrd.

"The voice will come," said the third.

"Why did the demon attack?" insisted Foxwood. "Did she take something?"

The Wyrd bent their heads and seemed to whisper together, muttering words that did not pass beyond their own ears.

"The future," one said at last. "She wished to take the future."

"But not for herself, for another," said the second.

"And then she attacked," uttered the third.

"Show us the future!" demanded Tamar.

The eyes of all three heads rolled back to show nothing but white, and the fingers on the painfully thin hands seemed to clutch and claw at things unseen.

"There is a price," said the third face.

"There is always a price," said Tamar.

Foxwood shivered. Everything existed in proportion. The price would be proportional to the status of the person seeking enlightenment. A mortal daring to foresee the future would pay a price heavy enough—a god, more so. And two gods? He lifted his stick and pointed at the withered women.

"You have seen the power of those who would oppose you. She did not kill you—that she can't do. But you have been given a warning, and so have we." He turned his stick on Tamar, who regarded him with a wary eye. "Queen Malanu meant to find out the future, perhaps, but also to alert us to her presence. Not good tactics."

"Unless she has already won," said Tamar. "Perhaps she has seen the future and let it come to pass."

"But the future can be changed. The Wyrd only warn."

"Then their warning failed."

"Name your price," he commanded. "And tell us the future of the world."

The second face opened its mouth, but only to laugh. "The price is never named before the prophecy is given. Promise to pay or forgo any revelation."

On Tamar's arm, the snake hissed and writhed, awoken instantly to life. It slid off her flesh, all bright green and yellow scales, eyes alight with fire, and slithered across the floor to the Wyrd. The women backed off, hissing in their turn, all three mouths open, all three tongues extended as if in mockery of the snake's voice. The reptile reared up as if to strike, but Tamar cried out: "Don't harm them!" The snake turned jewelled eyes on her, muscles pulsing and quivering down the length of its spine. The goddess held out her arm. "Return!"

It hissed at her. Foxwood raised his cane to ward off the creature but held back from striking it. The snake was not his to command or to punish. For a moment the beast wavered, the Wyrd on one side, a dark bundle of hideousness, and the faded goddess on the other, holding out her arm and almost pleading her servant to obey. Then, reluctantly, the snake condescended to wrap itself along her arm once more, sliding under her sleeve until only its tail appeared on her palm. Its head did not emerge from her collar, as if sulking.

"Your serpent fears," said the third face. "Do you?"

Foxwood glanced at Tamar, the feel of sweat on his brow. "Yes," he said. "We fear. But we will pay the price."

"Then we will show you what may come."

In the gloom of one corner they saw a table covered with a dark purple cloth on which stood a crystalline sphere on a wooden stand. If he hadn't appreciated the seriousness of the moment, Foxwood would have been disappointed. A crystal ball—any petty fortune teller could use such a mundane prop.

Except this crystal ball really did show the future.

"Step forward," said the first face. "Place your right hands on the sphere. Both of you."

With all the dignity he could muster, Foxwood bowed to Tamar and they stood on either side of the table, placing their hands on the crystal ball. A sensation of unutterable cold, of primordial ice, came over him. Then warmth flowed from the goddess's hand into his own, and he felt glad of her presence.

The Wyrd, still over against the wall, raised their hands in the air. Even then, Foxwood winced a little at the theatricality. In the Gypsy the orchestra would have played a dramatic minor chord. "Go to the future!" called the Wyrd, and the room faded.

III

Foxwood stood in his office at the Gypsy, but hardly recognised it. The old desk had gone, exchanged for a monstrosity of black metal. A human skull sat in the place of the vulpine one. The impressive shelves of books behind his desk remained, but every book was different, and one shelf held only stacks of old newspapers and journals. The shelves no longer surrounded a portrait of Queen Victoria; stains on the wallpaper showed where a picture had once hung.

To see what would happen, he conjured a glass of merlot into existence. It tasted peculiar.

I'm the god of wine. Surely I can do something to make it better.

He tried. No good. Watery, insipid, uninspired. His powers were weaker here in the future.

The clock on the wall showed ten in the morning. Sounds of preparation from the theatre below told him a matinee would start shortly. "What's the date?" he said aloud.

The view from the window had changed as well. It was still Grit Lane, but directly opposite, where the Lombard Theatre should have been, were only a broken wall and a pile of rubble. A glimpse of Hotspur Street could be seen through the wreckage. He recalled the broken buildings in Wallachia when he had visited Guang Jin—the same ruin of war, the same pathetic aftermath of fighting. Foxwood had no knowledge of what had happened to Sir John and Lady Rowley, or if they were still alive. The Lombard Theatre ruined, yet the Gypsy still stood. Questions buzzed in his mind.

At the Collingwood Road end of the lane rose a marble statue of a tall, slim woman with long hair bound with two black ribbons, holding her arms up and out as if to embrace the world. A black dog crouched at her feet. Around the base of the statue were smaller figurines of serpents, and carvings of poisonous plants. As he had feared: Lilitu, goddess of demons. A troublemaker from the dawn of time. So it was she who had been involved with the death of the Moon, who worked with the rakshasas. Typical of her meddling ways.

Above the buildings on the far side of Collingwood Road, black smoke rose into a sky already heavy with dust and yellow light. From the edge of perception came the boom and roar of war. Was London under siege, or perhaps the whole of England?

The door squeaked open and a woman entered. Auburn hair, bound up tightly in a severe bun, freckles, and a long nose, on which perched silver-rimmed spectacles. Thirty years old perhaps. The gold ring on the first finger of her right hand confirmed the sudden thrill that went through him: the woman was a maenad, but not one from the time he had left. A follower in the future.

"Master!" she cried. "You're here."

"Yes."

"Only…I thought you'd…"

"Gone? Yes, well. I came back."

The Wyrd had brought him to a future time when was known to be away from the Gypsy. He would need to be cautious. Somewhere roamed his future self, perhaps a different persona to what he was. Time changed even the gods.

"Excuse me for my intrusion," said the maenad. "I came to get the street key." She indicated a brass key that hung on the edge of his desk. Sounds from below revealed the staff were preparing for another show.

"Yes. Of course."

"I didn't mean to…I didn't think you were here."

"It's all right."

What was her name?

A long look between them. Should he reveal he was not her present master, but one from the past? This world had things wrong with it: the Lilitu statue, the black smoke, his diminished powers. Could he trust this woman, maenad or no?

"Thank you," he continued. "Um…what's the date?"

The faintest sign of a frown appeared on her face. "The twenty-first of August, master."

"And the year?"

The frown deepened. The barest hesitation before the response. "1855."

"Thank you. By the way, have you seen Mags?"

The face went blank again. "Who?"

Something cautioned him not to enquire further. The woman removed the key and clutched it tightly, eyes blinking behind her spectacles.

"Nothing," he said and drained the glass of disappointing merlot. "Return to your duties."

The woman disappeared as quickly as she had come.

So many questions he had to ask her, but again the doubt as to whether she could be trusted arose. No knowledge of Mags. That was a sign of something very wrong. Mags had been the Gypsy's maenad ever since he'd owned it, had hardly been more than a few blocks away from it in years. And yet this new maenad had never heard of her. August 1855. Slightly more than three years in the future. Much change in and out of the Gypsy. He'd give a good deal to have Mags's round face appear in place of this skinny woman's.

"Mags?" he said aloud, just to hear her name. "Leah?"

He put the wine glass on his desk and went downstairs to the Gypsy's backstage. The curtain was down and beyond it could be heard the shuffle of feet and scrape of chairs as the audience came in. Something was wrong. There was no high-spirited chatter, no coarse greetings or laughter. At a matinee performance the food vendors should be working the audience already, but their friendly shouts were absent. No sound of the five-piece band tuning up.

He walked across to the stage manager's desk. A new man sat there, talking to another man dressed in a dark, tailored suit. Where were Mr Simm and Fred Bastable? Both men stopped their talk and nodded to him as he approached.

"Good afternoon," he said.

The men made appropriate noises, no doubt wondering why the boss approached them minutes before the curtain was due to go up. Strictly speaking, Foxwood had no authority once the auditorium opened to the public. The show was the stage manager's responsibility.

"Is all well?"

The stage manager made a small noise in the back of his throat. The other man said, "As well as expected, sir, with the war and all."

"We weren't expecting you back so soon, Mr Foxwood," said the stage manager. "You said you'd be away quite some time, and it's only been a week."

"Yes. My business didn't take as long as I thought."

"Did you see the fighting, sir? Any reports? The papers don't say nothing, as usual."

"Er—no. Nothing new, at least."

"I heard there's been some scrap over near Bristol."

"I didn't go that way."

The stage manager looked behind Foxwood. "Clementine!"

The auburn-haired maenad came across to the desk, saw Foxwood and cast her gaze down to the floorboards.

"Did you clean in the gallery?" demanded the stage manager.

"Yes," she said. "Just this morning."

"I hope so. Got a special guest today, Mr Foxwood." He touched his cap significantly. "The Countess of Downham."

"Indeed? Then I'm sure Clementine did a good job of cleaning in preparation for her visit."

The look on the stage manager's face seemed to indicate that Clementine doing anything even approaching a good job would be an accident.

"Well, carry on then." He made a show of taking out his watch and inspecting it. "Nearly curtain time. Clementine, come with me please."

They re-crossed to stage left. A scene-shifter went by with a wooden crate—one of the old stage-hands from years past, so not all the staff were new.

"Who's our guest?" he asked.

She frowned. "Mister Callow said, master. The Countess of Downham."

It was not unknown for nobility to visit the Gypsy, although certainly unusual. Most toffs preferred the opera or legitimate theatres of the West End to the attractions of the two less reputable establishments he owned. However, something didn't ring true about this Countess. Despite his commoner status, Foxwood had rubbed shoulders with a few peers in his time. No memory of a Countess of Downham—or an Earl for that matter.

"Has she been here before?"

She gulped air and blurted, "I don't know, master."

"Stop calling me 'master'. My name's Mister Foxwood, or Dionysus, as you know very well."

"Yes, Mister Foxwood." The woman glanced down at the floor, her fingers twisting a delicate lace handkerchief. Her words came rushing out with all the speed of a contrite confession. "I'm sorry, master. I thought you knew she was coming. Mr Callow told me you asked her personally. I tried to ask him about her, sir, but he never tells me anything."

He had to trust her. She was a maenad after all, and only he could have made her one. At some time he must have thought her suitable for the role. Such a decision did not come lightly.

"Of course," he said, keeping his voice even. "My memory isn't what it was, my dear. Come with me."

"I have to do the curtain..."

"Not yet you don't. Five minutes."

They went to the stage door and looked into Gimble's booth. A strange doorman, too, a young man in striped shirt, black vest and bowler, reading a magazine. No sign of Tom Gimble. No tapestry on the back wall.

"The tapestry..." he said before he could stop himself.

Clementine stood away from the booth, or perhaps it was the doorman she avoided. He smirked at her the same way the stage manager had. Then his gaze followed that of Foxwood to where the tapestry had hung. "Lots more room now with that horrible thing gone."

"Yes, I guess so."

He walked over to Clementine and spoke quietly. "Listen to me. I'm going to have a long talk with you after this performance. I don't want to take you away from your duties. That might attract suspicion. I'll return after the show. Meet me in my office then."

She curtsied and as she rose looked him straight in the eye for the first time. Yes, something there all right. A smouldering fire deep inside. The maenad rage could be ignited if necessary even in this pale wallflower.

He raised his voice for the benefit of the doorman. "I'm leaving for a while. If anything goes wrong..."

The doorman chuckled. He probably expected him to say that if anything went wrong it would be Clementine's fault.

"...make a note of it."

"Yes, I will. Er...are you going that way?' She indicated the stage door.

"Shouldn't I?"

"Well, you usually avoid the lane, because of..." The flick of her eyebrows might have meant anything. "I mean...you know."

He smiled as if he understood. "Well, today's different. I must go, but come and see me after the show. Just do your job and no harm will come to you."

She retreated backstage. Foxwood hesitated at the closed stage door. Why did he not usually go out this way? Only one way to find out. He opened the door quickly and hurried down the steps. Without glancing at the lane, he looked up at the gargoyle.

It wasn't there.

Leah was.

Even in stone, the woman had a rare beauty. Even covered in barnacles and pitted extrusions of coral, her face had the same splendour of the real Leah. The mouth, slightly open so the tongue could protrude through, still had the firm line he remembered. The long hair hanging down either side of the face would still be as fetching draped over her shoulders. But her naked, oyster-adorned body, squatting in the same pose as the gargoyle, was obscene.

"Oh, Leah." He swallowed rapidly, unable to turn away from the ghastly sight. Blank stone eyes stared back. He wanted to say something more comforting, but what words could possibly succour her now?

For it *was* Leah, not a statue. No doubt about that. Leah transformed into shells and coral. He took a handkerchief from his breast pocket and held it over his mouth.

Oh, my dear. I'm so sorry.

What was his future self thinking, to let this come to pass? Mags gone, Leah turned to stone. His other maenads…well, where were they? Scattered around the world as usual. Perhaps his future self was off visiting them.

Or hiding.

This must not happen.

His feet raised dust as he stalked along the lane away from Leah, away from the wreckage of the Lombard, and came to the back of the Drum and Fiddle. Two corpses lay there, both male. No sign of wounds upon them, but quite dead, lying against barrels of ale. Someone might eventually move them, or they would continue to rot there. He could do something about the bodies, but such a move might anger whoever had killed them. At the foot of the statue of Lilitu he turned into Collingwood Road and strode along, not looking at the people, not looking at anything.

Only three years into his personal future. Three years, and the world so changed. Queen Malanu Negrashi had made good on her threat. Even now the war raged. London had fallen. Where else? He tried to recall what he knew of the rakshasas from the long-ago war between Heaven and Hell. They were certainly not foes to admit to any defeat. Malanu had mentioned her tribe, the Sevenat. Were there other rakshasa tribes involved?

After a long time, during which many unhappy thoughts passed through his mind, he became lost in the city. Perhaps he'd meant to lose himself—he should have stayed and watched the show at the Gypsy, to see the anticipated guest. The Countess of Downham might be Malanu. He'd left Clementine to face her—not a loyal move on his part. Perhaps even now he should return and confront the creature. But some other impulse kept him walking on.

Why had his future self allowed this to occur? Weakness? Fear? But the Wyrd only showed the future, they didn't explain it. He could observe, experience, sense, but not necessarily understand. Mags wouldn't have tolerated the changes for an instant. Mags would have...But there was no Mags.

He walked on, lost in thought, eaten up by doubt and guilt.

IV

Since so few people now worked at the Gypsy, Clementine had a lot of different jobs to perform. The matinee performance that day was no exception: the artists required help setting up their acts; Matthew, the lad who had replaced Fred Bastable as the master of ceremonies, demanded his dram of scotch whisky before he went on to announce the acts; and Clementine would also have to raise and lower the curtain, a heavy job assigned to her because of the lack of rope-men who normally did the hefty work.

As always before a performance, she spent a few minutes in the Gypsy's kitchen. This had few comforts, a stark grey-walled chamber which the acts avoided, given that the room was colder than their dressing rooms. That was why she chose the place, to have a drink of water and calm her shaking hands in private.

They shook every time, and more so on the days Foxwood was not there. It was mean of him to leave it all to her today, with the Countess coming! He had gone a week ago, after having said he would be away at least a month, and he was back, as grumpy and taciturn as ever. These were harsh days, with the rakshasas in control of England and fighting to conquer the rest of Britain, the rest of the world. Clementine looked back miserably to the time before the war, when she had enjoyed working here and at the now-ruined Lombard with Leah.

The fighting had begun a year ago, soon after she became a maenad. England before the reign of the rakshasas was like a dream, or a story she'd once read. With all Foxwood's talk of gods, none had come to help fight off the demons. Now, London was cowed and beaten, Queen Victoria murdered and a demon queen in her place, the government dissolved, the people frightened, dead or imprisoned.

She wondered at Foxwood's strange words just before he left—if anything was to go wrong, she was to make a note of it. *Everything* was wrong with the rakshasas in charge! Demons walked the Earth and her god wanted to know if anything went wrong. If only Leah hadn't left on some mysterious errand and returned as coral and shells, if only Gimble still sat in his booth and puffed on that noxious pipe of his. Clementine suspected she remained as the only maenad

Dionysus had left, and that possibility carried far too much responsibility. She hadn't asked to become a maenad, after all. And her knowledge of theatre—or wine for that matter, since she never drank the stuff—remained fragmentary despite a year at the Gypsy.

Not a good maenad at all. Even her first meeting with Dionysus had been an accident. She had been looking for work at a flower-shop when a gust of breeze snatched a five-pound note out of the hand of a man on the corner. She picked it up and handed it back to him. On seeing his face, she realised his divine nature—incredible to see a god walking the Earth! After he admitted himself to be Dionysus her world came undone. The fall of a five-pound note led her to this strange new life as a maenad.

But then the war with the demons started, Leah had left on some errand of her own, poor Tom Gimble had been arrested on a false charge and might even now been hanged or transported somewhere, and Clementine was alone with Foxwood under the rule of the demons.

Arriving back today, without any warning, Mr Foxwood looked slightly different, if no less divine. It was like he was not even sure of her true identity, as if they had never met before. The day Leah's petrified body had appeared above the stage door where the gargoyle had been had changed Foxwood: angrier, harsher, less tolerant. Until today. Today he was different, more like the old Dionysus. Ever since Leah's statue had appeared, Foxwood came and went via the front door of the Gypsy, but today he walked out under her frozen gaze as if he didn't know she was there. And his confusion about the date: Dionysus had a slim grasp of reality at the best of times, but to be doubtful of the year seemed extraordinarily odd.

She drank her glass of water, swallowing each mouthful carefully, lest the rancid taste of the Thames made her choke. Lifting the glass for each sip took both hands, but the slow action helped to control the shaking.

When the glass was empty, she pushed her dull coppery hair back from her face and readjusted a pin that held her shawl together. The sound of the arriving audience trickled through. "All right, missy," she said out loud, "it's just you and Mr Foxwood now, and since he isn't here at the moment it's just you."

A surge of laughter from the other side of the wall. For the hundredth time, Clementine wished the Lombard still existed. She had spent some time there before it was torn down, and much preferred it to the Gypsy. This rough vaudeville with its dubious artists, its low-brow acts, its coarse humour, were not to her taste. Of course, it was harder in the war to find more talented performers, but the line had to be drawn somewhere. But the real cause of her dislike was the bad relations the staff here showed towards her. They didn't know she was a maenad and gave her no deference whatsoever. They even thought her incompetent. If Foxwood stayed around to back her up things might be different.

"You can do this one more time. Just one more time."

For my master, she added silently, and went backstage.

Mr Callow, the stage manager who had replaced Simm, watched carefully from the other side of the stage as Clementine grasped the curtain ropes in readiness.

From the auditorium, the rumble of the crowd grew louder. Although she couldn't yet see them, Clementine could smell the cigar smoke and sweat, a vile concoction of stinks that had her breathing through her mouth. The first act, a weedy-looking man with a top hat on his head and a swagger-cane, gave her a quick look. He was not the best they had, but he could warm the crowd up sufficiently.

Matthew, the master of ceremonies, slipped through the stage right curtain and the audience went quiet. There came none of the applause or ribald comments, no good-natured hoots and hollers that had greeted Bastable's entrances. He started speaking, told a few jokes that went fairly flat, and then announced the opening act. Clementine strained on the curtain rope and the heavy wall of cloth slowly rose.

The top-hat man stepped forward as the lights came up. The music started at the same moment. Just the old man on the piano now. The rest of the band had quit like most of the other staff The singer launched into a popular ballad.

She settled her spectacles and peeked between the tormentor and the stage left wings. The spill of light from the stage illuminated the darkened auditorium enough to see the two front rows. Not many patrons at this matinee. A lone old woman sat by herself, and five men in a group—sinister, flat-faced men who didn't smile and drank from dark-tinted bottles. Behind them nothing but shadows, the seats not lit enough for her to make out the occupants' faces.

Clementine pursed her lips and looked up at the gallery. A few people there, among them no doubt their guest the Countess of Downham, avoiding the riff-raff below. None of them could be seen clearly.

Desultory applause as the act closed. Matthew let the noise continue for a few moments, then announced the next act, two girls who would dance dressed as fairies.

Clementine watched as they ran on stage and took up positions. No hoots or hollers from the audience, just a surly silence, as if daring the girls to entertain them.

Another day at the Gypsy.

V

The part of London in which Foxwood eventually found himself had pleasant enough streets, and the guards that patrolled it, armed with muskets and long knives, let him pass after asking his name. He recalled the statue of Lilitu and surmised these humans must be worshippers of hers; even the rakshasas needed help from their goddess to conquer the world.

Finally a sight that oriented him: the ruins of Trafalgar Square. Nelson's Column had been blasted by some diabolic means into a million pieces, and its wreckage lay scattered, perhaps not because the rakshasas liked disorder, but as a warning to any humans who still harboured dissent.

Tamar the Snake-Rider sat on the edge of the fountain and stared at the devastation. It had only been a few hours since he had last seen her in the Wyrd's cave, but she sat with hunched shoulders, her red-ribboned hat askew. He wanted to grasp her hand, to kiss it and blurt out something about his pleasure at seeing her safe. But the city depressed him too much.

"Hello, my dear."

The sky goddess nodded without looking at him but gave no other greeting.

He pointed at the dark gathering of clouds on the horizon. "A storm is coming," he continued. "Yours?"

"No. It must be nature crying, not me."

"I thought not. Yours would have more panache."

That raised a reluctant smile. "That's one description I've never heard before. On a good day I can raise a hell of a tempest."

"I'm glad to see you, Tamar."

And then she looked at him directly. The tear-tracks were plain.

"Did you just arrive here?" he continued. "Or have you come from somewhere else?"

"I've been in the future three days. You haven't?"

It seemed a little unfair they hadn't arrived together and at the same time, but not surprising. They had both wanted an answer to the same question, but the answers were no doubt different for each. They would each see things that were important to them in the future, but not necessarily at the same place and time.

"The Wyrd sent me to Georgia," she explained. "I met with one of my followers, a man named Mikheil, who has followed me for several centuries. He informed me of the war that humanity now fights against the rakshasas. England has fallen, and the Continent rings with conflict as the demons try to expand their influence."

"I thought as much." He snuffed the air: smoke and blood, and not only from London. All of Europe cried.

"Things are going badly for humanity," she continued. "Slowly but steadily the rakshasas push across Europe. There are many of them now, Mikheil told me. Only a few from the tribe of the Sevenat began the war, but others have arrived since. There are thousands now, using machinery brought from Hell, engines of war that kill many at once. And leading them in battle is a goddess, the one called Lilitu, as you feared. She converts new worshippers."

Lilitu. So he'd been right about her having human worshippers. Not content with being the goddess of demons, she sought to convert people to her religion. "The Sevenat tribe? Malanu is their queen. I met her in Romania."

"That's what Mikheil called her." She put out a hand and Foxwood took it and rubbed her fingers gently. The flesh, though warm, felt like old leather. "She and her son Prince Geneth entered the world by some means long ago, probably with help from Lilitu."

"Yes, a gateway between the worlds exists somewhere," said Foxwood. "Dire times indeed. Did Mikheil tell you how many of your followers remain to you?'"

"No. He's had no contact. I know of at least one here in England, but I haven't been able to contact him yet."

"I don't know about my maenads, either. One remains at the Gypsy. But the others..." He remembered Leah squatting above the stage door and clenched his teeth.

"I came to London last night riding on Ghame," she said. "Looking for you. I thought we might do something. We could seek to reverse what has been done."

"We are an anomaly, Snake-Rider. You and I hang onto existence by a thread. We have no power anymore. I can't even make decent wine."

She looked older. The lines on her face that had appeared so fetching now made her sallow, haggard. Her eyes had seen things not even gods should witness.

"Maybe some little power," she said. "My snake…"

The serpent slithered off her arm. Its eyes were no longer filled with fierce red light, its scales dull. It looked up at him, the tongue flicking in and out weakly.

"Yes," he said softly, "perhaps some vestige of power."

Across the square, a woman pushed a baby in a pram. A child born during the reign of the demons. It would never regard the rakshasas as mere folklore. It might grow up to be a slave, or a follower of Lilitu like one of his long-gone maenads, or might be offered as a sacrifice. Anything was possible.

He sat down beside Tamar on the stone edge of the fountain. "They stopped having faith in us," he said, taking off his hat and scratching his sparse hair. The wind stirred the dust of the square, which landed on his head. Just like it did in Grit Lane. "Not just us, in the new gods too."

"What do we do?" asked Tamar.

Two thousand years ago he had watched his maenads tear animals and people apart in orgiastic frenzy and he'd revelled in it as the drunken god of ritual madness, lord of passion. But those days were gone. Mags was nowhere to be found, Gimble had vanished, Leah was a statue. And as for Clementine—well, he had no memories of her, but on first impressions he could not imagine why had chosen her as a follower.

"We must return to the past," he said. "Get the Wyrd to cease the vision. We know what happens. It's our task to see it doesn't."

Tamar managed a smile. "You *have* changed, Joshua."

The woman with the pram reached inside and lifted the babe out. She clutched it to her breast while gazing at the two gods. A moment later she walked towards them, carrying the baby and pushing the pram. About ten feet away the woman stopped and stared directly at them once more. Both deities shifted slightly, noticing the way the woman's hair wafted from her scalp without a breeze, the vertical slits of her eyes, the long fingernails ending in needle-like points.

And the baby no longer a baby but a man's head, mouth twisted in agony, eyes wide open. Blood dripped from the neck.

Both gods rose, facing the woman. "You are a rakshasa," Foxwood muttered. "Shape-shifter. You're not welcome here."

The demon held out the severed head, shreds of flesh hanging from the neck. Foxwood wondered who the man had been, and what he had done to earn the wrath of the demon. The dead mouth moved, jaw opening and closing. After a few seconds a hissing voice emerged. "I have a message for both of you."

"Yes?" said Tamar. "From your marauding queen?"

"She who rules." The head's eyes rolled in their sockets until nothing showed but the whites.

"What's the message?" growled Foxwood.

"We rakshasas are taking back our world. You know this. But the old war with the gods is over. Her Majesty offers you both sanctuary. Once before, Dionysus, you were offered alliance, and you refused. You have the chance again. We rakshasas have a source of unlimited power and mighty engines of war. We drive the humans back further every day. Soon this world will once again belong to us. If you join our queen, you may stay and be a part of the new Earth. If not, then no mercy will be shown."

"And she sends such an important message through you?" Tamar laughed. "Hasn't she the courage to face us?"

Beside the head, the demon hissed, showing red-stained fangs.

"Get out of here!" roared Foxwood, taking a step forward. "Go back to Hell!"

The rakshasa gestured to encompass all the world. "Hell is here," said the dead man's head.

Tamar raised her hand to the sky. "We are strong still. It's not wise to defy us."

The rakshasa spat. "You are nothing to my race."

The mistress of storms said a single word, quietly, without force.

Foxwood blinked and flung a hand up to cover to his face as a lightning bolt flashed down from a clear sky and struck the demon. The scorched air filled with the stench of burnt flesh and the scream of the monster.

When Foxwood could see again, the thing lay on the ground, curled a little, smoking. And quite dead. The human head had fallen to the ground, bereft of its demonic possession, the eyes dull.

"Impressive," said Foxwood, extracting a handkerchief from his pocket and placing it over his nose to block out the reek of cooked demon flesh.

"I wasn't sure if I could still do that." Tamar rubbed thumb and index finger against each other.

"I'll remember you can," he said, tugging at his collar.

Sirens wailed in the air around them, and armed humans appeared heading towards the place of the killing.

"I think the rakshasas have received our answer," he said. "It's time I return to my theatre."

Tamar placed her hand on the ground and her snake slid up her sleeve.

"We'll come with you," she said.

VI

They found Clementine under the barnacled statue of Leah at the stage door of the Gypsy, hands clasped over her knees, staring at the broken remains of the Lombard Theatre. She looked up as they approached, and rose carefully, brushing her dress down and coughing as if from the dust. As they drew near she dipped in a curtsey.

"How is it?" Foxwood asked, nodding towards the stage door. "Has the show finished already?"

Clementine took off her spectacles and folded them, then immediately opened them again and perched them back on her nose. "No, master. It's just intermission. I came out to...to..."

He placed a hand on her shoulder. "It's all right, my dear. You're a maenad. I know you would never leave your theatre without a reasonable excuse."

Clementine regarded Tamar carefully, wrinkled her nose, then did another curtsey. "I'm honoured to meet you, goddess," she said.

Tamar almost broke into a polite smile but changed it to a frown. "You know me?"

"I know you are a goddess." Clementine glanced at Foxwood as if for confirmation, or forgiveness for her presumption. "I don't know which one. Please forgive me."

"This is indeed a divine friend of mine," said Foxwood, glaring at his maenad. "Tamar, goddess of the sky."

The maenad curtseyed again and placed her hands together in prayer. "I offer my respects, O Divine One."

"Call me Tamar." The goddess held out one hand, and the woman kissed it. "There's no need to do me worship. I'm not...There's no need."

"This is my maenad, Clementine." Foxwood tried to sound casual, as if he knew the woman well, but the name came strangely from his mouth. Someday, back in real time, they would meet. He hauled out his watch. "The interval's just finished." As if in response, piano music drifted out into the lane.

"The Countess is in the gallery," said Clementine. "I couldn't see properly, but Mr Callow saw her arrive."

"I'm interested in her," said Foxwood. "Something tells me the messenger we met in Trafalgar Square and her presence in my theatre are linked."

"You think she's the rakshasa queen?" Tamar glanced at the stage door, from which the doorman emerged, cigar between his teeth. He peered at them, then ducked back inside.

"Perhaps," said Foxwood. The thought of such a creature violating his theatre with her presence brought a bitter laugh from his throat. "Let's find out. There are a number of things I wish to say to her."

"How do you intend to meet her?" There was no hesitation in Tamar's voice, but she glanced again at the Gypsy's stage door with narrowed eyes.

"I hate it when things don't go according to plan," said Foxwood, "which is why I never make one."

Tamar drew herself up but her voice wavered a little. "That lightning bolt in Trafalgar Square...I garnered it from the distant storm. I can't produce such a thing indoors. If we must fight, I would have to change..."

A memory of seeing Tamar in her full divine glory long ago, in the true form she wore as goddess, rose in Foxwood's mind, still clear after centuries. He rubbed his jawline and said, "Ah. I see. I hope that won't be necessary. But I'm not asking you to come with me, my dear. You've already performed enough of a service. This observation is for me to do."

The sky goddess slapped him on the chest. "Don't be ridiculous! We came here together, and we'll finish this together. I've lost worshippers too."

He caught her hand, kissed her wrinkled fingers. "Very well." Then he saw Clementine, standing with head bowed, and raised her chin. At his touch, the woman started, but let him turn her face towards him. The usual fear there, the uncertainty, the distrust. He had to protect her, and not just because he depended on her for existence. She deserved his protection, maenad or not.

"Remind me, my dear, of your talent as a maenad. I suspect you used it just now."

She swallowed. "I know true natures, master."

"Er...yes. But for Tamar's sake, perhaps a bit more detail?"

"All I have to do is look someone in the face to know his or her true nature." She nodded to Tamar. "I knew you to be a goddess, like I recognised my lord Dionysus as a god when we first met."

A sense above and beyond the usual maenad second sight, which could not be fooled by the divine. The ability seemed almost fortuitous, but perhaps he'd already arranged things that way. He had selected all his ladies and gentlemen for their particular talents; perhaps Clementine had been chosen as a maenad for just this moment.

"You might be of service," he said. "I want to know who this Countess really is. Would your talent work on a demon?"

"It does, master. I can see through their human disguises, but I fear to look at them."

"Understandable. They aren't exactly attractive in their natural state. Will you come into the theatre with me now and look at the Countess?"

Clementine took a deep breath before replying. "I will obey all your commands, master." Perhaps her devotion to him would help her overcome her terror. But no, he could not force that on her. He kept forgetting that humans were...well, human.

"I don't require you to obey my commands, but would you willingly comply with my request?"

"Yes, master."

"Come if you wish, then," he said. "I won't order you to. But if you can know the true nature of our visitor, we won't be fooled by her in future."

Tamar indicated the stage door. "We can't just walk in. You expect this girl to face up to the Countess and stare at her? If she is Malanu Negrashi there'll be guards."

"As I always impressed upon Sir John Rowley," he said, trying not to let a superior tone enter his voice, "it's important to know your theatre. People are beguiled by appearances."

"What does that mean? Really, Joshua, you—"

"Don't be deceived into thinking the only entrances to a theatre are the visible ones."

If they entered by the stage door they would be quickly caught, and if they entered by the public doors in Ginger Street they would be even more obvious. Foxwood wanted to see without being seen at all. "All very well for gods to materialise where they will," said Foxwood. "But followers are a different matter. I suggest a more secretive route. Can your snake bear a maenad too, Tamar?"

The goddess placed her arm in the dust of the lane and Ghame slithered down. It raised its head off the ground and hissed as if it had understood the question.

"He can bear all three," said Tamar. "His mother is the great Sky Serpent, his father the Ouroboros. A maenad will be like a mote of dust as a burden. But where would you have him take us? His powers are limited to the open air. His dominion is the unsheltered sky and doesn't include the constructions of man."

Foxwood pointed upwards. "That's a problem solved with a bit of inconvenience. There's a smoke hatch in the roof. It leads to Mags's room. Well, the room that *was* hers. We can climb down from there."

Clementine peered upwards, the lenses of her spectacles two blank disks as they reflected the dull clouds above the London smog.

"Are you game for it, my dear?" asked Foxwood. "As I said, I put no pressure on you."

The woman nodded.

"Don't be afraid," said Tamar, lifting the serpent in both hands. "Take hold, both of you."

Foxwood placed his right hand on the snake and, seeing Clementine's hesitation, reached out and guided her right hand to put it on the creature.

The world shifted a little.

They stood on the roof of the Gypsy, tin roofing sheets under their feet, the chimney stack rising beside them. Next to the stack, grimed and with peeling paint, was a metal hatch with a ring for a handle.

"There," he said, smiling at his maenad. "Nothing to it."

A dusty breeze came from the south over the rooftops. He pulled out his pen-knife and ran it around the edge of the hatch, picking out flakes of rust.

"This hatch lets out smoke in the event of a fire inside, and so is designed to be opened by a rope and pulley from backstage. But no problem for us."

They tugged at the ring, but the hatch didn't move. Foxwood inserted the knife blade into the edge of the hatch near the ring and fumbled about for a minute.

"Try again."

They heaved and the hatch opened reluctantly. Rust and old paint fell to the metal roof.

"In the old days," observed Tamar, "a mere hatch would have been no obstacle."

"These are not the old days." Foxwood threw a grim smile and slid into the hole. His feet contacted a small platform between two rafters. From there a short ladder led down to the door of Mags's old loft room. He opened it and stared in. No sign remained that Mags had once lived there, no furniture, no possessions, just stacked timber, coiled ropes and the smell of paint. The heavy oak beams that formed the loft of the theatre creaked and groaned a under the afternoon sun. From below came the sound of a pianoforte and people singing.

He turned and helped first Tamar, and then Clementine, to make the descent. Both found it difficult in their gowns. Clementine tore the hem of hers on the edge of the hatch.

They proceeded along a walkway and opened a low door at the top of the stairs. Foxwood put his finger to his lips, even though the sound from the stage should mask any possible noise they might make descending.

"We'll go to the downstage lighting bar," he said. "The stairs creak a bit, so be careful."

Next to the lighting bar a catwalk hung twenty feet above the stage where the crew serviced the gas lights. They stepped onto this, their movement causing the attendant gas jets to wobble, but gaslight flickered anyway so it would not be noticed by the audience. They moved out to the middle of the catwalk. The heat from the blazing gas lights struck them like a wall, but from there they could see the stage clearly without being seen by the audience.

On stage, a man and a woman embraced in what passed for an amorous manner in vaudeville, his arm around her, her hands clasped together at her bosom in the typical ingénue pose. They sang a ragged duet. The quality of the acts at the Gypsy, never too high to start with, had taken a turn for the worse in the intervening years.

A typical theatre had many ways people backstage could view the audience without being seen themselves. Clementine's personal peephole near the curtain was an accidental one, formed by a slight warp in the tormentor's frame which opened a tiny gap. Other methods were deliberate, such as the speaking tube to Matthew's position in the master of ceremony's chair, or the prompt box placed in front of the orchestra pit, which could open both ways, either onstage or off, to pass instructions to the performers or the musicians.

In the case of the lighting catwalk, the viewing hole was not quite accidental. Repairs to the lights sometimes required tackling the gas tubes from more than one direction. At some time in years past a crew member had removed a section of the proscenium arch roughly centre stage in order to deal with some problem. A wooden patch had been put in place, but Foxwood—who knew his theatre— remembered it was not secured and could be removed if needed.

He lifted the square patch out a tiny bit, not to remove it completely, but to make a gap a quarter inch wide through which he could see. It was tricky to peek through without putting his sleeve too close to a gas light.

The gap gave him a view of the auditorium. At the front of the gallery sat a tall form. Her face was in darkness, but Foxwood could see a gleam of jewels about her neck. Anyone who wore jewellery openly to the Gypsy was either a fool or heavily guarded; by the bulky men seated on either side of her he guessed the latter.

"In the front of the gallery," he whispered to Clementine. "Take a look, my dear, and tell me if she is indeed a rakshasa."

Clementine moved to peer through the gap. "It's too dark, master. I can't see her face." She bowed her head. "I'm sorry. I must see the face to know her true nature."

He nodded. "I understand. Then we must cast some light."

He moved along the catwalk, which shifted a little under his weight but had been well-oiled to prevent creaking, to the gas-cage. If he turned a few taps the auditorium lights would spring into life. The gas man sitting in the cage looked about to say something, but Foxwood silenced him with a finger to his lips. Then, pointing to the peep-hole, he waited until Clementine was again in position, and turned three taps that controlled the gas flow to the gallery lights. The two lowest tiers of the gallery seats became brightly illuminated. Foxwood watched Clementine's face carefully and noted the little gasp she gave. She glanced at him and nodded.

He turned the gas back down and the glow in the gallery faded. The maenad made her way cautiously along the catwalk to stand beside him.

"There are four people there, master," she whispered. "Three men and a tall, thin woman. But they're not human. None of them. I know, I *saw*."

He placed a reassuring hand on her arm. Even now the woman flinched at the contact.

"They're all rakshasa demons," gulped Clementine. "One with green skin, one with eyes like a spider, one with the head of a horse." She shivered even in the heat of the gaslights. "And the Countess— she's their queen. I know true natures. She rules the others."

"Thank you," said Foxwood. "A true maenad." The woman seemed relieved at the description. "Now, as the great philosopher Sun Tzu said, 'Many calculations lead to victory, and few calculations to defeat'. Let's withdraw and calculate our next move. Back up the stairs, ladies."

They hustled along the catwalk single file, Clementine last. Foxwood glanced down at the stage manager, Mr Callow, who had at last noticed them. He was staring upwards at them, mouth open. Whatever had happened to the former stage manager, Mr Simm, Foxwood hoped the man still lived somewhere, that he hadn't fallen victim to the reign of the rakshasas. This Callow hadn't treated Clementine well. Mags would have dealt with that. He scowled. No Mags in this unfortunate future. Callow might even be in league with the demons or betray them through fear. But no: he would have condemned them already.

Foxwood stood aside at the base of the ladder and indicated for Tamar to go first. As her boots passed by his face a cry came from Clementine. A dark shape loomed behind her, long arms gripping the woman around the waist. A tusked and green-skinned face leered over her shoulder.

Foxwood raised his cane in one hand and sent a blast of white light to strike her attacker. It struck the demon on one shoulder. It howled and released that arm, but the other still held Clementine tight.

With a cry of "Euoe!" the maenad kicked backwards at her assailant's legs. A grunt from the rakshasa and a tighter squeeze on her body. Another kick and a twist from Clementine and she almost came free, but the demon wrapped its other arm back around her. Clementine bit hard on its arm, snarling, her eyes glaring with the animalistic fury of maenad rage. She would struggle relentlessly with all her strength and probably die without being aware of anything more than unfettered madness unless Foxwood helped her.

Another blast of white light. The demon let go, fell back with hands on face, and Clementine scrambled for the ladder. Tamar reached down to help and they clattered up the ladder and then the stairs to the loft. Foxwood slammed and bolted the door.

"Are you all right?" Foxwood gripped Clementine's shoulder.

"Yes," she gasped. A scratched line of red beads adorned her cheek. She put a hand up to wipe them and winced. The rage had settled, gone back to its lair in her soul.

"A demon not bothering to be in human form," said Foxwood. "I'm afraid my trick with the lights alerted them. Through the hatch. Then if Tamar produces her snake we can escape."

A crash at the top of the stairs, and at the same time the door smashed open. Human faces leered in, but the roars that came from them were those of rakshasa. All three held guns.

"Master!" cried Clementine.

Foxwood forced himself between her and the demons swarming in. "All right!" he cried. "You have us!"

He caught a glimpse of Tamar, who had the smoke hatch open. Afternoon light peeped in, along with a few drops of rain.

"No," said Foxwood. "Close the hatch. We will submit."

Tamar twisted her mouth in a sneer and her snake appeared from under the cuff of her dress. "Get into the open air and we can use Ghame," she said.

"They'll shoot Clementine before we could exit. Besides, I have a thing or two to say to the queen."

The rakshasa grabbed Clementine and hauled her first down the ladder, a gun pointed at her head. The gods and the other rakshasas followed.

Foxwood knew gods had their flaws. Besides being dependent on followers to exist, they were terrible at running the world. Things wouldn't be in such a mess if deities were better at taking care of things. All he had done for the last couple of thousand years—no, before that even—was drink wine and have a good time. Hardly an exemplary record. It made no difference. Even gods with more dedication to their duties also managed to ruin things for humanity pretty much all of the time. He had put Clementine in danger and now all three of them were paying the price. If Mags were here or Leah, or one of his other ladies spread around the world...but no, that was unfair. Clementine had done her best—more than that. But that realisation didn't change things.

On stage the curtain had been closed and the audience cleared. There was no sign of Callow or any other staff. The gas lights were turned up full and Queen Malanu stood centre stage. No pretence at being a Countess now: she appeared as she had in Romania, wings and all, her third red eye glaring defiantly as two other rakshasas held Clementine tight.

Standing beside Foxwood, Tamar kept a haughty expression, but her tight grip on his arm betrayed her true emotion.

Time for bravado. It was all he had left. The slightest show of power would only result in Clementine's death. He thumped his cane firmly on the boards and threw his head back exactly as bad actors did when about to deliver a soliloquy. Except there was no theatricality in Foxwood's demeanour, no sense of false drama.

"Rakshasas! This is the end of the show!"

The queen's low laugh echoed back from the loft. At a gesture from her Clementine's hands were bound and a gag tied across her face.

"Leave my maenad alone!" roared Foxwood.

"Shut up!" Malanu's voice rasped a fifth lower than any human woman's. "The maenad will not be harmed if you obey me."

It must have pleased her immensely to have a god under her command. Foxwood decided not to give her the pleasure. "I'm afraid you and your kind must leave the Earth for good," he said. "I do apologise for the inconvenience."

The demons growled. Foxwood gripped his fox-head cane until his knuckles went white.

"Careful, Joshua," said Tamar, glancing at Clementine. "Don't antagonise her. I fear for your maenad."

"It's all right," he muttered, but without enough conviction to convince even himself. Other gods might sacrifice a willing follower, but he had a soft spot for humans.

"An interesting disguise as a countess," he observed. "And Guang Jin was a masterful impression. Who else have you been in history? Genghis Khan? Napoleon Bonaparte? That's the trouble with you rakshasas: you can fool even the gods with your disguises. But such a talent did you no good in the old war—you lost to the gods and mankind. It will do you no good now." He swallowed. His enervated powers could barely fight one rakshasa in this future, never mind five of them.

"Dionysus," said Malanu. "And Tamar Snake-Rider. Yes, I know you. I've met many gods. Some I conquered, some I respected. I haven't decided on your status yet."

Tamar let go of his arm and rose to her imperious full five feet six of height. "But now we know your intentions we can learn much about you," she growled. "Find your weaknesses. When we do, we will force you to return this world to the way you found it and then leave forever."

Foxwood recalled the statue at the end of Grit Lane. "And what of Lilitu?" he demanded. "I see now she is your ally. Goddess of demons. Appropriate. But relying on deities can be a weakness, even if I say so myself."

"I see *your* weakness," the Queen sneered. "You care too much for humanity. As gods, you should exploit your worshippers."

"As gods," said Tamar, "we honour those who follow us. It's you we despise."

Again the harsh laughter.

"This is the future," said Foxwood. "Unlike the past, it can be changed."

Malanu nodded. "So you, too, consulted the Wyrd. I thought you might. My attempt to kill them must have failed. No matter."

"Knowing the future comes with a price," said Tamar.

"True. And you are about to pay it." She indicated Clementine. "A follower of yours. One dear to you, perhaps, or not so dear, since you put her in peril."

"Release her," said Foxwood as calmly as he could, feeling hot under his clothing. "She can do no harm. Yes, she is a maenad, but a mere human."

Malanu laughed. "No follower of a god is 'merely' human. But she's human enough to deserve punishment for her race invading our world."

"No!" Foxwood stepped towards the queen. "You didn't arise here. The rakshasas came to Earth from another place. But humans developed along with the planet. It was we gods who conquered you. Blame us if you will, but leave the innocent humans alone."

"Join us!" Malanu flung out her wings; gaslights strung on the battens over the stage flickered in the draft of air created. The momentary shadows cast over Clementine's face made the light in her eyes flash out. The woman was on the verge of going into a rage again, might harm herself in struggling against her captors. The barrel of the pistol stayed an inch from her left temple.

It would be easy to align with the rakshasas, even to pretend to do so in order to have them release Clementine. Then he might plot to overthrow these demons another time. But that could not be. This was the future. Better to work from the past to alter the present, better to return to the old world and seek to rework history a day at a time.

"No," he said quietly.

The demon queen gestured and the gun roared.

Foxwood saw Clementine's head shatter, the blood gushing forth like a torrent, saw the wild anger that remained in her eyes even as she died. They let her fall to the floor, and her blood and brains stained the Gypsy stage.

His legs went weak, and he gasped as if his lungs had ceased to work. His heart slowed.

A part of his existence tore from him. He fell to the stage, clutching his cane.

"My last maenad!" he gasped. "You have…"

The sounds continued around him, the roars of the demons, and over all the voice of Tamar, calling to him. The goddess started to transform, her upper body growing larger, her lower half narrowing. Her arms lengthened, became clawed. The goddess of the sky appeared in all her divine glory, and she fell upon the demons who had killed Clementine.

The red third eye of the demon queen shone clearly as her laughter rolled down to Foxwood.

"So," the queen gloated, "she was your last maenad? You are dying? You understand my power at last, Dionysus."

He said through gritted teeth, "Come here, you bitch!"

Queen Malanu Negrashi leaned over him. The ember of her third eye filled his universe, a glowing ruby in the darkness.

One chance.

He lifted his cane and stabbed towards the red.

A howl from the queen, not a roar of triumph but real pain, as his walking stick penetrated her eye. He thrust harder, driving the ferrule of the cane further in, pushing until it pierced the demon's brain.

Malanu staggered back, pulling the cane from his grip.

He rose, instantly wary of the other rakshasas, but Tamar had dealt with them. Two lay dead, ripped in half by the power of the sky goddess. The others had fled.

He tugged his cane from the queen's eye and flicked it to shake off the repellent gore stuck to the ferrule. "No, Clementine was not my last maenad," he said. "But as god of the theatre, I have some ability, perhaps, as an actor."

The body of Clementine lay in the stage. He stroked her hair. Nothing to be done for her; he hadn't the power to reverse death.

"It's time to leave," he said to Tamar, who had returned to her human form. "We can't do anything more here for the time being." He felt the grip of her hand in his, and called upon the Wyrd, wishing the vision to be over.

Foxwood lay on the floor of the Wyrd's cave under the castle of Ortega. Beside him was the table with the crystal ball. No darkness now. He remained there for a while, feeling the hard floor, breathing deeply of the close air.

"Tamar?"

No reply.

Slowly he sat up. No sign of the goddess. Against the wall huddled the three Wyrd sisters, exactly where they'd been before. He looked around for his cane, could not find it, and rose wearily to his feet.

"You have seen," said the second face.

"Yes." He glanced once more around the room. "Where's Tamar?"

"The price of omniscience is great," said the third voice.

"What? Tamar was the price? Where is she?"

"Still in the future."

He took two paces towards them, then halted, opening and closing his hands, shoving down the urge to attack them. A great sob emerged from his throat. The price of knowing all that would come to pass—even the gods had to pay it. The Wyrd themselves had paid it long ago.

Tamar was trapped in the future that would be, with the demon queen dead but the world still at the mercy of revengeful rakshasas.

"I would not have asked if I knew the cost."

"No one would. And yet many take the chance."

Mere platitudes. Clementine had died, and there lay nothing for him ahead. In a few short years Mags would disappear from the Gypsy and Leah would become a statue over the stage door. A mad desire filled him, to return to the future, to pay whatever price it took for him to rescue Tamar.

"What you saw will come to pass," said the third face, "unless you choose otherwise."

There remained a chance that particular future would not happen. He could do something to change it: find the demon queen now and slay her before the war began; close the gateway that had let them into this world; discover how Lilitu aided them. But he felt sick, weary of this place and these women. It was time to go home, back to his theatres.

He didn't speak to the Wyrd again, didn't thank them for what they had revealed. By the time he emerged onto the hillside and felt the bright sunlight on his face his resolve had returned.

VII

In Mrs Slattery's tea shop Mags paused with her cup halfway to her mouth and stared at the apparition in the street.

"Well, here he is at last."

Leah turned to look over her shoulder.

"It's him," said Mags. "It's really him."

They watched Joshua Foxwood enter the shop. Not in all her centuries had Mags expected Foxwood to walk into a tea shop, much less Mrs Slattery's, and much, much less while both she and Leah had tea there. Some things just didn't happen in the world, even in a maenad's rather odd one.

The god paused just inside, looking around until he saw them. His shoulders straightened up a little. He threw a thin smile at them and walked over, removing his gloves.

Sylvie the waitress scuttled up. "Good afternoon, sir, Will you be wanting tea?"

"Eh?" Foxwood turned his gaze on the girl. "What's that? Tea? No, no, I don't think so. No wine, I suppose? Oh dear. Never mind. Hello, ladies. It's a pleasure to see you."

Leah smiled. Mags put her tea cup down hard on its saucer. "Where have you been?"

"Yes," he said. "So good. You are both well?"

He lifted Leah's hand from the table and kissed it, then reached out to Mags, who drew back a little, paused, and then allowed him to grasp her hand and put his lips to the back.

"I am very pleased to see you both."

"I asked you where you've been. We haven't seen you for a month."

He resumed his usual stoop-shouldered form. Years appeared on his face.

"Travelling," he said. "With an old friend. I trust the theatres are both running smoothly?"

The women nodded. "Sir John's been running both houses. He thinks you're dead or something."

"No. Not dead. How good of Sir John to step in for me. I must see him immediately and thank him. Perhaps a raise in salary is in order as well."

"What do you mean travelling?" Mags couldn't recall when she'd last had a raise in salary.

"What one normally means by it. Moving from one place to another. Seeing new things. Meeting people. I'm not staying to take tea. I just wanted to see you were both healthy." He removed his hat to them and smiled. "My dear ladies, you are most precious to me."

Mags swallowed her indignation enough to observe the new lines of his face, the strain in his voice. Perhaps the old fox had been through a rough time.

"Are you all right?"

For a second a flash of what might have been pain passed across his face, but with a visible effort he thrust it aside.

"I am tired." He sat down next to Leah, who shifted her chair away a little to give his gaunt frame space. Her left elbow brushed against one of the potted petunias on the windowsill. "Ladies, I wish you to do something for me."

"*Anything, sir,*" signed Leah.

Mags noticed the use of the honorific and nodded in agreement.

"I want you to find a woman for me. Her name is Clementine."

Mags waited for more, and when it didn't come, said, "Clementine who?"

"I've no idea of her last name, I'm sorry, nor where she might be found."

"*A maenad?*"

"Not yet. Auburn hair, about thirty years old. Long nose. Wears spectacles."

"And that's all we have to go on?" Mags deliberately refilled her tea cup to show she wasn't going anywhere until further information could be provided.

"She's *going* to be a maenad in the next couple of years, so think about where you might find one of your own. Besides, she'll probably recognise you before you do her." He fidgeted with his top hat. "Find someone who knows you're maenads without you telling them. Really, ladies, use your common sense."

"*Is she English?*"

A sensible question. Trust Leah.

"I think so. Her accent might be Dorset, I think. And I have an additional task for you, Leah. Look into those books of yours and find out all you can about the rakshasas—a tribe called the Sevenat in particular, and their Queen Malanu Negrashi. And Prince Geneth—that's the demon that tried to sacrifice you, Mags. And the goddess Lilitu. It's her you met in London Field. See what you can turn up about all of them."

Mags recalled the demon she met on a rooftop while chasing the Moon across London. So the old god had been getting himself into trouble. "Sir," she said, and found herself putting out her hand to touch the cuff of his left hand, "please tell us what's happening."

"We deserve to know."

He looked at both of them, and for the first time in ages Mags found herself staring deep into his eyes. She'd done that a long, long time ago, when he had first tapped her on the shoulder while she watched a miracle play and seduced her passion for the theatre. The whole universe existed inside those eyes.

"The end of the world is coming," he said, "Unless we can prevent it. The rakshasas are set to conquer, aided by Lilitu—we must find out all we can about their movements. Now meet me at the Gypsy when you've finished your tea. I have a lot to explain."

Then, plopping the topper back on his bare skull, their god walked out into the street. They watched him head for the shadowed opening of Grit Lane.

That concludes Act One of *Fallen Gods*.

There will now be a short interval.

The adventures of Dionysus and his maenads will continue in:

<u>Act Two</u>

A Muse of Fire
Ladies Night
The Bane Machine
The Slaughter of the Innocents

and

<u>Act Three</u>

Full House
A Sea-Change
The Battle of Grit Lane
Night Music

Also by Russell Proctor:

Plato's Cave

Days of Iron
Shepherd Moon

The Red King
An Unkindness of Ravens
The Looking-Glass House

For middle grade readers:

Only-By-Darkness